PRETENDER TO THE THRONE

BY

MAISEY YATES

Published in Great Britain 2014
by Mills & Boon, an imprint of Harlequin (UK) Limited,
Eton House, 18-24 Paradise Road, Richmond, Surrey, TW9 1SR

© 2014 Maisey Yates

ISBN: 978 0 263 91217 3

Printed and bound in Spain
by Blackprint CPI, Barcelona

"You speak of the crown as though it's a poisoned cup," Layna said, her words muted.

"It is in many ways. But it is mine. And I have spent too many years trying to pass it off to others."

Yes, as far as anyone knew the crown was Xander's. It was the expectation. What he had trained for until he was twenty-one.

The truth was another matter. But it didn't change the reality.

It didn't change what had to be done.

"A conscience, Xander?" she asked, using his first name.

The sound sent a shiver through him. A ripple of memory.

"I'm not so certain I'd go that far. Maybe a bit of forgotten honor bred into me. Thanks to all that royal blood," he said, his tone dripping sarcasm. "Imagine my disappointment when I realized I hadn't replaced it all with alcohol."

"A disappointment for many," she said.

She sounded more like her old self now. He'd officially destroyed her serenity. Perhaps a lightning bolt would be in the offing after all.

"I'm sure. But I had thought there might be a way of softening the blow."

"And that is?"

"You," he said. "I'm going to need you, Layna."

THE CALL OF DUTY

When legacy commands they must obey!

Don't miss any of the books in this powerful trilogy
by Maisey Yates!

A ROYAL WORLD APART

Desperate to escape her duty, Princess Evangelina
has tried every trick in her little black book.
But where everyone else has failed will her
new bodyguard bend her to his will?
Pity the Princess who draws such a devastating gaze!

AT HIS MAJESTY'S REQUEST

Prince Stavros Drakos has ruled his country
like his business: with a will of iron!
And when duty demands an heir this resolute bachelor
will turn his sole focus to the task…
But will he have finally have met his match?

PRETENDER TO THE THRONE

Newly returned Prince Xander Drakos was raised
to sit on the throne… But was the crown ever really his
to wear? One thing is certain—this prince is determined
to right the wrongs of the past and do his duty
for his family and his country.
But first he'll need the woman he left behind at his side.

Maisey Yates was an avid Mills & Boon® Modern™ Romance reader before she began to write them. She still can't quite believe she's lucky enough to get to create her very own sexy alpha heroes and feisty heroines. Seeing her name on one of those lovely covers is a dream come true.

Maisey lives with her handsome, wonderful, diaper-changing husband and three small children across the street from her extremely supportive parents and the home she grew up in, in the wilds of Southern Oregon, USA. She enjoys the contrast of living in a place where you might wake up to find a bear on your back porch and then heading into the home office to write stories that take place in exotic urban locales.

Recent titles by the same author:

FORGED IN THE DESERT HEAT
HIS RING IS NOT ENOUGH
THE COUPLE WHO FOOLED THE WORLD
HEIR TO A DARK INHERITANCE
  (Secret Heirs of Powerful Men)

**Did you know these are also available as eBooks?
Visit www.millsandboon.co.uk**

To my readers.
This book exists because you asked for it.
And I'm so very glad you did!

CHAPTER ONE

"Either die or abdicate. I'm not particular about which one you choose, but you'd better make a decision, and quickly."

Alexander Drakos, heir to the throne of Kyonos, dissolute rake and frequent gambler, took a drag on his cigarette before putting it out in the ashtray and dropping his cards onto the velvet-covered table.

"I'm a little busy right now, Stavros," he said into his phone.

"Doing what? Throwing away your fortune and drinking yourself into a stupor?"

"Don't be an idiot. I don't drink when I gamble. I don't lose, either." He eyed the men sitting around the table and pushed a pile of chips into the pot.

"A shame. If you did, then maybe you would have had to come home a long time ago."

"Yeah, well, you haven't seemed to need me."

It was time for the cards to go down, and those who hadn't folded earlier on in the round put their hands face up.

Xander laughed and revealed his royal flush before leaning in and sweeping the chips into his stack. "I'm cashing out," he said, standing and putting his chips into a velvet bag. "Enjoy your evening." He took his black suit jacket off the back of the chair and slung it over his shoulder.

He passed a casino employee and dropped the bag into

the man's hands. "I know how much is in there. Cash me out. Five percent for you, no more."

He stopped at the bar. "Scotch. Neat."

"I thought you didn't drink while you gambled," his brother said.

"I'm not gambling anymore." The bartender pushed the glass his way and Xander knocked it back before continuing out of the building and onto one of Monaco's crowded streets.

Strange. The alcohol barely burned anymore. It didn't make him feel good, either. Stupid alcohol.

"Where are you?"

"Monaco. Yesterday I was in France. I think that was yesterday. It all sort of blurs together, you know?"

"You make me feel old, Xander, and I am your younger brother."

"You sound old, Stavros."

"Yes, well, I didn't have the luxury of running out on my responsibilities. That was your course of action and that meant someone had to stay behind and be a grown-up."

He remembered well what had happened the day he'd taken that luxury. Running out on his responsibilities, as Stavros called it.

You killed her. This is your fault. You've stolen something from this country, from me. You can never replace it. I will never forgive you.

Damn.

Now that that memory had surfaced another shot or four would be required.

"I'm sure the people will build a statue in your honor someday and it will all be worth it," Xander said.

"I didn't call to engage in small talk with you. I would rather strangle myself with my own necktie."

Xander stopped walking, ignoring the woman who ran

into him thanks to his sudden action. "What did you call about then?"

"Dad had a stroke. It's very likely he's dying. And you are the next in line for the throne. Unless you abdicate, and I mean really, finally, abdicate. Or you know, chain a concrete ball to your neck and hurl yourself into the sea, I won't mourn you."

"I would think you'd be happy for me to abdicate," Xander said, ignoring the tightness in his chest. He hated death. Hated its suddenness. Its lack of discrimination.

If death had any courtesy at all, it would have come for him a long time ago. Hell, he'd been baiting it for years.

Instead, it went after the lovely and needed. The ones who actually made a difference to the world rather than those who left nothing but brimstone and scorch marks in their wake.

"I have no desire to be king, but make no mistake, I will. The issue, of course, lies in the production of heirs. As happy as Jessica and I are with our children, they are not eligible to take the throne. Adoption is good enough for us, but not sufficient per the laws of Kyonos."

"That leaves…Eva."

"Yes," Stavros said. "It does. And if you hadn't heard, she is pregnant."

"And how does she feel? About her child being the heir?"

"She hates it. She and Mak don't even live in Kyonos and they'd have to uproot their lives so their child could be raised in the palace, so he or she could learn their duty. It would change everything. It was never meant to be this way for her and you know it."

Xander closed his eyes and pictured his wild, dark-haired sister. Yes, she would hate it. Because she'd always hated royal protocol. As he had.

He'd taken her mother from her. Could he rob her of the rest of her dreams, too?

"Whatever you decide, Xander, decide quickly. I would ask that you do so in two days' time," Stavros continued, "but if you want my opinion…"

"I don't." He hung the phone up and stuffed it into his pocket.

Then he walked toward the dock. And he wondered where he might find a concrete ball.

Layna Xenakos dismounted and patted her horse on the neck. Layna was sweaty and sticky, and the simple, long-sleeved shift she was wearing didn't do very much to diffuse the heat.

But she was smiling. Riding always did that for her. Up here, the view of the sea was intoxicating, the sharp, salty ocean breeze tangling with the fresh mountain air, a stark and bright combination she'd never experienced anywhere else.

It was one of the many things she liked about living at the convent. It was secluded. Separate. And here, at least, lack of vanity was a virtue. A virtue Layna didn't have to strive for. Vanity, in her case, would be laughable.

She pulled her head scarf out of her bag and wound her hair up, putting everything back in place. The only thing she could possibly feel any vanity about—her hair— safely covered again.

"Come on, Phineas," she said to the horse, leading the animal up to the stables and taking care of his tack and hooves before putting him in his stall and walking back out into the sunlight.

Technically, that had probably been a poor use of meditation time, but then, she rarely felt more connected to God, or to nature, than when she was riding. So, she imagined that had to count for something.

She walked toward the main building of the convent. Dinner would be served soon and she was hungry, since her afternoon's contemplation had been conducted on horseback.

She paused and looked over the garden wall, noticing tomatoes that were ready to be picked, and diverted herself, continuing on into the garden, humming something tunelessly as she went.

"Excuse me."

She froze when a man's voice pierced the relative silence. They interacted with men in the village often enough, but it was unusual for a man to come to the convent.

For a second, right before she turned, she experienced a brief moment of anxiety. Would he look at her like she was a monster? Would his face contort with horror? But before she turned fully, the fear had abated. God didn't care about her lack of outer beauty, and neither did she.

And moments like this were only a reminder that she did have to worry about vanity having a foothold. That it was an impediment to the service of others.

That, in a nutshell, was why she was a novice and not a sister, even after ten years at the convent.

"Can I help you?" The sun was shining on her face, and she knew he could see her fully. All of her scars. The rough, damaged skin that had stolen her beauty. Beauty that had once been her most prized feature.

The sun also kept her from seeing him in detail. Which spared her from whatever his expression might be, whatever reaction he might be having to her wounds. He was tall, and he was wearing a suit. An expensive suit. Not a man from the village. A man who looked like he'd stepped out of the life she'd once lived.

A man who reminded her of string quartets, glittering ballrooms and a prince who would have been her husband. If only things had been different.

If only life hadn't crumbled around her feet.

"Possibly, Sister. Although, I'm doubting I'm in the right place."

"There isn't another convent on Kyonos, so it's unlikely."

"I find it strange I'm at a convent at all." He looked up, the sun backlighting him, obscuring his features. "At least, I find it strange I haven't been hit by a lightning bolt."

"That isn't really how God works."

He shrugged. "I'll have to take your word for it. God and I haven't spoken in years."

"It's never too late," she said. Because it seemed like the right thing to say. Something the abbess would say.

"Well, as it happens, I'm not looking for God. I'm looking for a woman."

"Nothing but Sisters here, I'm afraid," she said.

"Well, I'm led to believe that she is that, too. I'm looking for Layna Xenakos."

She froze, her heart seizing. "She doesn't go by that name anymore." And that was true, the sisters called her Magdalena. A reminder that she was changed, and that she lived for others now and not herself.

And then he started walking toward her, a vision from a dream, or a nightmare. The epitome of everything she'd spent the past fifteen years running from.

Xander Drakos. Heir to the throne of Kyonos. Legendary playboy. And the man she'd been promised to marry.

Quite literally the last man on earth she wanted to see.

"Why not?" he asked.

He didn't recognize her. And why would he? She'd been a girl last time they'd seen each other. She'd been eighteen. And she'd been beautiful.

"Maybe because she doesn't want people to find her," she said, bending down to pick tomatoes off the vine, trying to ignore him, trying to ignore her heart, which was pounding so hard she was certain he could hear it.

"She's not hard to find. Simple inquiries led me here."

"What do you want?" she asked. "What do you want with her?"

Xander looked at the petite woman, standing in the middle of the garden. She had mud on the hem of her long, simple dress, mud on the cuffs of her sleeves, too. Her hair was covered by a scarf, the color given away only by her eyebrows, which were finely arched and dark.

One side of her face showed smooth, golden skin, high cheekbones and a full mouth that turned up slightly at the corners. But that was only one half of her face. That was where her beauty ended. Because the other side, from her neck, across her cheeks and over the bridge of her nose, was marred. Rough and twisted, her lips nearly frozen on that side, too encumbered by scar tissue to form a smile. Not that she was smiling at him. Even if she were, though, he imagined that grimace was permanent, at least on that part of her face.

This was the sort of woman he expected to find up here. Not a giggling, glittery socialite like Layna. She'd practically been a girl when they'd been engaged—only eighteen, on her way to womanhood. And beautiful beyond belief. Golden eyes and skin, and honey-colored hair that had likely been lightened via a bottle. But whether or not it was natural hadn't mattered. It had been beautiful—shining waves of spun gold mingled with deep chocolate browns.

He'd known even then that she would make a perfect queen. What was more important was that she'd been loved by the people. And she came with wonderful connections, since her father had been one of the wealthiest government officials in Kyonos, much of his success derived from manufacturing companies based out of the country.

As far as he could tell since his return two days ago, the Xenakos family was no longer on the island. Except for Layna. And he needed to find her.

He needed her. She was the anchor to his past. His surest ally. For the press, for the people. They had loved her, they would love her again.

They would not, he feared, feel the same way about him.

"We have some old business to discuss."

"The women who live here don't want to discuss old business," she said, her voice trembling. "Women come here for a new start. And old…old anything is not welcome." She turned away from him, and started to walk into the main building. She was going to walk away from him without answering his questions.

No one walked away from him.

He started toward the garden, and blocked her path. She raised her face to him, her expression defiant, and his heart dropped into his stomach.

He hadn't realized. Of course he hadn't. But now that he could see her eyes, those unusual eyes, fringed with dark lashes, he knew exactly who she was.

She was Layna Xenakos, but without her beauty. Without the laughing eyes. Without the dimple in her right cheek. No, now there were only scars.

Not very much shocked him. He'd seen too much. Done too much. He and the ugly side of life were well-acquainted. And he knew well that life's little surprises were always waiting to come and knock you in the teeth.

But even with that, this wasn't anything he'd expected. Nothing he could have anticipated.

From the time he'd left Kyonos, he'd very purposefully avoided news regarding his home country. Only recently, when his sister had married her bodyguard and when Stavros had married his matchmaker, had he read articles concerning his homeland, or the royal family.

Because he hadn't been able to stop himself. Not then. But every time he opened the window on that part of his past, it was like scrubbing an open wound.

And it took a lot to wipe his mind and emotions free of it all again. A lot of drinking. A lot of women. Things that made him feel like a different man than the one he'd once thought he was, than the one he was trained to be. Things that created happiness. Before they created a gigantic headache.

One thing he'd never thought to look for had been the fate of the woman he'd left behind. But obviously, something had happened.

"Layna," he said.

"No one calls me that," she said, her tone hard, her expression flat.

"I did."

"You do not now, your highness. You don't have that right. Do you even have the right to a title?"

That burned. Deeper than he'd imagined it could. Because she was edging close to a pain he'd rather forget.

"I do," he growled. "And I will continue to." His decision was made. Whether or not it made sense to anyone, including himself, his decision was made. He had come back, and he would stay. Though, no one knew it yet.

He'd felt compelled to come and see the state of things first. And then...and then he'd felt compelled to find Layna. Because if there was one thing he knew, it was that he had grown unsuitable to the task of ruling. And if he knew anything else, it was that no one was more suited to be queen than Layna.

He had thought it unlikely she would still be unmarried. He hadn't counted on her being both unmarried and at a convent, but he supposed it wasn't any less likely than what he'd been doing with his time for the past fifteen years.

No, he took that back. It was unlikely. Everything about this was unlikely. Layna Xenakos, the toast of Kyonosian society, renowned beauty and bubbly hostess, shut away in a convent, wearing a drab dress. With scars that made her mostly unrecognizable.

"I should like you to go," she said, walking toward him with purpose. He could tell she meant to go right on past him.

He stepped in front of her, blocking her way. She froze, those eyes, so familiar, like a shot straight out of the past, locked with his. "I would like for you to unhand me as well, then leave."

"So unhospitable, Sister, and to your future ruler."

"Hospitality is one thing, allowing a man to touch me as though he owns me is another thing entirely." She stepped away from him, her expression fierce. "You might rule the country, you might own the land, but you do *not* own me, or anyone else here."

"You belong to God now then, is that it?"

"Less worrisome than belonging to you."

"You did once."

She shook her head. "I never did."

"You wore my ring."

"But we hadn't taken vows yet. And you left."

"I let you keep the ring," he said, looking down at her hands and noticing they were bare.

"An engagement ring isn't very useful when there is no

fiancé attached to it. And anyway, I've changed. My life has changed. I suppose you thought you could come back here and pick up where we left off."

He had. And why not? It would be the story of the decade. The heir's return and his reunion with the woman the nation had always been so fond of. Except, for some reason, a very large part of him had assumed she'd simply been here in Kyonos, frozen in time, waiting for his return.

A large part of him had assumed that all of Kyonos had done so. But he had been mistaken.

There were casinos now. An electric strip by the beach. His brother Stavros's doing. The old town had been renewed. No longer simply a quarter where old men sat and played chess, it was now a place for hipsters and artists to hang out and "be inspired" by the beach and the architecture.

His sister was not the same. Not a dark-haired, mischievous girl, but a woman now. Married and expecting a child. His brother had become a man, instead of a rail-thin teenage boy.

His father was old. And dying. His father…

And Layna Xenakos had joined a convent.

"I will be straight with you," he said. "I am not the favored son of the Drakos family."

She nodded once but remained silent, so he continued.

"But I have decided that I will rule. For the next generation even more than for this one."

"What do you mean?" she asked.

"Stavros's children cannot inherit. And that would leave my sister's child. The changes it would require…it was never her cross to bear. I have done a great many selfish things in my life, Layna, and I intend to keep doing many of them. But what I cannot do, when it comes down to it, is condemn my brother to a life he never wanted. Or give to my sister's child a responsibility it was never meant to take on." He had ruined things for his siblings already. Their childhoods had passed by while he was gone. Children who'd had no mother.

Especially Eva. She'd been so young then. It was unfair. He couldn't continue to hurt her. He *wouldn't*.

"You speak of the crown as though it's a poison cup," she said, her words muted.

"It is in many ways. But it is mine. And I have spent too many years trying to pass it off to others." Yes, his. As far as anyone knew, it was his. It was the expectation. What he had trained for until he was twenty-one.

The truth, was another matter. But it didn't change Stavros's reality. It didn't change Eva's.

It didn't change what had to be done.

"A conscience, Xander?" she asked, using his first name, the sound sending a shiver through him. A ripple of memory.

"I'm not so certain I'd go that far. Maybe a bit of forgotten honor bred into me. Thanks to all that royal blood," he said, his tone dripping sarcasm. "Imagine my disappointment when I realized I hadn't replaced it all with alcohol."

"A disappointment for many," she said. She sounded more like her old self now. He'd officially destroyed her serenity. Perhaps a lightning bolt would be in the offing after all.

"I'm sure. But I had thought there might be a way of softening the blow."

"And that is?"

"You," he said. "I'm going to need you, Layna."

CHAPTER TWO

LAYNA FELT LIKE the world had just inverted beneath her feet, and only the wooden gate was keeping her from folding. "Excuse me?"

"I need you."

"I can't imagine why you think that, but trust me, you don't."

"The people love you. They don't love me, Layna."

"The people love me?" she spat, anger rising in her, anger she always thought was dealt with. Until something came up and reminded her that it wasn't. Something small and insignificant, like catching sight of herself in the mirror. Or burning her finger when she was cooking. In this instance, it wasn't a small something. It was the ghost of fiancés past, talking about the people. The people who had loved her.

She'd made her peace with some of the people of Kyonos. She served them, after all, but she didn't feel the way she once had about them—confident that she had a country filled with adoring fans.

Quite the opposite.

"Yes," he said, his voice certain still, as though he hadn't heard the warning in her tone.

"The people," she said, "behaved more like animals after you left. Everything fell apart, but I assume you know that."

"I didn't watch the news after I left. A tiny island like Kyonos is fairly easy to ignore when you aren't on it. And when you're drunk headlines look a little blurry."

"So you don't know, then? You don't know that every-thing…everything went to hell? That companies pulled up stakes, stocks went down to nothing, thousands of people lost their jobs?"

"All because I left?"

"Surely you knew some of this."

"Some of it," he said, his voice clipped. "But there's a lot you can avoid when you're only sober for a couple hours a day."

"I wouldn't know."

"I imagine vice isn't so much your thing."

"No."

"So the economy collapsed and I'm to blame? That's the sum of it?"

She shrugged. "You. The death of the queen. The king's depression. It was an unhappy combination, and no one was confident in the state of things. People were angry."

She looked at him and she tried to find a place of se-renity. Of strength. What happened to her wasn't a secret. It was in newspapers, online. It was widespread news. It was just hard to say out loud.

But you aren't going to show him that you care. You aren't going to be weak. It doesn't matter. Vanity. All is vanity.

"There were riots in the streets. In front of the homes of government officials, who were blamed for the economic crisis. There were different kinds of attacks made. Sev-eral attempts at…acid attacks. We were leaving our home when a man pushed up to the front and tried to throw a cup of acid onto my father. He stumbled, though, and the man missed. I was hit instead. I don't think I need to tell you where," she said, attempting to smile. Smiling could be difficult enough at the best of times since half of her mouth had trouble obeying that command, but when she didn't feel like smiling it was completely impossible.

But telling the story was easier when she imagined it was another girl. When she remembered what happened without remembering the pain.

She searched his face. She seemed to have succeeded in shocking him, which was something she hadn't imagined would be possible.

"So, I think it's fair to say maybe the people don't love me as much as you think they do." She pushed past him now, determined to put an end to this. To this strange bit of torment from the past.

He grabbed hold of her, his hand on her arm sending a rush of heat through her. She breathed in sharply, his scent hitting her, like a punch in the chest.

Her head was swimming. With glittering palaces and silk dresses. Dancing in a sparkling ballroom in a man's warm embrace. A trip to the garden where his lips almost touched hers. Her full, beautiful lips, unencumbered by scar tissue. It would have been her first kiss. And right then she wanted to weep for the loss of it because now there would never be one.

Not on those lips. They were gone forever.

Not even on the lips she had now. Because she had vowed to never know that pleasure of life. To forego it in favor of serving others, and release her hold on her own needs. Not that it should matter. No man would ever want to kiss her anyway.

But Xander was…he was too much. He was here, right when she didn't want him, and not fifteen years ago when she'd needed him.

Right now, she didn't need him. She needed distance.

The more Xander filled up her vision, the more faded everything else seemed to become. Xander was a look into a life that she didn't have anymore. Couldn't have. Didn't want.

She just needed him gone. So that she could start to forget again.

"I suppose you should go now," she said. "Now that you know how it is. If you're looking for a ticket to salvation, Xander, I'm not it."

"I'm not interested in salvation," he said. "But I do want to do the right thing. Novel, isn't it?"

"Well, I can't help you. Perhaps it's best you found your way back to the village."

"I'm staying here tonight."

"What?" she asked, shock lancing her.

"I spoke to the abbess, and explained the situation. I don't want the public knowing I'm here yet, not until I'm ready. And I intend to bring you with me."

"I see. And nothing of what I said matters?"

He shook his head, his jaw tight. "No."

"The fact that I'm not me anymore doesn't matter?"

He studied her face, the cold assessment saying more than any insult could. Before the attack, men…Xander… had never looked at her with ice in their eyes. There had always been heat.

"I'll let you know in the morning."

He turned and walked away from her, into the main building. She waited out in the yard, cursing silently and not caring that it was a sin as she stood there, hoping he was putting enough distance between them that she wouldn't run into him again.

She would speak to the abbess tonight and in the morning, hopefully Xander would leave. And he would go back to being a memory she tried not to have.

* * *

It was early the next morning when Mother Maria-Francesca called her into her office.

"You should go with him."

"I can't," Layna said, stepping back. "I don't want to go back to that life. I want to be here."

"He only wants you to help him get established. And as you want to serve, I think it would be good for you to serve in this way."

"Alone. With a man."

"If I have to concern myself with how you would behave alone with a man then perhaps this isn't your calling."

It wasn't spoken in anger or in condemnation, just as a simple, quiet fact that settled in the room and made Layna feel hideously exposed. As though her motives—motives she'd often feared were less than wholly pure—were laid out before the woman she considered her spiritual superior in every way.

All that ugly fear and insecurity. Her vanity. Her anger. And old desires that never seemed to fully die. Just sitting there for anyone to see.

"It isn't that," Layna said. "I mean, I'm not afraid of falling into temptation." And even less worried about Xander falling into temptation with her. "It's just that appearances…"

"Are what men look at, my dear. But God sees the heart. So what does it matter what people might think? Of the arrangement, or of you?"

Such a simple perspective. And one of the main reasons she felt so at home here. But that didn't mean her ease and tranquility transferred to every place she went.

"I suppose it doesn't matter." And what she wanted certainly wouldn't come into play. She could hardly throw herself on the ground and say she didn't want to. Of course she didn't. True sacrifice was hard. Serving others could be hard. Neither were excuses she would accept.

"This is an opportunity to do the sort of good that most of us never get the chance to do. You have the ear of a king, in heaven and now on earth. You must use this chance."

"I'll…think about it. Pray…about it." Layna blinked back tears as she walked out of the room. By the time she'd hit the hall, she was running. Out the door and to the stables.

She couldn't breathe. She couldn't think. She needed to ride.

And she did. Until the wind stung her eyes. Until she couldn't tell if it was the burn from the air that made tears stream down her face, or the deep well of emotion that had been opened up inside of her. Threatening to pull her in and drown her.

She rode up to the top of the hill, the highest point that was easily accessible, and looked down at the waves, crashing below, against the rocks. That was how she felt. Like the waves were beating her against stone. Breaking her down.

Like life was asking too much of her. When she'd already given everything she had.

She leaned forward and buried her face in Phineas's neck. Maria-Francesca was right. It hurt to admit it. Even in her own mind, it hurt to admit it. She'd never taken her vows. And so much of that was down to herself.

Was down to that piece of her that missed the ballrooms. That longed for a husband. For children. For the life she'd left behind.

If she stayed here, she would be safe. But she would be stuck. She would never take her vows. Because it wasn't her calling. And she'd been too afraid to admit it for so long because she didn't know where else to go.

You can go with him.

Not for him. For her. For closure. So that the ache she felt when she thought of Xander, and warm nights in a palace garden, would finally fade.

As it was, he'd been gone from her life with no warning. A wound that had cut swift and deep. An abandonment that had become all the more painful after her attack.

It was safe here at the convent. But it was stagnant. And she saw now, for the first time, that it shielded her, instead of healing her.

She could do this. She would do it. And when it was over…maybe something inside of her would be changed. Maybe she would find the transformation she ached for.

Maybe then…maybe then she would come back here and find more than a hiding place. Maybe then, she would be changed enough to take the final step. To take her vows.

Maybe if she finished this, she could finally find her place.

All of her belongings fit into one suitcase. When you didn't need hair products, makeup, or anything beyond bare essentials to wear, life was pretty simple. And portable, it turned out.

She shifted, standing in the doorway, looking at Xander, who had his focus on the view of the sea. "I suppose you have an ostentatious car ready to whisk us back to civilization?"

Xander turned and smiled, his eyes assessing. She didn't like that. Didn't like how hard he looked at her. She preferred very much to be invisible.

"Naturally," he said. "It's essentially an eight-cylinder phallus."

"Compensation for your shortcomings?"

The words escaped her lips before she even processed

them. They were a stranger's words. A stranger's voice. One from the past.

So weird. Being with him resurrected more than just memories, it seemed to bring out old tendencies. In her life at the convent, sarcasm and smart replies were not well-received. But when she'd been one of the many socialites buzzing around Xander, wanting to catch his attention, when she'd moved in such a sparkling and sometimes cut-throat circle, it had been the best way to communicate.

They had all been like that. Pretending to be so bored by their surroundings, showing their cool with cutting re-marks and brittle laughter. It struck her then that Xander had changed, too. He hadn't joined a convent, but he lacked the air of the smug aristocrat he used to carry himself with.

He still had that lazy smile, that wicked mouth. But be-neath the glitter in his eyes, she sensed something deeper now. Something dark. Something that made her stomach clench and her heart pound.

"I apologize," she said. "That was neither gracious nor appropriate. I'm ready to go."

He shrugged and took her suitcase from her, starting to walk across the expanse of green. She followed him, over the hill and to the lot where a red sports car was parked.

"I'm a cliché," he said. "The playboy prince. It would be embarrassing if it weren't so much fun."

"There's more to life than fun."

"But fun is a part of it," he countered.

"Certainly."

He deposited her suitcase in the trunk of the car. "I think you might have forgotten the fun part," he said.

"You have that covered for the both of us, I think." She moved her hand in a wide sweep, like she was presenting the car on a game show.

He smiled. "You have no idea."

For some reason that smile, that statement, made her stomach tight. "I imagine I don't."

"Why don't you get in the car and we can continue this while we head back down to Thysius?"

She hadn't been to the capitol in a couple of years, and just the thought of it filled her with dread. "What exactly are we doing?"

"Get in the car."

Fear wrapped its fingers around her throat, the desire to turn and run almost overwhelming. But she didn't. "Not yet. Where are we staying? What are we going to do?"

"The palace," he said. "You're familiar with it."

"Yes." Much too familiar. There was a time when it would have been her home. When she would have been the queen. Memories that seemed like they belonged in another life were crowding in, trying to remind her of all the things she'd tried so hard to let go of.

"The press will think it's all sensational." He opened his door and got inside and she stood outside, looking at her warped reflection in the slightly rounded window.

"That's what I'm afraid of." She pulled the car door open and got inside, closing it behind her.

The leather interior smelled new. And an awful lot like money. Such a strange contrast to the old stone walls of the convent. When he turned the key and the engine roared to life she couldn't help but think it was a very strange contrast. The pristine newness. The noise. So different than the ancient quiet she'd lived in for so long.

"This is the story that I need. You and me, collaborating on bringing the country into a new era."

"Why do I feel a bit like you just told me together we will rule the galaxy as father and son…."

"Are you saying I'm asking you to join the Dark Side?"

"I feel like it."

"Seems a strange reference for a nun."

"I'm not a nun, actually. Not yet. I'm a novice." And she had been for a near record amount of time. Speaking of movies, her life was becoming a bit *"How do you solve a problem like Maria."*

"And I do watch movies," she said. "There isn't a lot that happens up here, and we aren't all serious all the time."

He pulled out of the parking area and onto the road. And she wasn't "here" anymore, either. She was leaving. Heading into the world. Away from the convent, away from the village. Into the city. Toward people. And the press.

Panic clawed at her, a desperate beast trying to escape. But she held it in. Did she pray for serenity or was this part of her test? To do what she didn't want, for it to be hard. To have to persevere.

Suddenly, she just felt angry. She hadn't asked for any of this. Not for Xander to come back, not to have to be in the public eye again.

She hadn't asked to be attacked. To have her life stolen from her. And hadn't she taken it and turned it into something worthy? Why was she having to do this now?

Fear was doing its best to take her over completely. And its best was far too good for her taste. The farther she got from her home, the closer they drew to the capitol city, the more it grew.

She was shaking. A tremor that seemed to start from the inside and built outward until her teeth were chattering. She tightened her hands into fists, trying to will it to stop. But she didn't have the strength.

They took so much. He took so much. Don't let them have anything else.

That voice. That strong, quiet voice inside of her made the shaking stop. Because it was right. Too much of her pain belonged to Xander, to the people of Kyonos, and she wouldn't give them one bit more.

She would help. Help restore the nation, get it all back on track, get Xander into a good position. But she wouldn't give of herself. Her actions, her presence, yes. But nothing of her.

"It isn't just you," he said, his voice rough.

"What?"

"You aren't the only one who will be judged."

He was so in tune with her train of thought that she was almost afraid she'd voiced her fears out loud. "Maybe not. But I'm the only one of us who didn't earn the judgment."

It was true, even if it was unkind. So, okay, maybe she wasn't holding back all of herself from Xander. She was letting him have some of her anger.

He laughed and the car engine roared louder, the cypress trees outside the window turning into an indistinct blur of green as he accelerated. "Very true. I did earn mine. And I had a hell of a lot of fun doing it."

CHAPTER THREE

XANDER FELT LIKE he sometimes did after a night of heavy drinking. His head hurt. His stomach was unsettled. And memories pushed at the edges of his mind, threatening to crowd into the forefront.

Yes, it was just like the aftermath of being drunk. Or being hungover was a bit like coming home.

He paused the car at the gate. Stavros didn't know he was coming. It had been a phone call he hadn't been certain he could make. Stavros might bring up the option of hurling himself into the sea again and he might end up taking him up on it. Instead of returning to this.

He picked his phone up and dialed Stavros's number.

"Are you at the palace?" Xander asked when he heard an answer on the other end.

"I am not." Stavros's response was measured.

"Where are you then?"

"Vacation. My wife wanted to go to Greece and my children are enjoying a slight change of pace. Palace life is quite boring to them, I fear."

"I do remember the drudgery," he said, looking up at the turrets, bright white against a sun-bleached sky.

And he was walking back into it. Back into the past. Suddenly, he couldn't breathe.

He wanted to run again in that moment. Because he

could remember what had pushed him to it now, all too easily.

Blood. Death. Blame.

So much easier to run. To wrap himself in life's pleasures and ignore the pain.

"I can't imagine anything ever felt like drudgery to you. You never took it seriously enough."

"Maybe not then. But I'm here now. Oh, yes, I've decided to come back and assume the throne, I don't believe I mentioned that."

There was a long pause. He looked across the car at Layna, who was sitting there looking straight ahead, as though she was pretending she couldn't hear.

"I'm glad," Stavros said, at last, and Xander believed him. "But if this is a game to you, then I suggest you take your ass back to wherever you came from. It's been my life's work to bring Kyonos back from the brink, and I'll not have you destroy it."

"Don't worry, Stavros, I've only ever been interested in destroying myself."

"And yet, somehow, you seem to destroy others in the process."

Xander looked at Layna and felt an uncomfortable pang in his gut. "Not this time," he said. "Now, call and have them admit me, please."

"You'll find your quarters just as you left them."

He laughed. "I hope there's still porn under the mattress."

There was. Though it was hideously dated and nowhere near as scandalous as he'd imagined it to be when he was a young man only just starting down the path of debauchery.

The head of palace hospitality had ushered Layna to her room, and his father's advisor had walked him to his own quarters. The man, as old as the king, was blustering, shocked and trying to get answers from Xander who was, unfortunately for him, not in the mood to answer questions.

Instead he shut the man out, shut the door and looked around. That was when he found the magazines, just as he left them. They used to thrill him. He remembered it well. Now they just left him with this vague feeling of the stale familiar.

But then, life in general didn't thrill him much at this point. He'd seen too much. Done too much. He was less a carefree playboy than he was a jaded one. It was hard to show shock or emotion when one barely felt it anymore.

The glittering mystery had worn off life. Torn away the day his mother died. Forcing him to look at every ugly thing hidden behind the facade. And so he'd walked further into that part of life. The underbelly. Into all the things people wanted to revel in, but could never bring themselves to discard their morals—or their image—in order to do so.

But he'd done it. Morals didn't mean a thing to him. Neither did his image.

It was too hard to go on living in a beautiful farce when you knew that was all it was. So he never bothered. He was honest about what he wanted. He took what he wanted. As did those around him. Whether it was gambling, drugs or sex, it was done with a transparency, an unapologetic middle finger at life.

He'd found a strange relief in it. In being around all that sin in the open. Because it was the secrets, the pretense of civility, he couldn't handle.

And now he was back in the palace. Center stage for the show. Back in chains. Pretending to be someone he was never born to be.

He threw the magazines down onto the bed and looked

around. He'd expected a few more ghosts. Or something. But he felt the same as he had before returning home.

Shame and regret were his second skin. They existed with him, over him. And so he'd spent his life reveling in the most shameful things imaginable. He would feel it either way. At least if he sought it out, it was his choice. Not something forced upon him by life.

Like standing beneath water that was too hot. Until you were scalded to the point where you didn't feel it anymore.

In truth, it had worked to a degree.

But only to a degree.

He pushed his hands through his hair and turned toward where his suitcases had been put. He would need ties, he supposed. He didn't wear ties. One of the things he'd cast off when he'd left Kyonos.

For now, he just had his suits and shirts he wore open-collared, but it would have to do. Just the thought of ties made it feel hard to breathe. Or maybe it was the palace in general.

Her pulled open the door to his room and stalked down the corridor, not sure where he was going. He grabbed the passing housekeeper. "Where is Layna?"

"Oh!" She looked completely shocked. "Your Highness…"

"Xander," he said. He had no patience for station and title. "Which room is she in?"

"Ms. Xenakos is in the east wing, in the Cream Suite."

"Great." He started in that direction. Because there was nothing else to do. There was no one else in the palace he wanted to talk to.

He wasn't certain why that was. He should seek out his father's major domo. He should go and see his father, who was in the hospital. He should call his sister.

He didn't do any of those things. He just walked through

the expansive corridors, past openmouthed palace staff, and toward the Cream Suite. He got lost. Twice. It was an embarrassment, but he just kept going until he got his bearings again.

Then he pushed open the heavy wooden doors without knocking, and saw Layna, sitting on the edge of the bed. Her face snapped up, and again, he was shocked by her appearance.

It hit him like a slug to the gut. She had been so beautiful. So many beautiful things had been destroyed in that time. Either by his actions, or his very birth. The fault was bred into him, in many ways.

"What are you doing?"

"I'm here to speak to you. And to…escort you to dinner."

It had been a long time since he'd escorted a woman to dinner. Usually he had sex with them, then they ordered room service and ate it naked. Although, on a good night, he kicked the woman out quickly, then ate room service by himself.

She blinked. "Escort me to dinner? Where?"

"Here will do. The staff has been alerted to my presence, and I have no doubt they're eager to welcome me back with my favorite food," he said, his tone dry. "Or at the very least they won't let me starve."

"I don't suppose the heir is of much use to anyone if he's starved to death. I also don't suppose he's much use to anyone if he's absent and drunk."

"No, it doesn't seem that I've done any good during my time away," he said, his voice tight. "But I'm not sure what I could have done here, either. I was not the king then. I am not now. I'm simply in line."

"But you left us," she said, a note in her voice, so sad, so fierce, he felt it in his bones.

"I left you," he said.

"Yes."

"Did I break your heart, Layna?"

She shook her head slowly. "Not in the way you mean. I didn't love you, Xander. I was infatuated, surely, but we didn't truly know each other. You were very handsome, and I can't deny being drawn to you. I'm a bit of a magpie for shiny things, you know."

"I was shiny?"

"Yes. The shiniest prize out there."

"Not sure how I feel about that."

"You'll live." She looked down. "I loved the idea of being queen. I was raised for it, after all."

"Yes, you were." He didn't have to say that he hadn't been in love with her. That much had been obvious by his actions. When he'd left Kyonos he'd hardly spared a thought for what it would mean to Layna. He hadn't been able to spare a thought for anything but his own pain.

"But I thought I would find someone else. Maybe Stavros."

"You wanted to marry Stavros?"

She shrugged. "I would have. But then… Then the attack happened and I didn't especially want to see anyone much less marry anyone."

"So you joined a convent? Seems extreme."

"No. I spent years struggling with depression, actually, but thank you for your rather blithe commentary on my pain."

That shocked him into silence, which was a rare and difficult thing. He didn't shock easily. Or, as a rule, at all.

"When did you join?"

"Ten years ago. I was tired of muddling through. And I saw a chance to make myself useful. I couldn't fit back into the life I had been in, so it was time to make a new one."

"And you've been happy?"

"Content."

"Not happy?"

"Happiness is a temporary thing, Xander. Fleeting. An emotion like any other. I would rather exist in contentment."

He laughed. "Funny. I don't think I've been happy. Not content, either. I like to chase intense bursts of euphoria."

"And have you managed to catch them?" she asked, her voice tight.

"Yeah," he said, shoving his hands in his pockets and leaning against the doorjamb, "I have. But let me tell you, the highs might be high…the comedowns are a bitch."

"I wouldn't know. I strive for a more simple and useful existence."

"Do you want to dress for dinner?"

She looked down at the simple, shapeless dress she was wearing. It was blue and flowered, the sweater she had over it navy and button-down, hanging open and concealing her curves entirely, whatever those curves might look like. "What's wrong with this?"

"Really?"

"I'm not exactly given to materialism these days, and unless you were dead set on looking at my figure," she said dryly, as though it were the most ridiculous thing on the planet, "I fail to see why you should be disappointed. I'm clean, my clothing is serviceable. I don't know what more you could possibly need from me. If I am to be an accessory in your attempt at being seen by your people as palatable, then I'm sure my more conservative style could be to your advantage."

"I don't think that was what people liked about you."

"Perhaps not, but it can't be helped," she said, her voice tart.

She bowed her head, brown hair falling forward. "You used to sparkle," he said, not sure where the words came from, or why he'd voiced them.

She looked up at him, fire burning in her golden eyes. "And I used to be beautiful. Things change."

He pushed away from the door, and images from the past fifteen years—the casinos, the women—rolled through his mind. "Yes, they do. I'll see you at dinner."

He turned and walked out of the room, back down the corridor. And he got lost again on the way back to his room.

This damned palace was never going to feel like home. But he'd been a lot of places in the past fifteen years and none of them felt like home, either.

He was starting to believe it was a place that simply didn't exist for him.

CHAPTER FOUR

HE'D MADE HER feel self-conscious about her dress. More than that, his words had sliced through her like a knife, hitting her square in a heart she'd assumed would be invulnerable to such things.

I used to be beautiful. Things change.

Yes, they certainly did.

She was realistic about the situation with her face. Fifteen years of living with it, and there was no other option. It had been hard. She'd been a woman defined by her looks, by her position in the public eye, and in one moment, it had all changed.

She was still a woman defined by her looks. But people didn't like what they saw.

The press called her disfigured. The former beauty. The walking dead.

Going out into the town had meant a chance she'd get her photo taken, and that meant a chance she'd appear in the news the next day.

It had driven her deeper into her own darkness. Into isolation. It had been hell. And she'd had to escape.

Finding a way to a new life had been the hardest thing she'd ever done. Her family hadn't known what to do with her, they hadn't known how to help her. Their existence had been shaken, too. Their promised position as in-laws to the royal family vanished.

In the end, they'd all moved to Greece. Her mother, father and sisters. But Layna had stayed. And what she'd weathered should have made her immune to things like Xander's comments.

She was thirty-three. She wasn't a child. She knew now that life wasn't defined by dresses, balls and beauty. She did know it. So curse Xander for making her feel insecure. For making her feel like she should make an effort to look pretty when she met him for dinner.

Those things, they didn't matter. She had changed, and at the end of the day, she liked herself better now. At least now she didn't think the only way to live was by shopping the day away before going to a ball and pretending to be bored by all of it.

In some ways, she had more freedom now. If something made her feel joy, she had no problem showing it. Her face made it impossible for her to blend in, impossible for people to do anything but judge her. So why worry about trying to seem cool and unaffected? There was no reason at all.

"I'm glad you could make it."

Layna paused at the entrance to the grand dining room. Another unholy mash-up between her life then and now. The expansive banquet table held no one but Xander. In the past, there would have been fifty dignitaries in attendance. And Layna would have worn her best dress. Xander would have worn a tie. They would have sat beside each other.

He was wearing a black suit jacket and a crisp white shirt open at the collar, revealing a wedge of golden skin and a dark dusting of hair.

She tried to remember if he'd had chest hair during their engagement. He certainly hadn't been as broad or muscular. He'd been lean. Soft-faced and handsome.

His face was more angular now, his jaw more pronounced thanks to the black stubble there. And his eyes, those eyes were so much sharper.

He was a man now.

"I'm not late," she said, walking slowly into the room. She wasn't sure if she should walk up to where he was, at the head of the table, and sit near him or not.

"No, but I was still wondering if you would bother to join me."

"I said I would. So I did."

"You aren't a soft girl, are you, Layna?"

"Have I ever been, Xander?"

A half smile curved his lips and it sent a strange, tightening sensation through her stomach. "No. Now that you mention it, you never were. Though you used to look like you might be."

"All that blond hair dye and the pink gowns. I suspect it was deceiving."

"Maybe to some. I remember, though, standing out on the balcony with you while you looked at the other guests."

So did she. Making snide observations about how Lady So-and-so had worn that gown to a previous event, and how Madame Blah-blah-blah's hair looked like a bird had chosen to nest in it.

Yes, she'd had opinions on everyone's looks. Specifically their shortcomings. The irony of that still burned.

"Yes, well, I was young. I had a lot of growing up to do. And I've had a lot of years to do it."

"And have you?" He leaned back in his chair, an arm rested on the table, an insolent expression on his face.

"Of course."

"See, I thought you might be playing hide-and-seek."

She stiffened and walked toward his end of the table and sat down, leaving an empty place between them. "What about you?"

"That's certainly what I'm doing. But I've been found, and I am now 'it,' as they say. Means I have to face all this."

"You sound about as thrilled as a man facing the gallows."

Several servants entered with food on trays, laid out in front of them grandly, their glasses filled with wine.

"Are you permitted?" he asked.

She nodded. "Yes. So long as it's not to excess. And anyway, I haven't taken my vows yet, remember?"

He nodded slowly. "I do. That is significant."

"It is." The servants uncovered the platters and began to dish portions of rice, quail and vegetables onto her plate. She was surprised by how hungry she was. She hadn't eaten all day and she hadn't felt it. Because she'd been too filled up with nerves to do much of anything but worry.

"Why haven't you?"

Her face heated. "I haven't been permitted to take them yet."

"So it isn't your choice?"

She shook her head. "No. I'm committed." She hesitated to say the words because they felt false somehow. Especially after her revelation just before she left the convent. That part of her still wanted something from this life. From this palace. From Xander. She pushed her doubts away. "I was miserable before I went to the convent. I had no idea what to do with myself, no idea what I was supposed to… do with my life. Everything changed for me after."

"After I left," he said.

The servants cleared the room and they were left alone in the vast dining area. Layna looked out the windows, into the darkness, trying to find a point to focus on, something to anchor her to earth. Something to make her feel like the world hadn't changed entirely in the past twelve hours.

It was night out. There were still stars. She was still breathing.

"After you left," she said. "And then after the attack."

"I didn't think of you when I left," he said.

She laughed, and she surprised herself with her own bitterness. She'd done nothing but think about him. Worry for him. Pine for him. She'd lied a bit when she'd said he hadn't broken her heart. As much as she didn't believe she'd truly been in love with him, she'd cared.

Her heart and her future had been bound up in him. He'd been the man she'd imagined going to bed with at night. The man she'd thought she would have children with. The man who would make her a queen.

And then he'd gone, and taken with him her dreams. Her purpose.

Followed closely by the attack that took so many other things…gaining traction again had been nearly impossible.

"I didn't imagine you had."

"It was easier not to. But now I want to know."

"It was your father who told me you'd gone," she said. "And he asked that I return the ring."

"Did he?" Xander asked, his voice soft, deadly sounding.

"Yes. It was part of the Drakos family crown jewels, I could hardly keep it."

"Well, I'm sure it was badly missed in that dusty cabinet they keep it all in," he said, his tone dry.

"Are you really offended on my behalf?" she said, her throat tightening, anger pouring through her, hot and fast. "A bit hypocritical since you were the one who left."

"My leaving had nothing to do with you."

"No, as you said, you never thought of me again."

"I did. I thought of you after. It's true that when I ran, I only thought of me, and I am sorry for that. But later, I thought of you. I couldn't have been a husband to you, not under those circumstances."

She took a bite of the rice and the rich flavor knocked out some of her anger. She did not eat food like this at the convent. Even considering the unfortunate nature of the conversation, the food was amazing. As was the wine.

She let silence fall between them while she enjoyed her meal. She made a mistake when she looked up, and her eyes caught his. And she couldn't look away. Everything in her went taut, her breath pausing, her heart slamming forward. All she could do was stare at him.

He was so familiar. A face she tried never to remember. That perfect golden skin, the dark brown eyes fringed with thick black lashes. Lips that promised heaven when he smiled, and made a woman imagine he could take her to a beautiful sort of hell with a kiss.

All of that was so familiar.

But the lines around his mouth were harder now. Marks by his eyes showed the ghosts of his smiles.

He had been beautiful at twenty-one. At thirty-six he was no less stunning.

Time had not been quite so kind to her. And anyway, she had absolutely no business looking at him like she was. No business memorizing the new lines on his face. It was like she'd been in a coma, and she was slowly waking up. Slowly seeing new things. Or, remembering old things. She didn't like it. She was starting to remember why she'd worked so hard to forget.

"I wasn't meant to be your wife," she said, looking back at her food.

"You don't think?"

"Clearly not. I found a new calling. The place I'm supposed to be."

"You think you're better off hiding in the mountains than you are as the queen of Kyonos?"

She'd always thought she would be a good queen. But with a girl's insight. She'd loved the idea of the status and power. That everyone else was so jealous of her for having caught Xander's eye, or, more honestly, the eye of his parents.

Now she understood it had been her father's merit more than her own that had earned her the consideration. At the time it hadn't mattered. She'd only thought how beautiful she would look wearing the crown.

But now, ironically, that the position was no longer on the table, she saw all the good she could do. All that needed to be done to fix her country.

Prince Stavros had done an admirable job with it, more than admirable, but there were still things to be done on a humanitarian level, and as someone who had done nothing but serve for the past ten years she was well familiar with what tasks needed to be tackled head-on.

Nice that she knew all that. Now that there was nothing she could do about it. That would be for the woman who married Xander. And that woman would not be her.

A twinge of anger hit her in the chest, burned like a pinprick and spread outward. This had been her future. And she was sitting in it now, not a part of it.

She looked back up and saw him watching her, and it hit her then. What she'd lost. They would have been married for nearly fifteen years by now. There would have been children. She wouldn't be scarred.

It did no good to dwell on the past. It did no good to turn over what-ifs. But it was so hard when your biggest what-if was sitting across from you eating dinner, like he might have done if you'd married him way back then.

Yes, it was a whole lot harder not to what-if in that situation. Easier when cloistered in a convent, away from any part of the life she'd once lived. Impossible here and now.

"I wasn't meant to be queen," she said, her tone strong, a sharp contrast to what she actually felt.

"Perhaps I wasn't meant to leave." His words burned through her. Because he had left. It didn't matter what should have happened, only what had.

"Why bother turning it over, Xander? It's what happened. You did leave. And things have changed. We didn't freeze in time here while you were gone like I'm sure you imagined we did. We went on. Things have happened, things that can't be undone. I would have been…a silly and selfish princess back then anyway. And now…now it just couldn't be."

"It's hard not to turn it over here, though, isn't it?"

She put her palms flat on the table, her heart pounding, blood rushing through her ears. "Why did you come back? Really. I mean…what changed? You left, and no one ever thought you would be back, but here you are now, and you're dragging me into it, so I want to know why."

He shook his head, didn't say anything. He only stared out the windows into the darkness outside.

"Answer me, Xander," she said. "I have a right to know why you've crashed back into my life."

"Because there was nothing out there," he said. "No answers. It fixed nothing. If Stavros wanted the throne, if it didn't throw Eva's future into disarray, I would never have come back. But I don't do any good by being gone. I'm not sure I'll do much good being back. I'm not sure I'm even capable of doing good. I think that where I'm concerned, all of the bad might run too deep." When he said it like that, she believed he might be right. "But I came back, because if I didn't it would stay broken. And now that I'm here, it might all remain that way, but at least it's my broken mess and not theirs."

"You love them, don't you?"

"I don't love easily," he said, his voice rough. "But I would die for them."

"That's something."

"A sliver of humanity?"

"Yes," she said, taking a deep breath. "What am I doing here, Xander? You've given me a reason. The press. But I have to tell you, I'm not sure I believe it."

"It's part of it," he said.

"I need all of it."

"Do you want an honest answer?"

"If you know how to give one."

"I don't lie, Layna, it's the one sin I don't indulge in. Do you know why?"

She put her fork down. "I'm on the edge of my seat."

"Because people lie to protect themselves. To make people like them. To hide what they've done because they're ashamed. I have no shame, and I don't care if people like me. My sins are public property."

"Then give me an honest answer."

"I thought I might marry you," he said, his tone conversational, light. As though he'd mentioned that it was a clear night and the food was lovely, and not that he'd been considering asking her to be his wife.

"You did?" she asked, her lips numb, her entire body numb suddenly, from fingertips on down.

A wife. *Xander's* wife.

It was impossible. And she didn't want it anyway. Her life was in the convent, it was serving people and living simply. It was shunning the frivolous things in the world. Denying passions and finding contentment in the small things. In the things that were worthy.

It was this palace. This man. They washed those old memories in brilliant colors, where for years they'd always been faded.

And now she could see again, so clearly, how lovely it had all been. She could taste the excitement of it. That secret ache bloomed, flourished, let her dream. Let her see the glitter, the sparkle and what might be for one beautiful moment.

But it only lasted for a moment. Until a root of bitter anger rose up and choked out the bloom.

"Obviously," he continued, "that can't happen now."

She felt the sting of his words like a slap. "Obviously not. What would people think if you took me as a wife?"

"I only meant because you've chosen to forego marriage by joining a convent. Had I found you anywhere else I would have stuck to my original plan and proposed on the spot."

She bit down hard and tried not to say what she was thinking. Tried. And failed. "I would have told you to go to hell. On the spot," she said.

"You haven't changed as much as I initially thought."

She stood up. "That's where you're wrong. Everything's changed. I've changed, my whole life has changed."

He stood and started to walk toward her, dark eyes pinned to hers. "No, Layna, see I don't think you've changed as much as you think you have. When I look at you, I can so easily see the girl you were. You were blond then."

"Because I used to dye it."

"I suspected. But it did suit you."

"It's pointless vanity," she said, waving her hand.

"How is it pointless if you enjoy it? It can still be vanity, but it doesn't mean it's pointless."

"Yes it does. But make your point and be done."

He took another step toward her and her heart climbed up into her throat and lodged itself there. "You had fire. Beneath that airhead, mean-girl surface, you had more to you than anyone guessed. You were a little flame ready to become a wild fire."

She shook her head. "It doesn't matter. I've changed now and…"

"No. You're still doing it. You're still hiding who you are beneath something else. Beneath a shield. The flame is still there, you just want to hide it. Up in the mountains."

"It's not my fire I'm hiding. It's my face. And if you want to pretend it doesn't matter then I'm going to tell you right now, Xander, no matter what you said before, you are a liar." Rage rattled through her, fueled her, spurred her on.

It hit her, as the force of it threatened to consume her, that of all the emotions she'd felt since her attack, she'd never been angry. Sad. Depressed. Lonely. She'd hit rock-bottom with those. Then she'd found a sort of steady tranquility in her existence at the convent.

But she'd never been angry.

Just now she was so furious she thought she might break apart with it. "Look at me," she said, "really look. Can you imagine me on newspapers and magazines? The face for our country? Can you imagine me trying to go to parties as if nothing had happened? Trying to continue on as if I was the same Layna as before? That's why I went to the convent. Because there it didn't matter if my face was different. There it's practically a virtue and here…here it's just not. I'm ugly, Xander, and whether or not I accept myself there will always be people who want to point it out. I've never seen a reason for putting myself through it."

He shoved his hands into his pockets, his eyes hard. "It will be commented on. I won't lie about that. But do

you think people will resent your scars or my abandonment more?"

"Don't tell me you're honestly still considering me as
queen material."

"I was very interested by the fact that you haven't yet
taken your vows."

"My intent remains the same, whether or not I've taken
final vows."

He reached out, took a piece of her hair between his
thumb and forefinger. She froze. She hadn't been touched
by a man in longer than she could remember. Male doctors
were the last ones, she was certain. And then she hadn't
registered the touch in any significant way.

But Xander had never been easy to ignore. Now, with
his hand on her hair, just her hair, a flood of memories
assaulted her. The catalog of moments when Xander had
touched her in the past opened, forcing her to remember.

His hand over hers, or low on her back. An arm around
her waist. His warm palm on her cheek as his lips nearly
brushed hers.

If they had married then, they would have kissed thousands of times by now. But as it was, they had never kissed
once.

"But nothing is final," he said.

He lowered his hand, releasing her hair, and sanity
flooded in a wave. She stepped back, blinking, that fresh
and newfound anger coming to her rescue.

"Yes, Xander, everything is final. I have made my decision, like you made yours. I'll help you in any way I can,
but don't insult me by pretending, even for a second, that
you would consider making me your wife. Don't consider
that I might allow it."

She turned and walked out of the room and when she
hit the halls she suddenly realized that she was gasping

for breath. She put a hand on her chest and blinked hard, fighting tears, fighting panic.

Xander was reaching into places inside of her no one had touched in so long, she'd forgotten they were there. Longings and regrets she'd buried beneath a mountain of all that lovely contentment she'd learned to cultivate from the sisters at the convent.

Xander made her restless. This palace made her remember. It made her want things.…

She shook her head. No. She wouldn't let this happen. She wouldn't be shaken. She would help him. If only to help her country, her people.

But she wouldn't forget who she'd become. Who Xander's actions had forced her to become.

CHAPTER FIVE

XANDER UNBUTTONED HIS shirt and threw it onto the bed. He hadn't intended to bring up the marriage proposal like that. Hell, he hadn't meant to bring it up at all. She was a nun. Well, close enough to being one, anyway.

And then there were the scars. He couldn't pretend they didn't matter. She was right on that score. He needed a wife that would help improve his image in the public, and before he'd seen her, he'd imagined that she could do that. That their reunion would be seen as a true romance in the eyes of the media.

But how would they respond to a scarred princess? A princess who had been scarred during the turmoil caused by his leaving? A constant reminder of dark times for all of them. It had to be considered.

As for him, it didn't much matter. He would marry someone, he had to. But just because he had to marry didn't mean he had to be monogamous. He would be honest on that score with whomever he married, of course. But marriage was a necessity because he had to produce heirs, and preferably sooner rather than later. At thirty-six he was hardly getting any younger, and added to that, the people needed assurance that he could provide what was needed.

His plans were officially screwed.

Tomorrow, he was taking Layna to Kyonos's largest

hospital, where he would make his first public appearance. And where he would be giving a sizable donation of his personal fortune, and making his intentions of ruling Kyonos known.

Because nothing eased the way like throwing charitable donations around. At least, he hoped it would ease the way.

The people loved Stavros. They wouldn't accept the change lightly. Come to think of it, he was sure it was why his brother remained out of the country, even knowing Xander was back. The bastard.

He nearly laughed out loud. No, Stavros wasn't the bastard here. He never had been. The bastard had always been him.

But it was too late to worry about that now. His decision was made.

He thought of Layna, of his need for a wife. Some of his decisions were made, but not all of them.

He would have to figure that part out as quickly as possible. Of course, in order to have it all figured out, he needed to know what he was dealing with.

He turned to his desk, to his laptop, sitting there, open. He typed in his name on the search engine and hit enter.

It had hit. The servants must have called. Someone had said something, because there were headlines already.

The Disgraced Heir's Return. He clicked the link and skimmed the article. It was filled with bile and innuendo. About all he'd done with his life since he'd been gone.

Prince Alexander Drakos, abandoned Kyonos like a rat when it was a sinking ship, saved, of course by Prince Stavros. All while Xander partied in Monaco, wasting his family fortune, sleeping with countless women while indulging in alcohol and illegal substances.

One source from an exclusive casino was quoted.

"One night, he was so drunk he could hardly stand straight. He put his arms around two women to brace himself and they helped him back to his room. I didn't see them leave until the next morning."

And this is the man who presumes to come back and be king of our great nation.

Xander closed the laptop, heat streaking up the back of his neck. He couldn't remember the night being referenced in the article, but he couldn't say it was a lie.

It wasn't going to be like he'd thought. It was going to be worse. And all he could do was go forward with the plan.

There was no other option.

"I assumed asking you to put on something more appropriate for the occasion would make you look at me like I'd grown a second head."

Layna was at the breakfast table, wearing an insipid pale pink shift and a sweater that was the color of a dirty rose. She looked up, her gaze serene. But it didn't cover the fire beneath. He'd spoken the truth to her last night. The fire was still there, fire she'd always been so desperate to hide. "I have no idea what you're talking about. My dress is the picture of appropriate."

"For a nunnery."

She arched a brow. "Funny that."

"You're not in the convent anymore, Dorothy."

"I don't suppose if I tapped my heels together three times I might find my way back."

"Unlikely. I doubt nuns are allowed to possess magic shoes."

"Novice."

"Either way," he said, crossing the room and planting his hands on the back of one of the dining chairs, "I am wearing a tie. And I don't think you understand just what a concession that is, so all things considered, perhaps you would allow me to get you a more appropriate dress for what I am certain will end up being a press conference."

Her expression went blank at the mention of the press. "What's the point? I'm not speaking in your press conference. I'm there to be your…what am I exactly—some homely, saintly representation of your good intentions? Or am I just supposed to stand close so that the lightning bolt you were concerned about earlier doesn't hit you?"

"I thought God didn't work that way."

She lifted a shoulder. "I said that before I'd spent this much time with you."

"I won't lie to you, you are here to give me a bit more of a savory appearance. And also because I think it lends nice closure to our story. If you can forgive me…"

"Oh, I see. Another layer to my usefulness." She stood, color slowly blooming in her cheeks as her voice rose. "You thought that if I would forgive you the country would follow suit. That if you came back and the woman you were engaged to before you left opened her arms to you, your people would do the same." And then she did something wholly unexpected. She started laughing.

Not just a giggle, but a laugh that seemed to take over her whole body. She put her hand on the back of the chair in front of her and doubled over, laughing so hard he thought she might choke.

"Oh, poor Xander," she gasped. "You came back to find your queen, your key to your redemption and you found a scarred woman who'd given herself to the church. Your plans just aren't going well, are they?"

He wouldn't even mention the unflattering news pieces going around about him.

"You could say that," he said, his words clipped. He did not find the situation as funny as she did. But then, in his mind, none of this was terribly funny. It was all his worst nightmare as far as he was concerned.

He was back here, in the suffocating atmosphere of the palace, trying to pretend like he fit when he didn't. Trying to pretend the scars the past had left on him didn't hurt when they did. Trying to act like this was a future he was entitled to when he knew full well it wasn't.

But he was the only one who did know that. The only one who was still alive who knew it, anyway.

"Sorry I'm making it difficult for you to use me," she said, wiping her eyes. "I'm sure that must really mess things up."

"I thought you lived for the service of others."

"The poor and downtrodden, not entitled royal princes who don't know you can't find responsibility, honor or purpose in the bottom of a gin bottle."

He laughed, bitterness in the sound. "No, I know you can't, but that's not what I was looking for."

"What were you looking for?" she asked.

"I wasn't looking for anything. I was trying to lose something. Now are you ready to go or not?"

"I'm ready," she said, her eyes far too assessing for his liking.

"Fine then, let's go. And do your best to look saintly. If you can cultivate a halo on our way there I would really appreciate it."

Layna held her breath until she thought she would pass out. The press was already waiting at the hospital when they pulled up, so clearly someone on staff had leaked the news. It would be huge, of course it would. The heir to the throne back on Kyonos.

The implications were huge.

And all she could think about was that they would be taking her picture. That people would look at her.

Xander made her revert to a stupid, silly girl who cared about insubstantial things. It was annoying beyond belief.

Just focus on all the good you can do with the kind of budget he has.

Yes, that was the key. She would direct him to the needs she knew existed. It would benefit Kyonos and it would benefit him. Everyone came out a winner. Having her picture in the paper was a small price to pay for doing that kind of good.

It really was. It didn't matter what they said. It didn't matter what they thought. Her body was just the place her soul lived, and the only beauty she had to be concerned with was the kind that was inside.

She repeated that, over and over again, but still when the car came to a stop and Xander got out, her hands started to shake.

They were taking pictures already. Xander's return would be the biggest news since his abandoning the island and it would be on every news station, in every paper.

He opened the limo door and before she could fully process her movements, she got out and was assaulted by a barrage of flashes and shouts. He took her arm and she kept her face tilted down as they walked into the hospital.

He released his hold on her when they were near the doors, then stood in front of her, the gesture oddly protective as he turned, addressing the press. "I will speak to you when we are done here. For now, my priority is to see how the most vulnerable of my country are getting on.

I have brought with me an ambassador, one who knows the struggles of all of you. Please treat her with respect."

He turned back to the doors, his hand on her arm again as he led her into the hospital.

The hospital administrator was waiting for them and after making introductions it was clear Xander was waiting for her to lead things. "Is the hospital large enough to accommodate all of the patients that you need to see?" she asked.

"Prince Stavros has done an amazing job of building up our research center," the woman said. Her manner was reserved. Almost cold. She was trying to be friendly, especially since Xander was there to give money, but there was a brittleness there she wasn't hiding well. "As a result we're well-equipped in many areas, but yes, things are starting to feel understaffed, and the children's ward especially is very small. People travel here seeking treatment."

"A wonderful thing," Xander said, for the first time, his confidence sounding blunted. He knew when to tone himself down, which was a surprise to Layna, and a credit to him.

"Yes," Layna said. "What about emergency medical services?"

They finished the tour of the hospital, which included a trip through the cafeteria. Layna nearly laughed at Xander, trying to deal with a hospital version of a gyro. He was clearly not impressed.

"She was not thrilled to have me here, was she?" Xander asked as he took another bite of food.

"Not as much as one might have hoped," Layna said.

"Well, I imagined that's what I'll be contending with across the board. Stavros is well-liked. And I am not." He looked down at his meal. "I do have an idea of where we might increase the funding," he said, his voice low, only for Layna.

"Better idea, Xander, why don't you put some money aside to send the hospital cooks through a culinary course? Then they have transferable skills."

He paused, a half smile curving his lips. "This is why I brought you."

"I do have my uses," she said. "Even if I can't be made a queen."

He stared at her, for far too long in her opinion. It made her face hot, made her aware of her face. Annoying man.

"Are you ready to leave?" he asked. The hospital administrator had gone back to her office and they were standing in the lobby, staff and patients passing through. Some trying not to stare, some staring openly as they tried to decipher if the larger-than-life man standing there was a Drakos. If he was the long lost heir.

"Yes. As ready as I can be. I appreciated what you said to everyone before we came in. Hopefully they'll find it in them to be human. To both of us."

"Aren't you looking forward to the press ripping into me? They already have, you know."

She paused, waiting to feel some kind of relish at the thought, but she just didn't. "I actually don't want that. A surprise, I know. But I'm tired of this country feeling torn. I'm tired of grieving our losses. Tired of the unrest. Stavros has done an incredible job rebuilding, unifying, and the people love him. But there is a sense that everything isn't settled. That the royal family itself isn't healed. With the king so sick… Xander, I would rather you be accepted with open arms. And then I would like for you to take the people's trust and use it well, not abuse it. That's what I would like."

"And you want to go back up to your mountain then?"

"It's my years on the mountain that are helping you now. You have to admit, this wasn't your area of expertise."

"I've been a patient in hospital emergency rooms," he said, looking around them, "but I've been short on philanthropy in them."

"You have?" She was honestly shocked by that.

He laughed. "I've done no shortage of dumb-ass things in my time away, Layna. Just trust me on that. Too much speed in cars, too much drink, too much…everything." He paused. "Another advantage, I suppose to your being committed elsewhere. If you aren't my queen, you don't have to deal with my past."

"Is it so bad?"

He nodded slowly. "And there's a lot of it. Ready?"

She knew he was talking about facing the press. "Yes."

He walked out of the hospital and she followed slowly, dread filling her, her brain fuzzy, the world titled slightly.

"As has already been reported, in less than flattering words," he said, his voice loud, the microphones unnecessary, "I have returned, and I intend to take my place as heir to the throne. Of course, while my father is unwell, that doesn't mean it will happen now, or even in the next year, but I am here, and I'm here to stay. Layna Xenakos has graciously agreed to partner with me as I get familiarized with my home again. She's been living in service to this country, and she is the best choice, in my opinion, to show me where the greatest needs lie. If Layna can forgive me my choices, and welcome me back, I hope that her forgiveness is the start of my earning forgiveness from everyone. Though, I know that is a lot to ask. We all want what is best for the country. If you can't trust me, at least, for now perhaps, we can stand united in that."

The air roared with questions as the press crushed in on them both. Xander took her hand and pulled her through the crowd. She tried to keep her head down, tried to keep them from being able to snap shots of the worst of her damaged face. Tried to let all of the questions blend into an indistinct blur so that she didn't hear any of them.

But she heard words. *Attack. Scars. Beauty. Ugly.*

She'd never spoken to the press after her attack, and neither had her family. There were so many unanswered questions for them. Between her and Xander the press had the most salacious bits of the past, right there before them, and they were rabid now.

"In the car," Xander said, opening the door. She obeyed and slid inside. He followed, slamming the door behind them. "Back to the palace," he said before putting the divider up between them and the driver.

He let out a rough breath and put his head back on the seat. "Well, that went a bit better than anticipated."

"Did it?" she asked.

"They let me make a statement before mobbing us."

"Okay, yeah, there's that."

"It was better than they can be."

She looked at him. "How have you managed to avoid the press all these years?"

"Easy, actually. I don't go to places where they hang out. There will be no place to avoid them in Kyonos, but in the rest of Europe? In the States? No one cares. I made brief splashes in tabloids for the first couple of years. 'Dishonorable Heir Gambles Away His Fortune,' et cetera. But then people lost interest."

"I suppose it was the same for me. After the attack it was news. But they weren't allowed in the hospital to interview me. Then I was in too much pain to even consider talking to anyone. For a long time. I had a lot of surgeries." She didn't even like to say how many. "After that I didn't go anywhere. My parents moved to Greece where, you're right, no one cares about the drama that happened here, and I stayed on in their house with their servants for a while."

"Why didn't you leave?"

She frowned. "I…I was too tired." It was a terrible thing to admit. Even to remember. The depression had controlled her, not just emotionally, but physically. Breathing had often seemed too big of a trial. To move to Greece? It would have been unthinkable.

Those years were a haze, where she kept herself cradled by the gentle hands of painkillers that helped her sleep, helped her ignore the pain from her most recent surgery, and helped her live her days with blunted senses.

She preferred never to remember them. She'd come too far since then, and that place had been too dark. Although, there were times when it was important to remember it. It reminded her just how bright the sun was. How much better things were now.

Even sitting in the limo with Xander, with the press all but chasing the limo, it was better than that place. Because above all else, she had control now. She could leave if she chose. Could get up and walk away from Xander, from whatever she wanted to.

She had the power now. The energy and strength inside of herself to do it. She would never be stuck again.

"And has it been better here? Are you happy with your decision to stay?"

"It was terrible here, at first. That first five years…it was hell. The recovery was awful, Xander, I won't lie. It wouldn't have mattered where I was, not really. But when I got…well, when I got the worst, and I knew I had to figure out how to get better, it was right to change things as radically as I could. And that's why the convent was best for me. It's impossible to worry too much about your own drama when you have to confront what's happening with others."

"How did you connect with them?" he asked.

She looked down at her hands and smiled. "Some of the Sisters visited me in the hospital when I was recovering. And after every surgery. They checked on me sometimes. They cared. And they didn't look at me and see my scars. But they did see my pain, and they...cared."

"Your family?"

She sighed. "They didn't realize how bad it was. How bad it had gotten for me. Mainly because I lied to them. I told them I was fine when I wasn't and they wanted to believe I was telling the truth because it was so much easier. I don't blame them at all."

"Do you blame me?"

His words were stark in the silence of the car. Emotionless. He was asking, but he gave no indication that he cared either way.

"Yes," she said, and only realized just when she spoke the words that she meant them. That she did blame him, deep down, for the pain, for the isolation.

If he had stayed, at least she would have had a husband to stand by her. And maybe it would never have happened. Maybe the economy wouldn't have crashed, that she could never know. But she could have had someone.

She wouldn't have lost everything.

He nodded slowly. "I think that's fair. And I can handle having another sin added to the list."

"Do you think so?"

"Confession would take too long at this point, Layna. I'm beyond it. I might as well just accept it for what it is and move on from there."

Her heart thundered, anger burning through her veins. "At least you can move on. Gloss over it, pretend it didn't happen. It's a lot harder to do that when you have to look at the effects of the past in the mirror every day."

"Then how about I wake up to the effects of the past every morning?"

"What?" she asked, her stomach hollowing out.

"I've changed my mind about changing my mind." He put his legs out straight in front of him, his eyes fixed ahead. "After thinking about it, I believe the best idea is for you to marry me."

CHAPTER SIX

SHE HAD BEEN silent the rest of the ride back the palace. He supposed that it was probably a no, but he wasn't going to let her get away with not giving an answer. In his mind, it just meant he had to change hers.

"I'm tired," she said, once they reached the entryway of the palace. "I'm going to my room."

"I shall accompany you."

"No, you shall not," she said, starting to walk away from him, down an empty corridor, away from where the servants were bustling around.

"Then we will speak here."

"No, we won't."

He went to stand in front of her and she stopped and backed up quickly, her back making contact with the wall. "Yes," he said, advancing on her. "We will."

He studied her face, really studied it, for the first time since that day at the convent. It was a shame what had been done to her beauty. She'd been uncommon. He could remember her clearly. Those full pink lips, smooth skin, perfectly arched brows. Oh, he had wanted her badly. He could still remember that.

Being twenty-one and wanting his fiancée with a ferocity that he could scarcely understand. He'd been no virgin, even then, but she'd made him feel like one. And his father had made it clear Xander wasn't allowed to touch her, at least not until closer to the wedding. Something about respect and honor. About preserving the people's vision of their future queen.

So he had obeyed.

But they never would have made it that long. The chemistry had been too potent.

He'd nearly kissed her once. He remembered because it had happened the day before his mother's death. The day before the revelation about who he really was.

After that, he hadn't seen her.

He lifted his hand and put his fingertips on her scar-roughened cheek, drawing them down her neck. He could imagine the attack clearly, how it had made these particular scars. A hard hit to her cheek, spray over her nose, eye and forehead, down one side of her neck.

The other side of her face was virtually untouched, but it made her scars all the more shocking. It gave them contrast. A living, breathing before-and-after shot.

"Can you feel that?" he asked.

She nodded slowly. "Some. Where the grafts are."

"Some of this is a graft?"

"Yes. Not…nothing more than was necessary because I couldn't bear for them to add more scars to my body and… it would never have looked normal anyway. As it is, it's kind of Frankenstein's monster."

"You're hardly a monster," he said.

"Flattery won't get you your way," she said, her tone guarded, hard.

He dropped his hand back to his side. "I don't need flattery. You must see that this is going to be a challenge. We were going to marry, we *wanted* to marry."

"A lifetime ago. A face ago."

"Your face doesn't matter to me."

She laughed, a bitter sound. "For God's sake, Xander, don't lie. It insults us both."

"It doesn't matter. I won't be coy with you, Layna. I have to take a wife someday and when I do it will be because she specifically brings a benefit to my position and to Kyonos as a country. At the moment I think you're the most beneficial wife for me. My personal feelings for you as an individual, or for your looks, have no bearing on anything. I doubt I should be faithful to any woman I marry, so I don't see how wild attraction is an issue, either."

She jerked back as though he'd slapped her. "You're asking me to marry you, knowing you don't truly want me, and admitting to me that you will sleep with other women?"

"I'm being honest with you. It's how I would treat any marriage to any woman."

"And why is it you won't be faithful?"

"Does it matter if you aren't truly vying for the position?"

"Pretend I'm considering it," she said, "indulge my curiosities."

He shrugged, a vague sense of shame washing over him as he looked at the woman he would have promised his life to years ago and spoke of planned faithlessness. As he realized that, had he married her as a beauty queen, he would have been unfaithful to her even then.

He'd been young. In lust, not in love. The center of his own universe. Certain of his absolute entitlement.

The moment he'd gotten hard for another woman he would have had her without a thought, no matter the vows he'd made to Layna, because that was the manner of man he'd been. Now…he had no practice in restraint. In turning away from the various and sundry pleasures of the flesh. He'd spent their years apart bathing in them because if he couldn't get clean, then he would at least cover his transgressions in new layers of sin and hope that people never looked deeper. Hoped that he never had to look deeper.

"I have no practice at being with one woman," he said. "I can't imagine a lifetime with the same person in my bed, and I have low expectations of myself in that regard."

"Especially if your wife is ugly," she said.

"It doesn't matter. It's how things are, it's how I am."

"I thought you were changing."

He shook his head, taking a deep breath. "I came back because it was right, not because I have any burning conviction about the rightness of it. I can't condemn Stavros and Eva to a life they don't want when I was the one who was raised for it from the cradle. And it's one thing to walk away and ignore responsibilities when actually having to rule the country is years in the future. But with the way things are now…with the way Stavros's marriage turned out and the fact that the heir will be up to Eva without me. The fact that my father could die at any moment and a decision had to be made, that changed things. But it didn't change me. The one thing I can give for sure is honesty, so I'm giving that. Or would you rather have lies?"

"I rather wish I would have known you, really known you, back when we were engaged. I don't think I would have been so eager to say yes."

"Back then you had other options, too, but now you only have two—the convent, or standing at my side, ruling a country."

Black fire lit up in her eyes, the kind of anger he'd never seen on her face before, not in the time since he'd walked back into her life, and not in the life before. "You're so quick to remind me of how low I've fallen, but let me take a moment to show you a mirror. Your face might be as beautiful as it ever was, Xander, but you are nothing more than a dead limb on the Drakos family tree. Stavros made something with this country after you destroyed it, Evangelina was brave enough to fight for something she wanted, she didn't just run away. And what have you done?"

"Nothing," he said, his voice rough, his heart beating, bloody and ragged. "I have done nothing, and I would seek to change that. I am *trying* to change that. I made mistakes, Layna, and I will not deny it. I was a hurt, frightened child when I left, and then I became jaded. Now I have no heart left to wound and about a thousand things to atone for. So I am here, and I am trying. I am offering you this, the chance to rule with me. To make a difference. To give you children. Or you can go back to your convent and hide—because you're too afraid to face criticism—and make a small ripple in a giant pond with your good deeds when you could be changing the world. You can accuse me of anything you like, and you're probably right. But if you turn me down, you're turning down a chance to make a real difference."

She snorted, her lip curled. "You say that like marrying you, sharing your bed, is an incidental I shouldn't have to worry my head about so long as I can do my duty."

"Lie back and think of Kyonos," he bit out. He didn't know why he was pushing this so hard. He should let her go. He shouldn't be standing in the hall of his palace all but begging her to marry him. And yet he was.

Because he'd decided that Layna Xenakos would be his wife and now he couldn't fathom it being anyone else. No one would make a better queen. No one would help his image, or his country, in a deeper way than she would.

And he wanted her. That was the end of the reasoning really. When he wanted something, he got it.

"You're disgusting."

"And yet you're still here." He put one hand on the wall behind her and leaned in. "Would it be so bad?"

"You realize that I was prepared to swear off sex for life, that if I take my vows it means no men ever. Do you honestly think you're going to entice me with your looks?"

"Your altruism, then. And the chance to rise above where you fell. The chance to show all of Kyonos that, in the end, you have triumphed. Or, keep hiding."

Layna struggled to catch her breath. Rage, sadness and a deep, dark need all pulled at her. Xander, near enough to touch, smelling like rain and sin and man, was enough to make her pulse go into hyperdrive.

She lied when she said sex wasn't the way to tempt her. She was a woman who was prepared to take vows in part because she believed no man would ever want her, and, he was right, because it was easier to hide than to be out in the world experiencing rejection.

She liked men. And had things not changed the way they had, she never would have chosen a life that meant no men. No marriage. No children.

Children. A chance to make a difference.

She looked at Xander, at his strikingly handsome features. He was as perfect as he'd ever been, and the idea of him stuck with her…it was laughable.

And why are you like this? Because of him. Because he left. Because he left the country to rot in its own hell. And he never once thought of you. You needed him and he was gone.

Yes. It had been his decision to leave. To steal the future she'd always dreamed of for herself. Why couldn't she have it back? But if she was going to take him, the decisions wouldn't be his alone. Not again. He'd had enough control for too long.

He would sacrifice, too. She would not be a martyr.

She would have something for herself. And why not? Why ache for a man's touch when she could have it? Why long for the glitter of the palace in deep, secret parts of herself when it could be hers? Why wish that she could have a baby when it could be her reality?

"You can have me," she said, her voice hard, "on one condition."

"What is that?"

"I am the only woman you'll ever have in your bed again."

"I told you already…"

"Yes, and I already told you I wouldn't marry you, but that didn't stop you from building your case and asking again. You don't get to name all the terms, Xander. I am giving up my future at the convent and as much as you belittle it, I did find something there. Peace. With myself. With God and with those around me. You're asking me to leave that, and I'm consenting. To put myself out there before the world and expose myself to ridicule. And I won't do it for free. I won't make all the concessions. From this moment on, you will have no other woman. And you won't have me until vows are made. As I know well given the current state of my life, nothing is final until vows are spoken."

"And if I am unfaithful? If I agree now, but transgress later?"

"I will shame you in the media, your children will know you for the faithless man you are and I will ensure I sign a document that means I get your worldly assets. That's expensive sex, Xander, she would have to be well worth it."

A slow smile curved his lips. "You are quite ruthless under those plain clothes, aren't you?"

"Life has a way of making us that way, doesn't it?"

"I suppose it does."

"You've managed to live through all of this with very little in the way of consequences. Well, consider me your punishment." She turned and walked away from him, shaking with rage and sadness, with the tears that were building inside of her, a hard knot of pressure in her chest that she could hardly breathe past.

She'd just agreed to marry Xander Drakos, to become queen of Kyonos. To share the bed of a man who didn't truly want to be with her. She would never be able to go back to the convent. To the women she considered her friends. Her family.

But she was resolved. She'd made the right decision.

She was taking back a piece of the life that she lost. The life she should have had. It wouldn't be everything, not for either of them. But if felt like her right. She would be queen. A goal she'd fixed herself on at sixteen, from the first moment she'd seen Xander in person at a ball. She would bear the heirs to the throne, children for her to love. The children she'd given up hope of having.

And she would force Xander to face the consequences of his actions, every morning when he woke, and every night when he went to bed.

And she would try to ignore the crawling humiliation that thought made her feel. Tried and failed. As she walked into her bedroom and closed the door, she dissolved into misery, and gave in to her tears.

"I won't be coming back," she said into the phone. It had been hours since she'd accepted Xander's proposal. And now she'd realized she had to call Mother Maria-Francesca and confess.

"I thought you might not."

"You did?"

"He's the reason you were running all this time," she

said, her tone calm, steady. "And he's the reason I never advised you to move ahead with your vows.

"He is?"

"You are dedicated, and I have never doubted your faith, so please don't take me wrong, but I always felt you were driven by your inner demons, and not your convictions. It was good that you had us, to give you the shelter that you needed. But this is a calling that requires your whole life. And it requires a drive that goes beyond fear of the world outside."

She nodded slowly. "I know."

Deep down, Layna had always known it was true. Because she had ached for other things. She used convent life to hide from her desires, desires she felt could never be met. So that she didn't have to see gorgeous men, and mothers with babies, clothes there was no point in her wearing, hairstyles that would make no difference because she would never be pretty again.

She was having some of what she wanted. She felt…in some ways she felt more in control than she had in years. This wasn't about Xander, or his hold on her. It was about claiming the life she desired.

But if she had known this was what she really wanted, she never would have imposed on the Sisters.

"I didn't mean to use anyone," she said, her voice choked.

"You gave back more than you ever took, Magdalena."

Layna smiled at the use of the name. "Thank you. I'm not sure that's true, but thank you. I hope…to continue on giving in my new position I…I suppose I'm going to be a princess. And queen one day."

"I'm glad to hear it."

"I won't forget what you taught me. I'm going to use this. I'm going to do good with my position." Something she wouldn't have cared about if she'd married Xander as a girl of eighteen. She would have just used it to increase her shopping budget.

"That's nice to hear. But you're allowed to want things. You're allowed to have dreams."

"I've tried hard not to have them," she said, wiping away a tear she hadn't realized had escaped.

"I know you have, Layna. You've tried very hard to keep yourself safe. But if I could give you one last piece of advice, it would be not to let fear decide things for you."

"I won't."

And she wouldn't. Her decision was made, and even though the enormity of it made her tremble, there was no going back now.

CHAPTER SEVEN

"I TRUST YOU slept well."

"Your trust is misplaced."

Xander laughed as Layna made her way into the dining room and sat down at the table. He hadn't seen her since she'd run dramatically from him in the hall last night, but he'd had a feeling hunger would ferret her out of her room eventually. And here she was, in time for brunch.

"That is too bad. You haven't changed your mind, have you?"

Hard eyes met his. "No. Sorry, if you were looking for a reprieve you aren't going to get one from me."

"I don't want one."

"Even though you won't be permitted to slake your lusts elsewhere?"

"I've slaked them pretty well over the past fifteen years. More variety than most, so I can't truly complain." Though the idea of monogamy was foreign. Even so, if he promised her fidelity, he would give it. He would hardly sneak around behind her back all for the sake of sex, when he could have it with her if he wanted.

Not for the first time, he was feeling curious about the body beneath those simple shifts. Quite simply, in terms of her looks, he'd been shocked at first. And every time he looked at her, he was shocked. How she'd changed. The extent of the damage. But it was getting easier to let go of. Easier to just accept that it was part of her now.

And honestly, it made him extra curious about her body and if that made him reprehensible, so be it. She was to be his wife, and he hadn't reconciled the scars yet. They didn't turn him off but he wasn't exactly overcome by attraction.

As if to goad his thoughts his gut kicked as she moved into the room, the sunlight spilling over the smooth side of her face, catching fire behind her hair and revealing a golden halo. He got a glimpse of that blonde he'd been missing, subdued without the aid of dye, but there was some there. There was something about her that pulled him to her, there was no mistaking that.

"You will have to be tested," she said, her tone dry as she took a seat at the table. "I'm not risking catching an STD from you, so I'm sorry if you find that a problem, but you've been around."

"I get tested every six months. I'm promiscuous, but I'm responsibly promiscuous."

"Oxymoron."

"Judge not," he said, looking back down at his food.

"You can judge me all you want in that area of my life. I find myself quite blameless."

He raised a brow and looked back up at her. And found himself unbearably curious. How long had it been since she'd been with a man? Since before the convent? Before the accident?

Had she ever?

A ridiculous thought. She was thirty-three. A woman would have had to have been living in a convent to be a virgin at her age. But then, she had been, so all bets were off.

He found himself unreasonably intrigued by the idea. As if there was any doubt of his debauchery. Being fascinated by her innocence confirmed it.

"I find myself lacking in regret," he said. "Which I suppose isn't the same as blameless."

"That would be a seared conscience," she said. "And I have no desire to hear about your exploits beyond looking at medical records and seeing a negative result on the test."

"You're a savvy little thing for a woman who's spent ten years in a convent."

"I wasn't born in one."

"I suppose not. I propose that we set the wedding for early spring."

"That's very soon. Only a couple of months."

"I know," he said, "but it will create a nice celebratory atmosphere. Also, you've told me I have to remain celibate until our wedding night so I'm not eager to put it off."

Red bloomed in her cheeks, visible even beneath her scars. "I shouldn't have thought you would be overly concerned with that."

"You thought wrong. Now—" he reached in front of him and pulled a black velvet drape from over a tray that contained six rings, all a part of the Drakos family collection "—I have a selection of rings for you to choose from. There is, of course, the one that you had back when we were engaged the first time. It's sized to fit you, assuming that's stayed the same. But I know that women often change their tastes, so I wanted to give you options."

Layna swallowed hard and stared at the jewelry in front of her. She'd come down hoping for some coffee and fruit. Maybe eggs and bacon. She hadn't expected diamonds. It was, in her opinion, a little early in the morning for diamonds.

She couldn't tear her eyes from the pear-shaped diamond, surrounded by citrines, glittering in the midmorning light that was filtering through the window.

It had been hers. She could still remember King Stephanos asking for it. He'd called her in with her father, deeply regretful to have to ask for it back. But it had also belonged to his wife, and since Xander was now gone and the wedding wouldn't be taking place, he simply couldn't bear to have it out of the palace.

Leaving, her hand had felt bare and her heart…

How could he leave her? How could he leave all of them? And why had she never kissed his lips?

Looking at the ring made her remember all of that. She hated those memories. They made her feel too much. They interrupted her contentment. But then, her contentment had been interrupted for a while now. Also Xander's fault.

She reached out, her fingers hovering over that ring. It was the one she wanted. She'd been allowed to choose back then, too, and it had been her favorite. But this wasn't the same moment. She wasn't the same girl. He was not the same man.

"I don't care," she said, putting her hand back at her side. "You can choose it for me."

He arched a brow and picked up a ring with a square cut solitaire and an ornate white gold band. "This one, then," he said. "If you don't care."

"I don't."

He stood from his place at the table and walked to where she sat, standing in front of her and taking her hand in his. Then, with her sitting and him looming above her, he slipped the ring onto her finger. "It fits fine, doesn't it?"

She pulled her hand back and curled her fingers into a fist. "Fine," she said, trying to swallow and failing, her throat too dry to manage it.

She looked down at her hand, at the completely different ring that was now on her finger. This was different. This wasn't just going back in time. Recapturing what might have been. He might have the same name, but he was a different man. Just as she was a different woman.

Time had changed them. Time had changed their circumstances. She was no longer half in love with him, that was for sure.

Neither would she be falling in love with him any time soon.

"I do need to go and see my father sometime soon."

She nodded slowly. "I imagine you do."

"And we shall have to plan a party. To celebrate my return, and to celebrate our engagement. And hope it isn't perceived as tacky since my father is ill."

"Maybe you can talk to Stavros about that?"

"Oh, yes, I could talk to Stavros, though it seems he would rather not talk to me."

"Eva, then?"

"I should talk to both of them."

She frowned. "I'm sure we can find a way to make sure it doesn't look tacky. If we try and portray it as a show of strength for the country. No matter how dark the night, the dawn is coming, and so on."

"See," he said, smiling, "this is why I need you."

Those words did something to her. Made her heart feel like it was unfolding, like it was expanding. Made her feel a little bit of pain, a little bit of pleasure. But it was stupid. It wasn't flattering. He only needed her because he was a gigantic PR nightmare. Such a gigantic PR nightmare that a scarred almost-nun looked good by comparison.

"Well, I'll do what I can to help. Though, it's not for you."

"I'm sure it's not."

"It's for my country."

"Do you owe this country anything?" he asked. "After

the way they treated you, do you really owe them anything?"

"One man with a cup of acid isn't Kyonos, Xander."

"And one man with a cup of acid shouldn't be your whole life, Layna," he said, his voice rough, his eyes suddenly serious.

"To what do I owe the sincerity?"

"I don't like seeing you hurt."

"Then why are you so often the one who hurts me?" she asked, her newly unfurled heart closing tightly again. Like a flower suddenly deprived of sunlight.

"It's a gift I have," he said, looking away from her, out the window. "It's what I seem to do. I hurt people who genuinely don't deserve it." He looked back at her. "I guess that's your warning. You can back out now if you want."

Something in his eyes sent a shock through her. It was a window into his pain. It hadn't been there fifteen years ago, but it was there now, as obvious as if he'd spoken about it out loud. In that brief moment she had the sense that she was standing on the edge of a chasm, looking down into an abyss that had no end.

It frightened her. And it made him impossible to turn away from.

"You couldn't possibly hurt me any more than I've already been hurt." Even as she said it, she had a feeling it was a lie. She hadn't kissed him yet, much less gone to bed with him. She hadn't heard about the wounds he carried deep inside of himself.

He knew it was a lie, too. She could tell by the way his lips curved up, could tell now, that the expression was false. That there was no real humor in it. No real warmth. "Well then, we had better make a formal announcement."

"I suppose we'd better."

"You will need a dress, for the engagement party. I

trust you won't mind if I use a professional shopper to select one for you?"

She blinked. "No."

"Then I shall have your measurements done and that will be taken care of as quickly as possible."

"What about your father?" she asked.

"I should go and visit him alone."

Except she had a feeling that he shouldn't. She wasn't sure why. And moreover, she wasn't sure why she should care. Why his pain should interest her or concern her in any way, and yet over the course of the past few seconds she found that it did.

"I'll go with you. It will help solidify your plans. When you announce your engagement… I think your father felt very bad about what happened to me," she said.

"He did?"

"He was consumed by his own grief."

"Yes," Xander said, "I know."

"But he came to see me once. I…I didn't want to talk to him so I pretended to be asleep, but I knew he came."

"Why didn't you want to talk to him?"

"I was just starting to realize, really realize, that nothing in my life was ever going to be the same. That my face wasn't going back to normal. That…that I had maybe twenty surgeries ahead of me."

"Twenty?" he asked.

"It ended up being twenty-one. Skin grafts and reconstruction. Some of the grafts didn't take and…anyway. I knew that I had all kinds of hell ahead and that everything I knew was behind me. I didn't…it was hard to face people. That way you looked at me at the convent, when you realized it was me…it was ten times worse than that every time someone saw me right after the attack happened. I looked like something from a bad zombie movie. And the press said that. More than once. I hardly looked real at all. And it made my mother cry. It made my father sick. I got tired of seeing the expressions so I would close my eyes when visitors would come. And then it was just easier to keep them that way."

"Then of course you can come," he said, his tone light, as though he was content to skip over the graveness of the subject matter. And that suited her just fine. Being with him had forced her to relive her past more than she was comfortable with. "I'm sure my father will be happy to see you."

"I'm sure he'll be overjoyed to see you."

That smile again. That fake smile. "I wouldn't bet on it. But it will be nice to have you there to take some of the focus off of me."

Xander kept finding reasons to put off visiting his father, although, Layna was hardly going to judge him for avoidance since she was a pro at it.

Not that she could blame him. She imagined he was hardly going to have the fatted calf slaughtered in his oldest son's honor when he learned of Xander's return.

The engagement had been announced. On that he hadn't procrastinated. And the date of the ball had been set.

In spite of the fact that he was being hammered by the press, he was soldiering forward.

Prince Stavros and his wife, Jessica, and Princess Eva and her husband, Mak, were set to attend. Which would make for an interesting evening, Layna was sure. She imagined that things wouldn't be easy between Xander and his brother.

She tried to breathe around the terror that started constricting her throat when she thought about exposing herself to all of those people. All of that scrutiny. And Xander had said a selection of dresses would be here soon.

As if cued by her thoughts, there was a knock at the door. But rather than the woman who had come in to take her measurements earlier in the day, she was greeted by Xander, who had a black garment bag in his hand.

"Where's Patrice?" she asked.

"Downstairs having a coffee. I told her this would be between me and my fiancée." He stepped into the room and closed the door behind him and her heart collided with her breastbone.

"It doesn't sound like she's busy. Perhaps you'd like to trade places with her."

"No," he said.

"You work too hard," she said, no conviction in her voice.

"Now, *agape mou*, you and I both know that's not true." He sat down on her bed, the grin on his face wicked, and she felt her entire body tighten like a spool of wire.

That endearment. He'd called her that during their first engagement, too. *My love*. He hadn't meant it then and she was sure he didn't mean it now.

"So what…I'm supposed to put on a fashion show for you?"

"If you wish."

"Some might call it a freak show."

He stood quickly, the motion fluid, shocking. "Let us get one thing straight here and now," he said. "I will not stand for the press speaking of you in any terms that are not flattering. I will not hear it from you, either."

"Why should you care?" she asked. "It's true enough. I'm more sideshow than beauty pageant and we both know that."

"I damn well do not," he growled, advancing on her. "Is that truly what you think?"

"Can you tell me I'm beautiful?"

The fire in his eyes cooled. "No," he said, his voice hushed now, an extinguished flame. "Can you tell me I'm good?"

"No." She ached now. His denial like salt on a wound, but then, what would it have mattered if he would have said yes? It wouldn't have. It would have been a lie all the same and they both would have known it.

"You are, though," he said. "Good, that is. And isn't that the better thing to be?"

"When a camera is pointed at me I think I would prefer the beauty."

"When trials come, it would be better to be you, trust me. Now—" he handed her the garment bag "—it is time for us to preview your dress."

She held the bag to her chest and walked into the bathroom. She wasn't beautiful, but she was good. Wasn't the sort of woman to drive a man to passion, but she was good. She turned that over in her mind as she put on the dress, too distracted, too numb to pay much attention to it.

The trouble was, with Xander, she didn't feel particularly good. He made her feel edgy. Angry. Hot and unpredictable. With him around she did things like accept marriage proposals and demand he sleep only with her.

Which meant he would be sleeping with her.

Her hands shook as she did up the zipper at the back of the dress. She'd sort of bet on dying a virgin. She wasn't thrilled with it, really, but she hadn't seen another way.

The idea of being with him… She wanted him. No point in denying it. She just wished she was certain he wanted her.

She opened the bathroom door and stepped out into the

bedroom. She caught sight of herself in the reflection of the mirror just behind the bed, behind Xander, and froze for a moment. The dress was…well, it was much more revealing than anything she'd worn in ages. And more sophisticated than the saucy dresses she'd chosen as a teenage girl.

It was black, with a neckline that plunged down to the middle of her chest. "I would need duct tape," she said, looking at her breasts, which were attempting to make an escape. The chiffon fabric skimmed her curves and fell to the floor in a ripple, flowing as she moved. It was nearly demure, understated. If not for that neckline.

She looked to Xander and realized that his focus was also on her breasts, not that she should be terribly surprised. Because he *was* a man. Still, she was surprised because he was a man who was looking at her. And she was even more surprised because far from being offended, it made her feel warm and a little bit excited.

"What do you think?" she asked.

"I like it," he said, his voice rough.

"It's…not anything like what I would normally wear."

"No, and that's a good thing. You aren't wearing one of those flowered monstrosities to our engagement party."

"But…people will look at me."

"Yes," he said, his voice rough. "I imagine they will."

"I don't want them to look at me," she said.

"But they will, *agape*. You're to be the princess, one day their queen. You were a woman they all cared about, a woman they adored, back when you were first engaged to be married to me. Their eyes will be on you no matter what you wear. Better that when they look they see a woman with confidence."

"But I don't think I have any," she said.

He moved to her. "You should."

"Why?"

"Because you are the woman most deserving of the crown. You should hold your head high if only for that reason."

He lifted his hand and reached behind her, taking hold of the pins in her hair and releasing the hair from its bun, letting it fall around her face in soft waves. He had touched her hair before, and it had been an oddly sensual experience. His touch, combined with the intense expression on his face, was taking things somewhere beyond sensual now.

He was making her knees kind of weak. Making it hard to breathe.

But he didn't even think she was beautiful.

"We should practice," he said.

"Practice what?"

"They'll expect us to dance."

"Will they?"

"Yes. See? All eyes on us, no matter what you wear. And we need to put up a good front. Because salacious details about my past keep ending up on the front page."

"What now?" she asked.

"'How Many Lovers for the Dishonorable Heir?'"

"Oh, my."

"Yes, indeed."

"And…how many?" she asked.

"Not answering. And I don't know."

"Oh."

"Yes, well. I'm not exactly proud of my behavior. But I am good at dancing."

"This is all so… Oh." He wrapped his arm around her waist and pulled her against his body. Then he took her hand in his, rough and hot, not an aristocrat's hands. But then, he hadn't been living an aristocrat's life.

"Do you know how to dance still, or is that forbidden

for a novice?" he asked, leading her into the first step of a slow dance to no music.

"I'm out of practice," she said, trying hard not to lose her breath. He was so warm and hard, and she was pressed up against him.

And in that moment she realized just how very much she wanted him. A deep, burning ache that spread from her core and ignited in the rest of her body. Such a strange thing. Lust was one of the little luxuries that had to be put away for the kind of life she'd been trying to lead, but she was all but bathing in it now.

She was so aware of his hand on her waist, his fingers entwined with hers. With each breath he took and how it made his chest rise to meet her breasts, how it made her nipples feel tight. Made her feel desperate for more. More of his touch. More of him.

"So am I," he said.

"You don't seem like it."

"Well, there isn't much in the way of formal ballroom dancing in the casinos I frequent."

"Is that all you've done since you left?"

"Basically. I live in the casinos, literally. I don't own a home. There's never been any point."

"You make money gambling?"

He lifted a shoulder and kept dancing. "I have a gift."

"You're a card counter, aren't you?"

"Not on purpose. But if I happen to be a bit more observant than the average person, is it my fault?"

"You really are a bad man."

He chuckled, slow and deep, the sound rumbling through him, and her, sending shock waves of sensation through her body. "And I don't even work at it. It just comes naturally. How about you?" he asked.

"How about me what?"

"Do you have to work at being good?"

She blinked. "Um…I don't know really. In some ways, no. But then, what I do…I don't do it because it's good. I do it because I don't have anything else to do. Because… maybe because it's easy to be good if you don't want much of anything. I could never have gone to hide out at a casino, for example, because I had no desire to be around anyone. I couldn't go sleep my way through Europe like you because I didn't want anyone to see me, much less sleep with me. And I could hardly go get drunk because you aren't supposed to mix alcohol and pain pills," she said, dryly. "All things considered, I don't know that I get any brownie points for good behavior."

"You haven't seemed particularly saintly since I've seen you, I'll tell you that in all honesty." His fingers moved down on her waist, just an inch or so, but enough to edge into somewhat erotic territory. At least, erotic for a woman who hadn't had a kiss in…ever, and was due. Past due.

"Maybe it's because I…I feel like I'm waking up." It was the strangest thing, but as she spoke the words she knew that was the best way to describe it. It was like she'd been sleeping. All those years after the attack, and then at the convent, it had been like hovering between reality and a dream. There was a cushion there, between her and life, and she had needed it.

Now, though, her eyes were wide open, and everything was clear. Frightening. And amazing.

"I thought women needed to be kissed awake," he said, lowering his head, his mouth a whisper away from hers.

"Sleeping Beauty maybe," she said. "But we both know that I'm not—"

He silenced her with the firm pressure of his lips on hers. She was almost too shocked to register the feeling of the kiss. She felt it deeper than she'd imagined she would.

Felt it in the pit of her stomach just as strongly as she felt it against her lips.

It was brief, and it was very nearly chaste, but it tilted her world on its axis completely. And he had no idea, she was sure of that. Because for him, it was just another kiss. But for her it was the first.

"How was that?" he asked.

"I…" She pulled away from him. "I don't think that had anything to do with dancing."

"It had to do with us, as a couple, making our debut at the engagement party, where we'll be dancing. It was a natural extension."

Yes, a natural extension for him, but not for her.

"Well, there's no need for any of that until after… until…"

"You aren't part of a convent anymore," he said, "you're a woman."

"I've been a woman the entire time, thank you. It didn't change when I went to the convent, it didn't change when I left. It didn't change just because you decided to kiss me. Our marriage is based on necessity, not on passion, so let's not pretend."

"Who said I was pretending?"

"Right, Xander, I'm sure you were overwhelmed by lust when you told me that I wasn't beautiful only twenty minutes ago."

"There is something else," he said, his voice tight, strange. "Something…"

She shook her head. "Just don't lie to me."

"This," he said, looking down, "it doesn't lie. I would put your hand on me but I think that would be a step too far."

"Put my hand on…" Her stomach tightened painfully

and she looked down, her eyes following the line his gaze had. "Oh."

"I thought it might be off-limits."

"Yes," she said, her throat dry. "It is. Definitely in the post-marriage vow zone. Anything below the belt."

"You look much more intrigued than you do offended."

"Do I? That's just the shock talking. Well, not talking, forming my facial expressions for me. I'm terribly shocked."

"I look forward to shocking you a bit more after our marriage vows then."

"Don't make it a joke, please," she said, suddenly feeling like she needed to lie down. Or dissolve into a gigantic puddle of wimpy girl tears. "I know you're experienced and cavalier and having pity sex with an ugly girl is just a witty anecdote waiting to happen for you. But this isn't funny to me. It's my life. And I'm the one who stands to be hurt the most by this. I'm the one…"

"You're the one who called yourself my punishment, Layna. I have said nothing cruel to you on that score. I don't look at you and think that you're ugly—neither do I feel like I'm doing you any great favors by marrying you and sharing your bed. In truth, you may find that you are more unhappy with the demanded fidelity than I am."

"Why is that?"

"Because it will ensure that I'm around more, and you may tire of me quickly. You have this idea that I'm somehow more desirable stock because I'm not scarred. Let me assure you that while I may be physically undamaged, you are not by any stretch getting the better end of this deal. I am selfish, I have spent the majority of the past few years battling demons and addictions, and doing neither very well at all. You may think that what I'm giving you is pity sex, but don't for one moment think that I don't realize what I have on my hands is a pity marriage."

She blinked back tears, his words settling over her like a heavy cloak, making it hard to breathe. "I don't pity you. I don't approve of you. I'm not sure that I like you, but I don't pity you. This is…a marriage of no one's convenience. What we do, we do for our country. And…I do it for children. Because I do want them. And I had thought that wasn't possible for me, so to have the chance…I do want it. Power is something I don't crave anymore, status is almost my enemy because it means I'll be under scrutiny."

"A marriage born of a sense of national duty and disdain then," he said, dryly. "You flatter me."

"I would imagine you've been flattered enough in your life that you don't require much from me."

"I'm sure my ego can weather it."

"I'm not sure mine will survive any of this."

"It will," he said, his tone certain, authoritative. And in that moment, she saw a hint of the king he would be. So strange, because she knew the boy he'd been. Cocky and obnoxious in so many ways, but handsome as sin and just as tempting. She'd barely gotten to know the man he was now, wounded, damaged and self-deprecating. As much as the boy had loved himself, she had a feeling the man hated himself just as much.

But for one second, all of that fell away. And she saw nothing more than confidence. Nothing more than a smooth, unswerving focus.

"This is why I'm marrying you," she said, her voice hushed now. "Because I believe that, no matter where you've been in the past, your future is tied to Kyonos. That with you we will rise or fall, and if we fall it will be because the people can't get past what has been done. You leaving…"

"Me killing the queen," he said.

"You didn't kill her," she said. "You were driving, but it was an accident. It was…"

"People think it, Layna. Just as the man who threw acid on you, trying to get to your father blamed him for his troubles."

"Then this is why," she said, suddenly feeling the need to close the gap between them. To make contact. "This is why I'm marrying you. Because if I can help in any way, if I can heal some of the wounds from that time, I will do it. Because you are the future here, Xander."

He frowned and lifted his other hand, touched her damaged cheek with his thumb. "It is a shame that time won't heal your wounds."

"It is."

"Sometimes I think it won't heal mine, either." He released his hold on her and turned and walked out of her room, leaving her standing there in an evening gown, in the middle of the day, more confused than she'd ever been in her life.

CHAPTER EIGHT

HELL. XANDER HAD forgotten how much he hated these kinds of events.

The engagement celebration was small compared to some of the parties thrown at the Kyonosian palace, due to the short notice and out of respect for the king's health.

Xander's recently noisy conscience pricked him. He should go and see the king. It was a hard thing to do. The last time he'd stood before the old man, his father said in no uncertain terms that he blamed Xander for the queen's death.

And because he hadn't been wrong, Xander had finally done what Stavros, and the man who believed he was Xander's father, had wanted. He left.

Because it had been easier for everyone. And it had been easy, most especially, for him.

He wasn't truly the heir after all.

You can't tell him, Xander. You have to be king. You are my firstborn son and the right should be yours, regardless of the mistakes I've made.

Xander shut out the sound of his mother's pleading voice. He hated reliving that conversation. Mainly because it was the last one they'd ever had. It had changed everything.

He straightened and looked across the room at Layna. She looked…well, she did look beautiful in her way.

She was wearing makeup. He'd brought in a team to help her get ready. He wondered if she'd ever bothered to put makeup on her face, or if it had been too discouraging. There was no hiding the fact that the skin was damaged on one side. It looked…aged with makeup on, rather than just scarred.

But her eyes were highlighted to perfection, and they glowed with golden warmth, her lips painted a deep rose. And that dress. That dress that made his body tighten. That made him want…

He wanted her, and that was the most surprising thing about this arrangement. He hadn't expected to want her. He'd had an endless array of models, mainstream actresses and actresses who did the kinds of movies that rarely had scenes outside the bedroom. Women who were perfectly beautiful, either by birth or with the aid of a surgeon's knife.

He'd hardly thought Layna would present a temptation to him, all things considered.

And yet…when he'd kissed her the other day, she had been a surprise. A burst of flavor on his lips unlike any he'd ever tasted before. And newness, to a man as jaded as himself, was so unexpected it was an aphrodisiac that was almost unmatched.

"Congratulations are in order, I suppose."

Xander turned to face Stavros, and Eva, who was standing next to him, a glowing smile on her face, her hand over her rounded belly. He wanted to embrace them both. But he didn't know if he could. And that was a strange thing.

Who didn't feel they could hug their siblings if they wanted to? Who didn't speak to their siblings for fifteen years?

Eva had gone from a child to a woman in that time. Having a child of her own. Stavros was a man as well, not the teenage boy he'd been.

Theos. He felt old.

And more than a little bit tired.

"For both of you as well," he said, keeping back, his hands clasped behind him.

"I'm surprised she agreed to marry you," Stavros said, his eyes flashing over to Layna, who seemed to be shrinking into the corner under the watchful eyes of their many guests.

"Are you?" he asked. "We had an agreement before I left."

"And things have changed."

"I've noticed," he said.

Eva smiled, shy but with a glimmer of that old sparkle in her eyes. "Xander, I'm glad you're back. I don't want things to be weird between us. So let's skip all of the regret and angry stuff. I'll leave that to you and Stavros, since I doubt he'll let it go as fast as I will. I, for one, have missed you for too long, and I won't waste a second of you being back here with anger."

"I appreciate that, Eva," he said, feeling strangely tight around the chest. "I plan on staying."

Stavros frowned. "I would love to never speak to you again. But you're going to be the king. And my wife tells me that I should be nice because not only are you the future king, you are the uncle to our children, and it would be wrong of me to deprive you or them of that relationship."

"She threatened you, didn't she?" Eva asked, smiling.

"I don't want to sleep on the couch for the rest of my life," Stavros said, his tone dry. "But someday…we'll have to talk more. And someday, perhaps I will not be so angry. But not today."

Xander nodded. "Yes." But he knew they wouldn't talk about everything. Never about everything.

He made the rounds with Stavros and Eva, meeting Stavros's wife, Jessica, and their two children, and Eva's husband, Mak.

He looked back at Layna, who was slinking into the wall now, fading. "Excuse me," he said, "I have to go and ask a woman to dance."

He didn't want to see her do this. Didn't want to watch her try and disappear, and he wasn't even certain why. Why it should matter.

It shouldn't. She would get him the positive press he needed, she was a worthy choice to produce heirs. Nothing beyond that should matter.

But it did.

"Are you trying to turn into another coat of paint?" he asked, when he was near to her.

"What?"

"You look like you're trying to become part of the wall," he said.

"You left me alone and I feel…I feel self-conscious."

"You look…"

She shook her head. "Don't."

"But you do."

"Compared to the way I usually look."

"So I'm not allowed to win?"

She blinked, dark lashes fanning over high cheekbones. "Thank you."

"Of course. Now, you will come and dance with me and stop acting like you wish you could melt into the floor."

She looked stricken. "We're really going to dance?"

"That's why we practiced, darling." He extended his hand and she looked at him like he was offering her forbidden fruit. He felt like he was. Like he was on the verge of bringing her into something he had no right to drag her in to.

But it was too late. She was here. In front of hundreds of people, his ring glittering on her finger, tomorrow's headlines being created right now, in the moment.

He didn't deserve to use her like this. To have her as a buffer between himself and the unflattering headlines about his past behavior. But he didn't see another choice.

Delicate fingers wrapped around his and she allowed him to lead her to the dance floor. He pulled her to him, much more gently than he'd done in her room.

"Relax," he said, his lips near her ear.

He breathed in deep, and her scent teased him. It wasn't false, or floral. It was the wind. The sea. The grass. Skin. It was Kyonos. It made his stomach tighten, opened up a well of longing, a strange sense of need and homesickness that washed over him like a wave.

This desire for her came from somewhere deep. It didn't come from looking at her, or even from touching her, it was her very presence. It seemed to be some part of her, some part deep inside, connecting with something in him.

Perhaps it was shared pain meeting a shared goal. Or maybe it was nothing more complex than a bout of celibacy that had gone on for too many months. Either way, it was beginning to feel too strong to fight. He was wondering if there was a reason to bother, anyway.

She was going to be his wife after all.

Not that she had any idea of what that truly meant. Of who he truly was.

"Everyone is staring, aren't they?" she asked.

"Have you ever worn makeup? Since your attack?"

She frowned. "Once. I tried it once. Not very long after my last surgery. It didn't really help I... But I thought tonight I should wear some because I needed to dress up and…"

"You look lovely. And I do mean that."

"They did a better job covering the damage than I ever managed to do."

"That isn't the only reason."

"Let's not do this mushy, stumbling lying thing now, Xander. You were perfectly honest with me the other day about my looks. So don't go trying to smooth it all over just because I tried."

"You are a stubborn woman," he said. "And I want you."

"I don't understand."

"You don't understand want? Desire? Do you know what it means to want someone?"

"I…yes. But I don't need you to lie to me about it."

"I'm not." he said, tightening his hold on her, bringing her curves flush against his body. And he let her feel what she was doing to him. He let his cock harden against her and he didn't bother to suppress his need, his fantasies. He imagined what it would be like to have her bare softness against him, without this damned tux in the way.

What it would be like to make her let go. To make her break out of the little cell she'd locked herself in. The one that meant there was no passion. No desire. Only boring, staid contentment.

He wanted to make her lose herself while he lost himself in her. Because for some reason he felt sure that she was the only one who could make him feel again. The only one who might make a change in him that could last.

The feeling that came with that thought was fleeting, but so intense it nearly buckled his knees. So intense he nearly dragged her from the dance floor and into the nearest dark alcove to make her his without any thought to vows.

But then it cleared. The fire dying down as suddenly as it had flared up.

No, there was no changing him. Not even she could do it. There was no magic to be found on her lips. But there was pleasure. And he was a man who'd spent years consumed by the desire for pleasure.

That was the simple answer to why he felt so drawn to her. It wasn't in his nature to deny himself anything he wanted.

"I'm sorry, I wasn't able to hold myself back this time. You accused me of lying about wanting you and I thought you should know this time, for yourself, that it's true."

She pushed out of his arms and walked away from him, leaving him there in the middle of the dance floor, shocked and hard as hell.

He followed her, through the crowd of people and out onto the balcony. Her shoulders were shaking and guilt stabbed him, low in the gut.

He'd had a lot of bad feelings since returning home. Guilt and regret. He preferred it when his life boiled down to being drunk and horny, but right now he had felt sober, horny and guilty. Which was a combination he wouldn't wish on anyone.

"What did I do? Did I offend you with my erection? Because you're going to have to get used to it if you honestly want to marry me."

She whirled around to face him. "Oh, please. Stop making this about you when it's clearly about me."

"I think we both think it's all only about us."

"Fine," she said, tears on her cheeks, "but…this is…why do you want me? Why…I don't understand this. Any of it."

"Is that really what upset you?"

"It's just a lot. A lot to take. Everything has changed in the past week. Everything I'm supposed to want."

"Do you want me?"

"Xander…"

He walked over to where she was standing and took her chin between his thumb and forefinger. "Do you want me?"

"That's not what this is about."

"But it's part of marriage."

"So is love. We barely have like."

"I'm not big on love," he said. "Personally, I would rather have want. So if that's all we have, I'm okay with it."

She shook her head. "I can't deal with this just now. Not when everyone is in there and we're on show. I've probably already ruined things by storming out."

"It's okay. I might have been a little bit inappropriate. But I'm out of practice when it comes to civilized behavior."

"You make me…you do make me want things, Xander. Things that I thought I'd let go of. And it scares me. Because in my experience, wanting things is just a long road paved with pain."

"That's emotion you're thinking of. Sex can be a lot more simple. And a lot more fun."

She laughed, a shaky, watery sound. "Well, I wouldn't know."

His gut tightened, blood rushing to his arousal. "I could show you."

"I don't understand this. I don't remember being this tempted by you back when I thought you were a decent human being, so how can I be so drawn to you now?"

"Lust doesn't have to make sense, Layna."

"I guess not," she said, looking at him with a weary expression. "Perhaps that's why the church has such a firm stance on it. It could potentially get someone into a lot of trouble. Particularly since our bodies seem to be indiscriminate."

"Is your body being indiscriminate for me?" he asked. So strange how badly he just wanted her to say it. How much he wanted to her to admit, from her prim little mouth, that she wanted him. That she was picturing sweaty, tangled limbs and screams of pleasure.

Yes, screams. He wanted it loud. And he wanted it dirty. He wanted it with a ferocity that shook him to his core.

With a woman who's most likely a virgin. You truly are a rare breed of ass.

Maybe. Did it matter? He was so past the point of redemption anyway. And she was going to be his wife, surely that made it at least partly okay.

And if not, why should he start caring now?

It was too late for him anyway.

"We should go back inside," she said.

"You didn't answer my question."

"And I'm not going to. Here I've stormed out of the ballroom and I'm supposed to be making you look stable. So I think it's time to go back and show solidarity, don't you?"

He nodded slowly. She really was good at this. He'd all but forgotten the ball happening inside. If she'd let him he probably would have just lifted her dress and taken her here on the balcony with the ocean as the backdrop. And people just inside.

He did a much better job of thinking of his own appetites than he did of thinking of his people.

"Can I do it?" he asked, not sure why the words came out just then.

"Can you do what?"

"This," he said. Too late to take them back now.

"Will I really be a good king? For some reason, you seem very confident in me when it comes to that part of things. You have no respect for me on a personal level, but you seem very sure that I'll rule well, why?"

"Because you don't want it," she said. "Because there's nothing easy about it, and the power itself doesn't seem to appeal to you at all. What better man to rule?"

"Because I *don't* want it?"

"Yes. From that I have to assume that your motives are pure."

"My motives are a lot of things. But I doubt they're pure. I doubt anything in me is."

"Are you ready to go back?" she asked.

He was humbled in that moment, by her strength. By the cost of this to her. It was costing him, but what really? His total waste of a life? His meaningless flings with random women? His chance to continue living in different penthouse suites?

It was costing her every shred of pride she had.

He would not let them take it. She was too strong. Standing there with her focus fixed on the ballroom, determined to go back in even though he knew it was difficult for her.

"Yes, *agape*, let's go and show them what the future of their country looks like."

CHAPTER NINE

SHE HONESTLY HAD no idea what her problem was. Why she'd melted down with Xander, why she'd had to run out of the ballroom.

Well, no, she did know why. It was because she had no idea what she was doing. She didn't know how to handle men. Didn't know how to deal with this desire that was starting to wrap itself around her like a creeping vine.

This wasn't supposed to happen.

She was supposed to be…at the very least she was supposed to feel nothing for him. And at most, she'd been willing to allow herself to be angry.

And she was angry. She was angry at him for leaving her. She was angry at life for making her the way that she was.

But in there somewhere, she wanted him, too, and that was the thing she couldn't quite deal with.

She breathed in the sea air. It was such a relief to be outside. To be on the beach instead of in that ballroom, which, as expansive as it was, had made her feel claustrophobic beyond words.

She'd escaped as soon as she could. Most everyone had gone and she'd made her excuses, as soon as was polite. She was dreading tomorrow's headlines. Dreading the future. So funny, because she hadn't thought of the future at all in a long time.

All of her days had been so alike at the convent. Her future had been so certain. So solid. She'd seen her days stretching out before, a calm and endless sea.

But now she was storm-tossed and she had no idea where she would land.

She sat down, not caring that the ground was wet, not caring that there would be sand on her gorgeous black dress. She would hardly be able to wear it again anyway. That was something she remembered from her socialite days. Never wear the same thousand-euro dress twice. Such a sharp contrast to her other life, where she wore the same threadbare shifts until they couldn't be mended anymore.

She felt like she wasn't wholly the girl she'd been before, or the woman she'd become, but damned if she had any idea who she really was. And she blamed Xander for that feeling.

She'd been fine before he'd walked back into her life. She'd been at peace with her choices. And now he was demanding so much from her. So much more than she ever thought she'd have to give to anyone.

"I thought perhaps I had seen a ghost." She looked up and saw Xander standing there, his shirt open at the collar, his tie and jacket discarded.

"That's how I felt the day I saw you at the convent."

"I'm sure."

"What are you doing down here?"

"I might ask you the same thing."

"I am…brooding. I think that's what this is called."

He sat down next to her. "I'll brood with you."

"Brooding is best done alone."

"Doesn't that get tiring, though?"

"What?" she asked.

"Being alone."

She looked out across the water, at the moon reflecting on the waves. "You're never alone, though, are you? I mean, you've never had to be. You've basically been at a giant party for the past few years."

"I've been surrounded by people, yeah. But it's amazing what a hell that can be."

"I doubt you've spent one night alone when you didn't want to be alone," she said, feeling bitter now. Because all she'd had was an endless void of alone. In that huge house without her family, with only a couple of servants to help her with things. Making sure she ate, making sure she didn't overdose on her pain medication.

Locking up her pain medication. And then, when they'd taken her one bit of solace, they'd felt like her enemies, not her allies. Even though she knew differently now.

Xander truly had no idea how isolating her life had been. How low she'd gone. How dark it had been. Because he'd walked away. Because he hadn't stayed. When things had gotten hard in his life he'd left her there, but there had been no way for her to unzip her damaged skin and crawl out of her own body. There had been no way to escape her pain.

"I'm sure getting smashed in a casino was terrible for you, but while you were doing that, I was by myself in my parents' old home in a prescription drug haze, so excuse me if I don't feel that sorry for your plight."

"Layna…"

"No." She stood up. "I wasn't going to tell you this, and for what? My pride? What pride have I got? No, you should know. You should know because you should have been there, Xander. You should have been there with me. I…" A sob broke through, tears spilling down her cheeks. "I needed you…" The words were torn from her, pulling at any thread of dignity she might have had, but they were the truth. A truth she'd never even allowed herself to think before, let alone voice.

She wiped a tear from her cheek. "Do you have any idea… Sometimes I just wanted to be held and there was no one there. And it should have been you. You were supposed to be my husband, you weren't supposed to leave me."

"I won't leave again," he said, his voice rough. "Though…I don't know that I would have done everything for you that you hoped I might."

"Anything would have been better than being alone. My days just kind of blended and…I got addicted to my pain medication. It was so much nicer to be out of it than it was to feel. And the medicine helped with that. Helped things seem nicer. Without them it was just endless despair and… and I would think things like…if I walked out to the beach and went out into the ocean and just…kept walking until the water went over my head, would anyone care? Would I care? Or would everything just stop hurting?"

He swore. "Layna, I'm sorry."

"Why couldn't you help me? Why couldn't you think of anyone but yourself?"

"Because," he said. "Because I killed my mother, Layna. Because my father looked me in the eye and told me he believed it was my fault, and my brother thought so, too. Because I couldn't stay here and face that. And I might never have thought of walking into the ocean but everything I've done has been about seeing that I shorten my days in a very spectacular fashion."

Her chest felt tight. And for the first time she really thought about him, and his loss. Not just her own need. "Did they really blame you?"

"Yes."

"That's not fair, it was an accident."

He nodded slowly. "But we were arguing. And no one

knows that but me. I was angry, and so I wasn't paying attention. I looked up and there was a truck cutting across the line and I swerved and hit the side of the mountain because I panicked and overcorrected. They were my mistakes, and they were brought about largely by my anger. Because I didn't take the time to pull the car over. Because I let emotion take over and I behaved… I was stupid. And it was my fault." He looked at her. "Maybe I should have stayed for you. But I don't think I could have been the man you needed. I know I wasn't the man that you thought I was."

"I've never told anyone before," she said. "I've never told anyone about wanting to…about having trouble living. I don't even like to remember it but…do you know what's nice?"

"What?"

"Even when I told you, even when I let myself think about it, I can remember how bad it was, but it doesn't make me feel the way I did then."

"The convent is what changed things for you?"

"It gave me a purpose. I didn't know what to do with myself. I didn't have you. The marriage wasn't going to happen, I wasn't going to be queen. No other man would marry me. My friends, who I took such delight in cutting down behind their backs, wouldn't see me. No one invited me to parties, and I wouldn't have wanted to go if they had. Everything changed for me and all of that combined with my depression just made me…I was just drifting. But after talking to the Sisters after my last surgery, about the work they did, about the life they led, I thought maybe the answer wasn't trying to go back, or even making myself want to go back, but to find something new."

"That's sort of what I did. Only without the altruism or chastity."

"How so?"

"I changed everything. Because things were too different to be who I'd been before."

"That's sort of how I feel right now," she said, turning to face him. "Too different to be the girl I was fifteen years ago, and not quite the woman I was a week ago when you found me again."

"I am sorry," he said. "I'm sorry I've uprooted your life again. And that you were alone. It's funny," he continued, "you're right, I never spent a night alone unless I wanted to. But it's a strange thing about sex. For a moment, there's this clash of heat. A connection of some kind. Ten minutes of euphoria, and then, in the end, you can be skin-to-skin with someone, inside of them, and feel more alone than you ever have in your life." He stood up, hands in his pockets. "There's nothing more terrifying than that. Because it's moments like those where you realize how far beyond human connection you are."

"Is that how you feel?" she asked, the picture he pained cutting a swath of pain through her heart.

"It's just not in me anymore. To love someone. To feel all that deeply. I care about the country, but what I do…it comes from my head."

"Is that a warning?"

He nodded slowly. "Maybe. I don't want to hurt you, it's clear to me that I've done that enough for one lifetime. But we will make a marriage, a real one. We don't need love for that. And…I will be faithful to you."

"You said that already."

"I did say it, but I'm not sure I meant it. I do now. Because I gave it some thought, and what it comes down to is that I know the kind of pain infidelity causes. Even if one party never finds out, there are always consequences."

"What else is there, Xander?" she asked. Because she

could sense, somehow, that there was more he wanted to say. That his pain came from somewhere even deeper.

"There isn't anything."

"Really?"

He shook his head. "It's not important." He cleared his throat. "Tomorrow we're going to go and see my father."

"Both of us," she said, confirming it.

"Yes."

"I was going anyway. For my part, Xander, you're not going to be alone anymore. And neither am I."

CHAPTER TEN

HE COULDN'T HIDE the headlines from her forever. But he would do his best. He had expected…something triumphant. Something about Layna's bravery. About her beauty, at least her inner beauty, to grace the pages of the newspapers. But he was disappointed.

There were before and after photos. Layna, young, radiant and golden, and Layna as she was now. With the scars that had changed the landscape of her face.

And they asked would she now be the face of the nation. And suddenly…suddenly they were acting like he was a saint. Honoring past commitments in spite of present circumstances.

Isn't that what you wanted?

His blood boiled. Rage spiking through him. At the media. At himself. He had used her. He had exposed her to this.

And he would protect her from it as long as he could. Because he needed her. Of that he was certain. He had no idea how he would rule without her.

He couldn't dwell on it now. Today he was seeing his father. Today, he was facing the hardest part of his past.

At least Layna would be beside him.

His father was an old man. That was his first thought when he walked into the hospital room and saw the man he'd always thought of as so imposing, hooked up to all the machinery.

He was asleep. Or maybe he was unconscious. Xander wasn't sure. He wasn't certain he could get close enough to find out.

Delicate fingers wrapped around his hand and he looked down at the top of Layna's head. Shocked that she was there. Shocked that she was touching him.

"I told you," she said. "You aren't alone."

"You don't owe me anything, Layna."

"I know. This isn't about owing you. This is about getting you through."

"I didn't help you get through."

"And I didn't help you. But that was then. And we're both here now."

He wanted to tell her he didn't need any help getting through, but the words stuck in his throat. "What do we do exactly? He isn't awake."

"Talk to him."

"I would feel stupid."

"King Stephanos."

She approached the bed, small and regal. Yes, it was she who belonged in this position while he…he was not sure he had a place in life much less in Kyonos.

"It's Layna Xenakos. And I'm here with Xander. He's home. He's here for you. For Kyonos."

She turned back to face him and the sun caught in her hair, catching the deep golds that were woven in with the browns. She was practically glowing, and he had a feeling he couldn't even blame the sun. She seemed to glow from the inside. "I don't feel silly."

"No," he said. "I can see that. But it's been longer since I talked to him so…"

"Yeah, like a week longer." She reached out and grabbed

his arm, squeezed it. "I understand, though. I know you left on poor terms."

"Understatement there."

He looked at his father and tried to find one part of himself there. Because part of him had always hoped his mother had been wrong. But he could see nothing of himself in the old man. Eva's stubborn chin, so many of Stavros's features. But nothing of himself.

The king wasn't his father.

He'd never for a moment believed his mother would lie about his parentage, but he had hoped off and on that she might be mistaken. Denial was a beautiful state. The one he chose to live in.

Suddenly, the room seemed too small. The beeping machines all too loud and antiseptic burned his nose. "Let's go," he said, undoing the top button on his shirt. Damn. He couldn't breathe. "I have to go."

He pushed through the curtain and out into the halls, gasping for air. It was a luxurious environment for a medical center. The sort of place you sent kings, of course. But no matter how comfortable, it couldn't ease him now.

He walked down the hall with long strides, pushed open the doors and went out to the parking lot, leaning forward with his hands on his knees.

"What happened, Xander? I know he looks sick…he's your father and…"

"No…Layna…" He couldn't say it. He could barely think it. He could barely think at all. So instead he did what felt right. And it felt right to take her arm and pull her up against him.

He stroked her cheek—the undamaged side—and he really couldn't see the point in holding back on what he wanted. Not now. Not when everything felt terrible and he just wanted to lose himself again.

Before he'd run. From Kyonos. From himself.

He couldn't do that now.

And there was only one other way he could think of to lose himself completely.

He leaned down and took her mouth. And he wasn't gentle. Because this wasn't for her. Madonna or whore, it didn't matter to him, all that mattered was the feel of her lips on his and what it did for him.

And oh, *Theos*, what it did.

It set him on fire. The flames so hot he could feel nothing else. Nothing but his desire. Nothing but this. He coaxed her lips open, sliding his tongue against hers as he delved in deep.

Yes. This was what he needed. He could drown in this. In her sweetness. She didn't know how to kiss him back, her rhythm a step behind his, her fingers curled into the front of his shirt like little claws.

And it was the most wholly erotic kiss he'd ever experienced in his life.

"Where is the car?" he asked, feeling beyond himself. Unable to think straight.

"Over...over there," she said.

He took her hand and led her over to the limo, which was parked near the front doors. He must have passed it on his way out of the building. He honestly couldn't remember it, though.

He jerked open the back door and got in, pulling her in with him, reaching across and closing the door behind him, with her half on his chest, her leg draped over his lap.

She had no makeup on today. Her dark hair was loose around her face, and she was back in one of those unflattering dresses. He needed to take her shopping. But he had no time to concern himself with that. Not now. Not when her touch, her lips, were so perfect.

He made sure the divider between them and their driver was up, and then he pulled her to him, kissing her deeper, harder than he'd done outside. He poured everything into the kiss. All of his anger. All of his desire. Everything.

He breathed her in, and he found he wasn't suffocating anymore.

He could forget himself like this. Because a woman like her would never kiss a man like him and that meant that it was easy to pretend he was different. A different man, in a different time and place.

But he knew it was Layna. He knew it when he cupped her cheek and brushed a thumb over her rough scars. When he lightened the pressure on her lips and felt the hardened tissue by one corner of her mouth with his tongue.

Layna, who the media called ugly. Layna, who he wanted more than anything. To possess, to protect. He wanted all of it. Everything.

He put his hands on her hips, bunched the thin fabric of her dress into his fists and pushed it upward. Her body was a treasure. Full, round hips, a slim waist and those breasts…the ones that had haunted his dreams since he'd seen them in that gown of hers.

He needed to see her again. All of her. Now.

He pushed her dress up farther and she pulled back, breathing heavily, her eyes wide. "What are you doing?"

"If you have to ask, clearly I've done something wrong." He was so hard it hurt. And his lungs felt tight now. Being deprived of her lips was like being deprived of oxygen. He needed her. He couldn't explain it, but he did.

But he would never let her know.

She shifted and moved away from him, tucking her hair behind her ear. "I mean, I know you were…that you were…"

"That I was about to make love to you?"

"Well, that. But we're in a parking lot. Our driver is just behind that divider and I seriously doubt these windows are that tinted."

He frowned and looked outside. "There's no one around."

Layna felt like she'd been underwater for too long. Her lungs were burning, her head was fuzzy and her body ached. Though it ached in very pointed and telling places. How was she supposed to think when he was kissing her like that?

He'd essentially devoured her. In a parking lot. She'd never been devoured by a man in her life, much less had it happen while she was in a parking lot.

It was scary, how he managed to steal her control, her common sense. How he made her lose sight of everything. That they were in public, that she was inexperienced. That she'd been about two minutes away from losing her virginity in the back of a limo.

Yes, he made her lose sight of a lot of things.

But when he'd run out of the medical building, his pain had been palpable. Coming off him in waves, a deep hurt that she knew he wouldn't share. One she knew he'd had to exhaust by kissing her. For some reason.

"It doesn't matter that there's no one around. People don't just...do that."

"I do," he said. His posture readjusted. To this sort of slouched position in the seat, a half smile on his face. Gone was the desperate man of a moment before, replaced by the Xander character that he was so very fond of playing.

"Well, I don't. So that's something you'll have to deal with being married to me."

"You're a prude?" he asked.

"Practically a nun," she answered.

"*Touché.*" He straightened and pushed the intercom

button that fed into the front half of the limo. "Back to the palace, please."

"Are you going to tell me what happened back there?"

"It's not important."

"You can just tell me that you aren't going to tell me. It's more honest than saying it's not important. Don't say things that affect you that deeply aren't important."

"Well, it's unimportant in terms of you and I."

"I see."

"You can't act like a miffed fiancée, Layna, not when you don't act like a fiancée when I need you to."

She frowned and looked at him, ignoring the kick in her heartbeat. "What do you mean by that?"

"If you were my real fiancée, and by that I mean, if you were with me for some reason that extended beyond the desire to heal the country and protect them from my wickedness," he said, his tone dry, "then you would have lifted your dress for me and given me the thing I really needed."

"What is that supposed to mean?" she asked, her voice tight.

"That it wasn't talking I needed, baby. It was f—"

"Stop it," she said. "Stop turning into a horrible…beast every time you encounter territory that wounds you. Whatever happened between you and your father isn't my fault. In fact, I've suffered enough due to all of those events, thank you."

"Why don't you take a little pleasure out of it?"

"Can we stop? Can we stop with this shallow, ridiculous nonsense. You aren't telling me what's really going on. And I'm not going to let you…not here."

"Still sticking with your wedding night plan?" he asked.

"Yes." Although it was more for self-protection now than anything else. To prove that she could wait. To prove she wasn't helpless against this thing. This…this attraction.

"Then I suppose we won't have much need of each other over the next few weeks. What I would like you to do is coordinate with Athena, my father's personal assistant. She has all of the information regarding Kyonos, the budget, various charities and so on. Make that your project. And I'm going to be sending you a new wardrobe. You're not allowed to turn it away. Burn those dresses you've been wearing."

"I'm donating them," she sniffed, irritated by his high-handedness. But she wasn't about to argue because what he was proposing meant that she got to avoid him.

"Do as you like, but you aren't wearing them anymore."

"No, I have a better idea," she said. "For every one outfit purchased for me, two new outfits—new—will be donated to a battered women's shelter."

"That is your affair, not mine."

"If I'm going to get something out of this arrangement I intend to start now."

He looked at her, dark eyes molten, and an answering heat started in her core. She knew challenging him was a bad idea. But she didn't really care. Something about him made her feel free. Made her feel like she could say anything. Made her feel like she was no longer bound up by a bunch of safe parameters.

She wasn't sure she liked it at all. Though, goading Xander had its merits.

"I will make sure you get something out of this marriage, *agape mou*," he said, his voice rough. "Several times a night if you're a very good girl."

Her cheeks heated. The bastard. "Perhaps I will endeavor to be a bad girl then."

A slow smile curved his lips. "Even better."

True to his word, Xander avoided her over the course of the next two weeks. And she kept busy. Athena had a lot of useful information and between the two of them, they had endless ideas for more efficient and helpful social programs and ways to help fund various charities.

It was the big picture of all she'd done at the convent. There, she'd been on the ground, physically handing out clothing and food, and it had been wonderfully rewarding. But this was like flying over Kyonos in a helicopter, being able to see every bit of it at once.

And even better because she had the resources to help.

The sad thing was, though, that she was unhappy not seeing Xander. Darn him. She should be glad to get a reprieve. And yet she wasn't.

She'd grown accustomed to his presence. To not feeling alone.

She missed riding. She would have to do something about that eventually, but she'd honestly been so busy. But then, she supposed that was the trade-off. Going from a life of service, reflection and meditation, to a life of high-octane service, balls and luncheons.

There were ever so many luncheons and she'd been invited to all of them. But people were shockingly nice to her.

It made her feel like she might be able to weather it after all. And the makeup artist Xander had hired to help her get ready for big public events didn't hurt. Neither did the new wardrobe that suited her figure so nicely.

She managed to look polished at the very least.

She glanced into the dining room and saw Xander sitting at the table, an expression of doom on his face, papers spread out in front of him. Her heart jolted. She hadn't run into him at all in days, and there he was, just sitting there.

"Hello," she said, coming into the room. She wasn't going to avoid him. He was her fiancé after all, and it would be silly.

He pushed the papers together, stacking them oddly,

his frown intensifying. "I would have thought you'd be ensconced in an office with Athena."

"We're done for the day. Athena had to go home and see to her sick child. Why are you glaring daggers at the headlines?"

"It is nothing," he said, waving his hand. "Just…the news is never good, is it?"

"I don't know. I've spent so much time cut off from it." She wandered over to where he was sitting and he shifted his elbow, like he was trying to hide something from her view.

Buried beneath the top pages, she saw the edge of what looked like her dress from the ball. "What is this?"

"It is nothing," he repeated.

"Then I can see it." She reached down and jerked the paper from beneath the stack and his arm, holding it up, her stomach sinking as she saw the headline and the accompanying photo. "The Zombie Princess," she said. "Oh."

"I will not have this," he said, his tone dark. "I will take steps to make it stop. I'll…"

"Abolish the freedom of the press?" she asked, feeling dizzy. "There's nothing you can do. They…they can think what they want and write what they want. After all. It's only…it's nothing. Vanity."

"You told me to stop pretending like the things weren't important." He took the paper back from her, throwing it down on the table.

"Yes, well, you didn't follow my advice, did you? Why should I follow yours?"

"Because this is garbage. They've hurt you. And I will not allow this to continue."

"It's clever. A joke. An old one. Because I look a little undead. All things considered there were worse things to be called, though."

"Name one."

She put shaking hands on her hips. "I…I can't think of any but it doesn't mean they don't exist. It could be Zombie Drudge, so…you know…Princess is better than that."

"I didn't want this," he said.

She took a deep breath. "I know. And now it's happened. The press did what I thought they would do. They took the easy route and insulted my looks. But that's not actually very surprising. It's what they do. It's how they operate. I can't exactly get upset about it." As she said it, a tear slid down her cheek. "Ignore that. I don't know why that happened."

Except she did. It was like being pulled from her shell, a defenseless crustacean exposed to the elements and scrubbed raw by the sand. This whole experience had been like that. Being with Xander, being back in the world. She'd lost her protection and it left her feeling wounded and fragile.

"Bastards." He picked up his cell phone and dialed a number. "This is Xander Drakos. I want you to track down the owner of *National Daily News* and let him know that if he likes his pants, he'd better print a retraction for his recent article featuring my fiancée. Otherwise, I'll sue them off of him." He hung up. "There. I feel better, I don't know about you."

"It wasn't necessary."

"Oh, come on, there's no point in having power if you don't abuse it a little."

"I take back what I said about you being perfect for the job," she said.

Xander stood, looking down at her, his dark eyes intense. For a moment she thought he might pull her into his arms. Thought he might kiss her again like he'd done yesterday. And she found she wanted him to.

"Can I see the rest of the article?"

"Why?"

"Please."

He handed the paper back to her and she skimmed the article. One thing that had changed about the tone of the articles was the way the press seemed to see Xander. He was being hailed as a man who had changed. As evidenced by his willingness to marry her.

"Well, they seem happier with you," she said. "That's good."

"Is it?"

"It's what you wanted."

"They seem to think I've reformed," he said.

"Have you?"

"I'm not sure."

"Are you going to run again?" she asked, arms crossed under her breasts, her chin tilted up, defiant. If he was, he'd better tell her now.

"No."

"Then you won't screw it up. Because I don't think it's in you to fail. You have to walk away from everything entirely in order to slack off last time."

"I'm not going to run permanently," he said slowly, "but I might need a day off. Do you want to come with me?"

"Where?" she asked.

"The beach. I think I need a day at the beach."

For the beach drive, Xander chose that ostentatious sports car rather than the limo. This moment really did feel like it was from another time. Strangely light. Strangely happy. The Zombie Princess headline lingered in the background, but right now, the mountains were green and beautiful and the beach was a glittering jewel. The windows were rolled down and the wind whipped through the car, smelling of salt and sand and sun.

"Now, this reminds me of the past," she said. "But in a good way."

"Me, too," he said, looking over at her briefly before putting his focus back on the road.

"There's that little window of life where you don't worry about much of anything. I think being seventeen was my favorite. I could drive and could do things I wanted with friends. But I wasn't quite to my dynastic engagement with you, so there was nothing too serious happening. Just parties and trips to the beach."

"I never had that. I mean, I was always raised to be the heir."

"You always seemed happy, though. Like you were having fun at life's expense."

"Yeah, well, I sort of was at that point. I always knew my responsibility, but I liked to have fun. Because, that's the flip side of the heir responsibility. I was assured of my place. Of my divine right to become the most powerful man on the island. How can a young guy not get off on that?"

"I suppose it's impossible."

They rounded a corner and she noticed Xander's knuckles get white on the wheel. She looked up at him, at the hard expression on his face.

"What?" she asked.

"Nothing." She could see his chest, rising and falling hard and fast as he struggled to breathe.

"What's happening, Xander?"

"I'm so stupid," he said, his lips white as his knuckles now. "I didn't realize where I was going."

She really thought he might pass out on her now. "Pull

over," she said. "Just up here, there's a place with beach access."

He nodded slowly and pulled the car into a gravel turn-out on the side of the road, killing the engine. There was silence except for the sound of his breathing and the crashing of the waves.

"What happened?" she asked.

He got out of the car without saying anything, the keys in the ignition, the door open. And he started down the stairs that led down to the beach.

And all she could do was stare after him.

She wondered what pain hurt so bad that he couldn't bring himself to speak about it. It was related to what had happened to him yesterday with his father, she was sure of that. She unbuckled and got out, following him down to the beach, white sand sifting into her sandals, piling into a warm ball beneath the arch of her foot. She kicked the shoes off and ran ahead to where he was.

He started walking into the ocean. She remembered telling him how she'd longed to do that. To disappear beneath the waves and never come back up. And then he dipped his head beneath the water, and Layna couldn't see him anymore.

CHAPTER ELEVEN

"Xander!" Layna shouted, following him out into the waves.

The waves were hitting her at chest level. She gave up on walking and tried to tread water, even though she could touch the bottom. But the waves washed her backward, away from him. "Xander!" she sputtered, water going over her head. She let the water draw her back toward the shore and stood hip-deep in the surf.

He came back up then, his dark head breaking the surface. A wave pushed him back so that he was near her.

"Are you trying to drown yourself?" she asked, feeling half-drowned herself. She knew all the beautiful makeup that had been put on in an effort to de-zombiefy her was gone.

"No," he said, his words heavy. "Not that. Just…I felt like there was blood all over my hands and I thought maybe I could get them clean."

She moved closer to him and took his hands in hers. And without asking why, without asking for an account of his sins, she held his hand up. "I don't see any."

"It's there."

"Tell me," she said.

"I couldn't go any further," he said. "I'm sorry."

"Don't apologize to me. Explain. Explain all of it. Yesterday, today. Something hurts badly enough that you have to run when it catches up with you and I want to know what it is."

"We were going to have to pass the accident site to get to the beach I had in mind and for some reason I didn't realize until we went around that last corner. It reminded me of that day."

"Oh…no, Xander I'm sorry."

"I'm sure it's horrible to watch someone die," he said, a shiver racking his body, "even if they're a stranger. But to watch your mother…to watch her get white, all of her color bleeding out of her, onto your hands…there is nothing worse." He met her gaze, the demons behind his eyes raging now, lashing him from the inside out. "I couldn't do anything but sit with her until help arrived and by then it was too late. But they couldn't get me to let go of her. The last thing she ever heard from me was anger. Those were the last sounds she heard on this earth. Me yelling at her. Swearing at her. I was…so angry with her, Layna."

"About what?"

"It doesn't matter," he said. "It doesn't change anything. It doesn't change what happened. It doesn't change the last moments of that relationship. I can never fix it. Can never apologize for the words I said. I can never go back and decide not to get angry. Decide to pull the car over. Decide not to go out that day. I can never go back and tell her that no matter how angry I was back then, I would have gotten over it and we would have been okay."

He shivered again. "Get on the sand," she said, "out of the water, and wait for me."

She scrambled back up the stairs, up to where the car was parked and took the keys from the ignition, fished a blanket and food out of the trunk, then closed all the doors before heading back down to where he sat.

She threw the blanket over his shoulders. "There. And I have sandwiches."

"I don't think I could eat," he said.

"Then we'll talk."

"Trust me?" he asked.

"Not really."

"Probably a good thing. But if memory from my misspent youth serves me, there's a cave over here. We could get out of the wind. And not have anyone stumble across the heir to the throne shivering and on the cusp of a mental breakdown."

"That might be for the best."

He kept the blanket on his shoulders and led the way down the beach and away from the water.

"This is all a little too perfect, Xander," she said, walking into the small stone alcove cut into the mountain.

"My break with reality and emotional meltdown?"

"How many women have you seduced in here?"

"Oh, this was my much younger misspent youth. Not my teenage years."

"I never really knew if you'd dated much before we were together."

He winced. "I didn't date so much as take advantage of women who liked the idea of getting dirty with a prince."

"I see."

"I take it you didn't?"

She blushed, but thankfully, in the dark she knew he couldn't see it. "I come from a political family and my mother was very blunt with me early on about what nets you a good husband. Purity, or at the very least the illusion of it, is quite important. Princes and the like don't want a lot of tabloid articles going around about their future wife's wild years."

He laughed. "I was expertly snared, wasn't I?"

"We both knew what our marriage was supposed to be. But yes, I did work to make my image one that would fit in with the Drakos family. I worked to be suitable."

"You did far too much for me," he said. "I never deserved any of it."

"I didn't do it for you," she said. "I did it for me. I don't think you fully grasp what a shallow little power grabber I was."

"You were far too pretty for me to care."

"Yes, and when life took that I had to work on developing my character a bit. A harsh wake-up call, and I resisted it for as long as I could."

"I'm still resisting it," he said. He put his hand on the rough stone wall and looked up. "I know a little bit about those hazy years, you know."

"Do you?" she asked, her throat tight all of a sudden.

"Yes. I was so high for the first couple of years after I left I could barely remember my reason for taking off in the first place. It was a lot harder to remember what it was like washing my mother's blood off of my body, too."

"It's terrible to live like that," she said. "Half alive."

"I tried to use things like sex and drugs to make myself feel. But in the end, it doesn't work. It's fleeting and the aftermath is so bad you wish you would have just stuck with empty."

"When did you stop?"

"The drugs? Probably twelve years ago. The drinking and sleeping around? It's been a couple of weeks. I've been walking with my favorite crutches for a long time."

"It's funny. I've been in a convent and you've been in a casino, but I think, at the end of the day we were doing the same thing."

"I think you might be right."

"I'm sorry about what happened. And I'm sorry I was

so angry at you. I didn't really stop and think about how you must have felt. All you must have gone through. My own tragedy overshadowed yours in my mind."

"I don't blame you for that, Layna. You were put through hell."

"We both were."

"Yesterday when I kissed you," he said, "I just wanted to lose myself. To forget who I was. Where I was. To forget that this was my life. That my father, who I haven't spoken to in so long, was unconscious. That he's dying. Another person I'll never reconcile with. When I kiss you it's hard to think about any of the bad things because…I just want you."

"Kissing me really works that well?"

"Yes," he said.

"The Zombie Princess?"

"I don't have time for people like that. They're idiots. They don't know what it's like to kiss your lips, or feel your curves beneath their hands. They know nothing."

She was really blushing now. "It's hard for me to think when we kiss, too. I didn't think I would miss touch. I thought I could live without being with a man because I didn't want to deal with the fact that I could be rejected for my looks. Or that any man who was with me might be with me out of pity. But when you kiss me, I care less about how you feel because I'm too focused on what I feel."

"I make you selfish?" he asked, moving closer to her.

"Yes. For that. For what you can give me. I've…never actually been kissed by anyone else. And the one thing I always regretted, in spite of myself, was that the night in the garden, you know what night I mean, we got interrupted."

"I regretted that, too. I tried not to think of you after I left, Layna, but I did regret that. I regretted you. If my life hadn't have changed, you would have been my future, and

I was always content with that vision. The life I've had has never been as beautiful as that dream. As that certainty I had for those few months we were engaged. I could see it all, you as my wife, us ruling Kyonos, and it felt right. Maybe that was really why I came to look for you after I returned. Because I hoped that somehow it wouldn't be too late to have some of that."

"And look what you came back to."

He put his hand on her cheek, a move he made often and one she didn't think she'd ever tire of. He was so comfortable touching her, even her scars. "But the feelings are the same. It's amazing how much we've both changed, only to come back to this point." He put his hand on her other cheek and lowered his head, kissing her, deep and long. "I do want you. As badly as I ever have. More even, I think, because I know how bitterly I've regretted the fact that I didn't claim you before. I will never make that mistake again."

She looked up into his eyes. They were still so bleak, so haunted. She could see it even in the dim light of the cave. "Do you need me?" she asked. "Do you need to forget?"

She did. She was wounded and hurting. For her, for him. For everything they'd lost. For the years of pain. For the years they suffered alone when maybe what they should have done was cling to each other.

"Yes," he said. "Please."

She kissed him then. Slowly traced the seam of his mouth with her tongue, asking for entry. He gave it, and with a growl wrapped his arms around her waist and held her tightly against him as he let her take the lead on the kiss.

She knew she was a little clumsy at it, but he really didn't seem to mind, his erection hard against her stomach, an air of desperation coming from him in waves.

She could feel it reflected in her, deep in her core. The need to feel like she wasn't alone. He'd said that he'd been inside of a woman before and felt utterly isolated, but somehow she knew that wouldn't be true with them.

Because they both knew rock bottom. And it seemed like they deserved to reach for the heights, even if it was just for a few moments.

He took the blanket off his shoulders and laid it down on the sandy floor of the cave. "I have never seduced a woman in here before," he said. "I know I told you that already but it feels like my current actions might make that assertion seem suspect."

"A little bit, but I don't really care," she said, blinking back tears. "I've been cold for a long time," she said.

"Because you were in the ocean."

She laughed and shook her head. "No, I've been cold inside for a long time. I feel like you could make me warm. I need you to make me warm."

"You deserve better than this," he said, kissing her again, cutting off any response she might have made. "You deserve so much better than this, but I don't have the strength to give it to you, because all I can do is take this for myself."

His desperation fed hers, the need that wrapped itself around his voice was like balm for the scars inside. She might be the Zombie Princess, but right then, the beautiful, damaged prince wanted her.

They were both broken. Barely limping through life. But maybe if they held on to each other tight enough they could hold each other up. Maybe she could be strong enough if they were braced on each other.

He swept his hand over the line of her back, a wave of sensation crashing over her. How long had it been since she'd focused on her body? On what she felt physically.

She'd been training herself to deny physical desire. To deny cravings of any kind. Of specific foods, rest, sex. Because it was important for a woman with her aims to deny herself.

But right now, Xander was making it impossible to think of anything else except what she felt. What she wanted. He was making her need, a deep, aching need that she couldn't possibly let go unanswered.

She wouldn't let it go unanswered. She knew what he meant now. Because she knew what she should do, too. She knew she should ask for a bed and soft sheets, and for him to be slow and gentle because it was her first time.

She knew she should demand marriage vows, because it was right.

But she was beyond that. None of it mattered. The cave floor would do, the commitment they had would have to as well.

She had a feeling that, if she had met him again and he hadn't offered marriage, they would be in the exact same position.

Because this was unfinished business. This was the chance to either bond her and Xander together for good, or to at least have him lose some of his power over her by answering some very important questions. The chance to turn regrets of missed chances into mistakes made.

She was honestly okay with the idea that it might be a mistake when it was over. Because she was short on those. Or maybe not. Maybe her life had been one long, steady, low-key mistake.

That sent a jolt of panic through her, spurred her on, made her kiss him all the more desperately. Xander made her feel so much. So many things she thought she'd let go of, and he brought it all roaring back, or to life for the very first time.

He pushed his hands beneath her shirt, repeating his earlier move, this time over bare skin. She moved her hands to his stomach, tugging his shirt out from his pants and slipping her fingers beneath. He was so hot, so hard. So very different from her.

She would have been shocked by her boldness in other circumstances. But not now. Not when they were in the dark. In this place that almost seemed removed from reality. Not when they were holding each other up.

Not when they were helping each other forget by filling the present with so much pleasure the past couldn't exist anymore, and the future couldn't be a concern.

He pulled his lips from hers and kissed her neck, teeth grazing her sensitive skin, his tongue sliding over her flesh to soothe away the sting. He knew just where to hit, just when to stop and suck at her skin, when to inflict pain. When to give pleasure.

He tightened his hold on her and drew her forward, raising his other hand to cup her breast through the fabric of her damp top. He moved his thumb, finding her nipple with ease, finishing the work of the cold water and tightening it to a painfully hard point.

A low growl rolled through his throat and he propelled her backward, pushing her against the wall of the cave. He pushed a thigh between her legs, then took advantage of her widened stance, his arousal coming into contact with the most intimate part of her.

There were layers of clothing between them but she still felt it, so devastating. So erotic. So unlike anything she'd given herself permission to want or feel for far too long.

She'd told him that she was a woman, and had been long before he'd walked back into her life. And it was true. But she'd suppressed an amazing part of what it meant to be a woman, and only now, with his lips on her skin, his hands on her body, his hardness against her softness, did she realize that.

She angled her head and caught his lips, kissing him deep, tasting him, reveling in the slide of his tongue against hers. For too long she'd had hazy. Gentle. Life on a near flat line with barely a blip, and now she felt like she was going to explode with the intensity of this encounter. With the rawness of it.

The rock at her back, the man at her front, the sound of the waves just outside the cave walls. It was sensory overload in the most perfect way. An infusion of sensation, bursts of flavor on her tongue. Years of bread and water dissolving into a sensual feast that she didn't think she would ever get enough of.

He forked his fingers through her hair and tugged, hard, guiding her away from the wall, down onto the blanket, his body covering hers, his lean hips settling between her legs. She bucked against him, chasing the promise of release that sparked through her with every touch of his body against hers.

He pushed her dress up, tugged her panties down to her knees, his hand at the apex of her thighs, thumb deftly finding the sensitive bud there. She didn't have time to be shocked or embarrassed, didn't have time to do anything but simply revel in the pleasure he knew how to give.

"You want me," he said, his voice feral, his words barely intelligible.

"Yes," she said, kissing his neck. "Yes."

The blanket was bunched up underneath them, only offering a partial shield between them and the ground, but she didn't care. It added to the intensity, to the depth of it all.

He slipped a finger inside of her and the wholly foreign sensation rocketed her to the brink of orgasm.

"You're a virgin, aren't you?" he asked, his voice hoarse.

"Yes," she said, pleasure rocketing through her as he slid his thumb over her clitoris again.

"And you're sure this is what you want?"

"I need it," she said. "I need you. I need it like this."

"It's not going to be romantic," he said, abandoning her body, reaching for the closure on his pants and unbuttoning them, then tugging his shirt over his head. "It's probably going to be fast."

"Are you trying to talk me out of it?"

"*Theos*, yes. Because if I have a soul left, this will damn it for sure."

She shook her head. "No. It won't. How could that be true? How can that be true when I feel like if I don't have you I'll die?"

He kissed her lips, gentle, searching, at odds with the ferocity of the moment. "That's absolute proof that I'm right," he said. "I'll try not to hurt you."

The blunt head of him probed at the entrance to her body and she tensed for a second before he started to push inside. The farther in he went, the more she relaxed. It didn't hurt. It just felt…new. And wonderful.

He put his hand under her bottom and lifted it, thrusting into her all the way. A harsh sound escaped from his lips, along with a curse that sounded more like a prayer.

He pushed her dress up higher, exposing her breasts, lowering his head and sucking a nipple deep in his mouth as he moved inside of her, driving her higher, faster than she'd imagined possible.

It seemed natural, having him like this, moving with him, finding her pace. She locked her legs around his lean hips and arched against him, meeting his every thrust, nails digging into his shoulders.

He lowered his head, his movements harder, faster now,

pleasure sparking in her, each thrust bringing the bursts of white heat closer together, turning it into a continuous flame that burned through her whole body, threatening to consume her as he ravaged her, pushed her to a point she hadn't imagined possible.

Xander growled, teeth closing down on her shoulder, his pelvis hitting hard as he froze above her and shuddered out his release. The pain ramped her pleasure up higher, the overflow of sensation an utter shock. Beautiful. Blinding.

And when the fire burned out, it was only the sound of their breathing echoing off the walls of the cave.

A chill stole through her blood, a slow trickle of ice that replaced the heat that had come before. And it hit her that she was lying on the floor, outdoors, kind of, almost, with Xander on top of her.

Her dress was still on, his pants only pushed down just past his hips. That she'd let him—no, begged him—to take her like this. When they weren't married. When they hardly knew each other. When they certainly didn't love each other.

He moved off her, standing and tugging his pants up, his movements fluid as he dressed. It all spoke of his ex-perience—experience he'd gained with other women.

Anger curled in the pit of her stomach. Anger she had no right to feel because she knew his past, she knew something of his experiences, and she'd just benefitted, mightily, from those experiences. It had been…amazing. Physically.

Emotionally she felt…an empty, crushing weight in her chest. The kind he'd spoken of. They'd just been as close as two people could possibly be and she felt alone. More alone than she'd felt in ages, with him right there, the scent of his skin still on her body. It made no sense.

Sex without love.

Yes, that had to be it. Lust. Empty lust that meant nothing.

But it had all seemed substantial in the moment. It had seemed necessary. Now she felt singed inside. Like she'd been burned, hollowed out.

No wonder she'd spent so many years content with… contentment. Happy to feel no brilliant highs so that she could avoid the lows. So that she could avoid this level of emptiness and confusion.

"Let's not talk," she said, scrambling into a sitting position and trying to put her clothes back in place. "Let's just…not."

"Why?" he asked, doing his belt and the final few buttons on his shirt.

"Because there's no point. I don't want to…I don't want."

"Do you regret it?"

"I don't understand it."

"What's not to understand? We wanted each other. We acted on it."

"Didn't I just say I don't want to talk?"

"Hiding?"

"Why not?" she asked, feeling like she was on the verge of tears. "It's what we're both best at. We hide from our pain and our issues and from anyone who might hurt us or ask anything from us, right?"

"Sums it up," he said, his tone hard. "And that right there is my favorite method of running. You have to admit, it's a lot more exciting than hiding in a convent."

"It was more *something*, but I haven't decided if I liked it or not yet."

He grabbed her arm and pulled her forward, kissed her hard on the mouth. "You liked it."

"I did?" she asked, keeping her voice monotone.

"You came pretty hard, baby, you can't hide that from me. I could feel it."

Her face heated. "Don't."

"Don't because you want to pretend that you're just a sweet, good girl? We both know you aren't."

"That's where you're wrong, Xander. Assuming I care about being good. I don't. I never have. I just cared about hiding. I've never needed to be good, and I think if I had, I wouldn't have given you my virginity on the floor of a cave."

"Then maybe our marriage will be a success, *agape*, because if neither of us care about being good, then we might have a lot of fun."

"More fun like that, you mean?" she asked, her tone disdainful.

"Yes," he said, "that's exactly what I mean." He hauled her against him for a kiss, his lips hard on hers. "And don't play wounded maiden with me. It doesn't suit you."

"What? All my wounds aren't convincing enough for you?"

He released his hold on her. "Whatever the hell your problem is? Get over it. I expect sex in my marriage and since you don't want me to have it with anyone else, I'll damn sure have it with you. Unlike you, running off into celibacy isn't my style."

"You are…you are…"

"Sexy?"

"Your ego is…"

"Yeah, I know. But I don't need ego in this instance. I know just how much you enjoyed that, so let's just skip this part."

She gritted her teeth. "I believe I'm the one who suggested that in the first place."

"So we'll continue with it then."

Layna dressed, careful not to look at Xander as she did, then headed out of the cave and into the sunlight. It was shocking that it was still midday. Shocking that the world seemed so normal outside while everything inside of her was rearranged to the point where she couldn't find a damn thing!

And, yes, damn again. She blamed Xander for her expanding vocabulary. Not that she hadn't known the words, just that she hadn't seen fit to use them until he'd come back into her life.

"For what it's worth," Xander said, his voice coming from behind her, "I do feel better."

"I think I might find that offensive."

"Don't," he said. "Because usually I feel worse when it's over, and I don't. Even after we've had a fight. Actually, I think I like that we had a fight."

"Why?" she asked, incredulous now.

"Because we talked. And I don't want to leave it on a fight because sometimes, you never get a chance to repair it when it's over."

Her heart squeezed. "I suppose that's true."

"A truce, then?"

She didn't really know how she felt about a truce with the man she'd just had sex with. She didn't know how she felt at all.

He stuck his hand out, as though she was meant to shake it and all she could do was stare. "A truce?" she repeated, sounding dumb.

"It's better than fighting, don't you think?"

But not very honest. Not when she felt all jumbled up. "Okay." She extended her hand and wrapped her fingers around his, shaking it slowly. This was silly, but it meant she was able to stop and collect herself. Shore up her defenses. It meant neither of them had to be particularly honest.

She was quite comfortable with that.

"Good," he said, releasing his hold on her. "Now, let's go. I think we both agree that a day at the beach has been had and there's no need to go any further."

No need for him to pass the site of his mother's accident. No need for them to confront what had passed between them. No need for them to talk about why he felt so dirty. Why he'd felt the need to walk into the ocean to get clean.

"Yes," she said. "I think I'm quite ready to go back."

He smiled, and she knew that he knew, as well as she did, what they were both doing.

Hiding.

"Excellent."

<h1 style="text-align:center">CHAPTER TWELVE</h1>

XANDER COULDN'T GET his tie right. And who the hell cared? He hated all of this. Hated that he had to dress for dinner because Stavros had invited heads of state and all other manner of dignitaries Xander could care less about.

Not when he was highly concerned with his feelings for his fiancée. Or rather, how his fiancée had felt when she'd been naked underneath him. Being with her yesterday had been a revelation. He swore succinctly and tossed his tie down onto the bed.

She had been… There were no words for the blinding flash of perfect oblivion and clarity he'd found when he'd pushed inside her body.

And wasn't that a damned funny thing? He'd always known sex had power. It had the power to wipe his worries from his mind. The power to make him feel. To bring his life, the emptiness of it, into sharp perspective the moment the buzz from his orgasm faded.

But this was different. He hadn't felt alone when he'd been with her.

Maybe it was because they were both so very much the same, though he doubted she would ever admit to that.

He looked down at the tie and frowned. Then picked it up.

He could call a servant, but he hated that nonsense. He

probably needed a valet or some such, no doubt his father had one.

But that wouldn't serve his purposes for the moment. Sure, it would get his tie on straight, but it wouldn't serve his purposes.

He flung his bedroom door open and stalked down the corridor. The servants were very good at ignoring him and his moods. But then, he supposed that was part of earning their salary.

He opened the door to Layna's room without knocking, hoping he might find her there. He was not disappointed.

"I need help," he said, his tone as stern as the walk he'd used to bring him here.

Layna frowned from her position on the bed. "You have a very bad habit of barging into my room."

"Since when does a fiancé need permission? And I have now seen all of your body, so let's not even pretend that your modesty is offended."

"Just because you've seen it once doesn't mean you have ongoing permission to see it whenever you like," she said.

"Of course it does." He sat down in a chair by the bed, one leg out straight, his arms on the rests. "I am to be king. I will see what I like when I like to see it."

She arched her brows. "Has being in your childhood home caused this regression or do you just always behave like a recalcitrant boy?"

"I need help putting my tie on," he growled. He was not going to dignify her question with a response.

"Then why didn't you call someone?"

"What the hell is the point of a wife who doesn't want me to see her naked and who won't tie my damned tie for me?"

"I'm not really sure, actually. Maybe it's the time for you to rethink your proposal."

"I won't." He stood up and walked toward her, draping his tie over his shoulders. "Fix this."

She let out a long, exasperated breath and gripped both ends of the tie. "It's been about a million years since I've done this. I did it for my father a couple of times. He felt it would be a good skill to know."

"For such a time as this, I should think."

"Clearly, yes, the idea was for me to be able to serve the every whim of my crabby husband. But you are not my husband yet, don't forget it."

"I made you mine in every way that counted today."

"Indeed," she said, her tone frosty.

"You don't agree?"

"Does every woman you have sex with belong to you? If so, we should start partitioning off a wing for the royal harem."

He pulled away from her and started working on the tie on his own again. "You need to dress for dinner."

"And the subject has changed."

"It bloody well has."

"Are you always such a horror after sex?"

"No, but I am always such a horror when I have to put on a tie and perform at some…state dinner I have no desire to partake in."

"So I should expect a lot of this then?"

He sat down again, his hands folded, his chin braced on his knuckles. "I have to get over it, don't I?"

"What?"

"The fact that I don't like this. Or want it. That I don't know how to do it anymore."

"How is it that you managed to lose all of what you were raised for? How did you lose so much of who you were born to be?"

Xander shifted in his seat. And he wondered if it was time she knew. "Because it's not who I was born to be."

It was too late to take it back now. There was no pulling back from a statement like that. She would never let him off the hook now.

"What do you mean?" she asked.

It didn't mean he wouldn't make her drag it out of him since just saying it seemed too hard.

"The way the system works here in Kyonos, it's almost as if our bloodline gives us some divine ruling powers. I mean, Stavros's children can't be in line for the throne because they're adopted, because they don't descend from our great and noble lineage. Are there magic powers in it, I wonder? I've always wondered that, even when I was a boy. Wondered how I'd been so fortunate to be born with such blood and the divine right to rule that came with it."

"No wonder you were so insufferable."

"Yes, it's no wonder at all when you're born believing that the simple act of your birth puts you above the common folks." He took a breath and looked out the window, at the slice of blue sky just barely visible. Not for the first time, he thought he would rather sail into the horizon than deal with all of this. But he'd made a promise.

He'd made a promise to Layna.

He wouldn't run again.

"But I found out…that I was not born with that right at all. I have no royal blood, Layna. I am not my father's son."

"What?" He had succeeded in shocking her. Her eyes flew wide, one eyebrow raised, the other, paralyzed by scar tissue, still managing to convey her surprise.

"That was what my mother and I were fighting about. She told me, on our trip to the beach that day that I was not of royal blood, but the product of an affair she had with her bodyguard. Ironic, considering Eva's marriage. But my sister had the courage to walk away from her arranged marriage when she decided Mak was the one she wanted. My mother made a different choice. She went ahead with the marriage to my father, knowing she was pregnant."

"What? How…"

"She seduced him quickly, is my understanding, and it was no hardship to convince him I was born just a few weeks early."

"But she's certain?"

"So she told me. She was already pregnant when she slept with my father for the first time."

"And the bodyguard?"

"Sent away with a grand payoff. She never took a test of any kind, and that was, in the end, why she told me."

"What do you mean?"

"She'd been getting increasingly paranoid, with the way technology was progressing. She was starting to fear that someday my DNA might be used against me. And so she begged me not to ever undergo any sort of analysis of my blood. Or to ever let my children undergo such a test, when you and I were married."

"But why would she…?"

"I think it was long-held guilt, starting to eat at her, making her see shadows where there were none. But the thing was, the economy had been having issues already and with the state of political unrest she was concerned for me."

"But if… Why couldn't Stavros rule then?"

"My father didn't know. She didn't want him to know. She loved him by then, you see? She hadn't loved him when they'd first married. So lying to him hadn't seemed so bad. But later…she wanted to keep it a secret. For her. For him. And for me. In her mind, I was her firstborn son and I deserved the honor. I think in some ways, I was her favorite son because of my real father. Because he was her first love. Because she had gone to such great lengths to protect me and ensure I was the heir."

He shrugged.

"I've had fifteen years to think this over. And I have. High, drunk, sober, alone and in the arms of a woman, I've thought about this. About what it meant. About what my responsibilities were. She did so much to ensure I could be named the heir. But the fact remains that I'm not."

"And that's why you left?"

"That. And the fact that I do blame myself for her death. I was so angry, Layna. I could hardly see straight and I was yelling, I just drove faster and…"

"You made a mistake. You didn't do it on purpose."

He shook his head. "I didn't. But it was a hell of a mistake. There are mistakes you can come back from, but then there are mistakes you make that someone doesn't walk away from, and those are the hardest ones to deal with. The hardest ones to seek forgiveness for. From yourself or anyone else."

"Tell me about the day you left," she said, sinking to the floor in front of him. "Tell me about what happened, now that I know everything."

"My father had called me into his office. Stavros was there, too." He could picture them both—his father ashen, angry and grieving. His brother, so young and sullen. A teenage boy still. "And then he proceeded to tell me that he found me responsible for the death of his wife. And how he had no idea how I could possibly be his son, when he would never have behaved in such a manner. And I had no argument. For I felt he spoke the truth. And I had just learned I was not his son. So there was no lie in what he said."

"And Stavros?"

Xander cleared his throat. He hated that the memory had this much power over him, even now.

"He looked at me and said he would always hold me responsible for the loss of his mother. His mother, as though she were no longer mine because I had taken her from the world. And remembering the words I'd yelled at her before the car hit the rocks? Where I had said she was no longer a mother to me? I couldn't argue with that statement, either."

"And you had nothing," she said, her voice a whisper.

"In one moment, I lost all my family. And I knew I had no real claim on the throne. I saw no reason to stay."

She rose up, planting her hands on his thighs, and kissed him on the mouth, the touch sweet, sincere. He raised his hands and gripped the back of her head, his fingers sinking deep into her hair, holding her tight to his mouth. He needed this. He needed her. He needed her so badly he was shaking with it already and it had been less than twenty-four hours since he'd last been inside her body.

He tugged gently on her hair, tilting her head back, exposing her tender throat, then he lowered his head and kissed her, slowly. She moaned, encouraging him, spurring him on. He bared his teeth, scraped her delicate skin and reveled in the raw sound she made in response.

She liked this. His little innocent. She liked him unrestrained. She liked to be at his mercy. Which naturally put him at hers. To have a woman on her knees before him, allowing him this kind of sensual feast? He might have the physical power, but she was holding the leash.

Keeping his hand in her hair, he reached down to his belt and undid the buckle, freeing himself from the confines of his pants.

She looked up at him, angelic eyes wide, her lips in a shocked *O*. There was something about that face that turned him on even more, and it shouldn't. He knew it shouldn't.

"You know what I want from you?" he asked, his voice strangled.

She nodded slowly and he tightened his hold on her hair. He watched the color in her cheeks rise, from arousal, not embarrassment. The flush spread down to her neck, her chest.

"Suck me," he said, his voice rough.

She leaned forward, guided by his hand, the tip of her tongue touching his rigid length.

"More," he said, tugging gently.

But she didn't comply. Instead, she just ran her tongue along his shaft. And he could do nothing but sit helplessly, let her have her way. She shifted then, taking all of him into her mouth, and he leaned back in the chair, a harsh breath hissing out through his teeth.

He swore, short and to the point, but it only seemed to encourage her. She wasn't shy. She seemed to have no qualms about tasting him, touching him, boldly changing the rhythm or stopping altogether, squeezing the base of him with her hand, pushing him to the brink.

"Careful," he groaned, when her tongue brushed the sensitive skin just beneath the head of his erection. "I don't want it like this. I don't want it over too soon."

The look she gave him was wicked, reminding him of Layna Xenakos as she had been. Confident. A minx. A flirt. A woman who had a sensual air about her, and an innocence, too. It had all called to him even then.

She had always called to him.

She lowered her head again and he tugged her hair. "No," he said, his voice sharp. "I want to be inside you."

She stood then, lifting her dress and tugging her panties off. He reached for her, hooked his arm around her waist and tugged her onto his lap, bunching her dress up around her hips, squeezing her bare butt before giving her an open-handed slap. Nothing too hard. Just enough to draw one of those sweet sounds from her lips.

Then he gripped her hips tight and positioned her over his body, testing her with the blunt head of him, finding her wet and ready. He starting to pull her down, sliding into her by inches. Her head fell back and he couldn't resist another nip on her throat.

When he was inside her all the way, she rested her head against his chest, her hands on his shoulders. "Yes, Xander," she said, and he knew she was still with him.

A relief, because he'd been so lost in his own need it would have been easy to forget her. To forget that she might not be ready for this. But she was. She was right there with him.

"My dress," she said, panting, "would you—?"

He tugged it up higher, pulling it over her head and throwing it to the floor, then undoing her bra with unmatched speed, exposing her breasts. "My pleasure," he said, lowering his head and sucking one rosy bud between his lips.

She arched against him, her internal muscles flexing around him. It was too much for him. But he'd already taken too much from this and she needed hers. He needed to watch her face as she came for him.

He reached between them, sliding his thumb over her clitoris as he thrust up into her.

Her fingernails dug into his back and for a moment she lost herself. But he didn't lose her. He held her the whole time. Watched as her lips parted, her eyes closed, her forehead creased. The way the scar tissue by the corner of her mouth folded, and how one brow never did match up with the other.

It was all her. No one else could have made this moment. No one else could have coaxed his darkest secret from him and then taken him to heaven on its wings.

She squeezed him tight, and the world exploded, his blood turning to fire and swallowing him whole while his orgasm burned through him, clearing out all the pain, all the regret, all of who he was and who he'd been, leaving him desolate in its wake.

And when he came back to himself, he was in her arms. And he wasn't sure who he was. Or why he'd cared so much about a tie only a few minutes ago.

"When is dinner?" she asked, her voice sleepy.

"Eight," he said.

"So we have five hours," she said.

He nodded and somehow, in spite of the fact that his legs felt like jelly, he managed to lift them both from the chair and carry her to the bed. He pulled back the covers and laid her down, then got in beside her, pulling her body up against his. He buried his face in her hair and took a deep breath, the air filling his lungs seeming all the fresher because it was infused with her scent.

"I should have done this after the first time," he said.

"What?"

"Taken you to bed. Held you close. You're so soft." He let his hand drift over her curves. Her hip, her thigh. "You are beautiful, Layna. I saw it just now. With that look on your face as you came. The most beautiful thing I've ever seen."

"You don't have to say those kinds of things."

"I know. But it's true. And you asked me only last week if I could say you were beautiful, and I said no. But I was wrong then. I know so much more now."

"A week to obtain wisdom. I wish I had that gift."

"Not wisdom in all things. But wisdom in how magical it is to watch you lose yourself in pleasure. To see the light catch your hair and pick up the hidden gold strands that always remind me of the past. Only the good parts of the past," he said, laughing. "And I don't know quite how I missed just what an incredible thing your smile is. Because you still have it. Because life has been cruel to you and you still smile."

"So do you," she said.

"Yes. But you mean it."

"You don't?"

He shook his head. "I already told you. I think we took different paths to accomplish the same goal. I tried to pretend everything was fine. I hid behind my smile. Behind artificial highs. So that I could pretend I felt something when I simply didn't. When I couldn't go back and face all that I needed to face. The only thing to do was never look at the past, and pretend everything was fine in the present."

He felt her nod, her body shifting slightly against his. "Yes. That sounds about right. I mean, I understand that."

"And you?"

"In my case, I thought if I could focus on other things, not myself, for a while, I would be okay. If I could have some purpose beyond living in a darkened mansion floating around like a tragic, gothic heroine, then maybe none of it would hurt so bad."

"Did it work?" he asked.

"Yeah. It did. I…I love helping people. And I was able to surround myself with women who had no love for clothing or fashion. I lived a life where outer beauty was a trap because it could lead to vanity. To pride. And since I had none…" She laughed. "In an odd way I suppose I soothed my pride that way. Because I was clearly the least in terms of looks, so I was starting at a greater advantage, and I could be proud of that. That it wasn't a challenge for me to avoid the mirror or to not long to spend ages on my appearance. So…I guess what I really did was try to find a new place I could be the best. But I wasn't that good at it to be honest. I had—I *have* faith. I believe. But I preferred to ride horses and not meditate indoors. I love food, and it was always hard to fast. But it was quiet. And easy to be content and nothing more. Nothing less."

"You always use that word to describe it," he said. "You never say happy. Content is the one."

"Because happiness is too big, I guess. Unlike you, Xander, I haven't been searching for the big emotional high. A return to feeling. It hurts too much to lose everything. And if you care…if you care then it's almost impossible to recover from. Not only did I lose everything, I had an audience. And the moment when I was attacked I had no control. I just stood there. Screaming and screaming, the pain…I can't even describe the pain."

He felt a tear splash onto his arm and an answering ache echoed in his chest.

"And I just let them all have it. Every drop of it. The protesters, the media, everyone. I never want to be like that again. I never want to feel so much. But I think…I think just having contentment doesn't work, either."

"You don't think?"

"I was starting to feel a little dry. Brittle. Does that make sense?"

"Like you needed to be watered," he said. "Like you would fade to nothing if you didn't have something new and fresh added to you."

"Yes."

"It makes sense, because I felt it, too." Nothing was real or substantial in his world, nothing truly passionate in hers. And for people like them, it was a recipe for death.

"I think that's why I like the way you are with me," she said, turning her face into his arm, muffling her words.

Heat assaulted his face. A strange thing. Almost like he was embarrassed, which was ridiculous. "The way I am with you?"

"Yes. The way that you're…rough. I know this isn't how it is for everyone. I understand that the way I like it isn't the way everyone does."

"No," he said, his blood rushing south, "it's not."

"But I think the reason it works for me is that I spent so long filled with nothing but this sort of bland steadiness. And you… You fill me with sensation. Pleasure and pain so sweet I can't bear it. It lifts me up from contentment and takes me somewhere else entirely." She turned over to face him, her expression serious. "But it's only physical, so it feels safe. Does that make sense?"

"Yes," he said, ignoring the uncomfortable tightness in his lungs. "Yes, that makes sense."

"I don't shock you, do I?"

He had to laugh at that. "You shock me? Until yesterday you were a thirty-three-year-old virgin fresh from the c—"

"Convent, I know," she said, sighing, sounding exasperated. "But look at it this way: I've had a lot of years of nothing more than fantasy. A lot of…desire building up inside me and all. And it was sort of by accident I discovered I liked a bit of rough. I blame the cave wall."

"Do you?"

"And you. I think you're corrupting me."

He laughed again, but this time not because it was particularly funny. "I'm afraid that might actually be true."

"I'm happy with it." She shifted against him. "So, what are you going to do?"

"About?"

"You aren't the heir."

"I know," he said. "And for years I was deciding to just not be the heir, but Stavros's circumstances and Eva's wishes have changed that for me."

"I understand that."

"But you don't approve?" he asked.

"It's not that I don't approve. It's just that I wonder if your father needs to know. If your family needs to know."

He tightened his hold on her. "I can't do that."

"Why not? Because you might lose your place?"

"Because I might…I won't have…"

"You won't have your family."

The tension released from him slowly. He was glad she'd said it and not him. "Silly, I know, considering I hadn't spoken to any of them in ages."

"But they were there. I understand that. My family is there, even though we don't really speak."

"Why is that, Layna?"

"It's easier not to. For all of us. I should think you would understand that."

"I do."

"Why don't we sleep for a while," she said, yawning. "Then…then maybe I'll do better tying your tie, and we'll have a hope of being on time for dinner."

CHAPTER THIRTEEN

THE PLAN TO make it to dinner perfectly pressed and on time didn't exactly go off without a hitch. Halfway through tying Xander's tie for the second time, Layna found herself tangled up in him, and the bedsheets, again.

That put them behind schedule by a good twenty minutes, and by then, she hadn't been able to have her makeup artist coat her face with all the paint she needed to begin to cover her scars, which meant she was rocking a much more natural look for the dinner than she'd intended.

But Xander didn't seem to mind.

And he'd called her beautiful.

Something bloomed inside of her, like a flower that had found the sun after a long battle with the clouds. And she wanted badly to crush it herself. But she couldn't bring herself to do it.

It was frightening, how much his words meant to her, and yet she found she wanted to hold them close, even knowing that doing that might be too costly.

She didn't know how today had happened. All that nudity, and not just in bed. It had been real honesty that had passed between them.

And their lovemaking was… She felt her cheeks heat even as they walked into the dining room together, where ten dignitaries were already seated. Yes, their lovemaking was explosive and far beyond anything she'd ever imagined.

If she thought way back to when she'd imagined she might have a sexual relationship with a man, then she remembered having fantasies about Xander. But she remembered them as being quite calm and hazy. Certainly not with her loving the bite of pain from his hands in her hair and rough demands issued from his lips.

She tried to look casual as the past few hours replayed in her mind. This was not the time. This was a formal dinner. Stavros and Jessica were seated near Eva and Mak, and the head of the table was empty, as was the foot. And just like it was choreographed, she and Xander parted and he walked up to his chair, while she moved down to hers.

It was choreographed, she supposed. From a time long passed, but even so, they both knew the steps. They were steps ingrained in them from years ago. It was the position they'd trained for. The marriage they'd trained for.

So strange to be here now, after she'd let go of it all. So strange to have it be so much the same to what she'd imagined and also so different.

They both had scars now. They had the kind of passion that had nothing to do with a bored, disinterested worldview. They might even be better people now than when they'd first been poised to slip into this roll.

"In the absence of my father," Xander said, "I will be acting as host."

"And how is the king?" One of the politicians to Xander's right posed the question.

"He is as well as can be expected. I would hope he makes a recovery."

"But of course we can't plan for that," Eva said, looking bleak.

"We can't plan for the worst, either, Eva," Xander said.

"We can prepare for it, but why not do that and then plan on a better outcome?"

She smiled. "I like that idea better than mine. I tend to be a catastrophist."

"I think this family has had enough catastrophes," he said.

Layna looked down the table at Stavros, who was looking at his older brother with an expression that was… almost like approval. It made her heart do strange and wonderful things. Because she found that she cared about what happened with Xander and his family. It made her ache for him. Made her appreciate how truly difficult things were for him.

Because he felt like he had a smaller foothold on the Drakos family than he should. Because he wasn't truly a Drakos at all, but the child of an unnamed man he would never know.

It made her want to go to him. Made her want to hold his hand. But that wasn't the proper thing to do. So she would help him by being everything a royal wife should be. She wasn't his wife yet, but today she was acting the part. It was what she could do for him, so she would do it.

The conversation turned to unchallenging things. No one questioned Xander on his years away, no one asked about her scars. No one compared her to a zombie. All in all it went very well.

And when it was over, Xander, Stavros and Mak adjourned to Xander's study—and it killed Layna not to follow and act as support—while Eva and Jessica stayed behind with her.

"We can take coffee in my study," she said, gesturing for them to follow her. She felt like a bit of a fraud considering Eva had lived in the palace until a couple of years ago, and Jessica was a frequent guest, where Layna was just learning the layout of everything.

Both women smiled graciously and followed her, and Layna waited until they were seated before settling herself in one of the armchairs that was positioned by the fireplace. It was lit and roaring already. She was used to having to see to things like that herself. But she wasn't going to complain.

"He's doing well," Jessica said.

Eva smiled, a kind of special smile a little sister has for her older brother. "He's brilliant."

"And both of you are happy?" Layna asked. "With the order of things, I mean. Jessica, I understand that when you married Stavros it was with the idea that he would rule. That you would —"

Jessica shifted in her seat, her red lips pursed. "Neither of us have ever really wanted it. He would have done it, because he believes so strongly in doing his duty. But he loves his business, and frankly, I love mine."

"Are you still a matchmaker then?" Layna asked, having been briefed on her future sister-in-law already.

"Yes. We both work less now that we have the children. Lucy and Ella take up a lot of time, after all, but we're both still heavily committed to the companies we've built. Stavros is so interested in bringing more business to Kyonos and he's thrilled to have more time to focus on that. And more flexibility for the girls. It would have been a hard life for them. Raised with the strictures of being the king and queen's daughters, with no hope of ever taking the throne. They would be considered second forever, because of their blood." Jessica's eyes glittered in the firelight. "The idea of that...I can't stand it. I'm so glad they were spared it. I had no idea how hard it would be until we were faced with the reality of what it would mean for them."

"I hadn't thought of that, either," Layna said, looking down at her hands. "How terrible it would be for them." And Xander, how terrible it would have been for him. To be the oldest child in the household and not be the heir. In some households, the matter of blood could be forgotten because love forged the bond. But in a royal house it was different. In a royal house blood was so much more important.

She swallowed and looked up at Eva. "And you, Eva? What about your children? Do you want this for them?"

Eva shook her head. "I've always chafed at what was expected of me. I don't see why my children would be any different."

"And Eva would be bored with palace life," Jessica said. "It's no wonder she had no desire to marry a prince."

Eva smiled. "Or perhaps I just liked what the bodyguard had on offer."

Jessica winked broadly and crossed her legs, her tulle skirt fanning out around her. "The prince does all right."

"Thanks, Jess."

"Oh, come on. Don't get prudish on me now, Eva. You didn't get that baby bump by eating a watermelon seed."

Eva sniffed. "How very American of you."

Layna laughed, genuinely enjoying the interplay between the two women. Between these women who would now be her family. And it was a relief to her to hear they didn't want the throne anywhere near them.

"Yep. I'm totally American like that. Another reason I probably shouldn't be the queen of anything," Jessica said.

It all made Layna appreciate the impossible place Xander was in even more. The reason he'd run. The reason everything had felt so hopeless.

It wasn't enough to have your father look you in the eye and lay the blame for your mother's death on you. He'd had to experience it knowing that the man wasn't really his father. That there was no magical bond between them. Not a blood bond.

And in a family like this, blood was everything.

"How about you, Layna?" Eva asked. "Are you all right with being in this position?"

"There is nothing holding me to the position. Nothing forcing my hand."

"Except for your relationship with Xander," Jessica said, her eyes narrowed.

She and Xander did have a relationship now, and she couldn't deny it. Not after they'd been together so intimately. Not when she felt this need to protect him.

"Xander and I have an understanding, based on our desire to see the country succeed. It has always been our goal. We were just derailed for a while."

The back of her neck prickled and she looked up—Xander was standing the doorway.

"Forgive me if I'm interrupting. But I'm ready to retire. I had thought you might come with me, Layna?"

There was something strange in his eyes. A raw, wounded look that she could see behind the careful facade he had in place.

She always saw through those walls, and sometimes, she wished she didn't.

Sometimes she wished she could go back to simplifying him. To not seeing him. Or at least to seeing him as nothing more than a playboy. Now she saw all of his wounds. Now she saw he was just as scarred as she was and it made it hard for her to hold onto her anger. Hard to keep her shields up.

And she needed her shields. Because when they were down, it burned like acid. And she knew, better than anyone, just how that felt.

Because she couldn't deny him now, even if she should. Even if they needed distance from today so that she could make sure she felt shored up again.

But she couldn't deny him. And she wouldn't.

"Of course, Xander." She stood and looked back at Eva and Jessica, who were giving her saucy raised eyebrows. She wanted to tell them it wasn't what they thought. Except it was what they thought and she knew it. Xander needed her, and if he needed her, it would be her body he required.

And she would give it.

She made her way to the door and took his arm, allowing him to lead her up the stairs and down the winding corridors until they were at his bedchamber.

"I had a maid send your things," he said. "I didn't see any point in pretending things weren't like this between us."

"Of course not."

He started to undo his tie, the one she had done earlier. It was a strange thing, to be a part of both rituals. The dressing and the undressing.

It made things feel very serious.

"I suppose you want—" She was going to say "sex" but he sat on the edge of the bed on a heavy sigh that seemed to demand silence.

Then he tented his fingers in front of his face, staring sightlessly ahead. "I feel like it's wrong not to tell them."

He wanted to talk? That really did shock her. More than that, it wasn't what she wanted. It was too much. Too challenging.

"Maybe you should think on it. You'll feel better after—" Again, she was going to say "sex," but he pressed on.

"Stavros is well-suited to the position. Listening to his thoughts on the economy I found myself quite humbled.

I am not uneducated in these matters, but he's a man who has examined the way things function on every level. From the workforce to the day-to-day running of things. Stockholders and traders, different kinds of industry. He's truly a man now and not the boy I often see him as. He makes me feel like the stupid boy, to be honest. He's been here holding everything up while I've been…" He paused and looked down. "Layna, I've done less than nothing. I didn't even have the decency to get employed somewhere, I gambled for room and board. And Mak…he's not royal and yet he's got a core of steel. Nothing would ever break him. His children, his and Eva's, would be well-suited to taking the throne one day."

"But they don't want it," she said.

He nodded slowly. "I know it. And I find myself in an impossible situation where I feel I must become a better man to make up for the fact that Stavros won't be the one on the throne, and I don't know how to be better."

Her heart ached, her throat tightening. This was too much. He was making her feel too much. Not in the delicious pleasure-pain way that came through sex. This was all in her heart. A heart she'd kept protected for so long that every lash of emotion felt like being hit with a battering ram.

"It doesn't seem like something we can solve tonight. Maybe we can—" She was going to say "have sex," but this time he cut her off with a kiss. And when he swept her into his arms, and into bed, she could focus on that.

On the sensations he created on her skin, not beneath it. The smooth and sensual, the rough and hard. And she let it all fill her. Until she was conscious of nothing more. Until the pain in her heart was overshadowed with sweeter physical pain, and much sweeter physical pleasure.

And when it was over, they didn't talk. They held each other until they fell asleep.

Layna's last thought before drifting off was that it was very strange not to be alone.

This was the second time in his life that Xander Drakos had woken up with a woman in his bed. The first time had been the previous afternoon, when he and Layna had napped after their pretty intense sex session.

And now, here it was, morning. He'd slept with her all night long, with her curves pressed up against him, his arms tight around her. Very tight. Like he was afraid she might escape.

But she wouldn't. Layna was so constant. So faithful.

If anyone could teach him how to be a better man, it was her. She didn't have royal blood and she was the epitome of steadiness and temperance. Well, maybe not really. But she did a wonderful job of acting like she was and maybe that was enough.

All he'd had practice at was indulging his more selfish whims.

Layna had spent years denying hers.

Perhaps he could learn something about restraint from her.

He shifted and looked down at the top of her head, at the golden highlights he could see, revealed by the shaft of sunlight breaking through the drapes.

"Layna," he said.

"What?" she mumbled sleepily. She wiggled against him then startled, drawing back to look at him, blinking like a mole who'd just come out of her burrow. "I forgot you would be here. Or that I would be here. With you."

"I was quite surprised to wake up with someone myself, but I find I don't mind it."

"You've slept with lots of women," she said.

"I've had sex with a lot of women," he said, heat bleeding over his cheekbones. "I don't sleep with them."

"Oh. Well."

"They never mind. They're usually staying in the same hotel."

"That's right. I forgot you didn't have a home."

"And if I had, I wouldn't have brought them to it."

"You are quite something, you know?" she asked.

"That's the thing, Layna, I do know, which leads me to what I was going to ask you."

"Which is?"

"Make me better."

"What?"

"I need to be…better. I have to be able to justify the fact that I'm the one taking the throne and not Stavros."

"No," she said, "you don't. You don't have to justify anything. Not to me. I talked to Jessica and Eva last night and they explained very clearly why they don't want it differently. Eva doesn't want her children raised in this environment and Jessica can't stand the idea of her husband being king while his children can't inherit because they're adopted. There. You're absolved."

"No, Layna, I'm not. Because that's not what ruling is. It's not being comfortable or making everyone happy. It's doing what's best. Stavros knows this. He would accept it if I were to leave."

"You said you wouldn't run," she said. Not accusing, just a fact.

"Is it running if you're simply trying to protect your country? Your people."

"What is it you need to do to feel like a better man?"

"I guess it's too late for me to join the church."

She blinked. "A bit. If you still plan on marrying me."

If he left, he would have no reason to marry her. Which drove home the point that he had to stay. Whatever happened. She was too important to him, and he didn't want to stop and examine why.

But she was changing him. Just being near her was changing him, and he needed that. Needed to be with her. Otherwise, what was there? Nothing more than that endless haze of neon lights and booze. And the idea of going back there now felt like the equivalent of walking into hell of his own free will.

He held her tighter. "And I am planning on it," he said. "You have my ring and my word."

"I've had both before."

"The man I was," he said. "Not the man I am now. And I'm vowing to change."

"So you'll stay."

"Yes. And does it matter to you so much that I do?"

She frowned. "I want you to have a place in the world, Xander. Everyone should. I don't want you to go back to the life that you were living. I don't want you separated from your family."

"And you tell me, since I imagine you know more about this than either of us, where is truth in all of this?"

"I don't know, Xander. Maybe there is no place for it."

"Seems like that might be heresy."

"Maybe. But isn't all of this? Life dealt us both an impossible hand. We either fold or we cheat. I'm becoming convinced of that."

"A gambling metaphor. You know me so well."

"Well, you were asking about the church, I thought I'd bring in the casino."

"Since we're aiming for heresy?"

She sat up, the blankets clutched to her chest. "Not exactly aiming for it." She pushed her hair off of her face.

She didn't seem so self-conscious of her scars around him anymore, and he found he quite liked that.

Especially since he didn't see them the same way he had at first. When he'd first seen them they'd looked like they weren't real. Like they were a mask over the face he remembered. Now it wasn't that way. He saw them as a part of her face. They didn't bear extra notice, not more than those mesmerizing eyes, or the shape of her nose. The stubborn set of her chin.

They weren't an intruder on his eyes or on her beauty. They were a part of who she was, what she'd been through.

Sometimes looking at them hurt, because it was a reminder of how much she'd been hurt. It was a reminder of her pain. But also a reminder of her strength.

"You're staring," she said, her eyes narrowing.

"Because I like to look at you." He let his eyes drift down lower. "But I do wish you'd drop the sheet. I could compose poetry about your breasts. And I don't even like poetry."

She surprised him by letting the sheet fall to her waist, her full, rose-tipped breasts on display for him.

He smiled. "Damn. I'm glad to be a man."

"That's the best you have, Drakos?"

"Shall I compare your nipples to a summer's day?"

"Okay, you can stop now."

"I don't think I can. Not ever."

She let out a long breath. "Xander, I don't know what I'm going to do with you."

Stay with me.

It was the first thought in his mind. It was the thing he wanted above all else.

"Reform me," he said, his throat tight.

"Sometimes," she said, looking away from him, "I'm not really sure I want you reformed."

He pulled her close and kissed her for that. And then more. Until everything faded away. And when they were done, Xander wasn't alone anymore. He was with Layna. And he felt it all the way through.

And he had never felt more alive. He had never felt more.

"Actually, Xander," she said, her voice a whisper, "I think you're already the best man I've ever known. You make me…you know you make me feel like I just might be…beautiful."

Light burst through him, bringing pain along with it. Like the sun hitting his face after a night of hard drinking. Only this didn't feel like stale regret. It was hope. It was something bigger, better than he'd ever known before. He didn't want to hide. He wanted to push off all the layers of rock and dirt, everything he used to hide himself, his secrets, from the world, to protect himself from the painful truths in his life, and emerge the man he was supposed to be.

But he could never do it, so long as everything was covered. He could never be free until he cut the ropes that bound him in the darkness.

With Layna by his side, the idea of it didn't seem so impossible.

"I have to tell him."

Layna looked up from her lunch and at Xander, a strange sense of dread filling her chest. "You what?"

"I have to tell him."

And she didn't ask who or what, because she knew. Somehow she knew what he was thinking without him saying it.

"But why, Xander?"

"Because he's my father. Or, he thinks he is, and for all

intents and purposes and everything that matters to me, he is. And moreover he's the king, and he has the right to choose who his successor is. With all of the information given to him."

"Xander, don't do this. He won't have a choice—"

"There is always a choice, Layna, and this is the thing I've been hiding from. It was horrible to lose my mother, but I couldn't fight against my father's anger, I couldn't stay because I was far too afraid that the truth would come out and then things would be…then they could never be fixed. I have to tell him everything, all of it. So that I can have forgiveness. So that I can have my life. So I can be free."

"But, Xander," she said, a desperate fear clawing at her now and she didn't know why. Didn't know why this was so terrifying. Only that it was making her feel like she was clinging to the ledge of a cliff, her hold slipping with each passing moment. "If you do this, he might send you away. He might…you might never be king. You won't even be a prince. You'll be the royal bastard."

"I'm the royal bastard whether anyone knows it or not," he said, his voice quiet. "And I can't keep hiding behind a lie. Because that's the key, I think. To reforming. To… to changing and being a man who's actually worth something. I have to stop hiding. And that doesn't mean leaving Monaco and returning to Kyonos, clearly I've done that already."

"It means taking less than you deserve because you've had a sudden attack of conscience," she said, shocked at the words coming out of her own mouth. Shocked at the vehemence behind them. She didn't know why she cared so much. Why it felt so vital and frightening.

"I can't argue with you about this."

"Why not?"

"Because I can't change my mind."

"You're just running," she said, anger and fear swirling in her and making her panicky. "You're running again."

"No, Layna. I've finally stopped."

Xander got up from his seat at the table and walked out of the room.

His father was awake this time when he went to see him.

"Xander?"

"I suppose you didn't hear that I was back," Xander said, standing in the doorway.

His father lifted a hand. Strange to see King Stephanos like this. So diminished and pale. But he was awake. Perhaps he would recover. Then, at least, the need for Xander, or Stavros to rule wouldn't be so pressing.

Then, at least, he might have some time left with this man. Time he'd wasted in fear.

"Are you back?" his father asked, adjusting his position in the hospital bed, fiddling with the lines from his IV.

"Yes. I am. But…and I know that this is a bad time to drop bombshells on you…."

"Xander, from where I'm sitting, there may be no time. I'm only glad you're here."

"You seem better," Xander said.

He nodded. "Better. I can speak again. Though it took a while. It was a bad stroke."

"I know."

"So say what you need to," he said, "and then I'll tell you what I need to say."

Xander took a breath. "It's about me. And mother."

King Stephanos closed his eyes and nodded. "Yes, we need to talk about that."

"Not the things you might think. There was a reason

for the crash. And that is that we were fighting, and I was reckless."

"Xander…"

"No, I need to finish. It was my fault, but I could never truly explain it to you. Not when the circumstances…not when I felt I couldn't tell you the truth of the matter. It seems cruel to tell you now, and if it weren't for the way things work in our family, if it weren't for the importance of royal blood, I wouldn't. I found out that day that I am not your son. She was certain of it."

King Stephanos nodded slowly. "I had suspected, of course. You were born quite early and yet quite healthy."

"You suspected?"

"Yes. But I was hardly going to accuse my new bride of faithless behavior. In truth, Xander, ours was a marriage of convenience. In the beginning. I do think we grew to love each other very much."

Xander nodded. "She did love you."

"There is no reason to condemn her for a sin that's thirty-seven years old."

"I'm afraid I didn't feel that way at the time."

"Of course you didn't. How could you?"

"You understand now why I had to leave," Xander said.

"You had to leave because of me," the king said, his voice heavy with regret. "I was hurting and I said things to you… I was not a loving father."

"But you aren't my father at all," Xander said.

King Stephanos frowned. "Xander, no matter what, you are my son. No matter the revelations, or the years that have gone by, or angry words that passed between us, you are my son."

Layna hung up the phone, her hands shaking. She had no idea how the reporter had gotten her line here at the palace. No idea why he'd felt the need to call and tell her they were doing a story, why he'd needed to recite the ugly things being written about her.

That they had photos of her, standing on the balcony off of Xander's room in a thin nightgown, her hair pulled back revealing the worst of her scars, no makeup on her face. And that they were publishing the photos.

Does he make love to you in the dark?

That was when she'd hung up. Her fingers had felt numb.

She hated this. Hated the way they were exploiting her. The way it made her feel. At first, she'd helped Xander's reputation, but was she helping him now?

He said he needed her, but when his rule was taken over by gossip about her looks, about their marriage, how would he feel then?

She sat down in her office chair and tried to catch her breath, failing as it dissolved into a sob.

What would happen when he didn't need her anymore? When he knew he didn't? When he could have any woman, why would he want her?

And he'd gone to confess all to his father. If that lost him his spot on the throne…he would never keep her with him. Never.

Despair washed over his as every word, every insult from the media, from now and fifteen years ago, played back through her mind.

Xander might not leave her now, but one day…

She'd survived losing him once. She couldn't do it again.

Xander walked into the palace with a strange, buoyant feeling in his chest. He felt lighter. He felt like he could breathe for the first time in fifteen years. And more than that, this felt like a place he could live. A position he could have.

Because his father, the man who would always claim him as his son, had said that Xander was the man he wanted on the throne.

The truth truly did set you free. Interesting. He wondered if Layna would be amused by his epiphany.

Layna. He needed to see Layna.

He needed to have Layna. With none of his walls between them.

He prowled through the halls and opened her bedroom door. She wasn't in the suite of rooms that were set aside for her. He walked out and continued on, toward the place she was using as her office.

He found her there, sitting behind a desk, staring off into space. She started when the door hit the wall.

And as soon as he saw her, every thought left his head completely. He'd forgotten why he was there. Where he'd just been. He forgot everything.

He could only stare at her, at her eyes, her high cheekbones. The extra fold by her mouth where her scar tissue was thick, a fold that deepened when she tightened her lips, like she was doing now. At her asymmetrical brows and her neat, feminine hands.

At Layna. All the pieces of her that combined to make the woman that had changed him on every level. That had changed him in a fundamental way he could neither name nor deny.

And he needed her. Needed to be close to her, inside of her, right now. Needed to affirm what he was feeling. To have her brand his body with her touch the way that she had branded his soul.

To brand her body, so that she would feel it, too.

"Layna…" His words evaporated on his tongue. He didn't know what to say. Or how to say it. He knew how to flirt, knew how to throw practiced lines at women and get them into bed for the night. But he'd never learned how to keep a woman with him for two nights, much less forever.

But he had to try. He had to try.

Because he'd gotten everything today—acceptance, forgiveness. And still things didn't feel finished.

"Layna," he began again, "you have been missing from my life every day since I walked away."

"Xander, what are you talking about?"

He went over to the desk and rounded to her side, hauled her up into his arms and kissed her. Then he kissed her cheeks, the damaged corner of her mouth, the winkled line of skin that ran along the bridge of her nose.

He pressed his forehead against hers. "I've been wandering in the desert for fifteen years. I have had no home. No one to call a friend. And I was okay with that because I didn't want anyone to get near me. I came back here, it was supposed to be the promised land, so to speak, and I didn't feel anything. I didn't feel home. Until I saw you."

"Xander, please…don't do that, I don't need it."

"I need to tell you."

"How did your meeting with your father go?"

"That isn't what I need to talk about."

"It's what I need to hear about," she said.

Layna tried to calm the wild beating of her heart, tried to do something to quell the panic that was racing through her. She didn't know what to do with this. With his words, his ferocity and sincerity, with such strength that it burrowed beneath her defenses and started pulling them down. Left her feeling raw and exposed. Reminded her of how it had been to lose it all, all of her control, all of her beauty, in front of hundreds of people.

To care so much and have it all torn away…

Zombie Princess. Does he make love to you in the dark?

She closed her eyes and kissed him. She didn't want

to hear him speak anymore. She couldn't hear more, not now. She could do this. They could kiss. They could make love. They could get married and live together and have children, and rule Kyonos.

So long as she could keep pieces of herself hidden, so that if the world ever fell down around her again, she wouldn't be left with nothing.

But she had to keep him from saying things like that. He could touch her skin, but she couldn't let him keep on touching her heart.

She couldn't risk it.

"Layna," he growled, kissing her deeper, longer.

It was working. He was focusing on her body now, his hands roaming over her curves. This was what she needed. This overwhelming tide of physical sensation that only he could make her feel.

Because it blocked out the other feelings. The ones that surrounded her heart and pushed at the walls. The ones that she'd made to protect herself.

When he'd said he was going to talk to his father her world had ended for a moment. When he'd made it clear he was willing to take a step that might end what they were building here, and it had made her feel like the earth had simply run out, and she was standing on the edge of a cliff waiting to fall, she'd known she had to shore up her defenses.

And now he was here, and he was saying things. Romantic things. Things that had nothing to do with sex or convenience or honor, and she couldn't do it. She couldn't handle it.

This she could do. This was all they needed. He just had to remember that. She would make him remember. That this was good. That it was enough.

"Take me," she begged against his lips. "Hard. Now."

But he didn't obey. He kept kissing her, his lips so tender and sweet it made her ache. She didn't want to ache. She didn't want to care.

She didn't want to love or be loved. She didn't want to care about anything. About whether or not they called her the Zombie Princess, or if Xander thought she was beautiful. If Xander stayed with her forever or only for a few months.

She didn't want to care about any of it.

It was too frightening. It asked too much.

"Stop it," she said, pushing against his chest, pushing him against the back wall. "Stop being gentle. Kiss me like you mean it." Like there was nothing else. Like the press didn't exist. Hard enough that he could made her forget, long enough that she wouldn't be able to breathe. That she might drown in it. In this.

She kissed him again, and she felt his fingers lace through her hair, and he tugged hard, drawing her head back. Yes. This was what she wanted.

"I have to look at you for a moment," he said. "You're lovely." He traced her ruined lips with his thumb, holding her still with his other hand, forked deep in her hair.

She shook her head. "I don't need you to lie."

"It's not a lie. Any man that misses your beauty is a fool."

"He's a man who has eyes, Xander." The whole world had eyes. And they didn't like what they saw.

He kissed her hard, a punishment for her talking back. The kind of kiss she wanted. The kind she reveled in. "You should know this, Layna," he said, his voice rough. "Beauty, the kind on your skin, is terribly vain."

"Inner beauty, Xander? Is that what we're talking about?"

"No. For the love of God, woman, do you honestly believe that a rough patch of skin takes away who you are? Takes away your allure? Your beauty? Your lips…your hair and eyes. *Agape*, they are worthy of any man's praise."

She could feel the cracks in her defenses widening. Could feel herself, her resolve, weakening.

"But I don't need praise," she said. "I need you, here and now."

"Sex is all you want?" he asked, a strange note to his voice.

"Sex and a partnership. Anything else is gratuitous."

He tugged her hair harder, kissed her throat. "I can show you gratuitous if you really want."

"Yes," she said.

He leaned down and picked her up, carrying her over to the desk, which was quite clean—and she had the vague thought that it was a good thing it was—and set her down on top of it, stripping himself of his clothes as quickly as possible. "Take them off," he said to her. "All of them."

And she obeyed. From her position on the desk she stripped off her top, pants, underwear and shoes, and stayed perched on the edge while he positioned himself between her thighs. He braced his hands on her hips and slid slowly, making her aware of every inch of him as he entered her.

He lifted one hand and gripped her chin. "Look at me," he demanded.

"No." She didn't know exactly why, but she couldn't.

"Look at me, Layna," he said, thrusting hard into her.

"Xander, please…"

Her eyes flew to his, shock preventing her from doing anything else. From thinking it through. And the minute she saw him, really saw him, her heart started to feel too big for its cage. She looked down again, squeezing her eyes closed.

"Don't shut me out," he said.

"Xander…"

"I love you."

"No," she said, shaking her head, closing her eyes tighter, a tear tracking down her cheek.

"Layna, I love you." He kept moving inside of her, his thrusts matching the terrified rhythm of her heart, as he drove her to the brink with his body while his words delivered fatal damage to the walls surrounding her heart.

"No. Don't love me. Don't ask me to love you."

He cupped her face and kissed her lips, moving hard and deep within her, his mouth covering hers, swallowing her denial, and the cry of pleasure that followed it as her orgasm crashed over her in a perfect storm of agony and ecstasy.

Just like everything with Xander.

Perfect pleasure. Perfect pain. Perfect misery mingled with joy.

When she came back to herself, his arms were around her, and he was holding her tight against his chest. She realized she was shaking. Sobbing.

Because of him. She pushed away from him.

"Xander, I can't…"

"You don't love me?"

"Why do you think you love me?" she asked, even though she didn't want to know the answer. Didn't want to hear any more. "No. Don't answer that. I can't…I can't breathe, Xander. I can't." She started hunting for her clothes, tugging them on as quickly as possible.

"Why not?"

"I thought I could…" She was gasping now, panicking. "I thought I could do this. But do you know why I cling to my contentment? Because at least if I don't…if I don't love anything, if I'm never excited, or overjoyed, I can't go back to the low place again. If I don't care about my looks then I can't be destroyed when people call me names. If I don't love you I can't fall apart when you leave. I can't fall into depression, and that…fog, Xander, that horrible fog. I won't do it again."

"I'm not going to leave you, Layna," he said, walking forward, gripping her arms. "Ever. I made a promise. And I will keep it."

"You didn't mean it, though. You still went to your father and told him the truth, even though it might mean you would lose this. Lose me…"

"I don't have to be king to have you, but I do need you to be a good man. I need you. You don't understand."

"That's just it! So what happens when you don't need me anymore? And you run."

"You don't trust me at all, do you?"

She wrapped her arms around herself, trying to hold it all, hold herself, together. "I don't trust in anything. Not you…not…"

"God?"

"Don't. You don't know what it's like. Fine if you have a trauma, you just get to run and run. But the rest of us are left with nothing. I couldn't run from my pain, Xander it was in me. And you don't know what that is!"

"Oh, I don't?" he growled. "Because throwing my life away on drugs and drinking and sex wasn't a horrible existence? It was, Layna. It was. It was every bit as dark, and every bit as rock-bottom."

"I don't suppose you ever thought about killing yourself. Because I did. I thought about it a lot."

"I never thought about it," he said. "I just assumed that running toward death at full speed like I was would eventually amount to it. One day you drink too hard, you take too much of the wrong thing, and you don't wake up again.

I was sort of hoping for that day, just too much of a coward to pursue it with any kind of real dedication. Or maybe it was the ties here. But for whatever reason, I didn't. Still, I know that place you're talking about. I know that kind of darkness. But I walked up out of it for real today and I want you to do it, too."

She shook her head. "I can't. I can't do it again, Xander. And I'm sure you think that I'm weak. And maybe I am. But I used up all my strength already and I can't possibly put myself at risk like this again. I can't just…put myself out there. All of me, and risk being pushed down into the darkness again."

Xander looked down at the desk. The desk where they had just made love. He was still naked. And he didn't seem all that concerned about it.

"My father told me that I was his son. No matter what the paternity test might say." He looked up at her. "He's my father no matter what."

"I'm happy for you. I'm happy for…you don't have to have a wife now, do you? Not one like me. You're accepted and your people love you. And I'm the Zombie Princess. You don't need me, Xander."

He hauled her against his chest, holding her to him. "I *do* need you, Layna."

"No, Xander, you don't. And more than that? I'm starting to hurt things for you. At first…at first maybe people loved you for sticking with me, but now I'm just a burden. An embarrassment. It's going to be…I'll be ridiculed by the world. Kyonos will be."

"Whether the people approve of you, or me, or not. I need you because you are the only woman for me. Because I love you beyond words. Because you have reached down deep inside me and shined a light on the real me. Made me look at myself and see who I am, and who I want to be. Because back when I was a selfish, entitled, wreck of a man, you were the only woman for me, and no matter what life has thrown at me in the meantime, at the end of it all, you're still the only woman for me."

"I can't be the woman for you." She pulled out of his hold, and he let her go. "I can't live like this. With…with the press closing in around me all the time. They took pictures of me, Xander. And a reporter called and…"

"What?"

"He asked if you made love to me in the dark."

"Layna…"

"So even if the people love me. Even if they love you being with me. Even if I don't end up embarrassing the nation I can't…I can't do this to myself. They'll never leave me alone. They'll harass me. Forever. For all of my life and I can't…do it."

"And you don't love me?" he asked, his tone flat.

She shook her head, the walls around her heart strengthening, folding in around it like a concrete blockade. "No."

"I see."

"I'm going to go."

"To your room."

"No. Away from here. Just…away from you."

"You're running?" he asked, his tone even, deadly. "I thought we agreed we weren't going to do that anymore. I thought we promised."

"No, Xander," she said, her voice a whisper. "You promised. I didn't. I don't want any of this. I don't want to be in the public eye, I don't want to be under scrutiny like this. I don't want your love."

"But you have it. I want you to want it all, Layna, I want you to have it all."

"How dare you?" she screamed, angry now, cracking apart inside. "How dare you take my safety away from me!

How dare you pull me from my home, from my quiet life and bring me here! You said we would be partners, you didn't say you would demand my soul."

"Nothing less, *agape*. Because you have mine."

"Well, you don't have mine. And I'm going. Goodbye, Xander. I wish you the best of luck in ruling, and in finding your future queen. She won't be me."

"What can I do?" he asked, a desperate thread in his voice that seemed tied to her heart, squeezing her tight, making it impossible to breathe.

"Show me the future. Show me nothing will happen. Show me that if I choose to want again, to feel again, to need again, that I won't have it all ripped from me. Prove to me you won't leave, you won't cheat. Prove to me that things will be well. Show me. Show me that when you don't need me anymore, when your reputation isn't helped by me, you won't want someone else. You won't regret me."

He ran his hand down his face, looking so impossibly tired, so defeated. "You of little faith," he said, laughing bitterly.

"I don't know how you can say that to me."

"I don't know how you can claim to be anything different. You spend fifteen years in a convent, pretending to be a woman of faith when you don't have enough to feel an emotion that transcends anything more than basic contentment. You're afraid to take a deep breath, Layna Xenakos, afraid to make a ripple for fear God might notice you and strike at you again. Afraid to live."

"I'm not. That's not it...."

"The hell it's not. At least I can do this. At least I can put the past behind me and walk forward. You don't want to go back to that hell you were living in, but you keep one foot in it to remind yourself. You keep yourself afraid. You keep yourself from ever feeling happiness. From ever feeling love. What's the point of protecting yourself if all you're protecting is a life half-lived?"

"Tell me why I should trust you," she spat, "when all your history proves that when things get hard, you'll leave. You haven't earned my faith, so don't stand there and talk about how I don't have it."

He jerked back like he'd been slapped. But he was only stunned for a moment. "I haven't earned your faith?" he asked. "All that I have given you, all that I have promised you, my body, my soul, and I have not earned your faith? Think of what I promised you before I ran the last time. Nothing. Engagements end, which happened with ours. I had not made vows to you, I had not promised undying love. I hadn't even promised you undying lust. I promise it all to you now and then some. I give you my word, my vow, that I will never leave you, no matter what comes. I give you everything I am. I'm laying it at your feet here, Layna. But now you tell me I have not earned your faith."

She looked at him, at his eyes, blazing with anger and hurt, burning inside her so that she had no choice but to look away. Because what she'd said was worthy of anger. Insults he didn't deserve.

She took her ring off. Shaking, she put it in his hand, forcing his fingers to close around it. "This is the second time I've returned a ring to your family. Maybe…maybe don't offer me one again."

"Is that really what you want?" he asked, his voice strained.

She nodded, trying to keep the tears from falling. "Yes. It is."

She walked out of the office and ignored Xander shouting her name. Ignored the sound of his footsteps behind her as she ran to her room. She looked around, at all the pretty things. And decided she didn't need any of it.

She wouldn't stop running again until she'd reached safety. Until she could feel safely hidden from the wall of grief that was threatening to overwhelm her.

CHAPTER FOURTEEN

LAYNA RODE UNTIL her thigh muscles burned and her lungs ached. Across the fields and up to the highest point on the hilltop, where she could look over the ocean. The wind was blowing her hair everywhere, her horse shifting his weight beneath her.

The drunken gambler didn't think she had faith, it would make her laugh if she didn't feel like she was cracking apart inside. Stupid man. Stupid, stupid man.

She closed her eyes and inhaled deeply, the salty air burning her throat. Mother Superior hadn't blinked overly much at her return, but this morning she'd called Layna into her office and told that she would have to make a choice now.

Either she would take her vows, or she would find somewhere else to go. The abbess hadn't been unkind, but the simple fact was, Layna's room had been filled and she'd been off living…well, unchastely. That was the truth and she couldn't deny it.

This wasn't a place for her to hide, while she was free to have bouts of going off and doing what she wanted. It wasn't fair. Or right.

Damn Xander. She had no idea who she was anymore. *You of little faith.*

It wasn't fair. He was asking her to have faith in him

but she didn't have a guarantee. She couldn't be sure that she wouldn't lose everything again.

That she wouldn't be left stranded at rock bottom alone.

For we walk by faith, not by sight.

Well, that was just inconvenient. She got off her horse and looked out at the ocean, over the rolling, gray waves. Everything seemed to have been leached of color to accommodate her mood and she appreciated it. At least something was working in her favor.

Suddenly she was hit by a wave of sadness so strong it crippled her. She went down to her knees, the moisture from the grass bleeding through her dress.

He was right. She had no faith. It took no faith to hide. You didn't need faith when you were safe. Didn't need it behind the walls of a convent, where you were protected from the world. When your every need was met daily and you were never challenged, you didn't need faith.

You didn't need faith when you were a novice who'd spent years managing to not take vows. Not taking the leap of faith and committing the trust it took to go wholly into that life, not having the faith to go back into the world and try to live.

She'd condemned herself to a halflife in exchange for safety. It wasn't the press that scared her. It was what he made her feel.

He made her feel so exposed. He didn't accept her excuses. Didn't let her scars keep him at a distance. He wanted it all. Worse, he wanted her to have it all.

And wasn't sure she was brave enough to ever take that risk again.

If ever there was a time Xander wanted to run, it was now. From the searing pain in his chest. From the burning in his eyes, from tears, damn it, and not because he was hung over.

He hadn't had anything to drink since she'd left.

It was like he'd well and truly changed. Fancy that. Change didn't feel all that rewarding when you were sober and you didn't have the woman you loved.

A pain shot through his chest. Yes, he did love her. He wondered now if he always had. If he'd been a shallow boy, in love with a shallow, beautiful girl. Until their world shook apart and he'd gone off licking his wounds.

He'd come back a man changed, to find her a woman changed. And to find that everything that had been there between them from the beginning was still there. That the tragedies of life had reshaped them, so much so that they fit together now even more perfectly than before.

And she was too afraid to see it. Too afraid to reach out and take it. To trust him. To be with him. She was choosing to be unhappy so that she wouldn't be devastated and that killed him.

Unless she just doesn't love you.

Well, that was always a possibility. But still, with him or without him, she was choosing fear over happiness and that ate at him. Because it was what he'd done for so long. Because he was an expert in empty, meaningless things. In pursuits that were vain and useless.

In turning away from everything pure and strong, and hard and wonderful, so that he could simply find some shelter from reality.

He was done with that now, though. He loved her. More than the throne. More than his own life.

So he could sit here and brood soberly, or he could go after her. Make a fool of himself. Again. For her love. And if he couldn't have her love, he would beg her to let go of all that pain and live the life she was meant to live.

Not shut herself away from the world, but shine in it.

Of course, he would beg her to be with him first. She could shine with him. Failing that, he would let her shine alone. But dammit, she would shine. Scars and fears couldn't keep her hidden anymore.

She was beautiful. She deserved everything. And he had to make sure that she knew it.

"Why don't you go for a ride? Or a walk?"

Layna turned toward Mother Maria-Francesca, feeling distinctly ashamed just looking at the other woman. She shouldn't still be here taking up valuable space and sulking. Though, sulking seemed like too weak of a term.

"That's probably a good idea."

"Where will you go?" She detected a hint of concern in her voice. Probably afraid Layna would do something dire since she looked like a specter of death.

But she wouldn't. She couldn't honestly say she wouldn't. "Just up in the hills. To get a view of the ocean. My favorite place."

"Will you take Phineas?"

"No. I need the walk. I need to move slow. I have a lot of thinking to do."

She folded her arms beneath her breasts and walked out of the church building and out into the stormy weather. Wind was blowing in off the waves, rain threatening to fall from swollen gray clouds.

Layna lowered her head and started up the hill, not thinking, just feeling. Just letting her emotions wash through her.

She felt like she was drowning even while she was standing there breathing air. But the strangest thing was, she didn't feel like she was losing herself.

She scrambled to the top of a grass-covered hill and

looked out over the ocean, tears blinding her. She hurt as much as she ever had, her heart smashed to pieces, shards embedded in her chest, but she wasn't fading into the mist.

Maybe it was because Xander's face was too strong in her mind. Maybe it was just because she had something, someone, to care about now.

Maybe it was because she finally knew who she was.

She wasn't a party girl with spoiled looks. Wasn't a princess who would never be crowned. She was Layna Xenakos, whatever her circumstances. Whatever her face. She was strong. She had run through hell and caught on fire along the way, left with scars that were inside and out, but she'd run through.

She had lost her faith, but for one blinding moment, she felt like maybe she'd found it.

Because this was that place again. That rock-bottom moment. But she wasn't alone.

She closed her eyes and tilted her face up to the sky, a raindrop landing on her cheeks. No, she wasn't alone. And she was strong.

A lump rose in her throat, a sob breaking through.

It didn't matter what happened. She could trust herself. She could trust Xander.

Oh, Xander.

She needed to go to him. Because she loved him. Because he was the one she wanted to be with, that was the life she wanted.

She had to get down and beg for his forgiveness if that's what she needed to do. To ask him if he would take her, as she was, so broken and scared, when she'd been so horrible to him.

To tell him she feared nothing. Not pain, or love, or the media, more than she feared a lifetime without him.

She turned and her heart nearly stopped when she saw

a dark head come into view, cresting the top of the hill, followed by a familiar face, and a heartbreakingly familiar body.

"Xander," she whispered.

And she ran to him.

Layna threw her arms around his neck and held him close to her, tears falling, her hands shaking. "What are you doing here?"

"I lied to you," he said, voice rough, his fingers forked through her hair, his face buried in her neck.

"You did?" she asked, pulling her head back so that she could look at him.

"I told you no more running. But I'm running now. To you."

She laughed as tears rolled down her cheeks. "Well, you're in luck because I just stopped running. So it looks like we're finally standing in the same place."

"It's about time," he said, kissing her lips. "It's about time."

"I love you," she said. "I was so scared, Xander. So scared to say it, or hear it, or feel it. But I found my faith. I found it and now I'm not afraid."

"I still can't give you your guarantee. Not as far as anything in life is concerned. But with me you have one. I'll always stand with you. I'll always stay with you. You will be my wife. The mother of my children. You're the only woman for me, Layna. Now and always. There are many uncertain things, but not my love."

"I don't need a guarantee. Not now. Faith is all about walking without sight. I don't need to see ahead, I just need to see you."

"You have no idea how glad I am to hear you say that."

She laughed. "About as glad as I am to say it?"

"I need to tell you this. I need you to understand—"

"I believe you, Xander, you have nothing to prove," she said, cupping his face and kissing him again. "I'm sorry I made you feel that you did. I'm sorry I doubted you. I'm sorry I let fear win. But it won't. Not again."

"But you need to hear this. I have walked down so many dark paths. I've chased pleasure in all its forms, and oblivion. I've tasted hopelessness. There was nothing there. No satisfaction. No answer. But with you, I find I am the man I'm meant to be. I find I'm the man I should have been all this time. You gave me the strength to face my father, to face this. I had to come and find you right away because somehow I knew I couldn't do it without you. I felt it."

She took a deep breath, of the sea and of Xander.

"I feel like we're standing at the beginning again. But better. Because I know so much more. I've been down those paths, too, and I know how dark they can be. So I know now just how important it is to always reach for the light. I know how weak I can be, but I also know how strong I can be."

"Very strong," he said. "You are so very strong."

"I wouldn't go back," she said, another tear spilling down her face. "I wouldn't take it back now. Because this is who I need to be. This is when we need to be. Not fifteen years ago when we would have made each other more vain and selfish, with equally vain and selfish children. But now."

"Now that I'm a broken-down playboy and you're a scarred novice? You are still only a novice, right? You didn't take vows, did you?"

"Nothing half so drastic, don't worry. But, yes, the scarred novice and the broken-down playboy with no pedigree. That's exactly who we needed to be."

"It was always going to be us in the end, wasn't it?" he asked.

She nodded. "I think so. How else would we survive all of this if we couldn't hold on to each other?"

"We wouldn't," he said. That simple. That certain.

"I'm just glad we got to become better versions of ourselves before it happened."

"I'm just glad that we're finally together."

"So am I."

"And we're together because of how much I love you, because of how much you love me. Not for Kyonos. Not for appearances. Not for any other reason."

He picked her up, and spun her in a circle, rain falling in earnest now, soaking them both. She flung her hands wide and let it fall on her, let it wash away the years. The regret. The pain. So all that remained was love.

"You know," she said, "I always felt the most free when I was riding my horse. But now I just feel that way. I just feel free."

"We both are, Layna. We both are."

EPILOGUE

Fifteen years later...

"He's going to outlive us all." Xander sat down on the edge of the bed and looked at his wife. He was exhausted from the ball, a sort of "coming out" affair for Jessica and Stavros's oldest daughter. His own daughters had been so excited about it they'd been driving him mad for weeks.

Now they were feverishly planning their own, even though it was some years off. Mak and Eva's oldest son had reacted to the entire thing with the same sullenness of his father, and nothing his squealing cousins had done to entice excitement from him had worked. The same had been true for Xander and Layna's son, who had copied his cousin's practiced disdain. They had succeeded very well in annoying the girls, which Xander privately assumed was their goal.

He sighed. How he'd become the father of two teenage girls and a sullen preteen boy he didn't know.

"Entirely possible," Layna said. She was standing by the vanity, all long elegant lines. He was always fascinated by the way she removed her jewelry. The way her fingers moved, the way she stood.

But then, everything Layna did fascinated him. Now and always.

"Can you believe the way he moves around the palace

in that motorized cart of his? It's…well, it's the funniest thing I've ever seen."

King Stephanos had firmly denied both death and doctors and was a very crotchety old man. Xander was the acting ruler at this point, his father not able to perform most of the functions required by the position, but that didn't mean he wasn't still acting the figurehead. With gusto.

"It's that Drakos spirit," she said. "You're all too stubborn to be defeated."

He smiled. "True enough." Ever since that day he'd reconciled with his father he'd felt like a Drakos, unquestionably. "I still hate wearing ties to these things," he said, tugging the black scrap of silk off and letting it fall to the floor.

Layna smiled and walked over to him, planting her hands on the bed on either side of him, leaning down for a kiss. "The torture you're subjected to," she said, smiling that special smile of hers.

He kissed the crease by the corner of her mouth. "I know it."

"So tell me, Xander Drakos, heir to the throne, have you ever regretted coming back?"

"Not once. I would wear a tie every day of my life so long as I spent those days with you."

"Now that was the right answer."

"I'm getting pretty good at this husband thing."

"You've been good at it for a while," she said.

She kissed him again, deeper, more passionately. And then he was lost. As he always was with her. Years hadn't diminished their need for each other, their love.

Much, much later, Xander held his wife against his chest, threading his fingers through her hair, stroking her scar-roughened cheek.

"Layna Drakos, you make me very glad that I stopped running."

* * * * *

'You win, Alessandro.'

Chase looked at him with green eyes that had once mesmerised him right out of the rigidly controlled box into which he had always been accustomed to piling his emotional entanglements with the opposite sex.

'But maybe you could tell me whether you would have been as hard-line if I hadn't been the person sitting here trying to talk you out of buying the shelter.'

'Oh, the sale most certainly would have gone ahead...' Alessandro drawled, without an ounce of sympathy. 'But I probably wouldn't have tacked on a ticking clock.'

Chase glared at him. 'I never took you for a bully.'

'I'll admit that I have no intention of pulling out of this purchase, but you could recoup the lost thousands...'

'Could I? How?' She stared at him. She knew that the finances for the shelter were in serious disarray. They would need all the money they could get just to pay off the debts and wipe the slate clean.

'We have an unfinished past...' Alessandro murmured. 'It's time to finish it. I want to know who the hell you really are. Satisfy my curiosity and the full price is back on the table...'

Cathy Williams is originally from Trinidad, but has lived in England for a number of years. She currently has a house in Warwickshire, which she shares with her husband, Richard, her three daughters, Charlotte, Olivia and Emma, and their pet cat, Salem. She adores writing romantic fiction, and would love one of her girls to become a writer—although at the moment she is happy enough if they do their homework and agree not to bicker with one another!

Recent titles by the same author:

HIS TEMPORARY MISTRESS
A DEAL WITH DI CAPUA
THE SECRET CASELLA BABY
THE NOTORIOUS GABRIEL DIAZ

**Did you know these are also available as eBooks?
Visit www.millsandboon.co.uk**

ENTHRALLED BY MORETTI

BY

CATHY WILLIAMS

Published in Great Britain 2014
by Mills & Boon, an imprint of Harlequin (UK) Limited,
Eton House, 18-24 Paradise Road, Richmond, Surrey, TW9 1SR

© 2014 Cathy Williams

ISBN: 978 0 263 91217 3

Printed and bound in Spain
by Blackprint CPI, Barcelona

ENTHRALLED
BY MORETTI

To my three wonderful daughters.

CHAPTER ONE

CHASE EVANS PUSHED aside the folder in front of her and glanced at her watch. For the fourth time. She had now been kept waiting in this conference room for twenty-five minutes. As a lawyer, she knew what this was about. Actually, even if she hadn't been a lawyer she would have known what this was about. It was about intimidation. Intimidation by a juggernaut of a company that was determined to get its own way.

She stood up, flexed her muscles and strolled over to the floor-to-ceiling panes of glass that overlooked the teeming streets of the city.

At this time of year, London was swarming with tourists. From way up here, they appeared to be small little stick figures, but she knew if she went down she would join foreigners from every corner of the globe. You couldn't escape them. You couldn't escape the noise, the crowds and the bustle although here, in the opulent surroundings of AM Holdings, you could be forgiven for thinking that you were a million miles away from all that. It was deathly quiet.

Yet another intimidation tactic, she thought cynically. She had seen a lot in the past few years since she had been a practising lawyer, but the antics of this company took some beating.

She thought back to meeting number one, when they

had imagined that buying up the women's shelter would be a walk in the park. For meeting number one, they had sent their junior lawyer, Tom Barry, who had become embroiled in a tangle of logistics with which he had patently been unable to cope.

For meeting number two, they had dispatched a couple of more experienced guys. Alex Cole and Bruce Robins had come prepared, but so had she. Out of all the pro bono cases in which she specialised, the women's shelter was dearest to her heart. If they had come prepared to wipe it out from under her feet, then she too had upped the stakes, pulling out obscure precursors and covenants that had sent them away scratching their heads and promising that they would be back.

Chase had had no doubt that they would. The shelter, or Beth's House, as it was nicknamed, sat on prime land in West London, land that could earn any halfway canny speculator a great deal of money should it be developed. She knew, through contacts and back doors, that it had been targeted for development by the AM group. An ambitious transformation—from a women's shelter to an exclusive, designer shopping mall for the rich and famous.

Well, over her dead body.

Staring down as the minutes of the clock ticked past and no one appeared, she knew that there was a very real possibility that she would have to let this one go, admit defeat. Yet for so many reasons she refused to let herself think that way.

After Alex and Bruce, her next meeting—this time with her boss by her side—had been with their top guy, Leslie Swift. He had cleverly countered every single magic act they had produced from their rapidly shrinking hat. He had produced by-laws, exemptions and clauses that she knew had been designed to have them running back to the drawing board. Now, alone in this sprawling conference room, Chase knew that she was in the last-chance saloon.

Once again she glanced at her watch before moving back to her seat at the thirty-seater table. Lord only knew who they would send this time to take her on. Maybe they would realise that she was mortally wounded and see fit to delegate her right back to the junior lawyer so that he could gloat at the woman who had sent him packing.

But she had one more trick up her sleeve. She wasn't going to give up without a fight. The memory of giving up without fighting was too embedded in her consciousness for her ever to go down that road again. She had dragged herself away from a dark place where any kind of fighting had never been a good idea and she wasn't about to relinquish any of the grit and determination that had got her where she was now.

Banishing all thoughts of a past that would cripple her if she gave it a chance, Chase Evans returned her attention to the file in front of her and the list of names and numbers she had jotted down as her final attempt to win her case.

'Shall I tell Ms Evans how long she might be expected to wait?'

Alessandro Moretti glanced up at his secretary, who stared back at him with gimlet-eyed steeliness. She had announced Chase Evans's arrival half an hour ago, longer, and had already reminded him once that the woman was waiting for him in the conference room. From anyone else, a second reminder would have been unthinkable. Alicia Brown, however, had been with him for five years and it had been clear from the start that tiptoeing around him wasn't going to be on the cards. She was old enough to be his mother and, if she had never tiptoed around any of her five strapping boys, then she certainly wasn't going to tiptoe around anyone. Alessandro Moretti included. He had hired her on the spot.

'You can't keep her waiting for ever. It's rude.'

'But then,' Alessandro countered drily, 'you've been with me long enough to know that I'm rude.' But he stood up and grabbed his jacket from where he had earlier flung it on the long, low, black leather sofa that occupied one side of the office.

In the concrete jungle where fortunes were made and lost on the toss of a coin, and where the clever man knew how to watch his back because the knives were never far away, Alessandro Moretti, at the tender age of thirty-four, ranked as one of the elite pack leaders.

Well, you didn't get to that exalted position by being soft and tender-hearted. Alessandro understood that. He was feared and respected by his employees. He treated them fairly; more than fairly. Indeed they were amongst the highest paid across the board in the city. In return, the line they trod was the line he marked. If he wanted something done, he expected it to be done yesterday. He snapped his fingers and they jumped to immediate attention.

So he was frankly a little put out that his team of lawyers had, so far, singularly failed in nailing the deal with the shelter. He couldn't imagine that it was anything but routine. He had the money to buy them out and so he would. Why then, four months down the line, was he having to step in and do their job for them?

He had elaborate plans to redevelop the extensive land the place was sitting on. His price was more than fair. Any fool should have been able to go in, negotiate and come out with the papers signed, sealed and delivered.

Instead, in a day which was comprised of back-to-back meetings, he was having to waste time with a two-bit pro bono lawyer who had set up camp on the moral high ground somewhere and was refusing to budge. Did he really need to take valuable time out to demolish her? Because demolish her he most certainly would.

He issued a string of orders as he left his office and threw over his shoulder, as he was about to shut the door behind him, 'And don't forget how good I am at sacking people! So I'd better not find that you've forgotten any of what I've just told you! Because I don't see your trusty notepad anywhere…' He grinned and shut the door smartly behind him before his secretary could tell him what she thought of his parting shot.

He was carrying nothing, because as far as he was concerned he didn't need to. He had been briefed on the woman's arguments. He didn't anticipate needing to strong-arm her at all into giving up. He had managed to unearth a couple of covenants barely visible to the naked eye that would subvert any argument she could put forward. Additionally, she had now been waiting for over forty minutes in a conference room that had been deliberately stripped bare of anything that could be seen as homely, comforting, soothing or in any way, shape or form, designed to put someone at ease.

He briefly contemplated summoning those losers who had not been able to do their job so that they could witness first hand how to do it, but decided against it.

One on one. Over and done with in fifteen minutes. Just in time for his next conference call from Hong Kong.

Having had plenty of time to mull over the intimidation tactics, Chase was standing by the window waiting for a team of lawyers. In bare feet, she was five-eleven. In heels, as she was now, she would tower over her opponents. The last one had barely reached her shoulders. Maybe, as a last resort, she could stare them down into submission.

She was gazing out of the window when she heard the

door to the conference room opening behind her and she took her time turning round.

If they could keep her waiting in a room that had all the personality of a prison cell, then she could take her time jumping to attention.

But it wasn't a team of lawyers. It wasn't Tom Barry, Alex Cole, Bruce Robins or Leslie Swift.

She looked at the man standing by the door and she felt the colour drain from her face. She found that she couldn't move from her position of dubious advantage standing by the window. Her legs had turned to lead. Her heart was beating so violently that she felt on the verge of a panic attack. Or, at the very least, an undignified fainting spell.

'You!' This wasn't the strong, steady voice of the self-confident twenty-eight-year-old woman she had finally become.

'Well, well, well...' Alessandro was as shocked as she was but was much more adept at concealing his response and much faster at recovering.

And yet, as he moved slowly towards her, he was finding it almost impossible to believe his eyes.

At the speed of light, he travelled back in time, back to eight years ago, back to the leggy, gloriously beautiful girl who had occupied his every waking hour. She had changed, and yet she hadn't. Gone was the waist-long hair, the jeans and sweater. In its place, the woman standing in front of him, looking as though she had seen a ghost—which he supposed she had—was impeccably groomed. Her shoulder-length bob was the same blend of rich caramel and chestnut, her slanting eyes were as green and feline as he remembered, her body as long and willowy.

'Lyla Evans...' He strolled towards her, one hand in his trouser pocket. 'Should I have clocked the surname? Maybe I would have if it hadn't been preceded by Chase...' He was standing right in front of her now. She looked as though she was about to pass out. He hoped she wouldn't expect him to catch her if she fell.

'Alessandro… No one said… I wasn't expecting…'

'So I see.' His smile was cold and devoid of humour. Of their own accord, his eyes travelled to her finger. No wedding ring. Not that that said very much, all things considered.

'Will you be here on your own, or can I expect the rest of your team…?' Chase tried desperately to regain some of her shattered composure but she couldn't. She was driven to stare at the harsh, sinfully sexy contours of a face that had crept into her head far too many times to count. He was as beautiful as she remembered. More so, if that were possible. At twenty-six, he had been sexy as hell but still with the imprint of youth. Now he was a man, and there was nothing warm or open in his face. She was staring at a stranger, someone who hated her and who was making no attempt to mask his hatred.

'Just me. Cosy, as it turns out. Don't you think? So many years since last we saw one another, Lyla…or Chase, or whoever the hell you really are.'

'Chase. My name is Chase. It always was.'

'So the pseudonym was purely for my benefit. Of course, it makes sense, given the circumstances at the time…'

'Lyla was my mother's name. If you don't mind, I think I'll sit.' She tottered over to the chair and collapsed on it. The stack of files in front of her, her briefcase, her laptop, they were all reminders of why she was in this conference room in the first place, but for the life of her she couldn't focus on them. Her thoughts were all over the place.

'So, shall we play a little catch-up, Lyla? Sorry…Chase? A little polite conversation about what we've been doing for the past eight years?' Alessandro perched on the edge of the sprawling conference table and stared down at her:

the one and only woman he had wasted time chasing, only to be left frustrated when she'd failed to fall into his bed. For that reason alone, she occupied a unique spot in his life. Add all the other reasons and she was in a league of her own.

'I'd rather not.'

'I bet. In your shoes, I'd plead the fifth as well.'

'Alessandro, I know what you must think of me, but—'

'I really don't need to hear any sob stories, Lyla.'

'Stop calling me that. My name is Chase.'

'So you became a lawyer after all. I take my hat off to you—although, thinking about it, you did prove you were the sort of girl who would get what she wanted whatever the cost...'

Chase's eyes flickered up to him. The expression on his face sent the chill of fear racing up and down her spine, yet how could she blame him? Their story had been brief and so full of things that had to be hidden that it was hardly surprising.

'And I notice that there's no telling wedding ring on your finger,' he continued in the same mildly speculative voice that wouldn't have fooled an idiot. 'Did you dispose of the hapless husband in your ever-onwards and upwards climb?'

When he had met her—sitting there in the university canteen with a book in front of her, a little frown on her face, completely oblivious to everyone around her—she had knocked him sideways. It was more than the fact that she'd stood out, that she possessed head-turning looks; the world was full of girls who could turn heads. No, it had been her complete and utter indifference to the glances angled in her direction. He had watched as she had toyed with her sandwich before shoving it to one side and heading out. She had looked neither right nor left. The canteen could have been devoid of people.

Standing here now, looking at her, Alessandro could recreate that feeling of intense, incomprehensible attraction that had swept over him then as though it had been yesterday.

Significantly, she hadn't been wearing a wedding ring then either.

'I'm not here to talk about my past,' Chase said, clearing her throat. 'I've brought all the paperwork about the shelter.'

'And I'm not ready to talk about that yet.' He sat on one of the chairs alongside her and angled it away from the table so that he had a bird's eye view of her as she stared down at the bundle of files and papers in front of her and pretended to concentrate. 'So…' he drawled. 'You were about to tell me where the wedding ring's gone…'

'I don't believe I was,' Chase said coolly, gathering herself. Eyes the colour of bitter chocolate bored straight through her, bypassing the hard, glossy veneer she had taken so much time and trouble to build like a fortress around herself. 'You might be curious about what I've been up to for the past few years, Alessandro, but I have no intention of satisfying your curiosity. I just want to do what I came here to do and leave.'

'You came here to lose to me,' Alessandro told her without preamble. 'If you had any sense, you would recognise that and wave the white flag before I start lowering the price I've offered to pay for that place.' He drew her attention to the clock on the wall. 'With every passing minute, I drop my price by a grand, so make sure your argument's a winning one, because if it's not you're going to find that you're not working on behalf of your client.'

'You can't do that.'

'I can do whatever I like, Lyla…Chase…or shall I call you Mrs Evans? Or perhaps *Ms*…?'

'This isn't about *us,* Alessandro.' She tried to claw the

conversation back to the matter at hand, back to the shelter. 'So please don't think that you can use empty threats to—'

'Look around you,' Alessandro cut in lazily. 'And tell me what you see.'

'Where are you going with this?'

'Just do as I ask.'

Chase looked around nervously. She could feel the jaws of a trap yawning around her, but when she tried to figure out what sort of trap she came up empty. 'Big, bland conference room,' she told him in a voice that hinted that she was already bored with the subject. When she looked around her, her eyes kept wanting to return to him, to look at his face and absorb all the small changes there. Seeing him now, she was beginning to realise that she had never entirely forgotten him. She had buried him but it had obviously been in a shallow grave.

'I like it bland. It doesn't pay to provide distractions when you want the people seated at this table to be focused.'

'*You* like it bland…'

'Correct. You see, I am AM Holdings. I own it all. Every single deal is passed by me. What I say goes and no one contradicts me. So, when I tell you that I intend to drop my price by a grand for every minute you argue with me, I mean it and it's within my power to do it. Of course, you're all business and you think you can win, in which case my threat will be immaterial. But if you don't, well, after a couple of hours of futile arguing… Do the maths.'

Chase looked at him, lost for words. In view of what had happened between them, the deceit and the half-lies that had finally been her undoing, she was staring at a man who had been gifted his revenge. She should have done her homework on the company more thoroughly, but she had been handed the case after her boss had done the preliminaries himself, only to find that he couldn't follow through for personal reasons. She had focused all her energies on trying to locate loopholes that would prevent the sale of the shelter to *anyone* rather than specifically to AM Holdings. Even so, would she have recognised Alessandro had his name cropped up? They hadn't afforded much time for surnames.

'Sounds ungentlemanly.' Alessandro gave an elegant shrug and a smile that was as cold as the frozen wastelands. 'But, when it comes to business, I've always found that being a gentleman doesn't usually pay dividends.'

'Why are you doing this? How could you think of punishing those helpless women who use the shelter because we…we…?'

'Had an ill-fated relationship? Because you lied to me? Deceived me? Does your firm of lawyers know the kind of person you really are?'

Chase didn't say anything but she could feel her nervous system go into overdrive. She had inadvertently stepped into the lion's den; how far did revenge go? What paths would it travel down before it was finally satisfied? Alessandro Moretti owned this place. Not only was it within his power to do exactly as he said, to reduce the amount he was willing to pay for the shelter with each passing minute, but what if he decided actively to go after *her*?

'Things weren't what they seemed back then, Alessandro.'

'The clock's ticking.' He relaxed and folded his hands behind his head. Against all odds, and knowing her for what she really was, he was irritated to discover that he could still appreciate her on a purely physical level. He had never laid a finger on her but, hell, he had fantasised about it until his head had spun, had wondered what she would look like underneath the student clothes, what she would feel like. By the time he had met her, he had already bedded his fair share of women, yet she had appealed to him on a level he had barely comprehended.

He hadn't gone to the university intending to get involved with anyone. He had gone there as a favour to his old don, to give a series of business lectures, to get students inspired enough to know that they could attempt to achieve in record time what he had succeeded in achieving. Six lectures charting business trends, showing how you could buck them and still come out a winner, and he would be gone. He hadn't anticipated meeting Lyla—or, as she now called herself, Chase—and staying on to give a further six lectures.

For the first time in his very privileged life, he had found himself in a situation with a woman over which he'd had little control and he had been prepared to kick back and enjoy it. For someone to whom things had always come easy, he had even enjoyed the hard-to-get game she had played. Of course, he had not expected that the hard-to-get game would, in fact, lead nowhere in the end, but then how was he to know the woman he had been dealing with? She had left him with the ugly taste of disillusionment in his mouth and now here she was…

Wasn't fate a thing of beauty?

'You're not interested in reliving our…exciting past. So, sell me your arguments… And, by the way, that's one minute gone…'

Feeling that she had stepped into a nightmare, Chase opened the top file with trembling fingers. Of course she could understand that he was bitter and angry with her. And yet in her mind, when she had projected into a future that involved her accidentally running into him somewhere, his bitterness and anger had never been so deep, nor had he been vengeful. He could really hurt her, really undo all the work she had done to get where she had.

She began going over some of the old ground covered

in the past three meetings she'd had with his underlings, and he inclined his head to one side with every semblance of listening, before interrupting her with a single slash of his hand.

'You know, of course, that none of those obstructions hold water. You're prevaricating and it won't work.'

Chase involuntarily glanced at the clock on the wall and was incensed that the meeting—all the important things that had to be discussed, things that involved the lives of other people—had been sidelined by this unfortunate, unexpected and worrying collision with her past.

And yet she lowered her eyes and took in the taut pull of expensive trousers over his long legs, the fine, dark hair that liberally sprinkled his forearms… Not even the unspoken atmosphere of threat in his cool, dark eyes could detract from the chiselled perfection of his face. He had the burnished colour of someone of exotic blood.

When she had first laid eyes on him, she had been knocked sideways. He hadn't beaten about the bush. He had noticed her, he said, had seen her sitting in the university canteen. She had instinctively known that he had been waiting for a predictable response. The response of a woman in the presence of a man who could have who ever he wanted, and he wanted her. She had also known that there was no way she could go there. That she should smile politely and walk away, because doing anything else would have been playing with fire. But still she had hesitated, long enough for him to recognise a mutual interest. Of course, it had always been destined to end badly, but she hadn't been able to help herself.

She tightened her lips as she realised just how badly things could go now, all these years later.

'Okay, so you may have all the legalities in place, but what do you think the press would make of a big, bad company rolling in and bulldozing a women's shelter? The public has had enough of powerful people and powerful companies thinking that they can do exactly as they like.' This had been her trump card but there was no hint of triumph in her voice as she pulled it out of the bag.

'I have names here,' she continued in the gathering silence, not daring to risk a glance at him. 'Contacts with journalists and reporters who would be sympathetic to my cause…' She shoved the paper across to him and Alessandro ignored it.

'Are you threatening me?' he asked in a tone of mild curiosity.

'I wouldn't call it threatening…'

'No? Then what exactly *would* you call it?'

'I'm exercising leverage.' It had seemed an excellent idea at the time, but then she hadn't banked on finding herself floundering in a situation she couldn't have envisaged in a million years. His dark eyes focused on her face made her want to squirm and she knew that her veneer of self-confidence and complete composure was badly undermined by the slow tide of pink colour rising to her face. 'If you buy the shelter in a cloud of bad publicity, whatever you put up there will be destined to fail. It's quite a small community in that particular part of London. People will take sides and none of them will be on yours.'

'I bet you thought that you'd bring that out from up your sleeve and my lawyers would scatter, because there *is* such a thing as bad publicity being worse than no publicity. It's a low trick, but then I'm not surprised that you would resort to low tricks.' He leaned forward, rested both arms on the shiny conference table and stared directly at her. 'However, let's just turn that threat on its head for a minute…'

'It's not a threat.'

'I have offered an extremely generous price for the purchase of the shelter and the land that goes with it. More than enough for another shelter to be built somewhere else.'

'They don't *want* to build another shelter somewhere else. These women are accustomed to Beth's House. They feel safe there.'

'*You* can wax lyrical to your buddies at the press that they're being shoved out unceremoniously from their comfort zone. My people will counter-attack with a long, detailed and extremely enticing list of what they could buy for the money they'll be getting from me. A shelter twice the size. All mod cons. An equal amount of land, albeit further out. Hell, they could even run to a swimming pool, a games room, a nursery…the list goes on.

'So, who do you think will end up winning the argument? And, when it comes to light that I will be using the land for a mall that will provide much-needed jobs for the locals, well, you can see where I'm going with this…' He stood up and strolled lazily towards the very same window through which she had been peering earlier.

Chase couldn't tear her eyes away from him. Like an addict in the sudden presence of her drug of choice, she found that she was responding in ways that were dangerously off-limits. She shouldn't be reacting like this. She couldn't afford to let him into her life, nor could she afford to have any deep and meaningful conversations about their brief and ruined past relationship. Heck, it had only lasted a handful of months! And had never got off the starting block anyway.

'So.' Alessandro turned slowly to face her. With his back to the window, the light poured in from behind, throwing his face into shadows. 'How are you feeling about your ability to win this one now?'

'It's Beth's place; she's comfortable there. Why do you think people fight to stay in their homes when a developer comes along promising to buy them out for double what their place is worth?' But he would be able to sell it across the board. He had the money and the people to make sure that whatever message they wanted to get across would be successful. She knew Beth. Was she fighting to preserve something for reasons that were personal?

'I can tell from your expression that you already know that you're staring defeat in the face. By the way, it's been nearly forty-five minutes of unconvincing arguing from you… So how much have you lost your client already? The games room? The nursery? The giant kitchen with the cosy wooden table where all those women can hold hands and break bread?'

'I never thought that you were as arrogant as I now see you are.'

'But then you could say that we barely knew anything about each other. Although, in fairness, I didn't lie about my identity…' He was unconsciously drawn to the way the sunlight streaming through the panes of glass caught the colours of her hair. Her suit was snappy and business-like and he could tell that it had been chosen to downplay her figure. In his mind's eye, he saw the tight jeans, the jumpers and trainers, and that tentative smile that had won him over.

Chase stared down at the folder in front of her. There was nothing left to pull out of the hat. Even if there was, this was personal. He was determined to win the final argument, to have the last word, to *make her pay.*

'So I'm guessing from your prolonged silence that you'll be breaking the happy news to… What's her name? Beth?'

'You know it is.'

'And can you work out how much I'll be deducting from my initial offer?'

'Tell me you don't really mean to go through with that?'

'Lie, in other words?' Alessandro walked towards her and perched on the edge of the table.

'You can't force them to sell.'

'Have you had a look at their books? They're in debt.

Waiting to be picked off. It may be a caring, sharing place, but what it gains in the holding hands and chanting stakes it lacks in the accountancy arena. A quiet word in the right banker's ear and they'll be facing foreclosure by dusk. Furthermore, if it becomes widespread knowledge that they're in financial trouble, the vulture developers will swoop in looking for a bargain. What started out as a generous offer from me would devolve into an untidy fire sale with the property and land going for a song.'

'Okay.' Chase recognised the truth behind what he was saying. How could this be the same man who had once teased her, entertained her with his wit, impressed her with the breadth of his intelligence…driven her crazy with a longing that had never had a chance to be sated?

'Okay?'

'You win, Alessandro.' She looked at him with green eyes that had once mesmerised him right out of the rigidly controlled box into which he had always been accustomed to piling his emotional entanglements with the opposite sex. 'But maybe you could tell me whether you would have been as hardline if I hadn't been the person sitting here trying to talk you out of buying the shelter.'

'Oh, the sale most certainly would have gone ahead,' Alessandro drawled without an ounce of sympathy. 'But I probably wouldn't have tacked on the ticking clock.'

He strolled round to his chair and sat back down. His mobile phone buzzed, and when his secretary told him to get a move on because she could only defer his conference call for so long he informed her briefly that she would have to cancel it altogether. 'And make sure the same goes for my meetings after lunch,' he murmured, not once taking his eyes off Chase's downbent head. He signed off just as Alicia began to launch into a curious demand to know why.

'I don't want to keep you.' Chase began stacking all her files together and shoving them into her capacious brief case. She paused to look at him. *Last look*, she thought. *Then I'll never see you again.* She found that she was drinking in his image and she knew, with resignation, that what she looked at now would haunt her in the weeks to come. It was just so unfair. 'But I would like it if you could reconsider your…your…'

'Lower offer? And save you the humiliation of having to tell your client that you single-handedly knocked the price down?'

Chase glared at him. 'I never took you for a bully.'

'Life, as we both know, is full of cruel shocks. I'll admit that I have no intention of pulling out of this purchase, but you could recoup the lost thousands.'

'Could I? How?' She stared at him. At this point, the images of those wonderful additions to any other house Beth might buy vanishing in a puff of smoke, because of her, were proliferating in her head, making her giddy. She knew that the finances for the shelter were in serious disarray. They would need all the money they could get just to pay off the debts and wipe the slate clean.

'We have an unfinished past,' Alessandro murmured. 'It's time to finish it. I wouldn't have sought out this opportunity but, now it's here, I want to know who the hell you really are. Satisfy my curiosity and the full price is back on the table…'

CHAPTER TWO

So WHERE WAS the jump for joy, the high five, the shriek of delight? For the sake of a little conversation, she stood to claw back a substantial amount of money. He might have expected some show of emotion, even if only in passing.

Alessandro didn't take his eyes off her face, nor did he utter a word; the power of silence was a wonderful thing. Plus, he didn't trust her as far as he could throw her. If she thought that she could somehow screw him for more than the agreed amount, then let her have all the silence in the world, during which she could rethink any such stupid notion.

'I would need any assurances from you in writing,' Chase finally said. He wanted to finish business between them? Didn't he know that that was impossible? There were no questions she could ever answer and no explanations she could ever give.

'You will be getting no such thing,' Alessandro assured her calmly. 'You take my word for it or you leave here with your wallet several shades lighter.'

'There's no point rehashing what happened between us, Alessandro.'

'Your answer: yes or no. Simple choice.'

Chase stood up and smoothed down her grey skirt. She knew that she had a good figure, very tall and very slender. It was a bonus because it meant that she could pull off cheap clothing; she felt she needed simply to blend in with the other lawyers and paralegals in the company where she worked. Fitzsimmons was a top-ranking law firm and it employed top-ranking people; no riff-raff. Nearly everyone there came from a background where Mummy and Daddy owned second homes in the country. She kept her distance from all of them, but still she knew where they came from just by listening to their exploits at the weekends, the holidays they booked and the Chelsea apartments they lived in.

Thankfully, she was one of only two specialising in pro bono cases, so she could keep her head down, put in her hours and attend only the most essential of social functions.

She didn't want her quiet life vandalised. She didn't want Alessandro Moretti strolling back into it, asking questions and nursing a vendetta against her. She just couldn't afford to have any cans of worms opened up.

Likewise, she didn't want to feel this scary surge of emotion that made her go weak at the knees. Her life was her own now, under control, and she didn't want to jeopardise that.

But where were the choices? Did she make Beth pay for what *she* didn't want? Did she risk her boss's disapproval when she turned up and recounted what had happened?

More than that, if she kept her lips tightly buttoned up, who was to say that Alessandro would conveniently disappear? The way those hard, black eyes were watching her now…

She sat back down. 'Okay. What do you want to talk about? I mean, what do you want me to say?'

'Now, you don't really expect us to have a cosy little chat in a room like this, do you?'

He began prowling around the conference room: thick cream carpet aided and abetted the silence; cream walls;

the imposing hard-edged table where the great and the good could sit in front of their opened laptops, conversing in computer-speak and making far-reaching decisions that could affect the livelihoods of numerous people lower down the food chain, often for the better, occasionally for the worst.

'I mean, we have so much catching up to do, Lyla… Chase…'

'Please stop calling me Lyla. I told you, I don't use that name any more.'

'It's approaching lunchtime. Why don't we continue this conversation somewhere a little more comfortable?'

'I'm fine here.'

'Actually, you don't have a vote. I have five minutes' worth of business to deal with. I trust you can find your way down to the foyer? And don't…' he positioned himself neatly in front of her '…even think of running out on me.'

'I wouldn't do that.' Chase tilted her chin and stood up to look him squarely in the eyes. As a show of strength, it spectacularly backfired because, up close and personal like this, she could feel all her energy drain out of her, leaving behind a residue of tumultuous emotions and a dangerous, scary *awareness*. Her nostrils flared as she breathed in the clean, woody, aggressively masculine scent of his cologne. She took an unsteady step back and prayed that he hadn't noticed her momentary weakness.

'No?' Alessandro drawled, narrowing his eyes. 'Because right now you look like a rabbit caught in the headlights. Why? It's not as though I don't already know you for a liar, a cheat and a slut.' He had never addressed a woman so harshly in his life before but, looking at her here, taking in the perfection of a face that could launch a thousand ships and a body that was slender but with curves in all the right places, the reality of their past had slammed into him and lent an ugly bitterness to every word that passed his lips.

'I notice you're not defending yourself,' he murmured. He didn't know whether her lack of fight was satisfying or not. Certainly, he wished that she would look at him when he spoke, and he was sorely tempted to angle her face to him.

'What's the point?' Chase asked tightly. 'I'll meet you in the foyer but...' she looked at him with a spurt of angry rebellion '...I won't be hanging around for an hour while you take your time seeing to last-minute business with your secretary.'

Alessandro's eyes drifted down to her full, perfectly shaped mouth. He used to tease her that she looked as though she was sulking when it was in repose, but when she smiled it was like watching a flower bloom. He had never been able to get his fill of it. She certainly wasn't smiling now.

'Actually, you'll hang around for as long as I want you to.'

'Just because you want to...to...pay me back for...'

'Like I said, let's save the cosy chit-chat for somewhere more comfortable.'

Only when he left the room did Chase realise how tense she had been. She sagged and closed her eyes, steadying herself against the table.

She felt like the victim of a runaway truck. In a heartbeat, her life seemed to have been derailed, and she had to tell herself that it wasn't so; that because Alessandro was the man with whom she was now having to deal, because their paths had crossed in such a shadowy manner, it didn't mean that he was out to destroy her. His pride had been injured all those years ago and what he wanted from her now was answers to the questions he must have asked himself in the aftermath of their break-up. Not that they had ever really had a *relationship*.

Of course, she would have to be careful with what she told him, but once he was satisfied they would both return to their lives and it would be as if they had never met again.

She left the conference room in a hurry. It was almost twelve-thirty and there were far more people walking around than when she had first entered the impressive building. Workers were going out to lunch. It was a perfect summer's day. There would be sandwiches in the park and an hour's worth of relaxing in the sun before everyone stuck back on their jackets and returned to their city desks. Chase had always made sure to steer clear of that.

In the foyer, she didn't have long to wait before she spotted Alessandro stepping out of the lift. As he walked towards her, one finger holding the jacket that he had tossed over his shoulder, she relived those heady times when she had enjoyed kidding herself that her life could really change. Every single time she had seen him, she had felt a rush of pure, adrenaline-charged excitement, even though all they ever did was have lunch together or a cappuccino somewhere.

'So you're here.'

'You didn't really expect me to run away?' Chase fell into step alongside him. It was a treat not to tower over a guy but she still had to walk quickly to match his pace as they went through the revolving glass doors and out into the busy street.

'No, of course I didn't. You're a lawyer. You know when diplomacy is called for.' He swung left and began walking away from the busier streets, down the little side roads that gave London such character. 'And, on the subject of your career, why don't we kick off our catch-up with that?'

'What do you want to know?'

Alessandro leaned down towards her. 'Let's really get

into the spirit of this, Chase. Let's not do a question-and-answer session, with me having to drag conversation out of you.'

'What do you expect, Alessandro? I don't want to be here!'

'I'm sure you don't, but you're here now, so humour me.'

'I…I…got a first-class degree. In my final year I was head-hunted by a firm of lawyers—not the ones I work for now, but a good firm. I was fast-tracked.'

'Clever Chase.'

Chase recognised that it hadn't been said as a compliment, although she could only guess at what he was implying. He loathed her so, whatever it was, she had no doubt that it would be offensive.

Yet, she *was* clever. In another place and another time, she knew that she would have been one of those girls who would have been said to 'have it all': brains and looks. But then, life had a way of counter-balancing things. At any rate, she had relied far more on her brains than she ever had on her looks. She had worked like a demon to get her A-levels, fought against all odds to get to a top university, and once there had doggedly spared no effort in getting a degree that would set her up for life. And all that against a backdrop that she had trained herself never to think about.

'Thank you.' She chose to misinterpret the tone of his voice. 'So, I got a good job, did my training, changed companies…and here I am now.'

'Fitzsimmons. Classy firm.'

'Yes, it is.' She could feel fine prickles of nervousness beading her forehead.

'And yet, no designer suit? Don't they pay you enough?'

Chase cringed with embarrassment. He had never made any secret about the fact that he came from money. Was that how he could spot the fact that her clothes were off the peg and ready to wear from a chain store? 'They pay me more than enough,' she said coolly. 'But I prefer to save my money instead of throwing it away to a high-end retailer.'

'How noble. Not a trait I would tend to associate with you.'

'Can't you at least try and be civil towards me?' Chase asked thinly. 'At any rate, most of my work is pro bono. It's sensible not to show up in designer suits that cost thousands.' It was what she had laughingly told someone at the firm ages ago and her boss had applauded her good sense.

They were now in front of an old-fashioned pub nestled in one of the quieter back alleys. There were gems like this all over London. When they entered, it was dark, cool and quiet. He offered her a drink and shrugged when she told him that she would stick to fruit juice.

'So...' Alessandro sat down, hand curved round his pint, and looked at her. He honestly didn't know what he hoped to gain from this forced meeting but seeing her again had reawakened the nasty questions she had left unanswered. 'Let's start at the beginning. Or maybe we should pick it up at the end—at the point when you told me that you were married. Yes, maybe that's the place we should start. After we'd been meeting for four months... Four months of flirting and you gazing at me all convincingly doe-eyed and breathless, then informing me that you had a husband waiting in the wings.'

Chase nursed her fruit juice. She licked her lips nervously. Her green eyes tangled and clashed with cold eyes the colour of jet. 'I don't see what the point of this is, Alessandro.'

'You know what the point of it is—you're going to satisfy my curiosity in return for the full agreed price for your shelter. It's a fair exchange. Tell me what happened to the husband.'

'Shaun...was killed shortly after I got my first job. He... he was on his motorbike at the time. He was speeding, lost control, crashed into the central reservation on the motorway…'

'So you didn't ditch him in the impersonal confines of a divorce court.' Nor would she have. Alessandro downed a mouthful of beer and watched her over the rim of the glass. Not, as she had told him on that last day in exhaustive detail, when he'd been her childhood sweetheart and the love of her life. 'And I take it you never remarried.'

'Nor will I ever.' She could detect the bitterness that had crept into her voice, but when she looked at him his expression was still as cool and unrelenting as it had been.

'Is that because there's no room for a man in the life of an ambitious, high-flying lawyer? Or because you're still wrapped up with the man who was…let me try and remember… Oh, yes, I've got it: the only guy you would ever contemplate sleeping with. *Sorry if you got the wrong idea, Alessandro. A few cappuccinos does not a relationship make, but it's been a laugh…*'

'We should never have seen each other. It was a terrible idea. I never meant to get involved with anyone.'

'But you didn't get involved with me, did you?' Alessandro angled his beautiful head to one side as he picked up an unspoken message he wasn't quite getting.

What was there to get or not get? he thought impatiently. The woman had strung him along, led him up the garden path and then had casually disappeared without a backward glance. Hell, she had made him feel things… No, he wasn't going to go there.

'No! No, I didn't. I meant…'

'I'm all ears.'

'You don't understand. I shouldn't even have even to you. I was married.'

'So why did you? Were you riding high on the knowledge that you'd managed to net the rich guy all the groupie students were after?'

'That's a very conceited thing to say.'

'I value honesty. I lost track of the number of notes I got from girls asking for some "extra tuition".'

If there hadn't been notes, she thought, then he surely would have clocked the stares he'd garnered everywhere he went. The man was an alpha male with enough sex appeal to sink a ship. Throw in his wealth, and it was little wonder that girls were queuing up to see if they could attract his attention. She'd never, ever been at the university longer than was strictly necessary but, if she had been, she knew that she would have become a source of envy, curiosity and dislike.

'So was that why you decided to keep your marital status under wraps? To take the wedding ring off? To string me along with the promise of sex?'

'I never said we would end up in bed.'

'Do me a favour!' He slammed his empty glass on the table and Chase jumped. 'You knew exactly what you were getting into!'

'And I didn't think… I never thought…'

'So you lied about the fact that you weren't single or available for a relationship.'

'If I remember correctly, you once told me that you weren't interested in commitment, that you liked your relationships fast and furious and temporary!'

Alessandro flushed darkly. 'Weak reasoning,' he gritted cuttingly. 'Did you lie because you thought that you might try me out for size? See whether I wasn't a better bet than the stay-at-home husband? Is that why you strung me along for four months? Were you hedging your bets?' He shook his head, furious with himself for losing control of the conversation, for actually caring one way or another what had or hadn't been done eight years previously.

'No, of course not! And Shaun was never a *stay-at-*

home husband.' Again, that bitterness had crept into her voice.

'No? So what was he, then?' Alessandro leaned forward, the simple shift of body weight implying threat. 'Banker? Entrepreneur? If I recall, you were a little light on detail. In fact, if my memory serves me right, you couldn't wait to get out of my company fast enough the very last time we met.'

Alessandro was surprised to find that he could remember exactly what she had been wearing the very last time he'd laid eyes on her: a pair of faded skinny jeans tucked into some cheap imitation-suede boots and a jumper which now, thinking about it, had probably belonged to the 'childhood sweetheart' husband. On that thought, his jaw clenched and his eyes darkened.

It hadn't taken her long to spill out the truth. Having spent months of innocent conversation, tentative advances and retreats and absolutely no physical contact—which had been hell for him—she had sat down opposite him at the wine bar which had become their favourite meeting place; at a good bus ride away, it was far from all things university. With very little preamble, and keeping her eyes glued to his face while around them little clusters of strangers had drunk, laughed and chatted, all very relaxed in the run-up to Christmas, she'd informed him that she would no longer be seeing him.

'Sorry,' he recalled her saying with a brittle smile. 'It's been a laugh, and thanks for all the help with the economics side of the course, but actually I'm married...'

She had wagged her ring finger in front of him, complete with never-before-seen wedding band.

Shaun McGregor, she had said airily. Love of her life. Had known him since they were both fifteen. She had even pulled out a picture of him from her beaten-up old wallet and waxed lyrical about his striking good looks.

Alessandro had stared long and hard at the photo of a young man with bright blue eyes and a shaved head. There was a tattoo at the side of his neck; he'd probably been riddled with them. It had been brought home to him sharply just what a fool he had been taken for. Not only had she strung him along for fun, but he had never actually been her type. Her husband had had all the fine qualities of a first-rate thug.

'Shaun did lots of different things,' Chase said vaguely. 'But none of that matters now, anyway. The fact is, I'm sorry. I know it's late in the day to apologise, but I'm apologising.'

'Why did you use a different name?'

'Huh?'

'You used the name Lyla. Not just with me, with everyone. Why?'

'I…' How could she possibly explain that she had been a different person then? That she had had the chance to create a wonderful, shiny new persona, and that she had taken it, because what she could create had been so much better than the reality. She had still been clever, and she had never lied about her academic history but, she had thought, what was the harm in passing herself off as just someone normal? Someone with a solid middle-class background and parents who cared about her? It hadn't been as though she would ever have been required to present these mysterious and fictitious parents to anyone.

And she had always made sure never to get too close to anyone—until Alessandro had come along. Even then, at the beginning, she had had no idea that she would fall so far, so fast and so deep, nor that the little white lies she had told at the beginning would develop into harmful untruths that she'd no longer be able to retract.

'Well?' Alessandro prompted harshly. 'You lied about your single status and you lied about your name. So let's take them one at a time.' He signalled to a waitress and ordered himself another glass of beer. There went the afternoon, was the thought that passed through his mind. There was little chance he would be in the mood for a series of intense meetings and conference calls later. He was riveted by the hint of changing expressions on her face. He felt that he was in possession of a book, the meaning of which escaped him even though he had read the story from beginning to end. Then he cursed himself for being fanciful, which was so unlike him.

'Lyla was my mother's name. I like it. I didn't think there was anything wrong in using it.'

'And so you stopped liking it when you decided to join a law firm?'

'You said we weren't going to do a question-and-answer session!' Her skin burned from the intensity of his eyes on her. Alessandro Moretti, even as a young man in his mid-twenties, had always had a powerful, predatory appeal. There was something dangerous about him that sent shivers up and down her spine and drew her to him, even when common sense told her it was mad. He certainly hadn't lost that appeal.

'It was easier to just use my real name when I joined Edge Ellison, that first law firm. I mean, my Christian name.'

'Why am I getting the feeling that there are a thousand holes in whatever fairy story you're spinning me?'

'I'm not spinning you a fairy story!' Chase snapped. Bright spots of colour stained her cheeks. 'If you want, I can bring my birth certificate to show you!' Except that would suggest a second meeting, which was not something that was going to be on the cards.

But what would he do if he found out where she really came from? What would he do if he discovered that the solid, middle-class background she had innocently hinted at had been about as real as a swimming pool in the middle of the Sahara?

He might be tempted to have a quiet chat with the head of her law firm, she thought with a sickening jolt. Of course, she hadn't lied about any of her qualifications, and she knew that she was a damned good lawyer. There was no way she could be given the sack for just allowing people to *assume* a background that wasn't entirely true, yet...

Wounded pride and dislike could make a person do anything in their power to get revenge. What if he shared all her little white lies with the people she worked with—the posh, private-school educated young men and women who weren't half as good as she was but who would have a field day braying with laughter at her expense? She was strong, but she knew that she was not so strong that she could survive ridicule at the work place.

'I should be getting back to work.' She drained the remainder of her orange juice and made to stand up.

Without thinking, Alessandro reached out and circled his hand around her wrist.

Chase froze. Really, it was the most peculiar sensation...as if her entire body had locked into place so that she was incapable of movement. His fingers around her wrist were as dramatic as a branding iron and she felt her heart pick up speed until she thought it might explode inside her.

'Not so fast.'

'I've answered all your questions, Alessandro!'

'What the hell was in it for you?'

'Nothing! I...just made a mistake! It was a long time ago. I was just a kid.'

'A kid of twenty and already hitched. I didn't think that kind of thing happened any more.'

'I told you...we were in love...' Chase looked away and

shook her hand free of his vice-like grip. 'We didn't see the point of waiting.'

'And your families both joined in the celebrations?'

She shrugged. 'He's dead now, anyway, so it doesn't matter whether they joined in the celebrations or not.'

'Spoken like a true grieving widow.' Why did he keep getting this feeling that something was out of kilter? Was his mind playing tricks on him? Had his ego been so badly bruised eight years ago that he would rather look for hidden meanings than take her very simple tale of treachery at face value?

'It's been years. I've moved on.'

'And no one else has surfaced on the scene to replace the late lamented?'

'Why is this all about me?' Chase belatedly thought that she might turn the spotlight onto him. If there was one thing to be said for going into law whilst simultaneously detaching yourself from most of the human race, it was that it did dramatic things to your confidence levels. Or maybe it was just her 'flight or fight' reflex getting an airing. She stared him squarely in the face and tried not to let the steady, speculative directness of his gaze get to her.

'What about *you*?' she asked coolly. 'We haven't said anything about what *you've* been up to…'

'What's there to say?' Alessandro relaxed back, angling his body so that he could cross his legs. She really did have a face that made for compulsive watching. It was exquisite, yet with a guarded expression that made you wonder what was going on behind the beautiful mask. Even as a much younger woman, she had possessed that sense of unique mystery that had fired his curiosity and kept it for the duration of their strange dalliance.

And now, yet again, he could feel his curiosity piqued.

'I'm an open book.' He spread his arms wide. 'I don't

hide who I am and I don't make a habit of leading anyone down the garden path.'

'And is there a special someone in *your* life? Is there a Mrs Moretti dusting and cleaning in a house in the country somewhere and a few little Moretti children scampering around outside? Or are you still only into the fast and furious relationship without the happy ending?'

'My, my. You've certainly become acid-tongued, Chase.'

Chase flushed. Yes she had. And there were times when she stood back and wondered if she really liked the person she had become. Not that she had ever been soft and fluffy, but now…

'I don't like being trampled.'

'And is that why you think I brought you here? To trample over you? Is that what you think I'm doing?'

Chase shrugged. 'Isn't it?'

'We're exchanging information. How could that possibly be described as trampling all over you? And, in answer to your question, there is no Mrs Moretti in a country house—and if there were, she certainly wouldn't be dusting or cleaning.'

'Because you have enough money to pay for someone to dust and clean for you. Are you still working twenty-four-seven? Surely you must have made enough billions by now to kick back and enjoy life?'

She used to listen, enraptured, as he'd told her about his working life: non-stop; on the go all the time. The lectures, he had said, were like comic relief, little windows of relaxation. She had teased him that, if giving lectures was his form of relaxation, then he would keel over with high blood pressure by the time he was thirty-five. She was annoyed to find herself genuinely curious and interested to hear what he had been up to. Having anything to do with Alessandro Moretti was even more hazardous now than it had been eight years ago.

'None of my business,' she qualified in a clipped voice. 'Am I free to go now?'

Alessandro's lips thinned. He had found out precisely nothing. None of his questions had been answered. His brain was telling him to walk away but some other part of him wanted more.

'Why did you decide to concentrate on pro bono cases?' He asked softly. 'Surely with a first-class degree, and law firms head-hunting you, there were far more profitable things to do?'

'I've never been interested in making money.' He had stopped attacking her and she realised that she had forgotten how seductive he could be when he was genuinely interested in hearing what she had to say. He would tilt his head to one side and would give the impression that every word she uttered was of life-changing importance.

'I'd always planned on becoming a lawyer, although the two other options that tempted me were Social Services and the police force.' She blushed, because she didn't think that she had confided that in anyone before—not that she did a lot of confiding anyway.

'Social Services? The police force?'

'So please don't accuse me of being materialistic.'

'I can't picture you as a social worker, even less a policewoman.'

'I should be getting back to work. I have a lot to do, and I'll have to visit the shelter later today and tell them what the outcome of my meeting with your company was. They'll be disappointed because they honestly don't want to move premises, not when they've been such a reliable fixture in the area for such a long time, and not when the majority of the women who use their services are fairly local to the area. A big place with a swimming pool and a games room in the middle of nowhere is no good for anyone.'

'What made the decision for you?'

Hadn't he been distracted from asking her personal questions? Having lowered her guard for three seconds, Chase now felt as though she was handing over state secrets to the enemy, and yet what was the big deal? Was she so defensive because Alessandro was on the receiving end of her confidences? And wasn't it possible that, the more secretive she was, the more curious he would become? She forced herself to relax and smile at him.

'The hours,' she confessed in a halting voice. 'I didn't want to think that I might be called out at any time of the day or night. I might work long hours at Fitzsimmons but I can control the hours I work.'

'Makes sense. More to the point, I suppose both other options would have involved an element of danger, and even more so for someone like you.'

'Someone like me?' Immediately, Chase bristled at the implied insult. 'And I suppose you're going to launch into another attack on me? More criticism of me that I'm a liar and a cheat? Although I have no idea how that would have anything to do with being in the police force or working for the council! I get it that you're angry and bitter about what happened between us, but attacking me isn't going to change any of that!'

'Actually,' Alessandro murmured, 'I meant that those two professions are the ones that are possibly least suited to a woman with your looks. You're sexy as hell; how would that have played out for you if you had found yourself in a dangerous situation…?' The lips he had never kissed and the body he had never touched…

Suddenly, his body jackknifed into sudden, shocking arousal. The sheer force of it took him by surprise. It pushed its way past his bitterness and anger and made a mockery of the answers he had told himself he demanded to hear. As his erection throbbed painfully against the zip of his trousers, his mind took flight in a completely different direction. He imagined her hand down there, her mouth wrapped around him…

Who the hell cared about answers when he was consumed with lust? He had to shift in the chair just to release some of the urgency that was becoming painful.

He was suffused with anger at his physical response to her. She represented everything he found most repellent, yet how was it that she could still manage to turn him on? Was his libido so wayward that it could defy cool judgement and rise to the challenge of the unavailable, the unacceptable…the out of bounds? He had never lost control when it came to any woman and he had dated some of the most spectacularly beautiful women in the world. So what the hell was going on here?

'I never gave that side of things any thought at all.' Chase was determined not to let that description of her take their conversation in a direction she most certainly didn't want.

Her voice was cool, Alessandro noted, yet her colour was up. And she couldn't meet his eyes. Now, wasn't *that* telling?

He knew that the last thing he should contemplate doing was to pay any credence to whatever her expression was saying or, more to the point, whatever his disobedient body was up to, and yet…

'You know what? I think I might like to see this shelter. Evaluate just how the land will play out for what I have in mind. I'm taking it you'll be my escort…?'

CHAPTER THREE

For the first time in years Chase felt helpless. Three days ago she had walked into the imposing glass building that housed AM Holdings with a simple mission: save the shelter. She had been in control—the career woman, successful in what she did, in command of the situation. She had hoped for a favourable outcome but, had there not been one, she would have left with a clear conscience—she would have done her best.

And now here she was, hanging around by the window in her house, peering out at regular intervals for Alessandro, who had made good on his request to be shown the shelter.

'What for?' she had demanded at the time. 'I don't see the point. You're just going to demolish it anyway so that you can put up a mall catering for rich people.'

'Be warned,' he had said, eyebrows raised, those midnight eyes boring straight through her, making her feel as though her whole body had been plugged into a socket. 'Do-gooders and preachers have a monotonous tendency to become self-righteous bores. Naturally, I have details of the land somewhere but I want to see for myself what the layout is. Since you're the one handling the deal, I can't imagine that would be a problem. Or is it? Does our past history make it a problem for you?'

Yes. Yes, it does, she had thought with rising desperation. 'No. Of course not. Why should it?' she had answered with an indifferent shrug.

So here she was now and she felt as though control was slipping out of her grasp. She knew that under normal circumstances a lapse in her self-control would be easily dealt with but with Alessandro...

Her frustration and anger was underlined by a darker, more insidious emotion, a swirl of excitement that scared her. It felt like a slumbering monster slowly reawakening. Even though she had taken care to dress as neutrally as possible, in a navy-blue suit that was the epitome of sexlessness—and an impractical colour, given the wall-to-wall blue summer skies and hot sunshine—she still felt horribly vulnerable as she hovered in the sitting room waiting for him to show up.

She had informed him that she would meet him at the premises, but he had insisted on collecting her.

'You can fill me in on the history of the place on the way,' he had said smoothly. 'Forewarned is forearmed.'

She had bitten her tongue and refrained from telling him that there was no point being forearmed when the net result would be a demolition derby. He was the guy with the purse strings and she had already seen first-hand how he could use that position to his own advantage. She had no desire to revive the ticking clock.

A long, sleek, black Jaguar pulled up outside the house just as she was about to turn away from the window and her attention was riveted at the sight of him emerging from the back seat, as incongruous in this neighbourhood as his car was.

He was dressed in pale-grey pinstriped trousers, which even from a distance screamed quality, and a white shirt, the sleeves of which he had rolled to the elbow.

For a few heart-stopping seconds, Chase found that she literally couldn't breathe, that she was holding her breath.

The mere sight of him was a full-on assault on all her senses. She watched as he looked around him, taking in his surroundings. She felt sure that this was the sort of neighbourhood he would be accustomed to telling his chauffeur to drive straight through and to make sure the car doors were locked. By no means was it in a dangerous part of London but neither was it upmarket. Well paid though she was, she wasn't so well paid that she could afford to buy a house in one of the trendier areas and, unlike many of her associates, she didn't have parents who could stick their hands in their pockets and treat her to one.

She dodged out of sight just as he turned to face the house and, when the doorbell rang, she took her time getting to it. Her heart was beating like a sledgehammer as she pulled open the door to find him lounging against the doorframe.

'Right. Shall we go?' she asked as her eyes slid away from his sinfully handsome face, returned to take a peek and slid away again. She gathered her handbag from where she had hung it on the banister and bent to retrieve her briefcase from the ground.

'In due course.' Alessandro stepped into the hallway and shut the front door behind him.

'What are you doing?'

'I'm coming in for a cup of coffee.'

'We haven't got time for that, Alessandro. The appointment has been made for ten-fifteen. With rush-hour traffic, heaven only knows how long it will take for us to get there.'

'Relax. I got my secretary to put back the visit by an hour.'

'You *what*?'

'So this is where you live.'

Chase watched in horror as he made himself at home, strolling to peer into the sitting room, then onwards to the kitchen, into which he disappeared.

'Alessandro…' She galvanised herself into movement and hurried to the kitchen, to find him standing in the centre doing a full turn. It was a generous-sized kitchen which overlooked a small, private garden. It had been a persuading factor in her purchase of the house. She loved having a small amount of outdoor space.

'Very nice.'

'This is not appropriate!'

'Why not? It's hardly as though I'm a stranger. Are you going to make me a cup of coffee?'

Chase gritted her teeth as he sat down. The kitchen was large enough for a four-seater table and it had been one of the first things she had bought when she had moved in three years previously. She had fallen in love with the square, rough, wooden table with its perimeter of colourful, tiny mosaic tiles. She watched as he idly traced one long finger along some of the tiles and then she turned away to make them both some coffee.

'Is this your first house?' Alessandro queried when she had finally stopped busying herself doing nothing very much at the kitchen counter and sat down opposite him.

He hadn't laid eyes on her in three days but he had managed to spend a great deal of time thinking about her and he had stopped beating himself up for being weak. So what if she had become an annoying recurring vision in his head? Wasn't it totally understandable? He had been catapulted back to a past he had chosen to lock away. Naturally it would be playing on his mind, like an old, scratched record returned to a turntable. Naturally *she* would be playing on his mind, especially when she had remained just so damned easy on the eye.

'What do you mean?' Everything about Alessandro Moretti sitting at her kitchen table made her jumpy.

'Is this the family home?'

'I have no idea what you're talking about.'

'The dearly departed… Is this the marital home?'

'No, it's not.' She looked down. 'Shaun and I… We, er, had somewhere else when we were together… When he died I rented for a couple more years until I had enough equity to put in as a deposit on this place.'

Alessandro thought of the pair of them, young love-birds renting together, while she had batted her eyelashes at him and played him for a fool. He swallowed a mouth-ful of instant coffee and stood up, watching as she scram-bled to her feet.

'Are you going to give me a tour of the place?'

'There isn't much to see. Two bedrooms upstairs; a bathroom. You've seen what's down here. Shall we think about going?'

Alessandro didn't answer. He strolled out of the kitchen, glancing upstairs before turning his attention to the sit-ting room. Why was she so jumpy? She had been as cool as a cucumber eight years ago when she had walked out on him, so why was she now behaving like a cat on a hot tin roof? Guilt? Hardly. A woman who could conduct an outside relationship while married would never be prone to guilt. Or remorse. Or regret.

Perversely, the jumpier she seemed to be, the more in-trigued he became. He shoved one hand in his trouser pocket, feeling the coolness of his mobile phone.

'For a cool-headed lawyer,' he mused as he stared round the sitting room, 'you like bright colours. Anyone would be forgiven for thinking that the decor here suggests a com-pletely different personality.' He swung round to look at her as she hovered in the doorway, neither in the room nor out of it. 'Someone fun…vibrant.' He paused a fraction of a second. 'Passionate…'

Chase flushed, and was annoyed with herself, because she knew that that was precisely the response he had been courting. He was back and he was intent on playing with her like a cat playing with a mouse, knowing that all the danger and all the power lay exclusively in his hands.

'And yet,' Alessandro drawled as he prowled through the room before gazing briefly out of the window which overlooked the little street outside, 'there's something missing.'

'What?' The question was obviously reluctantly spoken. As he began to walk towards her, she felt panic rise with sickening force to her throat. All at once she was overcome with a memory of how desperately she had wanted him all those years ago. Her eyes widened and her mouth parted on a softly indrawn breath.

Getting closer and closer to her, Alessandro thought he could *touch* the subtle change in the atmosphere between them. It had become highly charged and, for the first time in a very long time, he felt sizzlingly *alive*. Not one of the catwalk-model beauties he had slept with over the past few years had come close to rousing this level of forbidden excitement. The immediacy of his response shocked him, all the more so because he recognised that the last time he had felt like this was when he had been in the process of being duped by the very same woman standing in front of him now. Hatred and revulsion were clearly inadequate protection against whatever it was she had that was now pushing an erection to the fore.

The bloody woman had been elusive then, for reasons which he had later understood, and she was elusive now, this time for reasons he couldn't begin to understand.

'Are you afraid of me?' he demanded harshly and Chase roused herself from the heated torpor that had engulfed her to stare up at him.

'What makes you think that I'm afraid of you?' She tried to insert some vigour into her voice but she could hear the sound of it—thin, weedy and defensive, all the things she didn't want him to imagine she was for a second.

'The way you're standing in the doorway as though I might make a lunge for you at any minute!'

'I can't imagine you would do any such thing!'

Couldn't she? It was precisely what he wanted to do: behave like a caveman and take her, because she was tempting the hell out of him!

'I'm afraid of what you could do.' She backtracked quickly as her mind threatened to veer down unexpected, unwelcome paths. 'You've already shown that you'd be willing to punish Beth because you… Because of me.'

'And yet here I am now. Do you think I'm the sort of man who reneges on what he's said? I've told you that I intend to pay the full, agreed price. I'll pay it.' Not afraid of him? *Like hell.* She might not be afraid of him, but he was certainly making her feel uncomfortable. Uncomfortable enough to try and shimmy further away from him.

He extended one lean hand against the wall, effectively blocking any further scarpering towards the front door. He could smell her hair. If he lowered his head just a little, he would feel its softness against his face. Of their own accord, his eyes drifted to the prissy blouse and the even prissier navy-blue jacket. He was well aware that she was breathing quickly, her breasts rising and falling as she did her utmost to keep her eyes averted.

Just as quickly he pushed himself away, retreating from her space, and he watched narrowly as she relaxed and exhaled one long breath.

He wasn't going to lose control. He had lost control once with her and he wasn't about to become the sort of loser who made a habit of ignoring life's lessons and learning curves.

'I was going to say…' He led the way to the front door and paused as she slung her handbag over her shoulder and reached for the case on the ground. 'There's something missing from your house.' He opened the door for her and stood back, allowing her to brush past him. 'Photos. Where are the pictures of the young, loving couple, from before your husband died? I thought I might have seen the happy pair holding hands and gazing adoringly up at one another...'

Chase walked towards the waiting car, head held high, but underneath the composed exterior she felt the ugly prickle of discomfort.

'We didn't do the whole church thing.'

'Who said anything about a church?'

'Why are you asking me all these questions?' she burst out as soon as they were in the car. She had kept her voice low but she doubted the driver would have heard anything anyway. A smoked-glass partition separated the front of the car from the back. Presumably it was completely soundproof. The truly wealthy never took chances when it came to being overheard, not even in their own cars. Deals could be lost on the back of an overheard conversation.

Alessandro shifted his muscular body to face her. 'Why are you getting so hot under the collar?'

'I...I'm not. I...I don't like to be surrounded by memories. I think it's always important to move on. There are photos of me and Shaun, just not on show. Do you want to talk about the shelter? I...I've brought all the relevant information with me. We can go over it on the way.' Sitting next to him in the back seat of this car induced the feeling of walls closing in. She fumbled with the clasp of her briefcase and felt his hand close over hers.

'Leave it.'

Chase snatched her hand away. 'I thought you wanted to pick me up so that we could talk about this deal.'

'I'm more interested in the lack of photos. So, none of the husband. Presumably you have albums stashed away somewhere? But none of your family either. Why is that?'

Chase flushed. The adoring middle-class parents who

lived in the country. She was mortified at how easily the lie had come to her all those years ago, but then she had been a kid and a little harmless pretence had not seemed like a sin.

Who wanted a rich, handsome guy to know that you have no family? That your mother had died from a drugs overdose when you were four and from that point on you'd been shoved from foster home to foster home like an unwanted parcel trying to find its rightful owner. How wonderful it had been to create a fictitious family, living in a fictitious cul-de-sac, who did normal things like taking an interest in the homework you were set and coming along to cheer at sports days, even if you trailed in last.

She had loved every minute of her storytelling until it had occurred to her that she had fallen in love with a man who didn't really know a thing about her. The fact that she had been married was just one of the many facts she had kept hidden. By then, it had been too late to retract any of what she had said, and she hadn't wanted to. She'd been enjoying their furtive meetings too much. Okay, so she knew that they would never come to anything, but she still hadn't wanted them to end.

And now…

'My parents…er…moved to Australia a few years ago.' She hated doing this now but for the life of her she didn't know what to do. At least, she thought, sending her non-existent parents on a one-way ticket to the other end of the world would prohibit him from trying to search them out.

Although, why on earth would he do that? The answer came as quickly as the question had: revenge. Find her weak spots and exploit them because he hated her for what he imagined she had done to him. She felt sick when she thought of the number of ways he could destroy her if he set his mind to it and if he had sufficient information in his possession.

'Really?'

'It was…um…always a dream of theirs.'

'To leave their only child behind and disappear half-way across the world?'

'People do what they do,' she said vaguely. 'I mean, don't *you* ever want to disappear to the other end of the earth?' Although she was making sure to stare straight ahead, she could feel his probing eyes on her, and she had to resist the temptation to lick her lips nervously.

'I disappear there quite often, as it happens. But only on business.'

Chase could think of nothing worse than travelling the globe in the quest for more and more money and bigger and bigger deals. Stability, security and putting down roots had always been her number one priority. She had managed to begin the process, and she shuddered to think of him pulling up any of the roots she had meticulously put down over the past few years.

'I'm surprised that after all these years you haven't become tired of trying to make up for your parents' excesses.' It slipped out before she could think and Chase instantly regretted the momentary lapse. The last thing she wanted to do was establish any kind of shared familiarity. 'My apologies,' she said stiffly. 'I shouldn't have said that.'

The reminder of just how much she knew about him underscored his bitterness with a layer of ice. He had never understood how that had managed to happen, how he had found himself telling her things he had never told anyone in his life before.

But then, she had been different. He had never met anyone like her in his life before. Still and yet wryly funny; guarded and yet so open in the way she gazed at him; composed and brilliant at listening. Between the inane yakking of the students—who, at the end of the day, were only a few years younger than him, even though he had been light years removed from them in terms of experience—and the pseudo-bored sophistication of the people he mixed with in his working life, she had been an oasis of peace. And, yes, he had told her things. For a relationship that struggled even to call itself a 'relationship', he had confided and, hell, where exactly had it got him?

He clenched his jaw grimly. 'I'm really not interested in psychobabble,' he told her.

'That's fair,' Chase returned. 'But if I'm not allowed to talk about *your* history then I don't see why you should talk about *mine*.' For starters, the last thing she needed was detailed questions about her so-called parents and where exactly they lived in Australia. And how dared he imply that they somehow didn't care about her simply because they had fulfilled their lifelong dream of emigrating? She almost felt sorry for them...

She half-grinned at that and Alessandro's eyes narrowed. What was going through her head? He had a fierce desire to know.

'So the shelter...' He interrupted whatever pleasant thought had made her smile.

'The shelter...' Chase breathed an inward sigh of relief because this was a subject she was more than happy to talk about. He ceased being a threat as she began to describe life at Beth's House. She smiled at some of the anecdotes about the women who came and went. She told him about the plans Beth had had for upgrading the premises, and then assured him that he could see for himself what she was talking about as soon as he got there. She told him that he had a heart of stone for wanting to knock it down to build, of all things, a stupid mall for people who had more money than sense, but found it was impossible to generate an argument because he hadn't taken her to task for voicing her opinion.

As a professional, a lawyer in charge of the brief, voicing opinions was not within her remit but she hadn't been able to help herself.

By the time they made it to the shelter, her eyes were bright and there was colour in her cheeks. More to the point, her guard was down. Alessandro felt that he was watching the years falling away. He wasn't about to be sucked into believing that she was anything but the liar she undoubtedly was, but he was certainly enjoying the hectic flush in her cheeks and the lively animation on her face.

They made it to the shelter on time. He immediately understood its potential for investment.

The large Victorian house, clearly in need of vast sums of money for essential repair, sat squarely in the midst of several acres of land. For somewhere that was accessible by bus and overland rail, it was a gem waiting to be developed.

The car swung through iron gates that were opened for them only after they had cleared security and they drove up to the house which was fronted by a circular courtyard, in the centre of which stood a non-functioning fountain.

'Beth was left this property by her parents,' Chase told him. 'It's another reason why she's so reluctant to sell. It was her childhood home. She may have converted it into the shelter, but there are a truck load of memories inside.'

'Is this when you begin to repeat your mantra that I have no heart and that my only aim in life is to make money at other people's expense?'

'If the cap fits…' Chase muttered under her breath in yet another show of unprofessionalism that would have had her boss mopping his brow with despair.

Alessandro raised his eyebrows and she had the grace to blush before stepping out of the car into the sunshine.

Alessandro was more than happy to follow her lead. He had never been to a place like this before. They were greeted at the door by Beth, who was in her sixties, a woman with long, grey hair tied back in a ponytail and a warm, caring face. Whatever she felt for the big, bad developer who was moving in to sweep her inheritance out from under her feet, she kept it well hidden.

'Some of the girls who come to us are in a terrible way,' she confided as they toured the house which was laid out simply but effectively inside. 'Chase knows that.'

'And that would be because…?'

'Because I've taken an interest in the place from the very start,' Chase said quickly. 'This sort of thing appeals to me. As I told you, I was very tempted to go into Social Services or the police force, some place where I would be able to do good for the community.'

Alessandro personally thought that it was priceless that she could come over all pious and saintly in his presence but he kept silent. He made all the right noises as he was shown through the house and introduced to girls who looked unbearably young, many of whom had nowhere else to go and were either pregnant or with a child.

'I try and keep them busy,' Beth told him as they went from room to room. 'Most of them don't see the point of continuing their education and it's very difficult for a fifteen-year-old to go to classes when they have a baby to look after. Many of my dear friends are teachers and volunteer to hold classes for them. It's truly remarkable the goodness that exists within us.'

Alessandro's eyes met Chase's over the older woman's head and his lips twisted into a cynical smile. 'It's not a trait I see much of in my line of business,' he said.

'I'm sure,' Beth concurred with a sad shake of her head. 'Now, Chase tells me that you're a very busy man.'

'And yet,' Chase inserted blandly, 'he's managed to make time to come here and see what you're all about. Although, I guess that mostly has to do with him judging the potential for knocking down the house and developing the land as soon as the money changes hands.'

Alessandro was cynical enough to appreciate the underhand dig. No one could accuse her of giving up without a fight. Their eyes tangled and he gave a slight smile of amused understanding of where she was heading with that incendiary statement.

'I will personally see to it that your…operation is transferred to suitable premises,' he affirmed, raking fingers through his dark hair.

'Not the same. Is it, Beth?'

'I will certainly miss the old place,' Beth agreed. 'It may not seem much to you, Mr Moretti, but this is really the only house I've ever known. I've never married, never left the family house. You must think me a silly old woman, but I shall find it very difficult to move on. Well, in truth—and I haven't said this to you, Chase, and you must promise me that you won't breathe a word to anyone else—my thoughts are with retiring from the whole business once I move on. Of course, I shall make sure that some of the money I get from the sale goes towards another shelter—perhaps smaller than this—and Frank and Anne will run it.'

'Frank and Anne?' Alessandro made a point of avoiding the scathing criticism in Chase's eyes. He had absolutely nothing to feel bad about. He knew for a fact that there were vultures hovering over the place, waiting to pick it to pieces, and those vultures would not have parted with nearly as much cash as he was prepared to.

'My dear friends. They help me here. As for me, perhaps a retirement place by the coast… So, I expect you would like to see the land, Mr Moretti? There's a lot of it. My parents were both keen gardeners. Sadly, I haven't had the money to look after it the way it deserves, but if the place is to be redeveloped then I'm sure you won't find that a problem. Chase tells me you have grand plans for it to be an upmarket mall.'

Alessandro marvelled that 'an upmarket mall' could be made to sound like 'the tower of Babel', although when he looked at the older woman there was no bitterness on her face.

'It will bring a great deal of useful traffic to the community.'

So he made money. It was what he did. It was what he had always done. And he was still doing it. He frowned as he remembered Chase's barbed comment about his lifestyle.

He had enough money to retire for the rest of his life and still be able to afford what most people could only ever dream of. So was he trying to make up for his parents' excesses? He was angry and frustrated that he should even be thinking along these lines. His parents were long gone and he had barely known them. How could he have, when, from a toddler, he had been in the care of a succession of nannies who had all fallen by the wayside in favour of boarding school abroad?

His parents had both been products of ridiculously wealthy backgrounds and their marriage had provided them with a joint income that they had both happily and irresponsibly squandered. Untethered by any sense of duty, and riding high on the hippie mentality that had been sweeping through Italy at the time, they had zoned out on recreational drugs, held lavish parties, travelled to festivals all over the world and bought houses which they had optimistically called 'communes' where people could 'get in touch with themselves'. And then, to top it all off, they had seen fit to throw away yet more of their inheritance on a series of ill-advised schemes involving organic farming and the import of ethnic products, all of which had crashed and burned.

Alessandro, barely through with university, had had to grasp what remained of the various companies and haul them back into profit when his parents had died in a boating accident in the Caribbean. Which he had done—in record time and with astounding success.

So what if he had learnt from his parents that financial security was the most important thing in life? So what if nothing and no one had ever been allowed to interrupt that one, single, driving ambition?

A woman in whom he had once rashly confided things that should have been kept to himself was certainly not going to make him start questioning his ethos.

Beth was now chatting amicably about the wonderful advantages of the place being developed, which would bring much-needed jobs to the community. To Alessandro's finely tuned ears, it sounded like forced enthusiasm. It was clear that she hated the thought of leaving the house, and he couldn't help wondering what someone who had always been active in community life in London would do in the stultifying boredom of the seaside.

It was after midday by the time they were standing outside the house saying their goodbyes. His chauffeur had returned for them but Chase pointedly made no move in the direction of the car.

'I'll make my own way back,' she said politely.

'Get in.' Alessandro stood to one side and then sighed with exasperation as she continued to look at him in stubborn silence. 'It's baking hot out here,' he said, purposefully invading her space by standing too close to her. 'And that outfit isn't designed for warm weather.'

'I'll take my chances on avoiding sunstroke.'

'Which is something I would rather not have on my conscience.'

'You don't have a conscience!'

'And you do?'

Chase looked at him with simmering resentment. *He* didn't look all hot and bothered. *He* looked as fabulous, cool and composed as he always did. Plus, he had charmed his way into Beth's affections. She could tell. He hadn't come on too strong, he had pointed out all the benefits of selling the place but in a perfectly reasonable way that no one would have been able to dispute. He was just so... damned *persuasive*! She hated it. And she hated the way she had found herself staring at him surreptitiously, hated the way her imagination had started playing tricks on her, hated the way she had had to fight against being seduced by the dark, deep, velvety tones of his voice.

'You can drop me to the bus stop. It's about a mile from here.'

'Are you going back to your office? Perhaps I could go in, meet all these people you work with... Tell your boss what a great job you've done even though the shelter will be sold. At least you've got me to thank for a reasonably happy Beth.'

'She's not happy.' Chase slid into the back seat, barely appreciating the terrific air conditioning as she grappled with the horror of having him invade her work space as well as having invaded her house. 'And I'm going home, as a matter of fact. I have work I can do there.'

'I've noticed that you try and avoid looking at me as much as possible,' Alessandro said softly. 'Why is that?'

As challenges went, that was about as direct as they came. *Avoid looking at him?* She wanted to laugh at the irony because all she seemed to do was look at him—it was just that she was careful with her staring. She looked at him now and the silence seemed to go on for ever as he gazed right back at her. Her mouth had gone dry and, although she knew that she should be breaking this yawning silence with a suitably innocuous remark, her mind refused to play along.

When he reached out and trailed one finger along her lips, she gasped with shock. There was a sudden, ferocious roaring in her ears and she couldn't breathe. All the strategies she had adopted to keep him at arm's length, to make him know that there was nothing whatsoever between them now aside from a brief, dubious past that no longer meant a thing, disappeared like mist on a hot summer's day.

She was no longer the lawyer with her life under control and he was no longer public enemy number one, the guy who could ruin everything she had built for herself in one fell swoop. She was a woman and he was a man and she still, against all rhyme or reason, wanted him with every incomprehensible, yearning ounce of her being.

'What are you doing?' She finally found her voice and pulled back.

Alessandro smiled. If he had had any doubts that she was still attracted to him, then he had none now. 'Maybe you're right,' he murmured, obediently removing his hand and observing her neutrally. 'Your friend really doesn't want to leave her home. The memories…the experiences… I don't see a bungalow on the coast cutting it, do you?'

'No.' Chase glared at him suspiciously. Her lips were burning from where he had touched them but she refused to cool them with her fingers.

'So I have an interesting proposal to put to you. You'd like me to believe that you're all bleeding heart and caring for the defenceless. Well, how would you like to prove it?'

CHAPTER FOUR

CHASE DIDN'T ANSWER immediately. Alessandro slid back the partition and told the driver to deliver them to a well-known French restaurant. By the time that sank in, the car had already altered course.

'What the heck do you think you're doing?'

'We're going to discuss my proposal over food. It's lunchtime.'

'And I've told you that I need to get back to do some work! Besides, I can't imagine what sort of proposal you have for me that involves you kidnapping me!'

'I like your use of language. Colourful.'

Chase was still burning from where his finger had touched her lips. Her mouth tingled.

'What made your friend decide to go into the good Samaritan business?'

Chase looked at him with unbridled suspicion. He was leaning indolently against the door and she got the feeling that it was all the better to see her. Like the big, bad wolf in the fairy story. 'I don't know what good it will do for you to hear Beth's potted history.'

'I've never known anyone who erects so many obstacles to complicate a perfectly harmless conversation.'

'That's because everyone kowtows to you, I imagine,' Chase offered ungracefully. While he was supremely relaxed, legs slightly open, one arm along the back of the seat, the other hanging loosely over his thigh, she was as tense as a block of wood. Her legs were tightly pressed together. Her lips were tightly compressed. Her fingers were interlinked and white at the knuckles.

'Rich people seem to have that effect,' she continued, avoiding his speculative eyes. 'I've seen it. They like throwing their weight around and they take it for granted that everyone is going to agree with everything they say.'

'You're getting all hot and bothered over nothing,' Alessandro murmured with mild amusement. 'The food at this restaurant is second to none. Have you been there? No? Then you should be looking forward to the experience. So why don't you relax? Tell me about your friend.'

'You didn't seem that interested in her when you were downgrading the price of the place by a thousand pounds per minute.'

'That was before I met her.'

Every argument she engineered seemed to crash into a brick wall. He wasn't interested in arguing with her. She, on the other hand, felt driven to keep arguing because something inside her was telling her that, if she didn't, she might find herself in dangerously unchartered territory. She might start remembering how funny he could be, how thoughtful, how engaging.

'She obviously comes from a fairly wealthy background,' Alessandro murmured encouragingly. 'And yet the road she decided to travel down wasn't exactly the predictable one.'

When he had first laid eyes on Chase after eight years, he had been shocked. And hard on the heels of that shock had come rage and bitterness. It seemed that he had badly underestimated the effect she had had on him. He hadn't put her behind him after all. Had he succeeded in doing that, he would have felt nothing but indifference and contempt. So, yes, revenge had been an option but why make a third party suffer? Weren't there other ways of handling a situation that had landed in his lap?

Rage and bitterness were corrosive emotions and there was one very good way of permanently eliminating them. He smiled with slow, deliberate intent.

Chase took note of that smile and wondered what the heck was going on.

'She hasn't had a…normal upbringing,' she said reluctantly. 'I know this because I knew her before this whole business with the shelter cropped up. Actually, she came to me when she was approached with your company's interference because we were already friends.'

'Interference? I'll overlook your take on my generous offer to buy her out. How did you become friends? Oh no, don't tell me—you were drawn to her because of your "care in the community" approach to life.'

'I'm glad you think it's funny to want to help other people!'

'I don't. I think it's admirable. Like I said, I just find the sentiments hard to swallow when they're coming from you.'

'If I'm such an awful person, why are you taking me out to lunch? Why didn't you let me find my own way back? The sale's agreed. Your legal team could take it from here on in.'

'But then I would miss out on the pleasure of watching you.'

Chase flushed and wondered whether he was being serious or not. She told herself that she didn't care and squashed the unwanted sliver of satisfaction it gave her when she thought of him watching her and *enjoying* it. Suddenly, it felt safer to talk about Beth than to sit in silence, as he looked at her, and speculate on all sorts of things that threw her into confusion.

'Her parents were both really well off,' she blurted out,

licking her lips nervously and wishing he would just stop looking at her in that pensive, brooding way that made the hairs on the back of her neck stand on end. 'They were missionaries. Beth says that as though it's the most normal thing in the world.'

She began to relax and half-smiled as she remembered the conversation they had had years ago when she had first met her. 'I mean, they didn't want to convert anyone, but they wanted to help people in the third world. They rented out their house, which is now the shelter, and took themselves off to Africa where they spent their own money on various irrigation and building projects. In fact, there's a plaque dedicated to them in one of the little villages over there.'

'Good people.' Alessandro thought of his own feckless parents and marvelled at the different ways money could be spent.

'They returned to London to live when Beth was a child. I think they wanted her educated over here. Maybe they thought that they had done what they had set out to do. At any rate, they found that they couldn't just do nothing once they'd come back, so they did lots of volunteer work at various places. They were both in their fifties by then. They'd had Beth when they were quite old. Beth went to university and studied to become an engineer, but found herself drawn to helping others, and when her parents died and she inherited the house and land, the stocks and shares and stuff, she turned the house into a shelter and hasn't looked back.'

'So effectively it's really the only house she's ever lived in and the only work she's ever done.'

'Yes. So there you have it. I don't suppose you can really understand what makes someone like Beth tick.'

'Do me a favour and stop trying to pigeon-hole me because I happen to have a bit of money.'

'A bit of money? You're as rich as Croesus.' They were now in front of the restaurant and Chase stared down at her formal working suit in dismay. 'I don't feel comfortable dining in a place like this wearing a suit.'

'Don't wear the jacket and undo the top three buttons of the shirt.'

'I beg your pardon?' She looked at him, her cheeks bright red, and he grinned at her. A full-on charming grin that knocked her sideways. It was that same grin that had turned her life on its head eight years ago and had made her continue to see him even though everything in her had been screaming at her to stop.

'You heard me.' He stepped out of the car and leaned through to give his driver instructions; when he straightened, it was to see that the prissy jacket, at least, had been left behind in the car.

'What about the buttons?' he asked, with the same sexy grin that made her toes curl and her skin feel tight and prickly.

He didn't give her time to think about it. With their eyes still locked, he undid the offending buttons. The softness of her skin under the starchy top... The glimpse of a cleavage... His breath caught sharply in his throat, mimicking hers.

'Don't do that!' Chase clasped the top and stumbled back a few steps.

'Much better. After you?'

Chase barely took note of the restaurant as they were ushered inside. She had been to a few fancy places since she had started working at Fitzsimmons. Her inclination to stare in awe had thankfully subsided. Nor was her mind in full working order just at the moment, not when her body was still in a state of heightened response at that intimate gesture of his undoing those buttons as though...as though she was his; as though they were the lovers they never, actually, ever had been.

'You said you had a proposal to put to me,' was the first thing she said tightly as soon as they were seated.

Alessandro perused the menu and made a few helpful suggestions which Chase ignored.

'This isn't a social occasion,' she said, choosing the first thing off the menu and shaking her head when he tried to entice her into a glass of wine.

'But it could be,' he returned smoothly. 'Couldn't it?'

'What do you mean?'

'I mean that eight years ago you were a married woman, albeit without my knowledge. Now, you're not. Your husband is no longer around and, unless you have another one stashed up your sleeve somewhere…?'

Caught unawares, Chase laughed shortly. 'Marriage isn't an institution I'll be going near again. Been there, done that, got the tee-shirt.'

Alessandro maintained a steady smile but his jaw hardened. 'Still in mourning?' he asked softly.

'Too wrapped up with my career,' Chase answered steadily.

'You haven't answered my question, but no matter. It really doesn't make any difference to the proposal I have in mind.' So she was still wrapped up in the ex. Why else would she have been at pains to avoid his question? He harked back to his image of the man, good-looking in a thuggish sort of way, her type of guy.

And yet, wrapped up or not in the past, she was still affected by *him*. He knew that with some highly developed sixth sense. As affected by him as he was, unfortunately, affected by her. She was an itch that needed to be scratched and he intended to do just that. Scratch the itch, and he would get her out of his system once and for all.

'So what's your proposal?' Had she ordered crab

mousse? It seemed so, as one was placed in front of her. She tucked into it without appetite.

'Do you get as personally wrapped up with all your clients as you do with this particular one?' Alessandro watched as she toyed with the starter in front of her.

'I told you. I knew her before… She's been a friend for years.'

'She's in her sixties.'

'What does age have to do with anything?' Chase looked at him defensively. Yes, she knew where this was going. Why was a young girl in her twenties friends with a woman in her sixties? Of course, age was no barrier to friendship. Many young people had friends who were much older than they were. What was the big deal? But Beth was one of her few friends, one of the few people in whom she had confided to some extent.

'Nothing. It's laudable. Although…'

'Although what? I suppose you're going to tell me that my friends should all be young and frivolous? That I should be spending my free time going to clubs and drinking instead of hanging out with a woman old enough to be my mother?'

'Although…isn't there something that suggests you shouldn't be working for someone with whom you're personally involved? I wasn't going to lecture you on hanging out with anyone. You choose your own friends, Chase. Interesting, however, that you never seemed to have a lot of those when I knew you eight years ago.'

'I…' She stared at him and, as their eyes tangled, she had the strangest sensation that he could see what was going on in her head. 'How would you know what friends I had or didn't have? You were only around part of the time. We met occasionally. You didn't know what I did in my spare time.'

Alessandro sat back as their food was placed in front

of them. He was surprised to see that he had eaten his starter although he couldn't even remember what he had ordered. She could barely meet his eyes and, again, he had the strangest feeling that there was something going on which he couldn't quite see.

He cursed himself for even being curious. 'True,' he concurred. 'And yet I remember a couple of occasions when kids from your course came up to you. You barely acknowledged them. Once they asked you if you were going to a party and you turned white and got rid of them as soon as you could.' The memory came from nowhere, as though it had been lurking there, just waiting to be aired.

'I…I had a husband.'

Alessandro found that he didn't like thinking about her husband. In fact, the thought of that shaved head, the tattoos, set his teeth on edge.

'Who would have been the same age as you were. Practically a teenager.'

It struck him that that was one of the things that had drawn him to her, the fact that she hadn't acted like a typical teenager. She had been old beyond her years in ways he couldn't quite pin down.

'I've never been into clubs and partying.'

'Never?'

'Why the thousand and one questions, Alessandro?' Her cheeks were bright red. Once upon a time she had actually enjoyed going out. She must have been fourteen or fifteen at the time, unsupervised, hanging out with older kids because most of the kids her age had had some form of parental control.

Schoolwork had been a breeze. She'd never had much need to bury her head in books. Absorbing information had come naturally to her. Oh yes, she had had plenty of time to go to clubs and parties. She frowned and wondered now whether she actually had enjoyed those parties, the dancing, the dim lights…and the confused, angry feeling that she shouldn't be there, that there should be someone in her life who cared enough to try and stop her.

'We're here. Why don't you just tell me what you want to say?'

'How does saving your friend's house sound to you?'

'Saving her house? What are you talking about?' Chase barely noticed that the starters had been removed, to be replaced with yet more exquisite food which she couldn't remember ordering. Despite having said no, her wine glass had been filled, and with a small shrug she sipped some of the cold white wine which tasted delicious. 'Are you going to build your mall around it?'

'Somehow I don't think that people on a quest for designer shoes would feel comfortable having to circumnavigate a shelter for women in need of help, do you?'

Chase thought about that and laughed. It was the first truly genuine laugh he had heard from her since they had met again and, God, how well he remembered the sound of it. Even back then, she hadn't laughed a lot, and when she had it was the equivalent of the sun coming out from behind a cloud. It was exactly the same now and he looked at her with rampant male appreciation.

'I know.' She grinned and leaned towards him confidingly. 'But wouldn't it be a great ploy? They'd all feel so guilty that they would contribute bags of money just to clear their conscience before they went to the shop next door to buy the designer shoes! Beth would never have any financial problems in her life again!'

'It would certainly be a solution of sorts to her financial problems,' Alessandro concurred.

'But you don't mean that, do you?' Her laughter subsided. She nibbled at the edges of her food and decided not to bother trying to second-guess what he had brought her here for.

'Not quite what I had in mind but the image was worth it just to hear the sound of your laugh.'

'Then what?' She ignored the tingling those words produced inside her. 'Will it involve getting any lawyers in? I can't honestly make any far-reaching decisions without reference to my boss.'

'How will he feel when you tell him that you'd had no option but to sell the place to me?' Alessandro asked curiously and Chase gave it some thought.

'A favourable outcome would have been for our client to hang on to the premises. The truth, however, is that our clients don't earn the firm money. The big money comes from our corporate and international clients. Intellectual property lawyers, patent lawyers, even some family lawyers…they earn the big money. I'm just a little cog subsidised by the big-fee lawyers, and I'm there because Fitzsimmons is a morally ethical law firm that believes in putting back some of what they take.'

Alessandro wasn't interested in hearing a long speech on the moral values of Fitzsimmons. 'Wonderful,' he said neutrally. 'But this particular decision won't require involvement from anyone else in your firm.'

'Okay.'

'Nor is it illegal.' Alessandro read the suspicion in her eyes and looked at her with wry amusement. 'However, yes, it will involve the house remaining in your friend's possession. More than that, what if I told you that I would be prepared to pay off all her debts and inject sufficient cash to make sure she can keep the shelter going for a very long time to come?'

Chase gaped at him. For a few seconds, she honestly believed that she had misheard what he had said. Then she thoughtfully closed her knife and fork, wiped her mouth with her linen serviette and searched his face to see whether this was some way of making a fool of her.

'So Beth…' she said slowly, giving him ample time to cut her short and rubbish what she thought he had said, 'gets to keep the house, plus you pay off her debts, plus you put money into renovating and updating the place… am I getting it right?'

'That would be about the size of it.'

'And you would do this because…?' Brow furrowed, she suddenly smiled at him with genuine delight. 'I know why. You were impressed with what you found at the shelter, weren't you? I don't suppose you were expecting it to be as well run as it was. Beth spares no effort when it comes to doing good for those girls. It's hard to go there and not be moved by what you find. I'm so pleased, Alessandro.' She reached out impulsively and covered his hand with hers.

Alessandro looked at the shining glow on her face and was extremely pleased with himself for being the one to put it there.

'Can I call and tell her?' Chase asked excitedly. 'No, perhaps I'd better not do that.' She flashed him an apologetic smile. 'You'll have to forgive the lawyer in me, but we'll have to get this all signed on the dotted line. But, once she knows, she'll be over the moon. Between you and me, I don't honestly think she was looking forward to a quiet retirement by the seaside.'

'So you agree with me that this is a good idea?'

'Of course I do! I'd be a fool not to.' Even with her defences up, knowing how he felt about her after what she had done to him, she knew that there was a blazingly good streak in him. Those lectures he had given had been given for free, and he had taken considerable time out to individually help some of the students, had actually offered internships to a couple of them. He hadn't just been as sexy as hell, he had shown her a glimpse of humanity that she had never seen before and that, amongst other things, had roped her in and kept her tethered in a place she had known was desperately dangerous.

'Naturally, there's no such thing as a free lunch in life.' Alessandro shook his head ruefully, the very picture of a man who regrets that there wasn't. 'I wish I could say that I was the perfect philanthropist, but you have to understand that all this will cost me a small fortune.'

The smile died on her face. The bill was brought to them and she automatically reached for her bag but it had been settled before she could rummage out her wallet and pay her fair share. 'Of course it will,' she agreed coolly. 'And you'll want to be repaid for your largesse. Will your rates be competitive?'

'Shall we go?'

Chase could feel disappointment rising inside her as he waited for her to gather her things, standing aside so that she could precede him out of the restaurant. Once outside, she didn't bother with her stupid jacket. He had been right when he had remarked that it was impractical for the weather.

What had he been playing at? Stringing her along with all manner of empty promises only to yank them all back at the last minute? Didn't he realise that, if Beth had wanted to borrow money so that she could clear her debts and get the shelter really going, she would have gone to the bank? Of course, Chase thought uncomfortably, she *had* tried that some time ago but to no avail. She simply hadn't had the collateral to get a loan of the size she required, even though the bank manager had known her parents. Money was just not being lent, not to ventures that had nothing to gain. Had Alessandro checked that out himself and come to the conclusion that he could provide her with the money but jack up the interest rates?

'I really believed you for a minute,' she simmered, barely noticing that she was being ushered into the back seat of his car. 'I really thought that you had been so impressed by what you saw that you decided to do the right thing. I really thought that there was a part of you that was the same guy who gave internships to those girls years ago, and the same guy who put in extra time helping that little group of Asian students through their language barriers with some of their papers.'

'You remember. Those girls have been promoted several times. One left a year ago to have a baby and returned a few months ago to resume work. Two of the Chinese students work in my Hong Kong offices.'

'You kept in touch with them.' She fought against the pull of a connection that threatened her valued self-control. She severed the incipient connection. 'Where are we going?'

'To discuss my proposal further. Out of public earshot.'

'Beth can't afford to pay you back for a loan.' Back to business, but her mind was still straying dangerously close to memories of the man she had once been so irresistibly drawn to—the man she knew still existed even if those complex sides, revealed all those years ago, would never again get an airing in her presence.

'Whoever mentioned loans?'

'You're confusing me, Alessandro.'

'Ditto,' he murmured under his breath. He looked at her in silence, his searing attraction laced with a poignant familiarity that wasn't doing his libido any favours, until she shifted uncomfortably and took notice of her surroundings. They were away from the hustle and bustle.

'And you haven't said where we're going. This isn't the way back to my house.'

'Well spotted. It's the way to mine.'

'What?' Chase immediately felt her pulses begin to race. She didn't want to be here, in this car! Far less heading to his place, wherever that was! He had just pulled a cheap trick, whatever he had said about his offer not being a loan. He had really shown his true colours, aside from which she knew that she should steer clear of him. But the memory of how much she had craved to see where he lived eight years ago slammed into her with the force of a freight train. 'Let me out of this car *immediately*.'

'Calm down.'

'I'm *perfectly* calm.'

'You're as perfectly calm as a volcano on the point of eruption. Relax. We'll be there in ten minutes.'

Chase felt ill at the thought of stepping foot into his private space. She had never thought that she would see him again and, now that she had, she should be laying down clear boundaries. Instead, the lines were blurring. He had come to her house, seen the way she lived, formed his opinions. Now she was going to his.

She watched with growing panic as the sleek, black car manoeuvred through quiet streets, finally turning into an avenue through imposing black wrought-iron gates. The houses here were beyond spectacular. No superlative could do justice to the pristine white-and-cream facades, the ornate foliage, the lush greenery, the air of indecently wealthy seclusion. The cars were all top of the range, high end.

So this was where he lived. Never in her wildest, twenty-year-old's dreams could she have come up with this.

'I'm not comfortable with this,' she said automatically as his driver opened the passenger door for her.

'I wasn't comfortable conducting a private conversation in a public place.'

'There was nothing private about our conversation. It was a business deal.' But she couldn't help staring at the enormous house in front of her, the perfectly shaped shrubs on either side of the black door, the highly polished brass of the knocker. Nor could she help feeling, in some deep, dark part of her, that their conversation had been threaded with undercurrents that were anything but businesslike.

'I love the way you constantly argue with me,' Alessandro remarked drily as he opened the front door and stood aside so that she brushed past him. 'It's refreshing. You did that eight years ago as well. And it was refreshing then.'

There had been times, countless times, when he had just wanted to scoop her to him and silence those feisty arguments with his mouth…just kiss them away. But he had been prepared to bide his time. He had been prepared to do way too much to attain the eventual goal of just having her. She had taught him the art of patience, damn fool that he had been.

Chase didn't say anything. She was too busy being impressed. It wasn't just the size but the pristine perfection: marble flooring, the colour of pale honey, was broken by silky rugs. The paintings on the walls varied in size but were recognisable—who on earth had paintings on their walls that were *recognisable*? The impressive staircase leading up gave onto a landing which was dominated by a massive stained-glass window that did magical things to the sunlight filtering through it.

She came back to planet Earth to find that Alessandro was watching her, hands in his pockets.

'You have a beautiful place,' she said politely.

Alessandro dutifully looked around him, as though taking stock of where he lived for the first time, then he shrugged. 'It works for me. Come through.'

'I honestly don't see why you couldn't have laid out your terms and conditions for this so-called "not a loan" at the restaurant.' But she followed as he led the way towards a kitchen that looked as though it had never been used. He didn't do cooking; she remembered him telling her that way back when.

'Have you *ever* used this kitchen?' she asked, perching on one of the top-of-the-range chrome and leather bar stools by the counter and watching as he attempted to make sense of the complicated coffee machine.

'You don't want coffee, do you?' he eventually asked, turning to glance at her over his shoulder.

'If I did, would you be able to figure out how that thing works?'

'Unlikely.'

'Tea would be nice.' She hadn't appreciated just how rich he was. These were the surroundings of a man to whom money was literally no object. She bristled when she thought of him holding her to ransom by reducing his offer for the shelter just because he could.

'I'm very good with a kettle and some tea bags.' He hunted them down, opening and closing cupboards. 'I come in here very rarely,' he offered by way of explanation. 'I have a housekeeper who makes sure it's stocked and a chef who does all my cooking on the occasions when I happen to be in.'

'Lucky you.'

There wasn't a single woman on the planet, Alessandro thought, who would have offered that sarcastic response when confronted with the reality of his wealth. 'You don't mean that.'

'You're right. I don't.' She took the cup of tea from him. The cup was fine-bone china, weirdly shaped, with an art deco design running down one side. When she thought of him trying and failing to work out how his high-tech appliances worked, she could feel a smile tugging the corners of her mouth, but there was no way that she would be seduced by any windows of vulnerability in him.

'Why do you have all these gadgets in here if you don't cook and barely use the kitchen?'

'I remain eternally optimistic.'

Chase wished he wouldn't do that, wouldn't undermine

her defences with his sense of humour. She didn't want to remember how he had always been able to make her laugh. She didn't want him to make her laugh now.

'Well, now we're here, maybe you could explain this business with the shelter?'

Alessandro looked at her. He wondered what it was about her that just seemed to capture his imagination and hold it to ransom.

'You have no idea what goes through me when I think of what you did eight years ago,' he murmured.

'You brought me here so that you could talk about that?' Chase fidgeted uncomfortably. She wanted to drag her disobedient eyes away from him but somehow she couldn't.

'But the past belongs in the past. What's the good dredging it up every two seconds? The best thing I could do right now is send you on your not-so-merry way, out of my life once and for all. Unfortunately, I find that there's something holding me back.'

'What?' It was a barely whispered response. She cleared her throat and did her utmost to remember that this was just an opponent whom she happened to have known a long time ago. It didn't work. She still found herself hanging onto his every word with shamefully bated breath, watching him watching her, and letting those deep, dark looks penetrate every fibre of her being. Dampness pooled shamefully between her legs, physical proof of something she was loath to admit, and her nipples tingled, sensitive and taut against her lacy bra. 'What's holding you back?' She shifted, felt her slippery wetness making her panties uncomfortable.

'You.' Alessandro allowed that one word to ferment in the lengthening silence between them until it was bursting with significance.

'I have no idea what you're talking about.'

'Of course you do,' he drawled smoothly. 'We can both

waste a little time while I indulge your desire to feign ignorance but what would be the point? We'll end up getting to the same place eventually. Despite what happened between us, despite the fact that my levels of respect for you are lamentably non-existent, I find that I'm still sexually attracted to you. And I wouldn't be telling you this now if I didn't know that it was a two-way street.

'And don't bother trying to deny it. I've seen the way you look at me when you think my attention is somewhere else and I've seen the way you respond whenever I get within a two-foot radius of you. We had it once and we have it again. It's a shame but…' He shrugged with graceful elegance.

'You're…you're mad…' Her words said one thing; her treacherous body however, was, singing a different refrain.

'Am I? I don't think so.'

Chase watched, mesmerised, as he slowly stood up and breached the short distance separating them to plant his hands on either side of her chair, locking her into place so that she could only raise her eyes upwards to stare at him. She could feel the pulse in her neck beating wildly, a physical giveaway that every word he was saying struck home.

'I'm the lawyer working for Beth; sure, we know each other…' The word faltered and died in her throat as he cupped her cheek with his hand and stroked it with his thumb.

Years ago, their chaste relationship had pulsated with unexplored passion and unspoken, untested lust. Now, as his hand remained on her cheek, she shuddered and resisted the urge to sink into the caress.

'Please, Alessandro, don't.'

'Your body is telling me something different.'

'I don't want to start any kind of relationship with you.'

'Relationship?' Alessandro queried huskily. 'Who's talking about a relationship? I could no more have a relationship with you than I could with a deadly snake. No, I'm not interested in a relationship. I'm interested in having sex with you, plain and simple. Just like you're interested in having sex with me. Don't you want to touch what you spent months staring at eight years ago? Don't you want to finish what you started? I do. A lot.'

Chase opened her mouth to tell him to get lost but nothing emerged. His cool, brilliant dark eyes held her in a trance even though she knew that every word that left that perfect mouth was offensive and insulting.

And yet...her imagination was going crazy. The fantasies she had had of him touching her all those years ago sprang from the box into which they had been firmly locked and attacked her on all fronts. She weakened at the thought of his fingers stroking the wetness between her legs, his mouth kissing the twin peaks of her breasts, nipping the tight buds of her nipples, suckling on them while he continued to stroke her dampness...

'So here's the deal.' Alessandro was finding it hard to contain his excitement at the prospect of netting the prey that had once escaped him and putting to bed, once and for all, feelings that had no place in his life. Her skin was like satin beneath his fingertips. 'You sleep with me for as long as I want you to and the shelter stays. Renovated, updated and modernised. Your friend's debts will be cleared.'

'You want to *pay* me for services rendered?'

'I want to take what you want to give. In return, you get the shelter. And please don't try and tell me that you don't want to touch me. You do.' His mouth met hers and Chase braced her hands on his shoulders, determined to push him away. But instead she was horrified to find that she was caressing him; that her mouth was returning his kiss with equal urgency; that she was sinking into him like a person starved of nourishment; that she was whimpering, little mewling sounds that shocked and excited her in equal measure and, worse, when he finally pulled back that the sudden space between them felt cold and unwelcome.

'I think I've proved my point.' There was a betraying unsteadiness in his voice. He might not like her or respect her but, God, did he want her. More than anything or anyone. 'Let's finish this business. A couple of weeks, tops, and you can disappear back to whatever life you have, having made your friend a very happy bunny.'

Chase had withdrawn and was rising to her feet, arms tight around her body.

'I'll never do that, Alessandro!'

Alessandro shrugged and tried to wrestle back his self-control, even though just watching her was affecting him in ways he could barely quantify. 'You have forty-eight hours to give me your answer then the deal is off the table.'

'I've already given you my answer!'

'Forty-eight hours…' he repeated, his eyes roving over her flushed face and her defiant yet tellingly shaken expression. 'And let's just wait and see if your answer remains the same after you've…thought things through.'

CHAPTER FIVE

BETH TELEPHONED THAT evening. She could barely contain her excitement. She might be able to hang on to the shelter!

'What do you mean?' Chase asked tentatively. She had spent the past few hours unable to get down to work. Alessandro's offer kept playing in her head over and over again, like a tape recording on a loop. She had stalked out of his house, her head held high, and he had made no attempt to stop her. She thought that that, in itself, displayed a level of arrogance that should really have had her turning her back on him for ever. She loathed arrogance.

Unfortunately, along with her determination not to be browbeaten into making a pact with the devil, there lurked the uncomfortable awareness that, devil or not, he roused something in her she didn't want but couldn't resist. He had kissed her and her whole world had felt as though it had been tilted on its side. It was the same something that had been there eight years ago; the same something that had made her behave in a way she had known she shouldn't. Sexual attraction: he had put his finger on it. Sexual attraction and more...

'I had a call from Mr Moretti.'

'Ah...' She drifted over to the sofa and sat down.

'He's a lot more compassionate than I originally gave him credit for. You know, when this whole business started, well, I just thought of him as a human bulldozer, not caring what or who got in his way.'

Chase smirked. 'What did he say?'

'That he's spoken to you and you've both come up with a plan to secure the future of the shelter; you're both trying to iron out the creases. Chase, my dear, I can't tell you how overjoyed I would be if this worked out. I've been dreading telling the girls that they'll have to go, plus the waiting list is so long of people who need us. Not to mention the seaside idea. Never could quite see myself retiring by the coast and having coffee mornings with all the other retirees.'

'I'm sure there's more to life by the coast than coffee mornings.' Her mind was in a whirl. She was also incensed. So much for the forty-eight hours after which her decision would be final! How could she have been foolish enough to believe that Alessandro wouldn't exert influence over a decision he wanted? 'Lots of people go down there to…er…sail…' she said vaguely.

'Can't think of anything worse. Drive me mad!'

'Did he mention what this idea of…ours happens to be?' Chase prodded gently.

'Not a word!' Beth hooted. 'Said it was something he wanted kept up his sleeve. Probably to do with tax!'

'Sorry?'

'Well, don't these awfully rich people enjoy tax breaks by giving money to charity? We *are* a registered charity…'

Chase sighed and decided to lay off the details of any such scheme. Despite a sharp brain and her degree in engineering, Beth's interest in all things financial was sketchy at best.

'Sometimes,' she said, noncommittal.

'At any rate, it all sounds very promising. I know what you're going to say, my dear! Don't count your chickens… But I get a good feeling from that young man. Did the minute I met him. Showed a real interest in everything we do here at the shelter.'

Alternatively, Chase thought, the man was a skilled actor with a golden tongue. Take your pick.

She spent another twenty minutes on the line as Beth waxed lyrical about Alessandro, and as soon as her friend was off the phone she hunted down the business card he had given her and telephoned him on his mobile.

'Well, that was a low trick!' was the first thing she said the minute she heard his voice on the other end.

At a little after nine, Alessandro had just finished wrapping up a two-hour conference call and was about to leave the office, which was deserted aside from him. In the act of reaching for his jacket, he flung it down on the leather sofa instead and relaxed to take her call. 'So Beth called you,' he drawled without an ounce of shame. 'I thought she might. She certainly was over the moon when I spoke to her. Charming woman.'

'You're a low-down, sneaky rat!'

Alessandro grinned. Whatever Chase's downsides, she was by far and away the most outspoken, feisty woman he had ever met in his entire life. It would probably be a tiresome trait in the long run, but just for the moment it was certainly invigorating.

'Now, now, now…is that any way to speak to your friend's knight in shining armour?'

Chase detected the wicked grin in his voice and gritted her teeth in frustration. 'What did you tell her?'

'Long conversation. I'll fill you in when we next meet.'

'How could you?'

'How could I what? Make that delightful woman one very happy lady?'

'Try and twist my arm into accepting your…your… No, I take that back; I understand perfectly how you did that!'

'It's comforting to know that you can read me like a

book. That way, there will be no mixed messages between us. Now, why don't you carry on working and I'll call you in the morning?'

'I haven't been able to do a scrap of work today!'

'Too busy thinking about me?'

Chase made an inarticulate sound of pure frustration and racked her brains for a clever riposte.

'Well, why don't you get some well-deserved beauty sleep and we'll talk in the morning…or later, if you'd like. After all, your forty-eight hour deadline won't yet be up. Don't worry. I'll be in touch.'

She was left clutching the phone which had gone dead because he had hung up on her. He'd barely heard her out! She felt that there was a lot more anger to be expressed. Unfortunately, without an adversary at which to direct her attack, she was left simmering and fuming on her own as she flounced down in front of the television, having abandoned all attempts at reviewing her caseload.

She was barely aware of what she was watching. It appeared to be a crime drama with an awful lot of victims and an extremely elusive murderer. She had fully zoned out of the story line when, at a little after ten, she heard the insistent buzz of the doorbell and was jerked into instant red alert.

Alessandro.

Surely he wouldn't have the cheek to show up at this hour at her house?

Of course he wouldn't. Why would a shark bother to stalk a minnow when it knew full well that the minnow would swim into its gaping jaw of its own free will?

Much more likely that it was Beth; as she slipped on her bedroom slippers and padded out to the front door, she was already trying to work out what she might say to begin killing her friend's already full-blown optimism.

She pulled open the door to Alessandro and her mouth fell open in surprise.

'Rule one,' he said, strolling past her to take up residence in the sitting room before she had had a chance to marshal her thoughts into order. 'When living in London, never open the door unless you know who's going to be standing on your doorstep.' He turned towards her, which instantly made her feel like a guest in her own home. 'I could have been anyone.'

'And, unfortunately for me, you're not!' She folded her arms and looked at him with gimlet-eyed stoniness. 'What are you doing here?'

'You said that you were finding it impossible to get down to work because you were thinking of me, so I thought I'd drop by.'

'I never said any such thing!' He was not in work clothes but in a pair of black jeans and a grey polo-necked shirt. He looked drop-dead gorgeous, which did nothing for her composure, because she felt far from drop-dead anything in her tatty old jogging bottoms and a tee-shirt that had lost its shape in the wash years ago. She also wasn't wearing a bra and she was conscious of her nipples poking against the cotton of the tee-shirt.

'I must have misunderstood. My apologies. But I'm here now, so maybe you could offer me a cup of coffee? Nothing stronger. I'm driving.'

'I wasn't about to offer you anything!'

'Don't you want to let off steam? You were breathing brimstone and fire down the line less than an hour ago.'

'Because you went behind my back and led Beth to believe that you were going to save her shelter—worse, led her to believe that the decision lies with *me*!'

'Oh, but it does, doesn't it?' He stared at her with a mixture of cool certainty and mild surprise that she should question the obvious.

'What on earth did you tell her?'

'That you and I were working on a plan to see whether the place could be saved and money invested.'

'Because you're such a good guy, right?'

'Let's not go down the tortuous route of moral ethics, Chase. However non-existent you think mine are, you're not exactly in a position to point fingers.'

Chase chewed her lip and glared impotently at him. 'I'll make you some coffee.' She shrugged and turned away. He was here now, in her house, smug and self-satisfied at the awkward position into which he had shoved her; sooner or later they would have to talk, so why not make it sooner? She couldn't see herself getting to sleep in a hurry.

She returned with two mugs of coffee to find him ensconced in one of the deep chairs, the very picture of a man totally relaxed in his surroundings.

'You gave me your word that I would have forty-eight hours.'

'And nothing's changed on that front,' Alessandro said smoothly. 'You still do. I've just thrown an extra something into the mix.'

'And that wasn't fair.'

'Between us, the gloves are off. You're as scheming as I am, so don't even bother to try and play the wounded party with me.' He had not been able to get her out of his head and, the more he thought about her, the more urgent his need to have her became. The sooner he had her, sated this voracious lust, the faster he would be rid of her. He couldn't wait.

Nudging the back of his mind was the uncomfortable truth that he was not a vengeful man by nature, that this sort of revenge was born from emotions which he had handed over to her eight years ago only to find them thrown back in his face. She had shown him his vulnerability and the force of his reactions now lay in that one, unmentioned reality. It was something he could hardly stand to admit even to himself and it lay there, buried like a pernicious weed, even when he had told himself over the years that he had had a narrow escape; that getting involved with a woman such as she had turned out to be would have been an unmitigated disaster.

'You think you know me,' Chase muttered bitterly, and Alessandro narrowed his eyes to look at her.

'By which you mean… Tell me.'

'Nothing,' she said in a harried undertone. 'This is an impossible situation.'

'No, it's not. It's the sound of the wheel turning full circle.'

'You don't like me, you don't respect me, so why on earth would you want to sleep with me? You must be able to snap your fingers and have a thousand women standing to attention and saluting. Why bother with the one who doesn't want to fall in line?'

Chase projected into the future. So she turned him down and the shelter became a shopping mall with her friend retreating to the seaside, where she would live out the rest of her days, bored, grumbling and dissatisfied. Furthermore, what would happen to their friendship? Alessandro had put her in an invidious position, for would her friend ever forgive her for being the one who failed to 'iron out the crease' that would have enabled her to hang on to what she loved?

She would never be able to tell Beth what that particular crease was and eventually the wonderful friendship they had would wither and die under the weight of Beth's misunderstanding and simmering resentment. How could it not?

'I've always considered myself a man to rise to the challenge,' Alessandro said coolly.

'And I'm your challenge.' There was no point moaning

about the unfairness of fate. He had seriously upped the ante by involving Beth and now she had to step up to the plate one way or another. He might well consider himself a guy who couldn't resist a challenge, but when had *she* ever been the sort of woman to back down? Her days of doing that had been put behind her.

And he talked about unfinished business… Wasn't it the same for her? Over the years, through everything that had happened, hadn't he been the burr under her skin? Hadn't she had broken nights dreaming of him? Hadn't she re-played scenarios in her head during which what they had had came to fruition?

More to the point, hadn't all those scenarios sprung back into instant life the second she had laid eyes on him again? Common sense had wrestled with what she consid-ered her stupid weakness, because he was as out of bounds now as he had ever been, despite the fact that Shaun was no longer on the scene. But common sense was failing to win the battle. She knew she looked at him, wondered…

'Are you going to tell me that I'm not yours?' Alessan-dro asked softly. Two adults, he thought, who wanted each other and this time no hidden obstacle lurking in the way. On top of that, so much for her to get out of it. So where was the problem? He had never had the slightest curiosity to plumb the hidden depths of any woman, yet now he had a sudden, urgent desire to reach into her head and discover what was going on behind that beautiful, enigmatic facade. The thrill of the unexplored was heady and erotic and it took a surprising amount of will power to remain where he was, holding on to silence as a weapon of persuasion.

'It feels…odd. Just not right.'

'But you can't deny that what I'm saying makes sense. If we cut through all the redundant emotion, if we leave bitterness and the past aside, don't we still fancy the hell out of one another?'

Chase thought of his hands on her body, touching her. She had stayed far away from the opposite sex over the past eight years. Offers had been plentiful, some of them horribly insistent, but there was no way she was going to get involved with any man ever again.

So here she was, nearing thirty, unattached, with barely any social life to speak of. Wasn't it time for her to rejoin the human race? And wouldn't she be able to do that once, as he had put it, business between them was finally finished? If she were brutally honest with herself, hadn't Alessandro been as much a reason for where she was now with her life, as Shaun had been? He had had such a dramatic hold on her all those years ago and the way things had ended between them had scarred her to the extent that she had just simply withdrawn.

'It just feels so…cold and detached. So businesslike.' She rubbed her lightly perspiring hands along the soft cotton of her jogging pants.

'You're looking for flowers and chocolates and courtship?' His mouth curled into a cynical smile. 'I believe I fell into that trap once before. I don't repeat my mistakes twice.'

Chase thought she could detect the rapid beating of her heart as he stared at her broodingly. She felt as though she had one foot raised over the edge of a precipice as she made her mind up as to whether to jump or not. Yet, she knew that that was a fallacy. She was older, wiser and tougher and, if this felt like a business arrangement, then it had to be said that business arrangements came with definite upsides. For starters, she would know all the parameters. She would not be hurt. She would be taking from him just as he would be taking from her and, when they walked away from each other, she would be freed from the strange half-emptiness of regret that had been her companion for the past eight years.

It was a tantalising thought.

As though she had opened a door to a gremlin, she was suddenly released from the constraints of having to fight the attraction that had been gnawing away at her. She *imagined*...and the images were so vivid that she felt faint.

'I can't think of anything I would want less than a courtship,' she informed him with as much cool detachment as she could muster. Certainly not flowers or chocolate. He had given her those once before. He must have realised, in the aftermath of her dumping him, that those tokens had hit the bin before she had had time to make it back to her flat. Thank goodness she had bluntly refused to accept anything else. At least he would never be able to add 'gold-digger' to all the other bitter insults he had heaped on her.

Watching her closely, Alessandro knew that he had won. She was going to be his. And yet, instead of the satisfaction of accomplishment, he was irked by the notion that she didn't want a courtship because she had already had a courtship from the one guy who had really counted in her life.

Who gave a damn about the ex-husband? The bald fact was that the man was no longer around and the one woman who had eluded him was going to be his. He was not now, and never would be, in competition with a ghost. When he was through with her, he would discard her and she could return to the photo albums she had stashed in a drawer somewhere. He didn't care. He would have got the one and only thing he wanted from her and for which, essentially, he was prepared to pay a high price, bearing in mind all the money that would need pumping into that shelter if it was to achieve habitable status.

'Is that because you've decided to limit yourself to one and that role was filled by your dearest, departed ex—or because you've had so many in the intervening years that you're sick of them?'

'I've been so busy in the past few years that I haven't had time for…for any kind of relationship.' How strange it felt to be sharing this kind of confidential information! Over time, she had become defined by her need for privacy. She knew that most of her colleagues her age thought she was weird. She knew they thought that, with her looks, she should be putting herself out there instead of working all the hours God made before scuttling off to a house to which none of them had ever been invited. She didn't care, and she had become so accustomed to self-containment that she now looked at Alessandro, wide-eyed, startled by her outburst.

'You mean…?' Curiosity kicked in with cursed force.

'There's actually nothing out of the ordinary about that. Relationships require time and I haven't had a lot of that while I've been trying to climb up the career ladder.' Chase knew how she sounded: tough, hard, cold. This wasn't the person she had ever set out to be but she wasn't going to apologise for the fact that her life hadn't been a round of parties, late nights and sex with random men.

'So ever since your husband died…?' he encouraged.

Chase tilted her chin defensively. 'I know how it must sound to someone like you.'

'Someone like me?'

'I expect you have an active sexual life. Lots of women. You're rich, you're good-looking, you're self-assured. You wouldn't have a clue how I could…hold off on relationships for quite a long time.'

'I managed it eight years ago. With you.' He shook his head, impatient with himself. And he did, actually, understand. Grief and mourning could do all sorts of things and have all manner of consequences. That said…

'It's not healthy,' he said brusquely.

Chase reddened. 'I haven't asked for your opinion,' she

said defensively. 'And the only reason I'm telling you this is because you might want to have a rethink.'

'Not following you.'

'I'm a little rusty in that particular area.' She gave a brittle, nonchalant laugh, but inwardly every part of her felt exposed, vulnerable and uncertain. What on earth was she doing? She wasn't like the women she imagined him being drawn to; she lacked the finesse and the experience. Did she want to risk the humiliation of having him look at her with amusement and disappointment just because she needed to know what she had missed all those years ago? Because, sure, the shelter would be a happy bonus, but she was already yielding for reasons that were far more complex than the desire to save her friend's shelter. Shelter or no shelter, she would never have allowed herself to be manipulated into doing something she didn't want to do.

Alessandro frowned. He had been quick to assert that his proposal was a non-negotiable arrangement designed to assuage the inconvenient need he had to sleep with her and thereby get her out of his system. He had been even quicker to inform her that he would not be investing it with any bells and whistles. It would be sex, no more or less. Yet, he found that he didn't care for the cool approach she was taking. Hell, she was still sitting a million miles away from him!

'I'll cope. Does that mean that you've made your mind up?'

'Perhaps you're right. Perhaps I've been curious. Maybe we do need to…eh…take what we have a step further.' Her heart was beating like a drum. 'But if I accept,' she continued firmly, because it was important for him to know that she wasn't making a decision based on blackmail or unfair persuasion, 'it's not to do with the shelter. Much as I love Beth, I would never do something I didn't want to because of her.'

'Right now, the only thing that matters is that we're going to be lovers.' He gave her a slashing, sexy smile and patted the space next to him on the sofa. 'So why don't you come and sit next to me and we can continue *bonding* with a little less physical distance between us?'

Chase thought she could actually hear her own painful breathing. Fear and apprehension at touching him, being close to him, warred with unbridled excitement. She had stepped off the side of the precipice and she had no idea what she had let herself in for but it was an adventure she needed to have. It was a situation over which she could only hope to exercise control and, for someone who had constructed walls of control all around her, it was a daunting prospect. But she had done daunting before. Many, many times. She could handle daunting.

'How long do you think this will take?'

'Come again?' Alessandro had never had to fight this hard for anyone. Sexual attraction had proved stronger than his very justifiable bitterness and dislike. He had had to swallow a lot and yet, having done that, having got her to the place he wanted, surely the going should get less tough?

'How long do you think it will take before we get past this…thing? A night? A couple of days?'

'How the hell should I know?' Alessandro raked his fingers through his hair and frowned at her. 'And why are we talking about timelines, anyway? All I want to do right now is touch you, so why don't we dispense with the conversation and get down to business?' He sprawled back, arms extended on the back of the sofa, legs loose and open.

He was the very essence of man at his most physical, Chase thought with a shiver, utterly and beautifully masculine; she licked her lips cautiously. She wanted this so badly. It felt as though it was something she had never stopped wanting. She tentatively closed the distance between them to sit like a wooden doll next to him.

'I feel I should tell you,' she whispered as Alessandro lazily removed one arm from the back of the sofa to trail it along her neck.

'You talk a lot,' he growled and then, almost from nowhere, plucked from thin air, 'You always did. As though you had too many words inside you that needed to get out.' He laughed softly, caught unaware by the memory. 'Do you remember the way you would mention a case file and then force me to have an opinion so that you could practise shooting it down in flames?'

Hell, what was he going on about? He angled his body round and pulled her towards him and it was like the promise of heaven. The undiluted thrill of having her in his arms was incomparable and he urgently sought her mouth, plundering it while his hands moved down to circle her waist. His erection was steel-hard and painful. More than anything else, he wanted to rip down those unattractive jogging bottoms, pull aside her panties and then just thrust into her, hard and fast, until he got explosive relief. There would be time enough to do the whole gentle foreplay stuff later.

Chase could feel the raw energy emanating from him in waves but that soft laugh, that nostalgic memory he had laid out bare for her without really thinking, was strangely seductive, strangely relaxing. Fingers that had been curled into his polo shirt suddenly splayed against his chest and she struggled back from him.

'Wait...'

'I'm not sure I can.' But he reluctantly drew back, his breathing ragged and uneven. She was stripped of her tough, outer shell, the consummate lawyer and assertive career woman. He glimpsed a uniquely feminine vulnerability that startled him, because she was the last woman on the planet he would ever have labelled *'vulnerable'*.

Once upon a time, sure, but then once upon a time he'd been an idiot.

'I'm not into playing games,' he drawled just in case she got it into her head that she could string him along for a second time. 'And, just in case you think that you might be able to pull off any "one step forward, two steps back" tactic, then forget it. This time round, you're dealing with a different person, Chase. My levels of tolerance when it comes to you are non-existent.'

'I know they are!' Whatever the backdrop to what they had had eight years ago, it all seemed so innocent now in retrospect. 'It's just...'

'Just *what*, Chase?'

'Never mind.' She wasn't looking for sweet nothings whispered in her ear nor was she looking for any shows of affection. She told herself that she was perfectly comfortable with an 'arrangement', yet as she reached to hook her fingers under the tee-shirt to pull it over her head, she knew that she was breathing too quickly, close to freezing up.

'Oh for goodness' sake,' Alessandro groaned and caught her hands in his. 'Why tell me that this is what you want if you have to squeeze your eyes tightly shut and give every impression of a woman who has to grin and bear it?'

'I *do* want it,' Chase insisted but she could hear the give-away wavering in her voice and she hated it.

'Then what's the problem?' He took in the hectic flush in her cheeks. What was going on here? Shouldn't this be straightforward—two consenting adults getting something out of their system? 'Tell me.'

'You're not really interested.'

'Let me be the one who decides that.' He nuzzled her ear and smiled as she quivered, because it tickled.

'I'm... I've...' She took a deep, steadying breath. 'I've never really been into sex,' she said in a rush. 'I know you can't bear me, and your tolerance levels are low, but I can't just fall on this sofa with you and have wild sex.'

'*Never really been into sex?*' Alessandro's voice held accusatory disbelief. 'You were a married woman,' he pointed out with ruthless directness. 'Married at what age—eighteen? Younger? Are you telling me that you were a gymslip wife who didn't enjoy sleeping with her husband?'

'I don't want to talk about Shaun,' Chase said quickly. *Or,* she mentally tacked on, *anything to do with my past, the past you think you know but don't.*

Alessandro looked at her in silence for a long time. She was flustered as hell but trying hard to put on a show of strength and assertiveness. Did he need all of this? It was just sex and, yet again, that surge of curiosity that was more insistent than the cold logic he wanted to impose. 'Why don't you want to talk about him?'

'Because…there's no point. I'll just say that things are never what you think they are.' Too much information. 'But it's been a long time for me…' she concluded hurriedly.

'You just want me to take it slowly, do you?'

Chase nodded.

'In that case, what about a show of good faith?' He shot her a slow smile. 'Taking it slow is one thing,' he murmured, playing with a strand of her hair whilst he tried to halt his runaway mind, which wanted to ask her what she had meant by her enigmatic remark about things never being what you thought they were. 'A standstill pace, on the other hand, just won't do. So why don't we both get naked and see what happens next?' He watched her carefully, wanting her more than anything, prepared to do the complex if that was what it took. 'If you're not comfortable down here, then you could always give me a tour of upstairs and we can end up in your bedroom. How does that sound?'

Chase nodded. 'You might be disappointed at what you see.' She tried to make her voice as normal as possible but her pulse was racing as they quietly padded upstairs. 'The whole of my upstairs could probably fit into your downstairs cloakroom.'

He wanted a show of good faith and she couldn't blame him. She pushed open the doors to the small spare room, with its single futon, the desk at which she was accustomed to working until late into the night and the bathroom which was large and airy given the size of the house. They ended up in her bedroom.

Alessandro stood in the doorway and looked. The walls were a subdued cream but the four-poster bed was dressed and all romance. The prints on the walls were landscapes of deserted beaches. The dressing table, like the wardrobe, was old, doubtless bought at auction. He thought that he might be the first guy to step foot in this room and it gave him an unbelievable kick. Every single woman he had ever known had been keen to show him their bedrooms and the beds which promised inventive entertainment for as long as he wanted. Mood lighting had usually been a dominant theme. When he took in Chase's wary expression, he could see ambivalence there.

'Your sanctuary.'

'Not any longer. You're in it.'

'By invitation.' His hand reached to the button on his trousers, but first he removed the shirt in one easy movement.

Chase practically fainted. He was the stuff daydreams were made of and she had had enough of those over the years. His body was burnished gold and honed to perfection. When he moved, she could detect the ripple of muscle under skin. Her breathing picked up pace and her mouth went dry. Under her top, her bare breasts tingled, and she had the heady feeling that she wanted them touched, that she wanted her nipples played with.

'Your turn…' He liked the way her eyes skittered across his body as if helplessly drawn to stare at him. He remembered the way that used to do crazy things to him once and was uneasily aware that that should have changed—so why hadn't it? He found that he was holding his breath as her tee-shirt slowly rode up her belly, exposing her pale skin a slither at a time. She wasn't doing this because of undue pressure, yet there was an erotic hesitancy about her movements. The wealth of all her complexities crashed over him like a wave from which he had to fight to surface, to bring himself back in the moment.

He was a randy teenager all over again as he looked at her breasts, heavy and sexy and everything he had imagined. More. Her breasts were bigger than he had thought, tipped with perfect rosy-pink discs. She possessed a body that should never be constrained by a starchy lawyer's outfit. Her proportions were all feminine curves: bountiful breasts, a narrow waist and proper hips that swelled tantalisingly under the dreary track pants. He wanted nothing more than to stride over to her and feel her nakedness pressed against him.

With some sixth sense, though, he was aware of her skittishness. He didn't get it, but he could feel it. Any sudden moves and he got the feeling that she would take flight, even though she obviously wasn't embarrassed about her body, wasn't trying to be coy and hide her breasts behind her hands. He kept his eyes on her face as he removed his trousers and flung them to one side, still looking at her.

Chase felt her skin tighten at the glaring evidence of his arousal. His dark boxers could hardly contain it. She shakily reached to the elasticised waist of her joggers and stilled as he moved towards her.

'You look as though you want to run away,' he murmured. He swallowed hard because the tips of her breasts were almost brushing his chest and his hands itched to feel the weight of them. 'Believe it or not, this is taking it slow by my standards.'

'I believe you,' Chase said huskily. She touched his chest with one finger and felt his soft moan.

'Come to bed.' He stepped away from her. 'I'm not sure how long the slow plan can carry on for.'

When he turned his back to her, Chase knew that he was trying to hold himself back. She felt giddy with power. It was a wonderfully novel sensation and it afforded her a layer of strength she hadn't known she possessed. With Shaun, it had never been like this, never, not even in the very beginning. But she didn't want to think about her ex-husband. That was one very fast and very sure route to instant depression.

She slipped out of the jogging bottoms; his back was still turned when she crept into bed and under the covers.

'Now...' He wasn't used to taking sex slowly. He had never had to pace himself. He failed to consider that pacing himself with a woman for whom he harboured nothing more than a desire to even the score made no sense. 'Tell me...' he flipped onto his side so that they were lying under the covers, front to front, their bodies not touching but both of them vitally aware of their nudity under the duvet '...about the prints on your walls. And the four-poster bed...'

CHAPTER SIX

IF THERE WERE prizes for holding a man's interest, then Alessandro thought that Chase would be in line for all of them. He had planned on a straightforward conquest, aided and abetted by the trump card of saving the shelter. He would take her and, by taking her, he would rid himself of the allure of the inaccessible—which was the position to which she seemed to have been elevated over the years, apparently without him even having noticed. For him, the accessible had always had a short-lived appeal, especially when the quarry in question came with a truck-load of dubious cargo.

And she had played him at his own game, had not been browbeaten but had laid her cards on the table. But then that hesitancy, that tentative admission that sex wasn't her thing… She had lain in his arms but he could feel her tension and he had backed off, even though his body had been on fire for her.

The rapacious, lying, deceitful, manipulative woman had shown a shrinking violet side to her that had got under his skin. Since when had he become the sort of man who was content to hold off, especially in a situation like this, with a woman scarcely worth his time and attention? He had held off with her once and look at where that had got him! But had he done what he should have done? Had he sneered at her attempts to play the shy maiden and ploughed forward? Hell, no! He had lain with her in his arms like the virgin she most certainly was not, had *talked*, and then he had left to return to his apartment and a freezing-cold shower.

Then he had gone abroad for two days, giving himself time to figure out why he was behaving so out of character and giving her time to wise up to the fact that what they had was a deal—and one he intended to cash, because her time limit for playing shy had been used up. He had returned late last night with two flights to Italy booked and the decidedly uncomfortable realisation that there might just be a need to shift gears slightly—to woo her, despite everything he had said about what they had not being a courtship. Somewhere along the line the whole 'time limit' speech had been shelved.

He just knew that when she came to him she would come of her own volition. She would jettison whatever the hell it was that was holding her back. In the space of a heartbeat, it had become a matter of pride—actually in the space of time it had taken for the notion of a break in Italy to take root, which had been fairly instantaneous.

If she was holding back because she hadn't managed to put the premature death of her husband behind her, then she needed to move on from that place and come to him willingly. There was no way he was going to sleep with any woman unless her thoughts were focused one hundred per cent on him and, if it took some seduction to get her to that place, then he would play along with it. The end result would be the same, wouldn't it? And he was an 'end result' kind of guy.

He had phoned her from abroad and announced the whole Italy idea with far more conviction than he had been feeling at the time, but she had taken little persuading as it turned out in the end. She was due some time off and she would take it. A little more enthusiasm would have been appreciated but he had met his match in her. She hadn't pandered to him eight years ago and she wasn't going to pander to him now, even though she knew him for the billionaire that he was.

Now, standing in front of the check-in desk at Heathrow surrounded by crowds, he scowled as he felt himself inevitably harden at the tantalising prospect of having her; of touching that flawless body; of sinking against those breasts, feeling them against his chest, against the palms of his big hands, pushing into his mouth. He had once lost his head over a mirage and now he would take what he felt was his due, take the promised fruit and kill the bitterness inside him that made such an unwelcome companion.

Through the crowds he spotted her weaving and looking around for him and he gave her a brief wave.

'You're ten minutes late. You should have let my driver collect you instead of coming by public transport.'

Chase looked up at his frowning face and was tempted to snap because, however much she wore her hard-won independence like a badge of honour, he obviously had a Neanderthal approach to women in general. But she bit back the retort because she could remember the way he had always taken command when she had known him: paying for whatever they had before she could offer to go halves; impatient with second-rate service; intolerant of anyone in his lectures who'd failed to try.

'I told you. I had some work to finish before I left.' Left for a week in the sun. She had no idea where that idea of Alessandro's had sprung from. She had fought against going, because she was all too aware that their relationship was destined to crash and burn, and the last thing she needed was a plethora of memories she would later have to work out of her system, but he had been insistent. Maybe being out of the country would infuse this weird closure of theirs with an unreality that would be easy to box away.

Italy, he had told her, was his home and, hell, why not. It was a nice time of year over there and he had just closed a massive deal. She could see his house. His casual tone of voice down the end of the line had told her that it wasn't a big deal. He would be going over there himself, she figured, with her or without her, but he would take her along because, as far as he was concerned, she had yet to fulfil her side of the bargain. Lying naked in his arms, tense as a plank of wood, didn't count.

Had they had sex, she was sure that he would not have suggested the Italy trip. Revenge lay behind his motivation and revenge was an emotion that could be sated very quickly. Certainly, a week of her would be enough. Did she deserve that? Maybe she did, in his eyes, and she would never disabuse him of the complicated story behind her lies because that would open up a whole new can of worms far worse than the one she was dealing with.

'Isn't that the old hoary line used by men?' Alessandro queried, moving towards the check-in girl at the first class desk. It occurred to him that he would have quite enjoyed having her at his beck and call and put that down to a caveman instinct he'd never known he possessed. Or maybe he only possessed it when the chase was still on, and only with her because she hadn't followed the pattern of the women he slept with.

'You're very chauvinistic, Alessandro. Women who have careers can't just jettison them the second something better comes along. As it is, I'll have a mountain of work to get down to when I get back. I shouldn't really be here at all, even if I *am* due time off.'

'Are you telling me that being with me is more compelling than your career?'

'I'm not saying anything of the sort!'

'You work too hard.'

'How else am I expected to get on?'

'What are you expecting to *get on* to?' They had checked in and were now heading through Passport Control, towards the first class lounge. Years ago he had considered the possibility of a private jet, if only to cut down on the inconvenience of a bustling airport, but had ditched the idea, because who needed to be responsible for such a vast personal carbon footprint when it could be avoided? Shame, though, because, had he had one, he could have introduced her to some creative ways of passing time twenty thousand miles up without an audience of prying eyes.

'I'd like to head up my own pro bono department. Maybe even branch out on my own and concentrate on that area. Bring in a few other employees…who knows?'

'And what about another prance up the aisle? Is that up there on the agenda? Surely your parents would want to hear the patter of little feet when you visit them in Australia? Or do visits to Australia get in the way of your career?'

Chase temporarily froze. The passing lie was not one on which she wanted to dwell. She wanted no reminders of her non-existent family. She knew that the last thing he would want to discuss would be her ex or her past treachery. His only goal was to get her into bed; her only goal was to put this murky, tangled, haunting past to rest. He was motivated by revenge, she by a need for closure. It was a straightforward situation. She needed no reminders of white lies that had been told and could not now be un-told.

How would he react were he to know that, not only had she once lied to him about her marital status, not only had she dumped him in a way that now made her cringe with guilt and shame even though she knew that it just couldn't have been helped at the time, but that her entire past was as substantial as gossamer?

'Australia is a long way away…' she muttered vaguely.

'Yes. I know. I've been there. You've never told me which part of Australia they live in. It's a big place.'

'You wouldn't have heard of it.' She could feel beads of perspiration break out all over her body. 'It's just a small town on the outskirts of…um…Melbourne. Look, I really don't want to talk about this. Discussing personal issues isn't what we're about, is it?' Never had she realised how being trapped in a lie could prove as painful as walking on a bed of burning coals.

'No,' Alessandro said shortly. 'It's not.' He looked at her blank eyes and tight smile and felt a surge of rage that the thing most women gave naturally to him—the desperate openness which they always seemed to hope could suck him into something permanent and committal—was the one thing Chase steadfastly refused to give. It angered him that he was even going down the road of quizzing her because it reflected a series of inner challenges that he knew were inappropriate. The challenge to get her into bed so that he could assuage the treachery he felt had been done to him had been replaced by the challenge to get her into bed willingly and *hot for him*; the challenge to wipe her ex out of her head when they finally had sex, the challenge to get into her head, to know what made her tick.

Where the hell did it end? Did he need her to remind him that the rules of the game precluded certain things?

'Call it making polite conversation,' he offered with cool politeness.

'I overreacted. It's just that…'

'No need to explain yourself. I'm basically not interested in your past. Like I said, small talk…'

Chase was silenced. Of course he was basically not interested in her past. He was basically not interested in *her*. He was utterly focused on one thing and one thing only. She nodded, nonchalantly indicating that she understood, that she shared the same sentiment.

When he began telling her about some of the complex legalities of the deal he had just pulled off, she let herself slide smoothly into career-woman mode, and then the conversation flowed faultlessly onto the subject of Beth and the shelter. It was a happy story and Chase felt herself once again relax. This was an odd situation but she could handle it, just as long as she didn't start feeling angst over stuff, just as long as she maintained the composed exterior that was so much part and parcel of her personality. She couldn't let herself forget that she wanted this as much as he did. They both had their demons to put to rest.

They landed at Cristoforo Colombo Airport at Genova Sestri to a brilliant day. The wall-to-wall blue skies, which had no longer been in evidence in London after their brief appearance, were here in full force. As soon as they stepped into the waiting limo, she could feel a heady holiday spirit fill her.

'It's been ages since I've been away,' she confided as she settled back to watch the stunning scenery gallop past from the back of the car. 'In fact…' she turned to him '…my only trip abroad in the past few years has been a snatched week at a spa resort in Greece.'

'In that case, I shall make it my mission to see that you enjoy every second of my country…when and if we have the time; bed can be remarkably compulsive with the right companion in it.' His dark eyes roved over her face, encompassing her luscious body, enjoying the delicate bloom of colour that tinged her cheeks.

This holiday would put an end to the game playing which he had sworn he wouldn't tolerate, yet had ended up indulging that one night which should have seen this uncontrollable passion slayed. As she had pointed out in a timely reminder, this wasn't about getting to know one another, this was about sex. Getting to know one another had been a pointless game which he had mistakenly played a long time ago, little knowing that he had been the only participant.

This time round, there'd be no more messing around and taking things at a snail's pace. He would move only as slowly as he felt necessary to get her where he wanted her—which was out of his system so that he could return to normality.

Vaguely annoyed at the contrary drift of his thoughts, he was aware of telling her about the Italian Riviera, on autopilot, pointing out the grandeur of the mountainous landscape in such close and unusual proximity to the sea, giving her a little bit of history about the place. His voice warmed as he described the vast olive grove plantations stretching across the hills, vast tracts of which had once been owned by his ancestors, only to disappear over the years, mismanaged and sold off in bits and pieces—the last by his parents, who had needed the money in their quest for eternal fun.

'You could always come back here…buy more olive groves. It's so beautiful; I can't see why you would want to live in London.' Not even in her wildest, escapist fantasies could she ever have dreamt up somewhere as beautiful as this. The landscape was bold and dramatic, the colours bright and vibrant. Everywhere was bursting with incredible, Technicolor beauty. Alessandro might have had irresponsible parents but it had to be said that, whatever he had gone through, he had gone through it in some style.

'I have a house here. It's where we're going.'

'But how often do you visit it?'

'As you'll be the first to agree, taking time out gets in the way of a career.'

Chase bristled at the implicit criticism in his remark. It reminded her that what they shared was simply a truce but, behind that truce, there was a lot he just didn't like about her. 'My career is important to me.'

'I've gathered.'

'You say that as though you disapprove of women who work.'

'On the contrary. Some of the highest positions in my company are occupied by women.'

'But you would never actually go out with a woman who had a career…'

Alessandro shot her a sidelong glance. The car was air-conditioned but he had chosen to have the windows opened and the breeze blew through her hair, tossing it across her face in unruly strands. She was no longer the high-powered lawyer with the pristine appearance. She was the girl he had once known and he railed against the pull of memories. 'There's little I find attractive about a woman who puts her career first.'

Chase rolled her eyes and sighed, because the breeze was too balmy and the scenery too exotic for arguing. 'That is because you're a dinosaur.' He had old-fashioned ideas. Years ago she had teased him that that was a back-lash from his parents' excesses but she had liked those old-fashioned ideas, never having come across them before.

'And I take it that under normal circumstances you wouldn't choose to go out with a dinosaur? Tell me about your husband.'

'I no longer have a husband,' Chase said shortly, rous-ing herself from bittersweet memories of their brief, shared dalliance.

'I realise that. What was he like?' He was curious. He found that he wanted to know. This wasn't polite conver-sation, although the casual tone of his voice gave noth-ing away.

The last thing Chase wanted to do was to talk about Shaun but she had a sneaking suspicion that, if she backed away from the subject, it would arouse his interest even further. 'We met when we were young. I was only fifteen. Just. We met at the local disco.'

'Cosy. And was it love at first sight?'

'We found that we had a lot in common.'

'Always a good start to a healthy relationship. Even at the ripe old age of fifteen. Just.' He found that he didn't care for the idea of them having a lot in common at whatever the hell age they had happened to meet. Nor had he intended to get wrapped up in pointless conversations about the thug who had been lurking behind the scenes when she had taken him for a ride and played him for a fool.

'So they say,' Chase murmured tonelessly.

'I take it he wasn't sharp enough to make it to university?'

'Shaun was plenty sharp.' She couldn't help the bitterness that had crept into her voice but she kept it at bay. Talking about Shaun would inevitably lead to all sorts of questions about the sort of world she had really come from. Chase found that she had moved on from the fear of him discovering the truth about her and eking out some kind of belated revenge by spilling the beans to her work colleagues. She honestly couldn't see him doing that.

No, what she feared—and she hated herself for this— was to have him walk away in disgust at the lies she had told, at the person she really was and the life she had really led. His pedigree was impeccable and although she knew that they would be the archetypal doomed lovers— in it for the wrong reasons but driven to fulfil their destiny—she still found that she wanted him to believe her to be the sassy, smart lawyer with the perfectly ordinary background when they parted company.

Wasn't that to be expected? What if she bumped into him at a later date? What if he met some of the partners in her law firm and started talking about her? If he knew the truth about her, then wasn't it likely that it would slip out in conversation? And, even if nothing did slip out, surely he would never be able to disguise the contempt in his voice at the mention of her name?

'Sharp as in…?'

She snapped out of her daydreaming to find his eyes narrowed on her. 'Streetwise; sharp as in streetwise.'

'And did your streetwise late husband have a job?' He thought back to the picture she had shown him all those years ago.

'He…worked in transport but he…he lost his job shortly before the accident. I'd bought him that motorbike. I'd been putting aside some money and I wanted to celebrate getting my first promotion…'

'So you celebrated by buying him a motorbike. Shouldn't *he* have been the one doing the buying to congratulate you? Or am I just thinking like a dinosaur again?'

'Alessandro, please, let's move on from this. I honestly don't want to talk about Shaun. Tell me more about here. It's amazing to think that there can be snow on mountaintops that are just a short distance from the Med…'

Alessandro heard the soft plea in her voice. 'Why did you give me a second look if you were so clearly head over heels in love with your husband?'

'I…I'm sorry. I made a mistake.'

'Which doesn't answer my question.' He raked his hand impatiently though his hair and sat back with his eyes closed for a few seconds. 'Scrap that. Not sure I could stomach whatever fairy stories you decide to come out with.'

'Alessandro…'

He inclined his head towards her and linked his fingers loosely in his lap. She had the face of an angel, the body of a siren and he was furious with himself for wanting to probe deeper. He pointed to a spot behind her as the car turned left. 'My house.'

Chase turned just in time to glimpse a sand-coloured

mansion rising up from the cliffs, overlooking the placid turquoise sea with a backdrop of woods of chestnut trees. She forgot everything and her mouth dropped open.

'I have two housekeepers who live in, make sure everything is ticking over. Occasionally, it's used by some of my employees, a little bonus if they do well. The promise of an all-expenses-paid long weekend here generates a lot of healthy competition, and it does no harm for the place to get an airing now and again.'

'It's huge. What about family members?'

'Oh, completely off-limits to them. My parents ensured their place in the pecking order as the black sheep of the family and I've inherited their generous legacy. I have little contact with my extended family.

'My parents were both only children, so there are strangely few people who bear a belated grudge towards me. I see a couple of slightly less distant relatives now and again when I'm in Milan; a few more work in some of my associated companies, my way of making amends for my parents' appallingly hedonistic behaviour which was, if all accounts are to be believed, ruinous to both family names.'

He edged towards her and pointed. 'You can't see it, but there's a winding path that leads down to a private cove at the bottom of the cliff face. Excellent bathing. Once upon a time, fishing used to be big here. Not so much any more. Tourism pays better, it would seem. The wealthy find the sight of yachts far more uplifting than the reality of fishing boats.'

'What a shame you don't get here often,' Chase said. When he was like this—charming, informative, his voice as deep and as dark as the most pure, rich, velvety chocolate—she could forget everything. She could lapse back to the past where dangerous, taboo emotions still held a certain innocence, a time when he didn't hate her. 'Don't you sometimes long to have someone to share this with?'

'Oh, but isn't that what I'm doing now?' Alessandro drawled. 'Admittedly, only for a few days, and with a woman who is destined never to return, but it'll do for the moment.'

He reached across, pulling her towards him. 'I've given my loyal housekeepers time off,' he murmured into her hair. 'It's hot here. I thought it might be nice for us to live as naturists for a few days. Why bother with clothes? I want to be able to touch you anywhere…at any time… And you'll discover that my house is perfect for ensuring one hundred per cent privacy. I'll make you thaw, my sweet; on that count, you can trust me…'

Chase was still smarting from the insistent stab of hurt his words had generated. *Destined never to return.*

They approached the sprawling villa through wrought-iron gates which had been flung open, revealing perfectly groomed lawns stretching out on either side of the gravel drive.

'How many people does it take to look after these gardens?' She shouldn't have been, but she was still shocked by the splendour.

'A small army,' Alessandro admitted drily. 'I'm single-handedly trying to do my bit to keep the economy going. There's a very private pool to the side of the house. I have vague memories of my parents throwing some extremely wild parties there.'

'I had no idea the house belonged to them.' Chase turned to look at him and their eyes tangled. Instantly, she could feel her breasts begin to ache in expectation of his caresses. With Shaun, she had become conditioned to viewing sex as something that had to be done. But when she had lain next to Alessandro her body had been fired up in a way that was new and, whilst they hadn't made love, it now thrummed at the prospect of being touched by him. It was a heady, exciting feeling and she was sure that it was all wrapped up in the culmination of what had begun all that time ago, what had never come to fruition.

'It was their pride and joy. The one thing they both hung on to.'

'And you kept it for sentimental reasons?'

'I never do anything for sentimental reasons. It's a good, appreciating asset.'

It was dreamy. If she had been able to conceive of a place like this, she might have been more elaborate in her teenage fantasies about perfect lifestyles instead of just settling for average. Then she decided that it was just as well, because how much more awkward would life have been now had her naïve, happily married parents in their two-up two-down been turned into minor landed gentry living in a small castle?

They were greeted by an elderly housekeeper and her husband who had stayed on to welcome Alessandro, tugging him into the kitchen so that they could show him the freezer full of food that had been prepared and the well-stocked larder. He managed to shoo them away after an hour and they departed wreathed in smiles.

'They've been with me for longer than I care to think. As you know, my parents were firm believers in handing over care of their offspring to hired help,' he told her as he played tour guide, taking her from room to room. He absently thought how many of those little details of his past she had been privy to, courtesy of that small window in his life during which his self-control had gone on holiday.

'I'm treating them to a well-deserved rest in a destination of their choosing, which as it turns out happens to be France, where their eldest is a dentist. I tried to persuade them into somewhere a little further afield but they weren't having it. Mauritius, apparently, is no competition for two hyper grandchildren.'

Chase's heart fluttered. This was how he had managed

to get under her skin. This was why she never wanted to have him learn the truth about her. This was why the thought of what he could do to balance the scales of justice should he want to avenge past wrongs was no longer the only consideration. Underneath his ruthlessly cold exterior were these flashes of genuine thoughtfulness that kept reminding her of why she had risked so much just talking to him eight years ago; that ambushed all her good intentions to keep her distance. Whenever he made her laugh, her defences slipped just a little bit more.

This was a dangerous game because she would end up being hurt. She would end up losing her hard-won self-control. She would end up with someone else having power over her, someone who didn't care about her, who wanted her for all the wrong reasons. Maybe she had already ended up there.

She had walked into this with her eyes wide open but now she felt as though she had walked straight into a trap, having stupidly failed to take account of its power for destruction.

The whole sex thing… Yes, she had wanted it, had *craved* it, but she had been scared because of past experience and he had respected her when she had turned into a block of ice in his arms. That consideration he had shown her, as it turned out, was just something else that had nibbled away at the edges of her defences so that what had once been a fortress, protecting her from the slings and arrows of emotional involvement with the human race, was beginning to resemble a broken down old castle open to all the elements.

She felt exposed in a way she never had in her life before. She felt as she had eight years ago: like a woman *falling in love.*

'You've stopped using rapturous superlatives to describe my house.'

Chase blinked and realised that he was several metres ahead of her because she had stopped dead in her tracks. Her brain had been so wrapped up contemplating the horror of falling for this guy again that it hadn't had any room left to give messages to her legs to keep moving.

'I think I may have run out of them.' She blinked and took in the raw sexuality of the man lounging in front of her with that killer half-smile on his lips.

'Where is this famous pool you've been bragging about?' Her voice was normal but her brain was malfunctioning.

'I never brag.' Again that smile that hurled her back in time. He took her hand to lead her through the house, out to the kitchen and towards the sea-facing side of the house, which took her breath away. 'Except in this one instance.'

He gestured to the open view as though he owned it and then relaxed back to look at her response. He had never given a damn what women thought of his opulent lifestyle and was indifferent to their gasps of awe whenever they stepped foot into his house in London. Yet he rather enjoyed the way her mouth fell open as she stepped out to stand next to him.

The house looked down to the sea that was turquoise and as still as a lake. The garden on this side was just a strip of green, broken by distinctive Italian palm trees and bordered by thick shrubbery. To one side a gate announced the winding stone steps, which Chase imagined led to the cove he had told her about.

This was her dream come true. She had somehow been catapulted into the prints she had hung on her walls. The romance which had not been part of the plan clung to her in a miasma, giving her all sorts of stupid illusions that somehow what they had might be the beginning of something real. It was time to start unravelling that piece of fiction.

'Are you sure it's completely deserted here?' She

squinted against the sun to look up at him, shielding her eyes with one hand.

Alessandro looked down at her. She was in a flimsy sleeveless dress which was far too baggy for his liking but which, on the upside, provided terrific fodder for his imagination. 'As a ghost town. Why?'

'Because I think we should explore that pool area you were bragging to me about… Oh yes, I forgot: you never brag…' Her hand fluttered provocatively to the small top button of the dress. 'It's so warm. I think I might need to strip off, have a dip in that pool of yours, the one—'

'I keep bragging to you about even though I never brag?' He laughed under his breath and felt the bulge in his pants as that part of his body which had been in charge of his brain ever since she had reappeared to smash into his ordered existence rose to immediate attention.

He linked his fingers through hers and began leading her across the lawn, swerving to the side of the house where exuberant flora, lemon trees, shrubs sprouting with brightly coloured flowers and hydrangea enclosed an exquisite infinity pool. The air was aromatic.

'I feel as though I've stepped into a travel brochure.'

Alessandro frowned. A nagging thought occurred to him. Had he seen those prints on the walls and brought her here so that he could deliver her those dreams of sun, sea and sand that had clearly never been realised? Had that been some weird, unconscious motivation behind his invitation to bring her to his house? He irritably swept aside a suspicion with which he was not comfortable.

'You said you were hot…?'

'So I did.' She would have liked to enjoy the scenery a bit more. Well, a lot more. But business was business, wasn't it? The longer this game between them carried on, the deeper her scars would be when they parted company, when he had got what he wanted. She undid the small buttons of the dress and it fell to the ground, pooling at her feet.

Alessandro remained where he was, looking at her with lazy, predatory satisfaction. 'Will this be a full striptease?'

'I want you, Alessandro...' *And I love you. I loved you once and I think it would be very easy to love you again.* She schooled her features to conceal the chaos of her thoughts. 'And I think we've both waited long enough...' She walked towards him, reaching behind her as she did so to unhook her bra, which she tossed onto one of the low, wooden sun loungers, never taking her eyes off his face.

Alessandro found that he could barely control his breathing. The moment was electric. His jaw clenched when she was finally standing in front of him and he had to steel himself against an unruly, premature overreaction as she slipped out of her panties so that she was now completely naked.

'The sun's pretty fierce...' He curved his hand around her waist, idly caressing it and pulling her against him at the same time. 'And you're fair. Any doctor would tell you that you need to lather yourself in sunblock...' He kissed her slowly, tugging her bottom lip with his teeth, gently tasting her mouth, taking his time as their tongues melded, even though it was agony trying to keep his libido in check.

'So what do you want to do about it?' She wrapped her arms around his neck and flung her head back with a sigh as his lips traced a path along the slender column of her neck. She was wet and ready for him. She reached to fumble with the button of his trousers and he stayed her hand.

'One good striptease deserves another,' he murmured in a sexy, shaky undertone that sent her blood pressure skyrocketing. 'But first...'

He sauntered towards what she now saw was a vine-covered pool house and emerged a couple of minutes later with towels and various creams. He dumped them on one of the vacant loungers and she watched, heart beating wildly, as he did what she had done only moments before.

His shirt was tossed to join hers and he kept his eyes on her as he walked slowly towards her. Every inch that brought him closer did crazier things to her nervous system. Her breath caught in her throat as he removed his trousers, then, when she felt that swooning was a real possibility, the final item of clothing joined the rest and he was as naked as she was, his proud, impressive erection proclaiming that he was as turned on as her.

When he was inches away from her, she reached down and firmly circled it with her hand.

'Three days ago you were as tense as a violin string...' He led her towards one of the loungers which was shaded by an overhanging tree and he neatly spread one of the towels on it.

Three days ago, she thought, *I had no idea that my body could feel like this; three days ago it started to come alive. I may have been apprehensive then at what I was feeling but I'm not apprehensive now...*

'I'm not now,' she said huskily.

'Then lie down. I'm going to put sun cream on you and it'll be the best foreplay you've ever experienced...'

CHAPTER SEVEN

'It might be a little cold,' Alessandro murmured. He had to make sure to keep his eyes away from her breasts, away from her flat stomach, away from the soft, downy hair that lightly covered the triangular apex between her thighs. He would save himself. 'I keep the pool house air-conditioned. Lie on your stomach...'

'You honestly don't need to bother with sun lotion. It's perfectly safe here in the shade.'

'Doctor's orders. Safety first is the main thing.' She was on her stomach and very slowly he began to explore every exquisite inch of her body, rubbing the sun cream into her, feeling the silky smoothness of her skin and, with each stroke of his hand on her body, getting more aroused.

He pressed his thumbs gently against each vertebra so that she was moaning softly and melting under his touch. He massaged her neck, then her sides, so that her mind went blank and she sighed and squirmed; then the rounded cheeks of her bottom and the length of her glorious legs which parted temptingly, inviting him to go further, but it was an invitation he wasn't going to take up until he was good and ready.

'This is... I never knew...' It was an inaudible sigh.

'Now, shift over. Lie on your back. We can't let an inch of you go unprotected, can we? I would never forgive myself if you were to get sunburned.'

Chase, cynical when it came to interpreting everything he said, wondered if he meant that he would never forgive himself should she be out of action while they were over here. Four days in paradise without the sex he had been anticipating wouldn't do, would it?

She nearly laughed hysterically when she thought that four days in paradise with him without sex would still be four days in paradise for her as opposed to a wasted trip.

'And stop frowning. Just relax. Enjoy.' Her face was first and then his long, supple fingers moved to her shoulders. He did his utmost not to look at her breasts, at the large, pink discs that were responding so enthusiastically to what his hands were doing. He was aware, though, that the tips had tightened into hard peaks as she became more and more turned on.

He watched, fascinated, at the slight flare of her nostrils as he began to lavish his attention on her breasts. 'You can't be too careful in this Italian sun…especially for someone with as little experience of hot weather as you.'

'Don't be silly, Alessandro. London gets hot.' Her eyes were shut tightly and her fists clenched in an effort at self-control as he continued to massage her breasts. It felt so good. 'Are you sure we're on our own here?' This as he bent to take one pouting nipple in his mouth and she moaned weakly as he suckled on it while spanning his hand across her rib cage.

'No one else would have permission to see this body,' he broke off to tell her. 'It's for my eyes only.' Then he returned to the matter at hand, moving to pay the same attention to her other nipple.

How long could he keep this up? Straddling her, he nudged her legs apart. Protection for the full thing, naturally. But he couldn't resist the feel of her moistness against him and he rubbed himself along her wet crease, an insistent, rhythmic movement that made her gasp out loud.

'How does this feel, baby?' he asked, his voice raw and unsteady and she whimpered a response that was answer enough. 'I'm not going to come in you. I just need to do this…'

But he had to stop when he knew that a few more seconds and he would push them both over the edge. The anticipation of having full-blown sex with her was filling his mind and sensitising every inch of his body. When she half-raised herself to take him in her hand, he gently pushed her back down. He had to control this. If he didn't, he would come right here, right now and that was something he didn't want to do. This time, he was going to feel the silky smoothness of being deep inside her.

He smoothed the cream over her inner thighs and breathed her in. The sweet, sexy smell of her filled his nostrils and he half-closed his eyes before dipping his head between her legs. The flat of his hands were on her thighs, pushing them apart, and he felt her tiny convulsion as his tongue made contact with her clitoris.

Chase's fingers tangled in his hair. Here, under the shade of a tree, the sun's heat was pleasantly diluted. The breeze was soft and balmy. Half-opening her eyes, she saw his dark head between her thighs and, framing him, the glory of the Italian scenery with its vista of blue ocean and in the distance the striking cliffs of the peninsula, lush green interspersed with picturesque hamlets, which were tiny dots seen from this far away.

She was living a dream. She was here, with Alessandro, making love to him, having him turn her on in ways that were unimaginable. Why shouldn't she stuff reality behind a door and enjoy what was on offer for its brief duration?

She smiled, moved against his mouth and smiled more when he raised his head and chastised her for moving too fast.

'More doctor's orders?' she teased breathlessly.

'You said it.'

It felt to her as though she had been building up to this moment for years, from the very first time she had had that first latte with him, a sneaky, stolen latte. She had nervously told herself that it would be a one-off, that she was in no position to have lattes with him or with anyone else, but then, as now, what she had told herself had had no bearing on what had actually transpired.

They had had the most sexually charged yet chaste relationship on the planet. Every touch had been accidental and every touch had left her craving more. She had dreamt about him back then and had been terrified that Shaun would somehow climb into her head and see her dreams. And he had continued to steal into her dreams like a silent intruder all through the years, long after she had picked up the pieces of her life and moved on.

So now she was ready.

'Alessandro...' she breathed huskily and he lifted his head to look at her.

'Alessandro what...?' The spoils of the victor. Triumph surged through him. This was what he had wanted: to hear her plead for him to enter her, to know that she could no longer hold out. The grieving widow shedding her black and getting back into mainstream life. With him.

'Tell me how much you want me,' he encouraged thickly. 'I want to hear you say it. No, hold that thought— but don't even begin to think that you can start cooling down.' There were condoms in his wallet. He couldn't fetch one fast enough. His erection was so hard that it was painful.

Cool down? Chase thought that she wouldn't have cooled down if a barrel of ice cubes had been thrown over her. She was on fire, burning for him. She looked at him hungrily, watching as he put on the condom, enjoying the way he was looking right back at her, his dark eyes bold and wicked.

'I'd better just check...' he murmured, straddling her on the super-sized lounger which could have been made for sex and—who knew?—possibly had been because it was as comfortable as a bed. 'Make sure you're still hot for me...' He slid his finger expertly over her throbbing centre and gave a slashing smile of satisfaction. 'Hot and wet.'

'I'm glad you approve.' She wound her arms around his neck and pulled him down to her. Her nipples rubbing against him were doing all sorts of delicious things to her body, adding to the overload of sensation. She sighed and arched up so that she could kiss him and simultaneously opened her legs. 'God, Alessandro, I want you so much right now...'

'Are you sure?'

Their eyes met and she knew that he was asking her if she was ready. Given half a chance, he was always more than prepared to tell her the depth of his bitterness towards her, to inform her that her place in his life was temporary, a passing virus of which he needed to rid his system. Yet, as now, when she could see old-fashioned consideration in his eyes which could flare up almost against his will, he could be just so damned three-dimensional.

'I'm sure.'

Alessandro thrust into her and never had anything felt so exquisite. She wrapped her legs around his waist and he levered her up, his hand on her bottom, so that she could receive him even better as he began moving, fast and hard and rhythmically. Her fingers were digging into his back, driving him on, and her head was thrown back, her eyes closed, her mouth slightly parted.

For a split second, he had a crazy desire to know whether she had ever felt like this with her husband. He certainly had never felt like this with any other woman but, then again, what other woman had he ever had under such extraordinary circumstances? His last girlfriend, a model whose appearance in his life had not outlived the three-month mark, had been a clone of all the other beauties he had dated in the past. Was it any wonder that this one was special? That *this* just felt so damned special?

Chase had died and gone to heaven. On one final thrust, she tipped over the edge as her orgasm ripped through her, sending her body into little convulsions and spontaneously bringing tears to her eyes which she fought to blink back. She felt his groan of fulfilment with every ounce of her being and never had she wanted more to tell him how she felt. Instead, she swept his hair back and smiled drowsily as he opened his eyes to look at her, at first unfocused, and then smiling back.

'That was…good…' she murmured as he slid onto his side to prop himself up on one elbow so that he could look at her.

'"Good" is not an adjective I've ever had much time for. It's along the same lines as "nice"…' He idly circled her nipple with his finger and watched as it responded with enthusiasm. 'How *good* was it?'

'Very, very good…'

'I'll settle for that. In fact, I'll enjoy trying to squeeze more superlatives out of you.' He dipped his head and closed his mouth over her nipple, which was still sensitive and throbbing in the aftermath of their love-making. He was utterly spent and yet he felt himself stir against her leg. 'Let's have a swim,' he suggested. 'And then some food. And then we can play it by ear; see what comes up…'

'Oh, very funny.' But she was laughing as they jumped into the pool. After four lengths, she was happy to take to the side and watch as he continued to slice through the water. She had learned to swim as an adult. Four years ago, she wouldn't have been able to jump into the deep end of this pool, never mind swim four lengths. He, on the other hand, had probably been swimming since he was a toddler, taught by a member of staff in one of the many pools he had probably enjoyed in various locations over the years.

The differences between them were so glaringly obvious, reminding her of the shelf life of what they had and of the shadowy undercurrents lurking just beneath the surface of their sexually charged relationship.

'Tired?'

'Swimming isn't one of my strong points,' she confessed. 'In fact...' what would this one simple admission hurt? '...I only learned to swim a few years ago.'

'You're kidding.'

'No, I'm not,' she said with a shrug.

'That must have been awkward on family holidays. I'm surprised your parents didn't sort that out.' He kissed her again, a little more hungrily this time, and pulled back with a grin of pure satisfaction. 'Besides, don't schools in England have arranged swimming lessons for kids? Something to do with the curriculum?'

'Some of them do,' Chase said vaguely. 'But, you know, I kind of had a phobia of water.'

'A little private tuition would have sorted that out, wouldn't it?' He swung himself neatly out of the pool and held out his hand to help her up. 'Better than Mummy and Daddy panicking every time their precious little darling got within a foot of the hotel pool. Hmm...nice...'

He enjoyed her wet body, running his hands along it, holding her close to him so that their bodies could rub together. 'No matter. Competitive swimming isn't on the agenda while we're here. I couldn't care less if you can only swim four lengths or four hundred.'

Chase opened her mouth, toyed with the idea of revealing a bit more about herself but then kept silent. This fantastic side to Alessandro was only in evidence for a reason.

Further proof of her lying would kill that reason dead because, even for the sake of finishing unfinished business, lust still had its outer limits. And without lust how much greater would be his anger in the cold light of day? She didn't want his anger and she certainly couldn't afford for that anger to be directed at punishing her through her work.

A sudden tidal wave of sheer misery immobilised her and it took almost more effort than she could muster to get herself back on track.

'Tell me what there is around here,' she eventually said, falling easily into step with him as he tossed her a towel and they began walking towards the house. 'All those gorgeous little villages… What do the locals do for a living? Do you know any of them? Personally, I mean?'

Exactly four days later, Chase understood what it must feel like to be in love with someone, living on cloud nine, where everything smelled differently and tasted differently and every single experience was a unique Kodak moment to be committed to memory and brought out at a later date.

She had seen him at his most relaxed. She felt that she could almost be forgiven for thinking that he really liked her and she guessed that, in a way, he did. He appreciated her quick mind; he appreciated her responsive body; he laughed when she tried to tell corny jokes.

Just so long as they both pretended that the past had never happened, everything was good between them. For her, it was so much deeper than anything he could possibly feel, but she refused to think like that. What was the point? She had made her bed and she would lie on it. She had accepted his proposal and only now and again did she think that, whilst she was falling deeper and harder for him, he was gradually working her out of his system.

Wrapped up in his arms at night, lying in a bed that was roughly the size of her spare bedroom, she had let her mind wander, analysed and re-analysed everything he'd said and every gesture he'd made. The one sure thing that sprang to mind was that, the more relaxed he was with her, the more he was putting her behind him.

It was an argument that made sense. When he had seen her again for the first time after eight years, his rage had been raw, out in the open, targeted and deadly. But that had changed. He would never, ever forgive her for what she had done to him, she knew that, but he was in the process of getting over it. Rage was becoming indifference and indifference was allowing him to stop treating her as public enemy number one.

She hated herself for trying to find alternative scenarios but they all led to the same dead end. Very soon, he would completely lose interest in why she had done what she had done eight years ago. He would simply stop giving a damn. He would no longer consider revenge because he would not care less. He would just use her and walk away without a backward glance.

The only consolation was that she had not dropped her guard. She had not let him see just how vulnerable she was, nor would she let him discover how successful he had been at claiming the revenge he had initially considered his due. Without him even realising it, he had indeed wreaked the ultimate revenge, because he would leave her broken and in pieces, whatever show of bravado she employed for his benefit.

And now here they were, last night, sitting across from each other at the kitchen table with an almost empty bottle of Chablis between them.

'So tell me again why you don't come here at least once a month, Alessandro.' Outside, another hot day had gradually morphed into a mild, starry night. They had spent most nights in the kitchen, which was huge, big enough for a ten-seater table at one end, and leading to a conservatory which doubled as an informal sitting area with comfy sofas and a plasma television. From here, they had an uninterrupted view of the sea down below, vast and silent, and the small back garden where they had spent much of their time by the swimming pool.

She felt lazy and replete after another excellent meal which had been prepared in advance by his housekeeper. They could have done their own cooking, and she had suggested it on day one, but he had killed that dead.

'Why waste time cooking?' he had questioned bluntly, 'When there are so many other things we could be occupied doing?' He had pulled her onto his lap and slipped his finger underneath her panties, leaving her in no doubt as to what those other things they could be occupied with were. Enjoying any form of domesticity was off the cards. That was not the reason why he had asked her on this holiday.

'You know why I don't come here once a month,' he replied wryly. 'It's the same reason *you* wouldn't come here once a month. Work wouldn't allow it.'

'But it's different for you. You're the big boss. You can do whatever you want. I can't.'

'Pull the other one, Chase. You're not a bimbo who would be content to while away her time walking barefoot on a beach, no matter how powdery white the sand might be. You're one hundred per cent a career woman. You would be bored stiff in a job that allowed you to take time out every month to enjoy a holiday in the sunshine.'

He stood up, moved to the fridge to replenish the wine and remained there with his back against the counter, carefully looking at her with his head to one side. She had caught the sun. Her skin was the colour of pale honey and from nowhere a smattering of freckles had appeared on the ridge of her nose.

'I recognised that the first time I laid eyes on you,' he continued casually. 'You weren't going to be distracted by anyone or anything. You barely seemed to notice what was going on around you.'

Chase fidgeted. Trips down memory lane never turned out well between them. However, his voice was mild and speculative, not in the least provocative. More proof that, whatever fireworks there might be on the physical level, on the emotional level he was breaking away. The medicine was working. Sex was finishing the unfinished business between them.

'I liked that,' he continued and she looked at him in surprise. 'You once asked me if I'd ever go out with a career woman and I gave you a negative answer.' He strolled towards her and resumed his seat at the kitchen table, tugging a free chair with his foot so that he could use it as an impromptu footrest. 'The truth is, you were the anomaly. Before you and after you, I've only gone out with...'

'Airheads? Bimbos?' Chase dropped into the brief silence. She smiled tightly. 'Women who are never ashamed to admit that their only ambition is to hunt down a rich guy and bag him even if it means a lifetime of doing exactly what he wants her to do?' The stuff of nightmares, she thought bitterly.

'There's absolutely nothing about a woman like that I can't handle, and you'd be surprised how easily they've slotted into my lifestyle.'

'Because they make sure to always tell you what you want to hear and do what you want them to do?'

'Some might say that a compliant woman is preferable to a liar.' He noted the swift surge of colour that flooded her cheeks. 'You *have* succeeded in persuading me, however, that there's something to be said for a woman with a brain.'

'I have?'

'You have,' Alessandro drawled. 'Don't get me wrong, Chase—agile though your mind is, and challenging though your conversation can be, you'll never be a contender for the vacancy—just in case your thoughts were heading in that direction.'

'They weren't!' Chase was mortified to think that he might have spotted some weakness in her armour that she hadn't been able to conceal. 'You're not dealing with an idiot, Alessandro. I know the rules of this game as well as you do.'

'I'm glad to hear it.'

'Why would you have thought any differently?' Just like that, his dark eyes had turned cool and assessing, reminding her that the so-called rules of this particular game were different for both of them, despite what she might say to the contrary. Reminding her, too, that his red-hot passion had changed nothing of what he fundamentally felt towards her.

'Look around you and tell me what you see.'

'We're in your kitchen.' Chase frowned, confused and flustered by the softly spoken question that seemed to have sprung from nowhere. 'I can just about make out the little garden at the back, and I can see where the pool is… Look, why are you asking me this?'

'What you see all around you is evidence of my wealth,' Alessandro inserted smoothly. He killed dead the passing twinge of hesitation at the thought that he might offend her. He reminded himself that no matter how good the sex was, and how much he might occasionally enjoy her rapier-sharp mind, she was still a woman whom he had met going by the name of Lyla; who had strung him along and lied to him; who had dumped him unceremoniously and who, certainly, he would never have clapped eyes on again had fate not decided to deliver her to his premises. At the end of the day, whether he offended her or not was immaterial.

'But,' he continued as she stared at him, perplexed, 'I

guess you were aware of the extent of my bank balance the minute you walked into my London place.'

'I don't see what your bank balance has to do with anything,' Chase said tautly.

'No? Let's just say that I wouldn't want you to start getting any misplaced ideas.'

'Misplaced ideas about what?' But she knew what he was talking about now. Well, it didn't take a genius to join the dots, did it? She should be enraged, but instead she was deeply hurt, cut to the quick.

'This is all about the sex—and it's great sex, I'll give you that. But don't think for a second that I've somehow forgotten the person you really are. I think this is a good point at which to remind you that you're a visitor in my life. You won't be getting your hands on any of this...' He gestured broadly to encompass the visible proof of his vast wealth.

He couldn't have thought of a more pointed way of humiliating her but she pinned a stiff smile to her face. She hoped she looked suitably amused and unimpressed. She hoped that whatever expression she was wearing revealed nothing of what she was actually feeling.

'Do you think I would actually *want* to be anything other than a...what did you call it, Alessandro?... *visitor* in your life?' Her heart contracted, squeezed tight with pain. 'You might have all...' she mimicked his gesture '...*this*. You might have the fabulous house on a fabulous coastline in a fabulously beautiful country, and you might have a house in London big enough to fit ten of mine, but I've never pursued money and I certainly would never, ever, set my sights on getting hold of someone else's by...'

'Fair means or foul?' He took his time standing up, flexing his muscles while watching her. Then he leant across to place his hands flat on the arms of her chair. 'I felt it a good idea to make sure we were both still singing off the same song sheet.'

'I could never be serious about someone as arrogant as you, Alessandro.'

'And yet you gave such a misleading impression eight years ago.'

'Will you ever forget that?'

'It's been imprinted on my mind with the force and clarity of a branding iron.'

So much for thinking that he was becoming indifferent, Chase was forced to concede. So much for thinking that revenge was a dish in which he might no longer be interested. 'You weren't arrogant then.' She met his stare levelly. She wasn't prepared for the feel of his mouth against hers as he crushed her lips in a driving, savage kiss that propelled her back into the chair.

Her hands automatically rose to push him away. How the hell could he think that she might be interested in having him touch her when he had just insulted her in the worst way possible? And yet her body responded, went up in flames like dry tinder waiting for the burning match. Reluctant hands softened to cup the nape of his neck.

In one easy movement, he scooped her off the chair and into his arms.

'Alessandro!'

He was heading up the stairs, towards the bedroom with its shuttered windows and thin, cream voile curtains, pale wood and wicker furniture.

'We've talked enough.'

'You called me a gold-digger! Do you…?' She was breathless as he kicked open the bedroom door. 'Do you honestly think that I…I get turned on being insulted?'

'I didn't call you a gold-digger. I warned you of the pitfalls of becoming one. And, no, you don't get turned on by being insulted. You just get turned on by me…' He unceremoniously dumped her on the bed and shot her a wickedly sexy smile as she scrambled into a sitting position to glare at him. 'I'm sick of talking.' He stripped off his black polo shirt and flung it to the floor. 'Get naked for me.'

Chase continued to glare but already her flustered mind was forgetting the hurt inflicted and keening towards the feel of his hands on her body. Still, she didn't rush to obey, but as he led the way, removing his shirt then his jeans, she could feel herself melting.

Their love-making was fast and urgent. She wanted to lose herself in it and forget the things he had told her, the coldness in his voice when he had reminded her of what their relationship really was all about. Did he honestly imagine that she was the type of woman who could look at someone else's possessions and work out how she could get her hands on them? Yes, of course he did. The distance between a liar and a gold-digger was very small.

She wanted to make love until she lost the hurt, and she did. She touched him, kissed him, dominating him in one move before yielding in another. She caught a glimpse of his back at one point and saw the marks of where her fingers had scored into his skin. He ordered her to talk dirty to him and she wondered how she did it so easily when she hadn't a clue what she was supposed to say. It was a complete release of all her inhibitions and it turned her on. It turned her on even more when he talked dirty back to her.

This was what it was all about—having sex. The most amazing, fulfilling sex she could ever imagine. It was all he wanted and, if it wasn't all *she* wanted, then that was something she would just have to live with.

Her orgasm was long and deep and filled every single part of her body. It dispelled all her dark thoughts. It made her feel as though she was soaring through space, out of reach of anything that might hurt her. She longed for it to last for ever. In fact, she closed her eyes and kept them firmly shut even after Alessandro rolled off her. He was breathing as unevenly as she was. She could picture every inch of his face, every line, the sweep of his dark lashes, his gleaming black eyes that could make her body go up in flames with a single glance. She had absorbed all the details and stored them in her head with the efficiency of a state-of-the-art computer housing data.

'Are you going to fall asleep on me?'

'I'm dozing.'

'Should I be flattered that I can send a woman to sleep?'

'Actually…' Chase opened her eyes reluctantly and propped herself on her side so that they were facing one another on the bed, front to front, her breasts brushing his chest. 'I was thinking…'

What would happen if she ever told him the truth about how she felt? Would she find it liberating? 'About work. How much I'll have to get done when I return. I may even go in tomorrow evening after we're back. Have I told you about the work that's due to start on the shelter? Beth keeps asking if I'm sure that the costs will be covered.' She ran her finger lightly along his shoulder blade, tracing muscle and sinew. 'She has a morbid fear of bailiffs banging on the front door because she hasn't been able to pay her creditors.'

Alessandro frowned. As pillow talk went, it left a lot to be desired, yet he realised that he should be feeling relieved. He had laid down his dictates and she hadn't blinked an eye. In fact, he need not have bothered. She had no interest in taking things between them beyond their natural course. Thank God. And, to prove how misguided he had been in imagining that she might get a little too wrapped up in *this,* here she was now, chatting about work. Did it get less romantic?

But who the hell wanted romance? 'I need a shower,' he said abruptly.

'Are you okay? I shouldn't have mentioned the shelter. I wouldn't want you to think that I don't trust you...' She sat up, slightly panicked by his sudden mood swing, and it occurred to her that this was something she would have to get accustomed to if she decided to stick it out. He didn't care about her. Why should it bother him if he was dismissive, if he decided to have a mood swing?

'You clearly have a way to go if you think that I would ever back down on my word, despite my assurances.' Alessandro eased himself off the bed. 'I can bring the flight forward if you have work issues. In fact, might not be a bad idea. I have a couple of major deals about to reach boiling point. I need to be back sooner rather than later. A few hours makes all the difference sometimes.'

Suddenly backed into a corner, Chase nodded brightly. 'I'll begin packing while you're in the shower.' She waited for him to relent, to tell her that they should stick to the original timetable; what did a few hours matter? He didn't.

And what happened with them when they returned? It was a question she was reluctant to ask.

It hovered at the back of her mind for the remainder of the night and through into the following morning. Flights had been rescheduled and still nothing was said and she refused to weaken. His mood had disappeared as fast as it had come. On the surface, everything was bright and breezy. When she looked back at the villa from the back of the limo as they were driving away, she felt a pang of intense sadness that she would never see it again.

He seemed to be lost in his own thoughts and she acknowledged that he was probably projecting ahead, thinking about those deals of his that wouldn't go away unless he was on the scene to sort them out.

The silence between them became oppressive but it was

only when they had touched down at Heathrow that she turned to him and said lightly, 'So, what happens next…?'

Alessandro had had no idea how tense he had been until she asked that question. He had been infuriated with himself for not much liking her air of casual insouciance. Did the woman give a damn one way or another? But now, his keen ears tuning in to a thread of nervousness in her voice, he was satisfied that she did, and that did wonders for his ego.

'I'll call you.' He curved a sure hand on her cheek and bent to place a hungry kiss on her lips.

Chase was ashamed of the enthusiasm with which she returned his kiss. If she could have, she would have dragged him off to the nearest hotel room and picked up where they had left off in Italy. Instead, she pulled away with a sigh. 'I've never had much time for those women who hang around waiting for the phone to ring.'

Alessandro laughed. Her kiss conveyed a thousand messages and all of them were good. 'I haven't had enough of you by a long shot. I'll call you tomorrow. Save you doing too much waiting by the phone…although, if you *do* find yourself waiting by the phone, then give my imagination something to go on. It would work if you waited there in your birthday suit…'

So what if she hadn't said anything? Would he have posed the question himself? Would he have wanted to know what happened next? Was this going to be her destiny for the foreseeable future—a day-to-day existence, only coming alive when Alessandro was around; not daring to breathe a word of how she really felt; living in fear of the phone calls stopping, grateful for whatever crumbs continued to drop her way? Was this what she had spent the past eight years working towards?

She took a taxi back to the house. She couldn't face the vagaries of the underground.

It was a little after two in the afternoon by the time she was paying the taxi driver. A thin, annoying drizzle had started, accompanied by a gusty wind, and as she fumbled in her handbag for her keys there was nothing on her mind other than getting inside the house and out of the rain.

She certainly wasn't expecting the man that stepped out of the shadows at the side of the house. When he spoke, all thoughts of the rain, getting inside and even of Alessandro flew out of her head. She gaped in horror as he smiled and pulled his hoodie down a little lower so that most of his face was in shadow.

'Long time no see, Chase. Been anywhere exciting…?'

CHAPTER EIGHT

CHASE WOKE WITH a start to the sound of her alarm going off. She had a few seconds of intense disorientation and then memories of the afternoon before broke through the barrier of forgetfulness and began pouring through her head. She had no idea how she had managed to get through what remained of the day, how she had managed finally to get to sleep.

She began getting ready for work on autopilot, showering, fetching her smart grey suit from the wardrobe, twinning it with a crisp white shirt. When half an hour later she looked at her reflection in the mirror, on the surface she was the same diligent, nicely dressed professional her colleagues would be expecting back at the office after a few days in the sun, with a companion or companions unknown.

Under the surface, she was barely functioning.

She had not expected to return to her house and find Brian Shepherd on her doorstep. In fact, she had not expected ever to have set eyes on Brian Shepherd again, but then didn't bad things have a habit of bouncing right back? Wasn't it true what they said, that you could run but you couldn't hide?

She had foolishly imagined Brian Shepherd to be nothing but a distant memory from the bad old days. 'Blue Boy' had been his nickname, because of his bright-blue eyes. He had been Shaun's closest friend growing up, the one who, from the age of ten, had shown him all the clever ways they could break and enter houses and all the tricks of the trade for getting their hands on valuable scrap metal. Six years older than Shaun, he had been his mentor until finally she and Shaun had moved to London, leaving behind Blue Boy for good. Fat chance, as it turned out.

And now he was back.

'Heard you were doing well for yourself,' he had said, inviting himself into her house and scanning it with the shrewd eyes of a born petty thief. 'Heard you found yourself a replacement for Shaunie.'

She had flinched every time he had reached out to touch one of her possessions but past experience had taught her that any sign of weakness would be a mistake with Brian Shepherd. She knew all about his temper.

There had been no need to ask him how he had found out about Alessandro. He had volunteered the information with relish: a friend of a friend of a friend had spotted them together on their little love-bird holiday in Italy. At the airport, of all places. Wasn't it a small world?

'Angie—Angie Carson. Remember her? Fat cow. Took a picture of the both of you. On her phone. Bet you never spotted her! Probably wouldn't have recognised her cos it's been a while, hasn't it? Anyone would think you were ashamed of all your old mates...'

He didn't remove his hoodie the entire time he was at the house, prowling through from room to room, touching and picking things up and turning them round in his hands, as though trying to figure out what they were worth.

Chase remained largely silent until, eventually, when she could stand it no longer, she asked him what he wanted, because of course he would want something.

Money. He was in a bit of a tight spot. Just enough to tide him over, and he knew she could lay her hands on some, because they'd driven off in a flash car and the luggage…

He gave a low, long whistle and eyed her up and down in a way that made her stomach lurch. Nice luggage. Expensive. Angie had been impressed. Snapped a few pics of that on her phone and all.

So, just a bit of money, spare change for a bloke who could zoom off in a chauffeur-driven limo with all that nice luggage in the boot. Angie had gone off with her mates but he was betting that, wherever that flash car had driven to, it wasn't going to be a one-star dump with dodgy air-conditioning.

So, what did she say? Did she think that she could spare an old friend a bit of loose change? Maybe, he said, he could persuade her. He knew where she worked…had done a little digging after those photos fat Angie had shown him…

Remember that club, the one that got busted by the coppers….? Course, she'd been underage at the time and she hadn't actually been doing drugs or anything—not like him and Shaunie and the rest of the gang. But those posh people at the law firm, they'd be really keen to know that she used to mix with a crowd who all had police records, wouldn't they? Might even get to thinking that *she* had a police record! Wouldn't that be funny? And, being honest, just the fact that she and he used to be mates would get them wondering, wouldn't it?

He had chuckled. 'You know what they say about the smelly stuff sticking…'

Her mobile rang now just as she was about to enter the office. Alessandro. She switched it off. There was no way that she could talk to him. Not just yet. But talk to him she would have to, because Brian Shepherd wasn't going to go away until he got his wretched money which, as it turned out, was hardly what she would have called 'loose change'.

It was certainly more than she had set aside, which was precious little after her mortgage repayments had been made and the bills paid.

Her life seemed to be unravelling at speed and she had to force herself not to succumb to the meltdown she knew was hovering just around the corner. She had weathered a lot of things and she would weather this as well. It would just take a little working out.

By the time she pushed through the doors to their offices, she had glumly decided what needed to be done.

Her first port of call was her boss's office.

Tony Grey was a short, round man in his fifties who would have been a dead ringer for Father Christmas were it not for the fact that he was almost entirely bald and his dark-grey eyes were way too astute for someone who spent all his time laughing and chuckling. In actual fact, Chase had never seen her boss laugh out loud, but he had always been fair and supportive. She would miss that.

She would have to hand in her notice. She had come to that conclusion as she had left her house. Brian Shepherd wouldn't just do what he threatened; he would go further if she didn't do as he asked. Hadn't he been banged up for nearly killing someone in a bar brawl when he was fourteen? What if he took it into his head to release his explosive temper on *her* if she didn't play ball? If he could nearly kill someone at the age of fourteen because they'd accidentally knocked into him without saying sorry, then he could certainly kill her if he wanted money from her and she refused to pay. She loathed the thought of having to yield in a situation like this but pride was no match for sheer common sense.

Well, on the bright side, she would find a company specialising more in the pro bono work she enjoyed and, even if Brian hunted her down there, he would be able to see for himself that it wasn't a money-making machine.

She still couldn't work out how he had discovered her whereabouts but there was no point wasting time trying to figure that out. With social-networking sites stretching their tentacles into every area of everyone's lives, it wouldn't have been beyond the wit of man for him to ferret her out the second he'd figured he could get money from her.

'My dear,' Tony said when she had explained that she would have to hand in her notice for personal reasons. 'Are you sure this is really what you want to do? You're on course to go far with this firm. Your dedication is second to none.'

But he assured her that, if he couldn't persuade her to change her mind, then of course he would provide her with glowing references. With just that sympathy and fairness which she would miss so much, he also agreed that she could leave as soon as she had tied up loose ends on the cases she was currently working on so that they could be handed over in good order.

She had no idea what he concluded her 'personal reasons' for leaving might be, but she suspected that health issues might be at the heart of it, and he was right in a way. She certainly wasn't feeling very well at the moment. Not when she considered the way her nicely controlled life had been turned upside down.

Alessandro… She thought that this might not be as similarly smooth sailing. She ignored a further two calls from him, only picking up his last just as she was about to leave the office on the dot of five. Clock watching had never been her style, but tying up loose ends was a dismal procedure. Nor was she up to chatting to all and sundry about her decision to leave.

'Where the hell have you been? I've phoned three times!'

'I'm sorry. I was…busy.' Just the sound of his voice

sent little ripples of awareness racing up and down her spine as she took the lift to the ground floor and emerged into yet another cool and overcast day to do battle with public transport.

'Busy doing what?'

'I, well, I've handed in my notice at Fitzsimmons.'

For a few seconds, Alessandro debated whether he had heard her correctly. But there was something in her voice, a tell-tale tremor that she couldn't quite conceal; a nuance which he felt that only he would have been able to pick up. Something was different, *wrong,* a little off-kilter.

He stood up, restlessly moving away from his desk towards the windows and absently looking down. 'You're kidding.'

'No, I'm not. Can we meet? I can…um…come to your office.'

'I can think of a better venue.'

'I'd rather your office, Alessandro.'

'What's going on?' he demanded bluntly. 'And please don't tell me *nothing.* You tell me you've handed in your notice, even though you've expressed nothing but satisfaction at your job there, and now…you want to meet me *in my office*?'

'Please.'

Alessandro sighed heavily and raked his fingers through his hair. He was getting a very bad vibe about whatever the hell was going on but he acquiesced. Whatever was happening, he would be able to get it out of her and things would return to normal. He was nothing if not wholly confident in his ability to take her mind off things.

'I'd rather not parade my personal life in front of my employees,' he drawled. 'And *you* may be scuttling out of the office because you've handed in your notice and lost momentum in your job, but my people are all still at their desks. If you can't wait until later and meet me somewhere private, then I can see you in forty-five minutes at that brasserie round the corner from my office. You know the one?'

She did. She made her way there slowly, forgoing the speed and ease of a black cab in favour of a laborious trip by public transport. It suited her mood.

How had life changed so fast in such a brief moment in time? As she neared the brasserie, she felt a sickening lurch of déjà vu. Eight years ago she had met Alessandro here with one thing and one thing only in her head—the need to get rid of him. She had walked towards a conversation she had known would break her in half and she was doing the same thing now. History was repeating itself. But it was so much worse this time, she would be taking so many more regrets with her when she was finished saying what she had to say.

Sitting at the back of the brasserie, nursing an extremely early glass of red wine, Alessandro had been waiting for ten minutes. He had been unable to get down to work after her phone call. He would never have imagined himself as one of those sensitive, intuitive sorts but something wasn't right and, however much he told himself that he could sort out whatever the hell it was that was eating her up, he was still vaguely uneasy.

And yet, why should he be? They had parted company the day before and everything had been just fine and dandy. There'd been no inconvenient intuition then. So, really, what could have materially changed since then?

He spotted her the second she walked through the door. For the briefest of moments he felt a sharp, inexplicable pang of nostalgia for the carefree girl in shorts and tee-shirts who had been his companion for the past few days. She was in full lawyer mode: prissy grey suit, even prissier white blouse, black pumps. He wondered how long he could wait before he ripped the whole lot off her and bedded her.

On cue, his erection pushed hard against the zip of his trousers and he shifted position uncomfortably to release some of the insistent ache in his groin.

He had not expected this crazy lust to be an ongoing situation after the countless times they had now slept together. He had assumed she would be more than just disposable: he would take what had once been denied him and then discard her without preamble. It wasn't working out quite as he had envisaged, but he shrugged that off. The unexpected could sometimes be a good thing and getting turned on by her on a semi-permanent basis was definitely not to be sneezed at, especially for him, a man whose tastes had become lamentably jaded over time.

He watched with masculine appreciation as she glanced around her. Already he was undressing her in his mind. Slowly. Revealing those generous pale breasts inch by succulent inch; exposing the pink nipples to take them one at a time in his mouth as they pouted temptingly up at him.

He pictured the prissy grey skirt hitting the ground, followed by whatever suitably functional underwear she happened to be wearing... He could almost taste the honeyed sweetness between her legs, hear her broken little whimpers of pleasure as his tongue found her sweet spot and worked it until the broken little whimpers became moans and cries of pleasure. The more horny he became, just sitting and watching her and letting his imagination run wild, the faster he knew he would have to sort out whatever was on her mind just so that he could get her back to his place. They might not even be able to make it to the bedroom.

He grinned as she spotted him and lazily attracted the waitress's attention without taking his eyes off Chase's face. Her looks were really quite startling. There was a sexiness to her, a perfection to her features, that made her naturally guarded expression all the more beguiling. He could see other men surreptitiously following her with their eyes as she weaved her way towards him.

'Alessandro…' Chase said weakly. She could feel her heart thumping like a sledgehammer inside her.

'So you've handed in your notice.' He broke off to order her a cappuccino. 'And you don't look very happy about it.'

'I…I…' She could barely string two words together. This was so much worse than she had envisaged. There was just no way that she could pretend to be cool, calm and collected. Her nerves were all over the place.

'Sit down. Tell me about it. Why?'

'I…I didn't have much of a choice,' she admitted truthfully. 'Personal reasons.'

'What personal reasons?'

'I'd rather not talk about it.'

'Are you ill?' He felt a sudden mixture of fear and irrational panic. 'Is that what this is all about?'

'No,' she said, waving a wistful goodbye to what could have been a fantastic excuse. As if lies hadn't landed her here in the first place. 'No, I'm not ill.'

'Then what? What personal reasons, and why don't you want to discuss them?' Alessandro scowled. Since when had he ever been interested in women's life stories? Mysteries dangling at the end of a line like bait to hook him in had always left him cold.

He eyed her narrowly as a new thought began to take shape in his head. 'If you're not ill,' he said slowly, 'and yet you've reluctantly had to hand in your notice, then there's only one explanation that springs to mind…'

Temporarily diverted, Chase looked at him in bafflement. 'Is there?'

'Someone's made a pass at you. Who is it?' His voice was low and controlled but he clenched his fists. The second he had a name, he would personally make it his business to make sure that the culprit paid.

'Made a pass at me?'

'Even wearing that starchy suit, you're still sexy as hell, Chase. And I won't be the only one who can see that. So, spill the beans. Tell me who it is. Your boss? One of your colleagues? What did he do? Did he touch you inappropriately? Try to feel you up?'

He imagined one of those rich kids thinking that he could have a go at the sexiest woman in the office and he was overwhelmed by an explosive rage. He had met enough twenty-something lawyers in his time to know that the majority of them thought that they were studs.

'No one touched me, Alessandro! And no one tried to *feel me up*! Do you think that I'm so feeble that I would allow anyone to get away with that? Do you think that I'm incapable of taking care of myself?' But his show of possessiveness touched her. She folded her hands on her lap to stop herself from reaching out and covering his hand with her own.

'Then what's going on?' Looking at her, it was clear that she could barely meet his eyes. She was fidgeting nervously with the handle of her coffee cup. Alessandro felt that he could do with the entire bottle of wine, never mind one careful glass. Instead he ordered a black coffee while he tried to sift through some plausible explanation for her behaviour in his mind. 'You're not…pregnant, are you?' It was a thought that only now occurred to him.

Chase glanced up at his face, suddenly ashen, and for a few moments anger replaced gnawing anxiety and dread. It was obvious from his expression that the mere suggestion of pregnancy had knocked him for six. 'And what if I *was*?' she queried boldly. 'What if I told you that there was a mini-Alessandro taking shape right now inside me?'

She fancied she could see the colour drain away from

his face as she allowed him time to absorb the full horror of that scenario. 'Don't worry, Alessandro. I'm not pregnant. I told you once that I'm not a complete idiot.'

For a few fleeting seconds, Alessandro had found himself ripped out of his comfort zone, staring down the barrel of a gun. She was having his baby. *His baby.* The gun barrel, strangely, was less of a threat than he might have imagined.

'Accidents happen,' he said grimly.

'Oh, Alessandro…' She sighed and sat back, head tilted up, eyes half-closed as the inescapable hurtled towards her with the deadly force of a bomb. 'I'm healthy, there's no mini-Alessandro on the way and no one's made a pass at me at work. And I wish there was some other way of saying this but there isn't…' She straightened and took a deep breath. 'I need to ask you something.'

'What?'

'I need to…borrow some money from you.'

Deathly silence greeted this request. Chase didn't dare look at Alessandro. What choice did she have? she wondered helplessly. Brian wasn't going to go away until he had his money and she simply didn't have it. If she got it, gave it to him and then convinced him that she had broken up with Alessandro, then he would go away. If she didn't, then she was, frankly, scared of what he might do. Scared of all the old horrors landing on her doorstep once again.

'Tell me I'm not hearing this.'

'I'm sorry and, naturally, I'll pay you back every penny of what I borrow. With interest.'

Alessandro laughed mirthlessly. 'So finally,' he said in a lethally soft voice, 'the real face of Chase Evans is revealed. I'm surprised you managed to keep it hidden for so long.' He felt as though he had been punched in the gut. This wasn't just anger; this was a level of hurt that he could barely acknowledge even to himself. He didn't know who he loathed more—himself for having been conned a second time, or her for having been the one to do the conning.

'What do you need the money for?' He could scarcely credit that he was willing to hear her out, willing to give her an explanation that would allow him to make sense of the situation. That window of willingness died the second she looked at him and said steadily,

'I'm sorry. That's…none of your business.' The harshest of words, yet they would provide the clean break.

'Right. So…when did you decide that you could screw me for money?' he asked in the same ultra-controlled voice that was far more intimidating than if he had stood up and shouted at her. 'Was it when you came to my house? Or was it when we went to Italy and you saw just how much I had? Tell me. I'm curious.'

'You don't understand, Alessandro. I wouldn't be sitting here asking you for money if…if…I didn't have to.'

'And yet you refuse to tell me what you want the money for.' He threw up his hands in rampant frustration as she greeted this with stubborn silence. 'Are you in some sort of debt? Hell, Chase, just be bloody straight with me!'

'I told you, it's none of your business. If you don't want to lend me the money, then just say so.' Her heart was breaking in two.

'And, just for the record, how much money do you fancy you can bleed me for?'

She named the figure and watched as he threw his head back and roared with laughter, except there was no humour there. He was laughing with incredulity and his dark eyes were as hard and cold as the frozen depths of a glacier.

'Well…?' Chase cleared her throat and valiantly met his eyes.

'No explanations, no excuses, not even of the make-believe variety… Sorry, not good enough.' He signalled to the waitress for the bill. 'And consider this conversation over.' Hell, the woman could act. She was as white as a sheet and her hands were shaking—remarkable performance. He felt something painful twist inside him, an iron fist clenching on his intestines, and staunched it down.

'I think we can say that our unfinished business has been concluded. If you ever get it into your head to descend on me, either at my offices or at my house, I assure you I will have you forcibly removed either by the police or by my security personnel. Do you read me?'

Chase nodded. Had she expected him to part with cash just because she'd asked? Because she'd offered to pay him back? Was there some part of her that had hoped he might know her well enough by now to give her the benefit of the doubt? She couldn't tell him the truth. How could she? She was boxed in with no room to manoeuvre.

'I understand,' she said quietly.

'Question.' Alessandro was furious with himself for not walking away without a backward glance. He was even more furious with himself for the unwilling tug of compassion he was feeling for a woman who was nothing more or less than a gold-digger with great acting ability. And, underneath that maelstrom of emotion, he recognised the angry pain of disillusionment. 'If you're so desperate for money, why jack the job in?'

'I can't discuss that either.'

Alessandro stood up abruptly. 'Good luck finding your money,' he told her coldly. 'If anything needs to be discussed about the shelter, you might want another lawyer to handle it.'

'I've already begun tidying up all my ongoing case files. Someone else will be handling all the details with the shelter. I…I've been given permission to leave at the end of the week. I should be working out a month's notice but my boss—'

'Not really interested.'

Chase remained standing, watching his departing back. She told herself, bracingly, that it was always going to end—yet the hollowness filling her felt as destructive as a tsunami. If she wasn't a homeowner, if she had been one of the millions renting, she knew that she would have upped sticks and disappeared. No job, no Alessandro and a threat waiting for her when she returned: it took all her courage to gather herself and head back outside down to the underground.

Brian would be there. He had told her in a chummy voice laced with menace that he would be waiting when she returned, that he didn't mind just hanging out there, although if she wanted to hand her key over to him…

Chase shuddered.

Heading in the opposite direction back to his office, Alessandro angrily realised that the very last thing he was in the mood to do was work. He still had a conference call lined up for later that evening. He got on his mobile, spoke to his secretary and cancelled it.

Hell, could he have been *that* stupid that he had fallen for the walk up the garden path *yet again*? With tremendous effort, he side-lined the fury raging through him and tried to recall the details of their brief conversation in the brasserie.

She hadn't given him an answer when he had asked her why she had handed in her notice if she needed money. That, for one thing, made no sense. Whatever debts she had managed to incur, she wasn't so stupid that she could imagine settling them without a regular salary coming in. So had she been sacked? Had they discovered something? Had she been embezzling? It seemed a ludicrous idea, but hell, how was he to know when she had offered no explanation for her behaviour?

No, this was not going to happen again. He was emphatically *not* going to be left stranded with a bucket load of unanswered questions, as had happened last time round. Whether he ever laid eyes on her again or not was immaterial. He would pay her a little visit and would stay put until she answered all his questions to his satisfaction. Then, and only then, would he leave.

He called his driver to collect him. Rush-hour traffic meant that it took a ridiculously long time before his driver made it to the building, even though his car, parked outside his house, was only a matter of a couple miles away as the crow flew. It took even longer to navigate the stand-still traffic in central London.

His mobile buzzed continuously and he eventually switched it off. He was fully given over to trying to disentangle the conversation he had had with Chase. He felt like a man in possession of just sufficient pieces of a complex puzzle to rouse curiosity and yet lacking the essential ones that would solve the conundrum.

This, he told himself, was why he was sitting in the back of his car, drumming his fingers restlessly on the leather seat and frowning out of the back window. He had been presented with a complex puzzle and it was only human nature to try and figure it out, whatever the cost. Frankly, he would drag answers out of her if he had to.

It was considerably later than he had expected by the time the car swung into her small road. From outside, he could see that lights were on. 'You can leave,' he told his driver. 'I'll get a cab back to my house.' He slammed the door and watched as the Jag slowly disappeared around the corner.

If there was a small voice in his head telling him that his appearance on her doorstep made little sense, given the fact that she had never been destined to be a permanent feature in his life, he chose to ignore it. Finding answers seemed more important than debating the finer points.

He leaned his hand on the doorbell and kept it there for an inordinately long time. Where the hell was she? If the lights were on, then she was home. She had a thing about wasting electricity, just one of her many little quirks to which he had become accustomed. He scowled at the very fact that he was remembering that at this juncture.

Chase heard the insistent buzzing of the doorbell but it took her a second or two before she generated the enthusiasm to get the door. In the lounge, a fuming Brian was filling a bin bag with whatever he fancied he could take from her. There was nothing she could do about it; he was bigger and he had no conscience when it came to violence.

She'd have done anything to get rid of him, to have him out of her house. He told her to get rid of whoever was at the door.

'Too busy here for visitors, darling. Still a lot to get through before I leave!'

Chase pulled open the door and her mouth fell open in shock. Alessandro was the last person she had expected to find on her doorstep.

'You're not getting rid of me until you tell me what the hell is really going on with you!' were his opening words.

'Alessandro, you have to go.'

She was scared stiff; that much he could see. He pushed past her and halted as a man in his thirties sauntered out of the living room. In the space of mere seconds, Alessandro had processed the guy and reached his verdict. This was no smarmy, overpaid young lawyer. This was a thug and, whatever was going on, Chase was afraid.

'And you are…?' If there was going to be a fight, then he was more than up for it.

'Not about to tell you, mate. Hang on…thought you said you'd broken up with lover boy? Lying to me, were you? Don't like lies…'

Alessandro clenched his fists. Chase had backed away

and was stammering out some sort of explanation which he barely registered. No, this wasn't going to do. He had hold of the man's tee-shirt and felt roughly one hundred and forty pounds of packed muscle try to squirm away from him. Escape was never destined to be. He propelled the man back towards the sitting room. Out of the corner of his eye, he could see that the room had been decimated. A black bin bag was stuffed to overflowing on the ground. Another was half-full. Was this the 'spot of bother' she was in?

'You're going to tell me what's going on...' He addressed her but kept his eye on his frantically writhing captive. The man was a bully; Alessandro could spot the signs a mile away. The sort of loser who didn't mind throwing his weight around with anyone weaker than him but would run a mile if faced with stiff competition. Alessandro prided himself on being stiff competition. He listened intently while Chase babbled something about Brian wanting money...taking her stuff...

The missing pieces were beginning to fall into place. So the money had been a legitimate request. She hadn't been trying to con gold out of him. 'Here's what you're going to do, buddy.' His voice was low, soft and razor-sharp. 'You're going to unload that bin bag and return all the nice lady's possessions to her. Then you're going to apologise and, when you've finished apologising, you're going to leave quietly through that front door and never show your face here again. Do you read me loud and clear?

'And just in case...' He tightened his stranglehold so that the man was gasping to catch his breath. 'You get it into your head that you can ignore what I'm telling you, here's what will happen to you if you do. I'll employ someone to dredge up every scrap of dirt on you—and I'm betting that there's a lot—and then I'm going to make sure that you get put behind bars and the key is conveniently thrown away. And don't think I won't do it. I will. And I'll enjoy every second of it.'

He watched in silence, arms folded, as his orders were obeyed. Out of the bin bag came all the bits and pieces which, Alessandro knew, would have taken Chase years to accumulate. Some were worthless, some—such as her computer, her tablet, the plasma-screen television which she had laughingly told him had been an absolute indulgence because she really didn't watch much TV—weren't.

His apology was grudgingly given until Alessandro ordered him to try harder, to say it like he meant it...

He left as quietly as he had been ordered to do. Then there was just the two of them, standing in a room that looked as though a bomb had exploded in it.

'I'm sorry,' Chase mumbled. Yet she was so glad that he had come because now she felt utterly safe. She moved to begin picking up some of her possessions from the ground, stacking them neatly on the sofa, very conscious of Alessandro's eyes on her. 'Why did you come?' she asked.

'You need something stiff to drink.'

'I'm fine.'

'Do you have any brandy?'

'I'm fine.' She finally met his eyes and hesitantly perched on the edge of the chair with her hands on her knees. 'There's half a bottle of wine in the fridge,' she offered when he continued to look at her in silence. 'It's all I can do by way of drink, I'm afraid. I don't keep spirits in the house.' Shock was creeping over her. She didn't want alcohol but she had to admit that she felt a little better after she had swallowed a mouthful from the glass he placed in her shaking hand a minute later.

'I guess you want to know what all that was about,' she said wearily.

'Understatement of the decade, Chase.'

Chase stared down at her fingers. She'd been rescued

by a man who had only returned to the scene to find out what was going on because he was like that—would never have been able to accept a brush off without demanding answers.

She would have to explain how it was that she knew Brian, how he had happened to be in her house. She would have to come clean about her background and know that he would be filled with contempt. Contempt for a woman who had lied about a fundamental aspect of her life and maintained the lie all through the time she had been seeing him. But there still remained a part of her that she refused to reveal, because to reveal it would be to lower herself even more in his estimation.

'You'd better sit down and I'll tell you. And then...' She took a deep breath and exhaled slowly. 'You can leave and it'll finally be over between us.'

CHAPTER NINE

SHE WAS STILL in her work clothes, the same dreary grey suit, except she looked...*rumpled.*

'Did he lay a finger on you?' Alessandro asked suddenly. 'Did he touch you?' This was as far out of his comfort zone as he had ever been. Even with parents intent on squandering their inheritance—parents who had been shining examples of irresponsibility; who had opened the doors of their various houses to artists and poets and playwrights, most of whom had been pleasantly stoned most of the time—through all that, he had never come into contact with the seedier side of life. The side of life that threw up people like the thug who had just been thrown off the premises. Even with diminishing wealth, he had still lived a sheltered, privileged life.

'No. No, he didn't.' Chase could see the incredulity stamped on his beautiful face. He was shocked at what he had found, shocked that the woman he thought came from a solid, middle-class background could know someone like Brian Shepherd. 'Although it's not unheard of for Brian to lay into someone just for the hell of it, never mind if he thinks they've done something to him.'

'How the hell do you know that guy, Chase?' Alessandro frowned. 'When you said that you couldn't tell me why you needed the money, did you mean that you owed that creep money?'

'No, I did *not* owe that creep any money. He just…' She stood up, suddenly restless, but then immediately sat back down because her legs felt like jelly.

'What, then…?'

'If you would just sit down and stop *prowling*.'

Alessandro paused to look at her narrowly. 'If you didn't owe the guy money, then why would he have gathered half of your possessions and stuffed them into a bin bag?' He sat on the chair facing her. Their body language was identical, both sitting forward, arms resting loosely on their thighs although, whilst Alessandro's expression was one of intense curiosity, Chase's was more resigned and reflective.

'Brian and Shaun were friends,' she said quietly, not daring to meet his eyes, fearful of what she would see there. 'They were friends from before I met Shaun, childhood friends, even though Brian was older. They grew up on the same council estate.'

'Which calls into question the type of man you chose to marry.'

'When you're young, it's very easy to get drawn in to the wrong crowd.'

'I'm trying to picture your parents allowing you to get drawn in to the wrong crowd. Or didn't they have any say in the matter? Maybe they were too busy projecting to happy times ahead in Australia…?'

'There *is* no Australia.'

'Sorry, but I'm not following you.'

Chase nervously tucked a strand of hair behind her ears. She wondered what hand of fate it was that had returned Alessandro to her life, only to have her fall in love with him all over again. Instead of getting him out of her system by sleeping with him, by putting that unfulfilled fantasy to rest, she had managed to well and truly cement him into every nook, cranny and corner of her being.

'My parents don't live in Australia. In fact, I have no parents. I was a foster-home kid. I was shuffled from family to family, never staying anywhere for very long. I never knew my father. My mother died when I was very little from a drugs overdose. I pretty much brought myself up. So, you see, everything you think you know about me is a lie.'

Of all the things Alessandro had been prepared for, this was not one of them. 'Lyla…?'

'Was the name I chose when I met you. When I thought that I could create…make myself out to be…'

'You fabricated everything.'

'No. Not everything!'

Alessandro slammed his hand on the side of his chair and vaulted to his feet. He felt tight in his skin. He needed to move. Energy was pouring through him and he was at a loss as to how to contain it. This must be what it felt like to imagine your feet were planted on solid ground only to discover that you were trying to balance on quicksand.

'Everything about you has been a lie from beginning to end. God. Why?'

'I made stuff up. I was young! I met you and I wanted to make a good impression.'

'Not only were you married, not only did you choose to conceal that fact from me eight years ago, but you also chose to conceal everything else. So your husband was… what, exactly? And how did you manage to make it to university? Or maybe you weren't a student at all. Were you? Or was that another lie?'

'Of course I was!' Chase cried, half-rising to her feet in an attempt to halt the flow of his scathing criticism. She sat back down as quickly as she had stood up. What else might she have hoped for? That he might have been understanding? Sympathetic? Why would he be? To him, she was now a confirmed liar and, if she had lied about everything, all those significant details, then what else might she have lied about? Her emotions? Her responses? It felt as though she had built a relationship on a house of cards and, now the cards were all toppling down, she had no idea how to start catching them before they all fell to the floor.

'Really? What strands am I supposed to start believing now?'

'I *was* a student at university,' she said with feverish urgency. 'I never did a lot of studying…' At this she laughed bitterly. Studying, when she was growing up, had not been seen as something worth wasting time doing. They had all known where they were destined to end up: out of work and on the dole, or else in no-hope jobs earning just enough to scrape by with a little moonlighting on the side.

'But I discovered that I barely needed to. I had a good memory. Brilliant, in fact. I would show up at school after a couple of days doing nothing, playing truant, and somehow I'd still be ahead of everyone in the class. I'd skim through a text book and manage to have instant recall of pretty much everything I'd read…'

The handful of teachers who had noticed that remarkable ability had been her salvation. Because of them she hadn't become a quitter, although she had learned to study undercover. There had never been any mileage in standing out.

She looked at him and held his inscrutable gaze. 'I guess you must find all of this completely alien. I don't suppose you've ever known anyone from the wrong side of the tracks…'

The chasm between them had never seemed wider, now that she was revealing the truth about her background. Even if she had been the person she had once claimed to be, the middle-class girl with the normal parents, there would still have been a chasm between them. Of course, he would have been attracted to her because of how she looked. Sadly, physical attributes were not destined to last; she accepted that, in an ideal world, he would have dumped her sooner or later anyway. He had been born into privilege, whatever his disruptive background, and he would always have ended up looking to settle with a woman from a similar background.

Not only had she lied to him, but she had lied to herself for ever thinking otherwise. And she had. When she had met him again and when she had fallen in love with him again. When she had nurtured silly dreams of 'what if?'s…

'Coming from the wrong side of the tracks is one thing,' Alessandro said brusquely. 'Lying about it is quite another. Were you ever going to tell me the truth?' His sense of betrayal overshadowed every other emotion, including anger.

'What would have been the point?' Chase asked defiantly. 'As you pointed out…as *we* agreed…it's not as though we were ever going anywhere with this relationship. Why would I have spoiled things with lots of truths I know you wouldn't have wanted to hear?'

Alessandro's jaw hardened. He took in her beautiful, stubborn face and had a very vivid image of the teenager she must have been: wild, drifting, incredibly bright, incredibly good-looking. 'Shaun…' Just uttering her ex-husband's name left a sour taste in his mouth. 'Must have thought he had won the lottery the day he met you—clever kid who could be his passport out of whatever dead-end life he was looking forward to leading.'

Chase looked up at him with some surprise. 'I never thought about it that way,' she said truthfully. 'I…' Was that how he had seen her, whilst making her believe that it had been the other way around? That *she* had been the lucky one to have been noticed by *him*? 'I met him when I was fifteen. He was the leader of the pack, so to speak. Everyone looked up to him even though he was younger than nearly all the guys in the gang. He was fed up living on the outskirts of Leeds. He said he wanted more. He said that London was the place to be.'

'And of course, he encouraged you to sign up to university life he knew that it was the best way out for him.'

'I don't know how I managed to get through all my exams, and I did them all a year ahead of everyone else,' Chase confessed. 'Maths, further maths, economics, geography…' But she had. Her teachers had seen to it that she'd sat them all. They were the ones who had insisted on university, who had filled in all the applications on her behalf while she had been busy having fun and running wild.

She had landed herself a place at one of the top universities in the country and had been amazed that she had accomplished such a feat. Only in retrospect had she appreciated the energy behind the scenes that had got her there.

'So you went to university and you got married.'

'The other way around, actually. I got married. Yes. And I went to university. I never expected to meet someone like you. Or anyone, for that matter.'

'And yet you did. And, instead of being truthful, you thought that it would be a much better idea to concoct a fairy-tale story about yourself.'

Chase heard the undercurrent of contempt mixed with bewilderment in his voice and inwardly winced. She was not the person she had pretended to be and that mattered to a man like him, a man who occupied a stratosphere of wealth and power that few could even dream about.

She wanted to shout at him that he didn't have a clue, that he couldn't possibly understand, but shouting wasn't going to do. Losing control wasn't going to do. She would offer him the explanation he deserved to hear with detachment and lack of passion. She would demonstrate that she was already breaking away from him, just as he was with her. She would leave with her dignity intact, as much as it could be. She would save her tears for later.

'Yes.' She tilted her chin up and steeled herself to meet his eyes squarely and without apology. 'I was young. I just…gave in to the temptation to turn myself into someone I wasn't. I made up the background I always wanted for myself.'

Alessandro felt another unwelcome, piercing tug of compassion at the thought that a middle-class background could have constituted her dream life. Most girls would have dreamt up stories of money, overseas holidays and parents with fast cars. She, on the other hand, had dreamt of what most other young girls of her age would have grumbled about and considered normal and boring.

He squashed any notion of compassion as fast as it raised its inappropriate head. The bottom line was that she was a compulsive liar, not to be trusted, never to be believed. He had come to get some truths out of her and he was getting them—in shed-loads.

'Which brings us to that piece of rubbish who was filling bin bags with your possessions.'

Getting to the heart of the matter and the reason he had shown up on her doorstep, Chase thought. Because, the faster he could wash his hands of her and clear off, the better.

'When we went to Italy, one of the girls who used to hang out in our gang was at the airport. I didn't see her.' But then, she hadn't had eyes for anyone but the man silently judging her now.

'She took pictures of us on her phone and posted them on a social networking site. Brian saw them, clocked the Louis Vuitton luggage and the chauffeur-driven car and decided that he would turn up on my doorstep and squeeze me for money. I don't know how he got my address, but there are so many ways of finding people; I don't suppose he had much trouble. He may just have gone to the place we were renting before Shaun died, got in touch with the landlord and got the forwarding address I gave him all those years ago. Who knows? He threatened to tell the people at work about my background… It would have spelled the end of my career. And he might have done a lot more besides…'

It seemed ironic now that the life she had built for herself could have been undone by something as crazy as someone taking a picture of her with Alessandro at an airport. There was no point dwelling on what was fair or what was unfair, she thought. The only way was to move forward. She kept her voice as modulated and toneless as she could.

'He was waiting for me when I got back to my house from Italy.'

Alessandro felt rage wash over him, a perfectly normal reaction to the thought of any thug lying in wait for a helpless victim.

'He told me that he wanted money and…that's when I asked you. I didn't want to, and if you *had* lent me the money I would have paid you back every penny.'

'You mean from the proceeds of the job you jacked in? Why did you do that?'

'I thought it best to resign just in case… I've never brought my past to my work. What would happen if Brian decided to show up at Fitzsimmons…?'

'Catastrophe—because they too were victims of your lies. They believed what you told them about your background, just like I did, didn't they?'

'I've never discussed my private life with anyone,' Chase mumbled, feeling even more of a hopeless liar, even though her lies had been through omission of the absolute truth. 'I've kept myself to myself. I fought hard to get where I was.'

'If you had told me the truth, I might have been inclined to give you the money.'

Chase shrugged. 'He would have come back for more. He knew where to find me. It was stupid of me to even… Well, in moments of panic we sometimes do stupid things.'

'He won't be back.'

'I know. And…and I'm very grateful to you for scaring him away. You probably threatened him with the one thing he would have taken notice of.' She wanted to smile, because who would have thought that a billionaire businessman from a cushy background could have had sufficient forcefulness to intimidate someone like Brian Shepherd into running scared? 'Look, I know you probably hate me for all of this…'

'You mean the fact that you were prepared to perpetuate a piece of fiction about yourself?' Alessandro strolled to stand in front of her, legs planted apart, hands at his sides.

Chase looked up at him reluctantly.

'What other pieces of fiction did you perpetuate?' he asked softly. 'No. There's just one more thing I need to get straight in my head.'

'What's—what's that?' she stammered uncertainly. She watched as he slowly leant over her and she half-closed her eyes as she inhaled his familiar scent. It rushed to her head like incense.

'This…' His mouth crushed her in a savage, punishing kiss and Chase helplessly yielded. She arched back in the chair, pulling him towards her, tasting him hungrily. She knew she shouldn't. She knew that it should be impossible to feel this driving, craven lust for a man who felt nothing but scorn towards her, but she couldn't seem to help herself.

There was a refrain playing at the back of her head that was telling her that this was the last time she would feel his lips on hers.

He pulled her to her feet and somehow they found themselves on the sofa, still entwined with one another. She was breathing heavily and she didn't stop him when he began undoing the buttons on her shirt, very soon losing patience. She heard the pop as a couple were ripped off. She wanted him so badly that she was shaking. Pride or no pride, she felt that she *needed* this final joining of their bodies. Her hands scrabbled to open his shirt so that she could feel the breadth of his chest and she moaned when, eventually, her fingers were splayed against it.

Her nipples tingled against her lacy bra. He cupped her breast with his hand and then pushed it underneath the bra, shoving the bra up so that he could suck on her nipple, drawing the stem into his mouth and swirling his tongue against it until she was half-crying for more.

As he suckled, he nudged her legs apart and then his hand was there, not even bothering to pull down her undies but delving underneath them, finding her wetness and exploring every inch of it with his fingers.

He still hadn't taken off a stitch of his own clothes. She had managed to undo a few buttons on his shirt and had yanked it out from the waistband of his trousers. She feverishly tried to complete the task of undressing him but he wasn't helping. She couldn't get to the zip of his trousers, although she could feel the bulge of his erection.

She gave up as he continued driving his fingers against her, pausing in the rhythmic movement only to insert them into her, into that place where she knew she wanted his rock-hard shaft to be instead.

He reared up and yanked down his trousers and, with his hand tangled in her hair, he guided her to his erection and stifled a groan when she took him into her mouth.

Through half-opened eyes, he watched as she sucked and licked him. She knew just how to rouse him down there with her hands and her mouth and he let her.

She might be a liar; he might not be able to trust her as far as he could throw her—because who could ever trust

a woman who made a habit of fabricating her life story?—
but she certainly knew just which buttons to press.

He tugged her away from him and sank onto her. Her
breasts, with the bra pushed up above them, were full and
ripe and irresistible. With a groan of satisfaction, he covered them with his mouth, until the pouting buds were wet
and hard and he continued, giving her no respite, until she
was wriggling like an eel, desperate for more.

Her hair was all over the place and her cheeks were
flushed, her mouth slightly parted, showing her perfect,
pearly-white teeth. She had sunbathed in the nude by the
pool in Italy, and her body was a perfect honey colour.

How well he knew this body. How much of it he had
explored and committed to memory, from the freckle by
her nipple to the tiny mole on her upper arm.

He pulled down her panties, flattened his hand between
her legs and then stroked her down there, harder and faster,
until he could feel her orgasm building beneath his fingers.
He didn't stop and when she came he watched: watched
her eyes flutter; watched her breathing catch in her throat
for a few seconds; watched her whole body arch, stiffen
and finally slacken as the waves of pleasure finally subsided, leaving her limp.

'Alessandro…' She reached for him and he stayed her
hand, circling her wrist before releasing her and standing up.

For a few seconds, Chase was completely bewildered.
When he began to zip up his trousers, she clambered into
a sitting position and looked at him speechlessly.

'What are you doing?'

'What does it look like I'm doing?'

'We were making love.'

'I was proving to myself that the way you responded to
me wasn't yet another lie.'

'How could you say that?' She itched to pull him back

to her but he was already turning away, doing up his buttons and taking his time, as cool as a cucumber. 'I never, *never,* pretended with you. Not about that…'

Alessandro steeled himself. She had made him cry once. The memory of that rose uninvited like poison from the deepest recesses of his mind. He had given a lot to her and her betrayal then had rocked his foundations. Never again.

'So it would seem.' He turned around to look at her. She was utterly dishevelled and utterly bewitching. 'I came here to get answers from you and I got them, Chase. Now the time has come for me to tell you goodbye. It's been… I would say fun, but what I'd really mean is…it's been a learning curve. You can congratulate yourself on teaching me the dangers of taking people at face value.'

'Alessandro!'

'What?' In the process of heading for the door, he half-turned towards her. His eyes were flat, hard and cold. There was a tense silence that stretched between them to breaking point.

Chase found that she didn't know what to say. She just didn't want him to go. Not just yet. Her body was still burning from where he had touched her, where he had deliberately touched her, turning her on, bringing her to a shuddering orgasm just to prove to himself that the attraction she'd claimed to feel for him was real. It was humiliating, yet she still couldn't bear the thought of him walking away. How on earth had she let it go this far? How was it that the control she had spent eight years building, the ability to arrange her life just how she wanted it without reference to anyone else, had been washed away by a man who had always been unsuitable and inappropriate?

'Nothing.'

He looked at her for a few seconds, shrugged and then he was gone. Just like that.

Chase was left staring at the empty doorway. He was

gone and he would never be coming back. She disgusted him. Her awful life, her sleazy ex-friends…

And he'd had the nerve to look contemptuous because once upon a time she had given in to the temptation to make it all go away by pretending to be somebody else! She might not have known about his wealth back then, but she had known with some unerring sixth sense that he would not be the kind of guy who would find any woman who came from her background attractive or in any way suitable.

And of course, she *hadn't* been suitable. She had been married, for starters. But she had seized that window of forbidden, youthful pleasure and now, all this time later, she was paying heavily for it.

She spent two hours returning all the stuff Brian had hauled off shelves and from drawers back to their rightful places. She washed a lot of it. The thought of his hands on her things made her shudder with distaste.

She hoped that by occupying herself she might take her mind off Alessandro but, all the while, he was in her head as she remembered the things they had done together, the conversations they had had.

She shakily told herself that it was a good thing that they were finished. It had been destined to end and the sooner the better. How much worse would she have felt had they ended it in two months' time? Two months during which she would have just continued falling deeper and deeper in love with him! The longer they lasted, the more difficult it would have been to unpick and disentangle her chaotic emotions. She should be thankful!

And yet, thankful was the very last thing she felt. She felt devastated, tearful and…*ashamed.*

More than anything else, she was angry with him for making her feel that way. She was angry with him for being hard line; for not having an ounce of sympathy in him; for not even trying to see her point of view. She had known from the outset that his sole motivation for sleeping with her was to exact some sort of revenge, to have that wheel turn full circle, to take what he thought had been promised to him eight years ago. Yet, hadn't he got to know her *at all* during that period? Had she just been his lover and *nothing more*?

They hadn't been rolling around on a mattress all of the time. There had been so many instances when they had talked, when the past hadn't existed, just the present, just two people getting to know one another. Or so it had felt to her.

She hated him for wiping that all away as though none of it had existed. She hated him for finding it so easy to write her off as though she was worthless.

Over the next week, as she came closer and closer to her final day at Fitzsimmons, the frustration and anger continued to build inside her. If only she could have maintained the anger, she might have felt protected, but there were so many chinks through which she recalled small acts of thoughtfulness, his wonderful wit, his sharp intellect, his lazy, sexy smile. What they had had all those years ago had been unbearably intense and that intensity had given the times they had shared recently a deep level of communication that was almost intuitive. She missed that. She missed him.

She hadn't heard a word from him. He had truly disappeared from her life—although, by all accounts, he had been on the scene far more than anticipated at the shelter, where, from what Beth had blithely told her, he appeared suddenly to have taken a keen interest in all the renovations she had planned.

'He has so many good suggestions for how the money could be spent!' Beth had enthusiastically listed all the suggestions while Chase had listened in resentful silence. 'He's also been kind enough to put us in touch with contacts he has in the contracting business so that we can get the best possible deal!' Chase had muttered something under her breath which she hoped didn't sound like the unladylike oath it most certainly was.

Beth had no idea of the history she and Alessandro had shared. It would have been petty and small-minded not to have responded with a similar level of enthusiasm to the hard-nosed billionaire businessman who had previously threatened a hostile buy-out, only to morph into a saint with a positively never-ending supply of 'brilliant ideas' and 'amazingly useful contacts'.

On the Friday, exactly a week after he had walked out of her house, there was a little leaving drinks party for her at the office, to which far more people turned up than she had expected, bearing in mind she had not been the most sociable of the team out of work.

She would be sorely missed, her boss said in the little speech he gave to the assembled members of staff. Everyone raised their glasses of champagne. These were the people she had kept at arm's length, burying herself in her work and always feeling the unspoken differences between them. And yet, as various of her colleagues came over to talk to her, she could tell that they were genuinely delighted that she intended to pursue her pro bono work in a firm that was solely dedicated to doing that.

Numbers and email addresses were exchanged with various girls whom she had known on a purely superficial basis.

When she tentatively volunteered the information that she would find it tough financially because she had no family to help her out if she started going under, there were no gasps of horror. When she confessed to a couple of the girls that she loved pro bono work because, growing up on a council estate, she had seen misery first-hand and had always wanted to do something about it, they hadn't walked away, smirking. They had been interested.

By the end of the evening, she had drunk more than she had intended but had also made friends in unexpected places.

Had she made a mistake in erecting so many protective defence mechanisms around her that she had failed to let anyone in? Had her cool distance been a liability in the end, rather than an asset? Had her detachment, which had been put in place for all the right reasons, become a habit which had imprisoned her more firmly than the solid steel bars of a prison cell?

Her thoughts were muddled and all over the place when, at a little after nine, she hailed a black cab to take her back to her house. When she closed her eyes and rested her head back on the seat, she could see Alessandro, a vibrant image hovering in the deepest recesses of her mind.

She had told him bits and pieces of the truth. Was that sufficient? An enormous sense of lassitude washed over her when she thought about the rest of what had been left unsaid.

So, nothing would change. He would still despise her. He would still be repelled by the person he thought she had turned out to be, but wouldn't she feel better in herself? Wouldn't coming clean, laying all her cards on the table, leave her with a clear conscience when she walked away? And wouldn't a clear conscience be a far better companion when she lay down in her bed at night and allowed thoughts of him to proliferate in her head?

She had given away more of herself today with her colleagues than she had in all the years she had worked alongside them, and it had felt good.

She leant forward, told the cab driver to turn around and gave him Alessandro's address.

She had no idea whether he would be in or not. It was a Friday night and face it, he was once again a free, single and eligible guy who might very well have jumped back on the sexual merry-go-round.

The alcohol had given her Dutch courage. Even as the taxi pulled up outside his magnificent house, her nerves didn't start going into automatic meltdown. She had reached a point of realising that she had nothing left to lose.

Her hand only shook a little as she reached for the door-bell and pressed hard, the very same way he had pressed *her* doorbell when he had walked in on Brian depleting her house of all its worldly goods.

On his third whisky, Alessandro heard the distant peal of his doorbell and debated whether he should bother getting it or not. A package was due to be delivered by courier. Work related. Could he really be bothered?

His torpor exasperated him but it had dogged his every waking moment ever since he had walked out of her house. Try as he might, he hadn't been able to shake it. The confines of his opulent office had felt restricting. He had found himself avoiding it, not caring what his secretary thought, going to the shelter practically every day.

It was Friday night and, whilst his head told him that it was time to get back on the horse, to find a replacement for the woman with whom he should never have become entangled all over again, his feet had brought him right back to his house and towards the drinks cabinet. A bracing evening diet of whisky and soda had felt eminently more tempting than shallow conversation with the airheads and bimbos who would circle him at the slightest given opportunity.

Of course, there was a limit to how long this crazy state of affairs could continue. Swearing softly under his breath, and with the glass of whisky still in his hand, he strolled to the front door and pulled it open. On his lips were a few select curses for whatever imbecile of a courier had had the temerity to keep his finger on the buzzer when he, Alessandro, was in the process of working his way down to the bottom of his glass, through which he hoped to see the world as an altogether rosier place.

'Alessandro. You're…' Any hint of incipient nerves flew through the window at the sight of an Alessandro who, for the first time ever, did not seem to be completely in control of all his faculties. 'Are you *drunk*?'

Alessandro leaned against the doorframe and swallowed back the remnants of whisky in his glass. 'What are you doing here at this hour? It's after nine. And I'm not drunk.'

The woman he had walked away from. He tried to think of all the pejorative adjectives that had sprung so easily to mind when he had last seen her. Before he had endured the most hellish week of his entire life. Where the hell had his bullish confidence gone about the fact that she was not worth his while? And where had she been anyway? He checked his watch and saw that it was actually a little before ten. Had she been out *partying*? A tidal wave of jealousy left him shaken.

'Living it up, Chase?' His mouth twisted as he focused on the much less prim and proper attire she was wearing, a fitted burgundy dress rather than her uniform of suits which was all he had ever seen her in for work.

'I know you're probably surprised to see me here. Shocked, even.' Although there was a glass in his hand and it was empty. Had he company? A woman? Chase refused to let that thought take shape and gain momentum.

Alessandro noticed that she had neatly avoided answering his question. He shouldn't even care. In fact, hadn't he made his mind up that he wanted nothing further to do with her? That he could never trust a woman who had lied to him? Hadn't he? 'What are you doing here? Thought you might pay a little social call? On your way back from wherever you've been out partying?'

So his mood hadn't changed. He was still hostile and contemptuous, still ready to attack. 'I haven't been *out partying*, Alessandro. I… It was my last day at work today. There was champagne at the office, that's all. I…I've come because there are some things I still need to say to you.'

So she had just been cooped up at the office. He felt some of his dark mood evaporate. She had more to say to him? Well, why not? The choice was either that or the rest of the whisky to keep him company. He turned on his heels, leaving the door open and Chase, after a few seconds' hesitation, followed him into the house.

CHAPTER TEN

SHE FOLLOWED HIM into the sitting room and immediately spotted the bottle of whisky, which was half-empty.

'How much of this stuff have you *drunk*?' she gasped in amazement.

'I think it's safe to say that my drinking habits are none of your business.' The burgundy dress lovingly clung to her body and outlined curves in all the right places. He could feel himself getting turned on and he scowled because the last thing he needed was his wilful body doing its own thing. He subsided on the sofa, legs apart, his body language aggressively, defensively masculine.

'So, what are you here for?' he demanded, following her with a glowering expression as she hesitated by the door. He watched broodingly as she took a deep breath and walked to one of the pale-cream leather chairs by the fireplace, a modern built-into-the-wall affair which she had variously claimed to have both loved and detested.

'I didn't ask,' Chase said in a thin voice. 'But is someone here with you?'

'Is someone here with me? Does it look like I have company?' He gestured to the empty room.

'You're drinking, Alessandro...' She nodded to the whisky bottle which bore witness to her statement. 'And since when do you drink on your own? Especially spirits. Didn't you once tell me that drinking spirits on your own was a sign of an alcoholic in the making? Didn't you tell me that your parents put you off giving in to vices like that in a big way? That they were a bigger warning against drinking, smoking and taking drugs than any lecture anyone could have given you?'

Alessandro's expression darkened. 'And since when are you my guilty conscience?' he demanded belligerently. He couldn't take his eyes off her. It felt as though he hadn't seen her in a hundred years and, whilst he knew that that certainly wasn't a healthy situation given the fact that she had been dispatched from his life, he still couldn't help himself, and that helplessness made him feel even more of a sad loser.

'I'm not.' Chase stared down at her entwined fingers in silence for a couple of seconds. Now that she was here, sitting in front of him, the nerves which had been absent on her trip over were gathering pace inside her. She had come to tell him how she felt but her moment of bravery was in danger of passing. She wasn't his guilty conscience. She was nothing to him. She was surprised that he hadn't slammed the door in her face, and she took some courage from the fact that he hadn't.

'I've…I've…managed to get a couple of leads on some promising jobs,' she heard herself saying, a propos nothing in particular. 'Out of London. One in Manchester. The other in Surrey. I guess I'll sell my place and move sticks. It'll be cheaper, anyway. I would probably be able to afford something bigger.'

'And you've come here to tell me this because…?'

'I haven't come here to tell you that. I just thought… Well…'

'Get to the point, Chase.' When he thought of her leaving London, he felt as though a band of pure ice had wrapped itself around his heart like the tenacious tendrils of creeping ivy.

She sprang to her feet and began walking restively around the room. It was a big room. The colours were pale and muted, from the colour of the walls to the soft leather furniture. It was modern and, when she had first seen it, she hadn't, been able to decide whether she liked it or not. Certainly, right at this very moment, it chilled her to the bone, but then wasn't that just her fear and trepidation taking its toll? The hard contours of his face spoke volumes for his lack of welcome. He might not have slammed the door in her face but he clearly didn't want her in his house. She felt that little thread of courage begin to seep slowly away.

'Do you remember that…that day, Alessandro?'

'Be specific. What day in particular are you talking about? The day you lied about the fact that you were a happily married woman, or the day you lied about the fact that the loving parents in Australia were a work of fiction…?'

Chase fought against the sneering coolness in his voice and sat back down, this time on the sofa with him, but at the furthest end of it.

'We met at that pub. Do you remember? The one by the park?'

He remembered. He could even remember what she had been wearing. It came to him with such vivid clarity that he almost thought that it had been lying in wait for eight years, just at the edges of his memory: a pair of very faded jeans, some plimsolls which had once been white but were scuffed way past their original colour and a light-blue jumper, the sleeves of which were long enough for her to tuck her hands inside them. Which she had done as she had delivered her blow.

'I told you about Shaun.'

'Believe me, I haven't forgotten that special moment in my life.'

'Please don't be sarcastic, Alessandro. This is really

hard for me. I just want you to listen, because you were right when you said that we had unfinished business between us. We did. And, for me at least, we still have until you hear me out. Or, rather, *I* still do….'

The palms of her hands felt sweaty and she smoothed them over the burgundy dress. 'Eight years ago, I fell in love with you.' She braved his silent stare and willed herself to continue. 'I was married and, believe me, I shouldn't have looked at you, far less spoken to you, but I did. You have no idea what you did for me. Being with you was like being free for the first time in my life. I finally understood what all those silly romance novels were all about.'

Alessandro frowned. This was hardly the direction he'd expected the conversation to go in. 'If you're hoping to pull on my heart strings, then you're barking up the wrong tree. I have perfect recall of your little speech to me. It involved you telling me that Shaun was the great love of your life, that it had been fun seeing me, but you were only in it for some help with work…hoped I didn't get the wrong idea. I'm recalling the moment you waved your wedding ring in my face and pulled out a photo of your loved one.'

'Yes.'

'So where are you going with this, exactly? Why have you come here to waste my time?' Another shot of whisky would have gone down a treat but he *did* remember what he had said to her about his parents teaching him the horrors of having no control, by example.

'I was an idiot when I married Shaun…' Chase stared absently into the distance. 'I was incredibly young and it seemed like an exciting thing to do. Or…or maybe not, thinking about it now. *Shaun* told me it would be an exciting thing to do and I went along with it because I had already figured out that it didn't pay to disagree with anything he said.'

'Watch out. You're in danger of wiping some of the shine from your blissfully joyous married life.'

'There was never any shine on it, and I wasn't blissfully married,' Chase told him abruptly. She refocused on his face to find him watching her carefully. When she thought about the horror that had been her married life with Shaun, she wanted to cry for those wasted years, but the self-control she had built up over the years stood her in good stead.

Alessandro found that he was holding his breath. 'Another lie, Chase?' But he wanted to hear what she had to say even though he told himself that he wasn't going to fall for anything she told him. Once bitten, twice shy.

'I haven't come here to try and make you believe me, Alessandro,' Chase said with quiet sincerity. 'I know you probably won't anyway. I know I've lied to you in the past and you'll never forgive me. You've made that crystal-clear. I'm here because I *need* to tell you everything. And, when I'm finished, I'll walk out that door and you'll never see me again.

'When I met you for the first time, I began something that was dangerous, although you weren't to know that. I've thought about what you said, about Shaun hitching his wagon to me because he knew that he would be able to go further with me shackled to his side. I think you were right, although at the time I didn't see it that way. By the time I made it to university, I'd lost the ability to think independently. My studies were the only thing keeping me going. We'd come to London and I had been taken away from my friends, from everything I knew, although I guess you would find "everything I knew" hardly worth knowing anyway. Shaun was in his element. I was married to him and he was in complete control, and he enjoyed making sure he exercised that control.'

'What are you telling me?'

'I'm telling you that I was an abused wife. The sort of pathetic woman you would find contemptible. The sort of woman who can really understand how all those women at Beth's shelter feel. Why do you imagine I have such empathy for them?'

'When you say abused…?'

'Physically, mentally, emotionally. Shaun was never fussy when it came to laying down laws. He used whatever methods suited him at the time.' She tilted her chin defiantly. She had come to say her piece and he could save his contempt for after she'd left. That was what her expression was telling him.

'He was very clever when it came to making sure he hurt me in ways that weren't visible. He let me out of his sight to attend lectures and tutorials but I was under orders to return home immediately, not to hang around and certainly never to cultivate any sort of friendship with any of the other students. I was just glad to be out of his presence. Anything was better than nothing and, besides, I thrived on the academic work. I found it all ridiculously easy.

'One of the first things I'm going to do when I leave London is to find the teachers who encouraged me and tell them how valuable their input was.' She made sure that he got the message that she wasn't looking for anything from him, that she was moving on, that she had her independence, whatever her story was.

'You say you were…in love with me. Why didn't you leave him?' *Because,* Alessandro thought, *I was certainly head over heels in love with you. I would have protected you.*

It was the first time he had ever really and truly given that notion house room and, now that he had, everything seemed to fall neatly into place. The manner in which she had departed from his life had altered his view of women and had, more profoundly, altered the sort of women he went out with. He had developed a healthy mistrust of anything that remotely smelled of commitment and had programmed every single relationship he'd had to fail by systematically dating women in whom he was destined to lose interest after very short periods of time. In the wake of losing his heart to a woman who had deceived him, he had simply pressed the self-destruct button inside him.

And then she had returned to his life under extraordinary circumstances. He had held her to ransom and told himself that he was exacting revenge. In fact, he had told himself a lot of things. The one single thing he had failed to tell himself—because he could see now that he just couldn't have brought himself to even think it—was that he still wanted her because, quite simply, he was still in love with her.

Chase sensed the infinitesimal shift in him. Was it too much to ask that he at least believed her?

'I couldn't,' she said, flushing. 'I've become very independent over the years. It's been so important for me to stand on my own two feet, to give nothing of myself to anyone, to make sure that no one had control over me. But back then there was no way that I had the inner strength to try and escape. He had sapped me of all my confidence. Anyway...'

She stared down at her fingers, drained from the confidences she was giving away. 'I haven't come here to make excuses, just to tell you things as they were. I met you and it was wonderful but Shaun found out. He got hold of my mobile phone; I had been stupid enough to have one of your text messages there. I had forgotten to delete it. It was arranging to meet for lunch. He went crazy. I can't tell you, but I was terrified for my life. He threatened to kill us both if I didn't end it and, to make sure I did what he said, he made me arrange the location we were supposed to meet. He told me exactly what I was to say to you, and he was sitting at the table behind us the whole time I gave you that little speech about being a happily married woman...'

'My God.'

'I could never have told you about how things really were and I still didn't want to when I saw you again because I was...ashamed. I knew how you'd react. I knew all your opinions of me as a strong career woman with a mind of her own would evaporate and I would be just a pathetic, abused woman, like all those women you didn't give a hoot about when you were going to buy the shelter and have them dispossessed.' She took a deep breath and made eye contact with him but what she saw there was far from contempt. The silence stretched between them until it was at breaking point.

'If we had met later...' she said in a low voice, half-talking to herself '...then things might have been different. Even if I'd still been with Shaun, I would have had more self-confidence. I would have had my degree, a good job; I would have had the courage to walk away from him, but at that point in my life it just wasn't there.'

'And then,' Alessandro said heavily, 'we met again and I hardly inspired the trust you needed to open up. I blackmailed you into sleeping with me...'

'I *wanted* to sleep with you,' Chase confirmed in a driven voice. 'I would never have let myself be blackmailed into doing anything. I said so at the time and I meant it. I'd learnt the hard way not to let anyone else have control over me. I *wanted* to sleep with you and I don't regret it.'

'And what happened to the...love?' Alessandro asked so quietly that she had to strain to hear him.

'I still love you, Alessandro,' she said proudly. 'And I don't regret that either. So, there you are.' She stood up and brushed her skirt to distract herself from speculating on what was going on in his head.

'Not so fast!'

Chase looked up at him in surprise. His command was imperious but there was a hesitancy underlying it that wormed its way past her common sense.

'I'm glad you came,' he said, flushing darkly and looking so suddenly vulnerable that she wanted to sidle a little closer to him, just to make sure that her eyes weren't playing tricks on her. She remained where she was, resisting the impulse. 'I'm glad you were honest with me. Yes, when we met again…'

Alessandro raked his fingers through his hair and shook his head with a rueful smile that did even more disastrous things to her common sense. 'It all came rushing back at me. I hadn't realised how much I remembered and I certainly didn't get why it was that I remembered so well. I just knew that I still…wanted you. Somewhere along the line, I figured out that I had never stopped wanting you. I couldn't make sense of it, couldn't understand how I could still want a woman who I felt had betrayed me in the worst possible way. Don't get me wrong; I understand why you wanted to keep your secrets to yourself, why you felt that they would be too dark for me to handle, but if only I had known…'

'Nothing would have changed, Alessandro. Nothing has changed now.'

'No, nothing's changed and everything's changed. You're the same person you always were, Chase, whatever you went through. What you mean to me will always be the same, just as it was all those years ago. You will always be the girl I fell in love with but was too damned stupid to own up to. I let pride rule my behaviour and only now… Well, I'm still in love with you.'

Chase wondered whether she had heard correctly or whether wishful thinking had taken complete control. Was it even possible to hear something you wanted to hear because you wanted it *so badly*? She found that she was holding her breath.

'Um…did you just say… Did you just tell me…?'

'That I'm in love with you? Yes, I did. And I'll tell you again if you'd move a little closer so that I don't have to shout across the width of the sofa.'

'It's not a big sofa,' Chase said faintly.

'Right now, with you sitting at the other end of it, it feels as wide as a canyon.'

She shuffled along and slipped into his arms with a soaring feeling of utter elation. 'What if I hadn't come tonight?'

'I would never have let you go. The past week has been the worst of my life. I've never hated my office more. I lost interest in deals, going to meetings, reading emails… I know more now about that shelter than I would ever have thought possible.'

'Beth said you'd been a frequent visitor.' She curled into him and heard the beating of his heart.

'It made me feel close to you,' he confessed shakily, 'Although I never faced up to that. I love you, Chase. I love you for the person you are now and I loved you for the person you were then. I can't live without you. I want you to be my wife. Will you marry me? Within the next hour?'

Chase lifted her head and laughed, her eyes glowing with happiness. 'Within the next hour might be stretching it,' she said softly. 'But, yes, I'll be your wife.'

'And never leave my side?'

'You're stuck with me for ever…' And never had the thought of being stuck with someone for ever sounded so good.

* * * * *

Special Offers

Every month we put together collections and longer reads written by your favourite authors.

Here are some of next month's highlights— and don't miss our fabulous discount online!

On sale 21st March

On sale 4th April

On sale 4th April

Save 20%
on all Special Releases

Find out more at
www.millsandboon.co.uk/specialreleases

Visit us Online

Emma
DARCY
3 in 1 GREAT VALUE
AUSTRALIA
IN BED WITH A BACHELOR

Emma
DARCY
3 in 1 GREAT VALUE
AUSTRALIA
IN BED WITH A KING

Emma
DARCY
3 in 1 GREAT VALUE
AUSTRALIA
IN BED WITH THE PLAYBOY

Emma
DARCY
3 in 1 GREAT VALUE
AUSTRALIA
IN BED WITH THE BOSS

Emma
DARCY
3 in 1 GREAT VALUE
AUSTRALIA
IN BED WITH HER GROOM

Emma
DARCY
3 in 1 GREAT VALUE
AUSTRALIA
IN BED WITH A SHEIKH